Lee Carroll is a pseudonym for the writing partnership of award–winning novelist Carol Goodman and her poet husband, Lee Slonimsky. They live in Long Island, New York.

Black Swan Rising

Lee Carroll

BANTAM BOOKS

LONDON • TORONTO • SYDNEY • AUCKLAND • JOHANNESBURG

TRANSWORLD PUBLISHERS
61–63 Uxbridge Road, London W5 5SA
A Random House Group Company
www.rbooks.co.uk

BLACK SWAN RISING
A BANTAM BOOK: 9780553825572

First published in the United States
in 2010 by Tom Doherty Associates, LLC

First published in Great Britain
in 2010 by Bantam Press
an imprint of Transworld Publishers
Bantam edition published 2011

Addresses for Random House Group Ltd companies outside the UK
can be found at: www.randomhouse.co.uk
The Random House Group Ltd Reg. No. 954009

The Random House Group Limited supports The Forest Stewardship Council
(FSC), the leading international forest certification organisation. All our titles
that are printed on Greenpeace approved FSC certified paper carry the FSC
logo. Our paper procurement policy can be found at
www.rbooks.co.uk/environment

Typeset in 11/15pt New Caledonia by Falcon Oast Graphic Art Ltd.
Printed in the UK by CPI Cox & Wyman, Reading, RG1 8EX.

2 4 6 8 10 9 7 5 3 1

For our mothers, Elinor and Marge

acknowledgments

We would like to thank our first readers, Gary Feinberg, Harry Steven Lazerus, Wendy Gold Rossi, Scott Silverman, and Nora Slonimsky, for their wisdom and insights. We thank Maggie Vicknair for naming things and making up magic symbols.

To Ed Bernstein and Sharon Khazzam we express our gratitude for their expertise regarding Ddraik's computing skills and Garet's jewelry design, respectively.

Lauren Lipton gave us exceptional and comprehensive feedback that was as inspired as her own brilliant novels are.

We thank the Cloisters for letting us inside their library.

Our editor, Paul Stevens, has been of crucial importance for his belief in the project and his astute editorial perspective. Our agents, Loretta Barrett and Nick Mullendore, have been superb readers and energetic advocates for Lee Carroll from the beginning.

Nothing would be possible without our loving and supportive families.

Black Swan
Rising

The Silver Box

I'd never been in the antiques store before.

That was the first strange circumstance. I knew the Village like the back of my hand. I grew up in a town house in the West Village, which I'd just learned was so heavily mortgaged that even if my father and I sold it we would still be under a mountain of debt. It was that news – along with a litany of dire economic circumstances – that had left me so shocked and disoriented that I'd walked back from the lawyer's office in lower Manhattan in a daze. I hadn't even noticed the light rain that had begun to fall or the fog rolling in from the Hudson River.

Only when a sudden violent deluge forced me to duck into a doorway did I realize I was lost. Looking out through a curtain of rain, I saw I was on a narrow cobble-stone street. I was too far from either corner to see a street sign through the heavy mist. Somewhere in the West Village or Tribeca, maybe? Had I crossed Canal Street? This part of town had changed so much, become so much trendier, in recent years that it all looked different. I must be near the river, though. The wind was blowing from the south carrying with it the smell of the Hudson and, from beyond the bay, the deep Atlantic. On chill autumn days like this, with low-lying clouds obscuring the tops of buildings and fog softening the edges of brick and granite, I liked to imagine myself in an older Manhattan – a Dutch seaport where traders and merchants came from the Old World to make their fortunes – not the hub of the financial world on the edge of economic collapse.

I shivered – I was soaked to the skin – and turned toward the door to see if I could find an address. I found, instead, a tall, wild-eyed woman staring back at me, her long black hair hanging limply in front of her pale face like a vengeful ghost out of a Japanese horror film. It was my own reflection. I was pretty sure that when I left my house this morning I was a reasonably attractive twenty-six-year-old woman, but this is what bad news and rain had done to me. I tucked my hair behind my ears and leaned down to look for an address, but the gilt letters on the door had been worn away long ago, leaving a sprinkling of gold dust like a magician's veil and a few scattered letters. The only intact word was *mist*. Probably the tail end of *chemist*. It wasn't a chemist's anymore, though. It was an antiques store, that much was clear from the contents of the window – Georgian silver, sapphire and diamond rings, gold pocket watches – all beautiful, but a bit too precious for my taste. Peering through the glass door, I saw that the shop itself looked like a tiny jewel box, the walls paneled in dark wood, the sparkling glass cases lined with garnet-colored velvet, a curtain of wine-colored damask hanging behind a polished mahogany counter carved in sinuous art-nouveau curves. The white-haired man who sat behind the counter looked as if he had been set there as carefully as a pearl in an onyx brooch. He was examining something through a watchmaker's loupe, but then he looked up – one eye grotesquely magnified by the lens – and saw me standing in the doorway. He reached under the counter and pressed a button to ring me in.

I can ask for directions to the closest subway station, I thought as I opened the door. I wouldn't be so rude as to do it right away, though. I hated when tourists popped their heads into our art gallery to ask for directions. I'd look around first, although I doubted the shop carried the signet rings I used for my molds and I hardly ever shopped for myself anymore – and it didn't look as if I'd be doing so in the near future. I wore on my right ring finger the silver signet ring my mother had given me for my sixteenth birthday. Engraved in the silver was a swan, its neck arched and wings spread out as if about to take flight – or in heraldry terms, *a swan rising*. Encircling the swan, reversed so that they would appear correct when pressed into wax, were the words *Rara avis in terris, nigroque simillima cygno.*

'"A rare bird on earth, very much like a black swan,"' my mother had translated for me. 'That's what you are, Garet, a rare bird. Unique. Don't ever let anyone make you think you have to be the same as everyone else.'

Someone had rubbed his finger over the words so often they could barely be read, and fine cracks ran through the design, but when I had pressed the ring into hot wax, the image and words were remarkably clear. My mother, who had worked as an apprentice at Asprey's in London, had shown me how to make a mold from the wax print and cast a medallion from the imprint of the ring – the same medallion I still wore today, and every day. So many people asked about the medallion that I had gone out looking for more signet rings and made more medallions, which I had sold to students and teachers at my high school and to clients at the gallery. I'd made enough to put myself through a jewelry design program at FIT and to start a small company with a studio on the top floor of the town house. I called it Cygnet Designs after the Latin word for swan. It was doing pretty well four years later, but I didn't make enough to repay the enormous debt my father had incurred.

How many of my customers will feel like they can afford to buy little trinkets like my medallions, I wondered as I entered the shop. *How long will quaint little businesses like mine – or this one – survive if things really get bad?*

If the proprietor of the shop was anxious about his present prospects of making a sale, he didn't show it. He continued to tinker with the watch he was fixing as I browsed the shelves. They held a strange assortment of wares. There were lockets opened to show sepia-toned photographs under mottled glass, and brooches woven from the hair of the deceased. Many of the rings and brooches were adorned with urns, willow trees, and doves – all traditional symbols of mourning. One whole shelf contained nothing but brooches of painted eyes. I'd read about these in a jewelry history class. They were called lover's eye brooches, a Georgian style that had been made fashionable by the Prince of Wales when he commissioned his court miniaturist to paint just his mistress's eye so no one would guess her identity. I'd seen pictures of them in books and one or two in antiques shops, but it was disconcerting to see so many of the disembodied eyes in one place.

'Was there anything in particular you were looking for?'

The question was voiced so softly that for a moment I thought it was only in my head. I couldn't help responding, in my head, *A way out of my troubles, thank you very much.* But aloud I said, 'I'm always on the lookout for old signet rings. I use them in my jewelry designs.' I held up my necklace for the man to see. He held up his magnifying glass and leaned over the counter to get a better look.

The moment he saw the design he lowered the glass and looked up. His eyes were a curious shade of amber, all the more startling in a deeply bronzed face framed by snow-white hair and carefully trimmed goatee.

'Are you by any chance Garet James, the owner of Cygnet Designs?' he asked.

'Why, yes,' I said, pleased at the recognition. I'd gotten some good press, but I wasn't used to being 'recognized.' 'That's me. I'm surprised an antiques dealer would know it.'

'I like to keep abreast of modern times,' he said. When he smiled, a million fine lines spanned his deeply bronzed skin. I had the notion that he had spent time at sea, squinting into sun and rain at the helm of a ship, but it was more likely he'd just played a few too many rounds on the golf course. 'I read the piece in *New York* magazine last week. I admire the way you make use of old materials to make something new. You're a real artist.'

'Just a craftsman,' I said quickly.

'You're being modest.'

'Not really. I know the difference.' I'd grown up among artists – painters and sculptors – and I knew what it meant to be a real artist, but I didn't have to tell this stranger all that – or that the last thing I wanted to be was an artist.

He narrowed his eyes. 'I've looked at your designs on your website. But I don't believe I've seen this particular design there.'

'No. This was the first medallion I made . . . from this ring.' I held out my hand so he could see the signet ring. 'I've never reproduced it again.'

The jeweler took my hand in his and held it up to his loupe to see the ring better. His fingers were cold and powdery and he held my hand for what seemed like longer than was necessary. Maybe he was having trouble reading the quote.

'The words are backwards. It says, "A rare bird—"'

'I know the quote quite well,' he said, dropping my hand abruptly and looking up. 'In fact, I've seen this insignia before . . . wait . . . I'll show you.'

Before I could object, the jeweler rose from his stool. He was taller than I'd thought – and more robust. The long loose cardigan he was wearing had disguised his bulk while sitting, but when he stood he had quite a presence. He must have been close to my father's age – mideighties – but where my father had recently begun to look frail, this man looked powerful. Almost disconcertingly so, as if the cardigan and white hair were a disguise.

He excused himself and disappeared behind the

maroon brocade curtain. I took another turn around the shop but there really wasn't much space to turn around in and wherever I stood those disembodied eyes seemed to follow me. I stared out the fogged window at the rain-slicked street instead. Why was I even waiting? I certainly had no intention of buying anything. Not after the news I'd received this morning.

My father's lawyer, Charles Chennery, had laid it all out for me in his blunt, Connecticut lockjaw. Five months ago my father had taken out a $2.5 million home equity line of credit from a Wall Street firm against the $4 million value of the Jane Street town house. He'd used it to buy several paintings – *steals*, he'd assured Charles – which had been appraised at $5 million value for resale. But that was before the world financial and art markets had collapsed this autumn. Much of the artwork hadn't even sold at auction, and what had, sold for much less than what my father had anticipated. Now even well-collateralized loans were being called in prematurely. ('No one ever reads the fine print,' Chennery had somberly told me when I expressed surprise that investment banks could do that), and with the true value of the town house dropping every day, no creditor was likely to take chances. Indeed, the Wall Street firm was threatening to repossess the house and gallery in thirty days (*by January 11*, I mentally reminded myself) if we couldn't repay the loan. Chuck Chennery had outlined various ways of restructuring the loan, but none of the options had sounded even remotely feasible. If we re-structured the debt, we'd have more time to repay it but at a significantly higher interest rate. We'd owe $50,000 each month. Where would we get that kind of money in this market? And if we sold the gallery to repay the loan, what would we live on? And *where* would we live? The town house was our home as well as place of business. Just thinking about it made me feel seasick. No wonder I had gotten lost walking here.

'Yes, I was correct, the crest on this is nearly identical to the one on your ring and medallion.' The shop owner's voice broke into the ever-widening gyre of financial ruin spinning inside my head. 'In fact, I believe it might be the *same* crest.'

I turned and looked at the object the jeweler had laid atop a blue velvet cloth on the glass counter. It was a shallow silver box about the length and width of my thirteen-inch MacBook, and so tarnished it was hard to make out the etched designs even when I moved closer to it. I was surprised the proprietor of such a fastidiously clean shop would allow the object to remain so tarnished. I peered at the design on the top of the box, looking for the crest he had spoken of, but the decoration on the lid was an abstract pattern of concentric ovals.

'The crest is here,' he said, pointing to the front of the box along its seam, to the place where there should have been a clasp. Instead of a clasp – or perhaps *over* the clasp – was a round lozenge of silver sealing the lid of the box to its base. Its edges were irregular and bulged around the perimeter, exactly like a pool of wax that has been stamped by a seal. It looked, in fact, a great deal like the medallions I made from wax seals. *And* it looked exactly like the seal on my ring: the same swan flexing its wings, the same Latin motto, even . . . *could it be?*

I leaned closer to the box and the jeweler wordlessly handed me his magnifying loupe. I raised it to my right eye, startled by a tingle of electrical energy that ran along my eyebrow and cheekbone, as if the metal had picked up a charge from the jeweler. I bent down until the seal came into focus through the thick lens. Fine lines were impressed into the metal. I knew from experience that they came from cracks in the seal that made the image. I looked back at the ring on my finger and then back to the box. The lines were identical.

'That's amazing.' I straightened up, the loupe still in my right eye, to look at the jeweler. The old man wavered in my vision, the edges around him blurring and streaking like sunflares. A cloud of shimmering lights, like a swarm of fireflies let loose in the shop, hovered above his head. I put down the loupe and closed my eyes to clear my vision.

'Sorry,' I said, 'I get—'

'Scintillations? Metamorphopsia?' the jeweler asked, naming two of the symptoms of an ocular migraine, a condition I had suffered from since my teens.

'Exactly. You must be a fellow sufferer.'

'Many of us are,' he said enigmatically.

What did he mean by *us*? The man was definitely a bit strange. I should ask for directions and get out of here. I certainly had no intention of buying the box. Not that I didn't want to. I felt, in fact, as if the box *should* belong to me. What were the chances of coming across an object that had been made with the very same ring my mother had given me? And on this day of all days when everything else in my life seemed so bleak? But that was exactly the reason why I couldn't even think of buying such an inessential item – it would be frivolous and foolish in such dire economic circumstances. Still . . . I could imagine polishing the silver until it shone. . . . I placed the tip of my finger on the surface of the box, imagining the whirling pattern released from its carapace of tarnish . . . and was startled to see the finely etched lines glow blue. I leaned closer and watched in amazement as the incandescent lines rippled, swayed, and spread out from my fingertip, as if the box were made of water instead of silver and my touch had been the cast stone that disturbed its surface.

I moved my finger away and the lines stilled and turned dull again. I looked up and saw that the jeweler was staring at the box. Slowly he lifted his eyes up. They seemed to be glowing with the same incandescent light that I had seen in the box a moment ago. His look was so intense I was afraid I had done something wrong. Damaged the box, perhaps. But instead of taking the box away he pushed it toward me. 'I have a proposition for you,' he said.

'What?' I asked, alarmed at the wording of his request.

'I'd like to make a trade.' He fluttered his hands between the seal on the box and my ring. They were trembling. When I'd entered the shop his hands had held the delicate tools of the watchmaker without a tremor, but now his hands quivered midair like butterfly wings.

'I'm sorry,' I said, afraid of agitating the man further. 'I don't understand. I don't really have anything to trade—'

'A trade for your services.' He clasped his hands together and forced his lips into a polite smile.

'What services?' I was suddenly aware of how isolated we were, alone in this little shop on a deserted street, the front door locked, the heavy rain like a curtain of silver chain mail separating us from the rest of the world. Was the man crazy? A hectic gleam was in his eyes and he was wringing his hands as if he were afraid they would fly away of their own volition.

'Your soldering services. I've seen what fine work you do with Cygnet Designs . . . and you do metal sculpture as well, don't you? I believe you had a show last year in Chelsea. . . . I've been looking for someone just like you for this job. It's quite delicate, you see . . .' He released his hands and gestured toward the seam of the box. I noticed two things. He didn't touch the box and his fingernails were the same shade of yellow as his eyes. 'The box has been sealed all the way around.'

I looked down at the box and saw what he meant. Along the seam between the lid and the base was a thin line of metal, which, unlike the silver of the box, was untarnished. It gleamed like molten mercury. Someone had welded the box shut, then stamped the seal on it as if the box were a letter that should only be opened by the intended recipient. And *I* was the one with the matching seal.

'That's strange.'

'Yes, and rather inconvenient. I can't very well sell a box that's been sealed. If you open the box, I'll let you have the seal and pay you a thousand dollars.'

'That seems an awful lot . . .'

'Not for such a delicate job. It's worth it to me to have someone with your skill do the job . . . and besides, I believe it was fate that brought you in here today, and who are we to disregard the chances fate puts in our way?'

Who, indeed? After the dire financial revelations of the morning why not accept the one gift fate seemed willing to give me today? A thousand dollars wasn't going to solve my financial problems, but could I really afford to turn down any extra income at all?

'Okay,' I said, holding out my hands for the box. 'You've got a deal. I'll open the box this evening and return it to you tomorrow morning.'

The jeweler picked up the box cradled in the blue velvet cloth, which I saw now was a jewelry sack. As he held it out to me, I heard something move inside, a rustling sound like leaves in autumn stirred by the wind.

'Oh, and I'd like to have the papers that are inside it, as well,' he said as I took the box. It was heavier than I expected. I looked down at it and saw the lines move once again. *It must be a trick of the design – a trompe l'oeil.* But instead of spreading outward, this time the lines coiled, crested and rolled like the waves of the ocean pulled by the force of the moon. For a moment the room was full of the brackish breath of low tide. I shook myself to shed the illusion and then, before he could change his mind about giving me the commission – or I could change my mind about taking it – I slipped the box into the velvet sack and then into my capacious messenger bag – my Mary Poppins bag, my friend Becky always called it – thanked the jeweler, and went out into the rain.

The moment my foot hit the sidewalk a taxi appeared, its vacancy light gleaming through the mist and rain like a lighthouse beacon. Forgetting my vows to economize, I hailed the cab and sank gratefully into the backseat. I gave the driver my home address and closed my eyes to ward off any more of the ocular phenomena that came with my migraines. It was only when the taxi pulled up in front of the town house that I realized I hadn't gotten the name or address of the jeweler – or even noticed what street the shop was on. I had no idea how I would return the box after I opened it.

A Snowy Field in France

Although the gallery was closed Maia, the receptionist, was still there. Oddly, she seemed to be working longer and more energetic hours now that we could only afford to directly pay her three days a week. The 'consultant' status she'd been offered – with a small percentage of each sale in lieu of two days' salary – seemed to be much more to her liking even though we'd made no secret of the recession's risk to the gallery's survival.

'I wanted you to know that the Pissarros came back from Sotheby's,' she said as she slipped into a dove-gray brocade coat that looked as though it could have been worn by a Restoration courtier – only presumably not with a paisley velvet miniskirt and UGG boots. 'Mr. James took them into the back office, but I'm not sure he's had a chance to put them into the safe . . . Mr. Reese came by around the same time.'

'With a bottle of Stolichnaya, no doubt,' I replied. Zach Reese was one of my father's oldest and best friends, an abstract artist whose paintings had sold well in the early eighties. They still sold well, only Zach didn't actually get around to painting any these days. He preferred to sit in the back room of his friend's gallery and relive the glory days of Basquiat and David Hockney. 'What was the occasion this time?' I asked.

'A welcome-home party for the Pissarros,' Maia said, rolling her eyes. 'It's too bad they didn't sell,' she added. 'But you know what they say about snow scenes . . .'

'They don't sell in a recession. Speaking of which, any traffic?'

'Just a couple of Long Island matrons killing time after the Marc Jacobs sale. They spent the whole time comparing their new economies: bribing their colorist to come to their house at a fraction of the salon cost and limiting their daughters to one Marc Jacobs bag apiece.'

'Wow, things really *are* tough all over!' I forced myself to laugh even though the idea of Long Island matrons cutting back made me slightly ill. I did a brisk business in monogrammed pendants during the holidays and for sweet sixteens, confirmations, and bat mitzvahs yearlong. 'I'll make sure the Pissarros get locked up. Thanks for waiting for me.'

'No problem. I'm going to a show at the Knitting Factory anyway and I had some time to kill. Have a good weekend.'

I followed Maia to the front door and double-locked it behind her. Next I dimmed the lights and set the security system on 'Night,' activating the motion detectors. Then I let myself into the narrow corridor that opened onto the town-house stairwell and led to the back office. As I locked the door to the gallery behind me, I could hear Zach Reese's raucous laughter.

'. . . and then he said, "You pissed on it, you bought it," and handed him the bill.' It was an old story from Zach's early days at the Warhol Factory and one Zach pulled out to entertain Roman in particularly bad times. Usually it made my father roar, but this evening the only sound coming from the back office was Zach Reese's broad Midwestern guffaw.

My father looked up as I entered the office and I saw from the strain in his eyes that he'd been waiting for me. *He hasn't been eating well,* I thought, noting the sunken caverns under his cheekbones and the hectic gleam in his dark eyes, *or sleeping well.* I'd never minded having older parents – Roman was fifty-eight when I was born; my mother was forty-five – because Roman was so vital and my mother . . . well, she hadn't looked a day over thirty until her death at sixty-one. The town house had always been filled with artists and writers whom my mother had nurtured and entertained. But since my mother had died ten years ago in a car accident, I had become more aware of my father's health. Most of Roman's own family had died in Poland in the war, and my mother had been estranged from her relatives in France since the war as well. Roman was all the family I had in the world. I was sorry now for making him wait all afternoon. I should have come back from the meeting right away instead of wandering aimlessly around the city – browsing in antiques shops and talking to eccentric jewelers while Roman waited to hear how bad the news was.

'Hail the returning hero!' Zach Reese lifted a shot glass brimming with clear liquid that shivered in his trembling hands. 'We were afraid you'd been swallowed up by the gods of mammon. Sacrificed on an altar in Trinity Church to the Succubus of Greed and Subprime Mortgages.'

'You were gone so long,' Roman said with a tense smile. He passed a gnarled hand over his bald scalp, a gesture I'd come to recognize as a sign of stress. 'We thought the bank might be holding you as collateral on the loan.'

'If only I were that valuable,' I said, waving away Zach's offer of a drink and moving to the stove to put the kettle on. The back office – as opposed to the front office where we saw clients – was the old kitchen of the town house. Its cabinets held files and office supplies instead of dishes and plates now, and the pantry had been converted into a fire-proof, steel-lined safe with a state-of-the-art lock and alarm system. I noticed that the safe door was open and the Pissarro snow scenes, unpacked from their crates, were propped up on two kitchen chairs. They were positioned so that they blocked the windows and French doors that let out onto the back garden, replacing the view of rainy twilight Manhattan with crystalline expanses of snowcovered fields. *Why didn't snow scenes sell in a recession?* I'd buy the Pissarros for myself if I had the money. I'd step into that serene expanse of mauve-tinted snow right now if I could.

The whistle of the teakettle snapped me out of an oft-cherished childhood fantasy of being able to step into a favorite painting. I'd spent a large part of my childhood daydreaming myself into fields of van Gogh sunflowers and tidy Dutch street scenes. I spooned black Russian tea into a teapot and poured in the hot water. I brought the pot to the table, folding a striped-blue-and-white tea cloth under it, and two cups.

'So, how bad is it?' Roman asked as I poured his tea and handed him a cup.

'We'll talk later,' I said, sliding my eyes toward Zach.

'Uh-oh, I can see I'm in the way of a family confab. I'd better get going. One of my students has an opening I thought I'd check out.' Zach lurched unsteadily to his feet, six feet two inches of rangy Swedish farm stock teetering in paint-stained Doc Martens. *Even though he hasn't finished a painting in twenty years his clothes are always covered in paint,* I thought as I positioned myself in between him and the Pissarros. I wasn't sure he could even hold a paintbrush steady with the tremor that was always in his hands.

'Leave those college girls alone, Zach,' I said, tilting my head to receive an avuncular kiss on the cheek. 'It's not fair to the college boys.'

'Later, Jashemski,' he called to my father, using the name my father had changed when he moved to this country. I led Zach down the corridor to the front door and locked it behind him. When I got back to the kitchen, my father was sipping his tea. The Pissarros were gone and the safe door was closed but he was still staring at the spot where they had been.

'Last year they would have sold for six million each,' he said. 'Even after the '87 crash we still moved inventory.'

'I have a feeling things may be different from '87, Dad.' I sat down and wrapped my hands around my tea mug, but I might as well have been in that snowy field in France for how little the warmth penetrated the chill I felt deep down in my bones.

❈   ❈   ❈

Two hours later I went upstairs, exhausted from keeping up a false front of optimism. I'd outlined the plan of restructuring the loan that Chuck Chennery had offered as our last resort. My father had seemed to accept it, but even he must have seen that if the economy continued to worsen we didn't have a chance in hell of ever getting out of debt. Still he'd preserved the optimism of an inveterate gambler throughout our talk.

'Something will turn up!' he'd shouted after me as I left him at the door to his apartment on the second floor.

By the time I reached my third-floor studio I felt as if my whole body had been cast in metal. I slipped the strap of the messenger bag over my head, dropped it gratefully onto the hardwood floor . . . and heard a heavy clunk.

The silver box. I'd forgotten all about it. I'd meant to show it to my father, but there'd been too many monetary details to go over. He had traded in decorative objects a little after World War II and could possibly have dated it. I certainly couldn't.

I lifted the box, still in its velvet sack, out of my bag and carried it over to my worktable, which stood at the far end of the room near the floor-to-ceiling windows under the slanted skylight that faced the garden. In the daytime the light poured in through the south-facing windows, making it the ideal workspace. An old secretary desk fit into a small alcove to the right of the table; on the left a tall metal bookcase held my jewelry-making supplies and the scrap metal I collected for my metal sculptures. One of those sculptures, a six-foot-long dragon crafted of junk metal and chain links, hung from a hook in the ceiling. In the daytime his red headlight eyes caught the sun and gleamed mischievously, but tonight he cast a looming shadow against the rain-spackled windows that made me feel vaguely uneasy.

I switched on the high-intensity work lamps on either side of the table. The strong light immediately picked up what I'd missed in the shop – a pattern of silver and gold shapes stitched into the blue velvet – circles, triangles, and crescent moons embellished with curves and squiggles. The shapes looked vaguely familiar.

I turned to my desk, flipped open my laptop, and hit the power key. While waiting for the screen to come to life I slid the box out of the velvet sack and brushed my fingers over the finely etched pattern of concentric ovals. The high-intensity studio lamps picked up a bluish cast in the lines – a delicate inlay of enamel, perhaps. I'd have to be careful not to damage it while opening the box.

I turned from the box to the laptop, placed my fingers on the touch pad . . . and recoiled as sparks flew off my fingertips. The screen flickered and the laptop let out a low shriek that sounded like a Siamese cat in heat.

Damn! I shook my hand in the air and watched the computer screen reset to my home page. I approached the machine again warily, gingerly touching the keyboard. There was no shock this time. I typed in *Symbols.com* and entered the parameters for the signs on the cloth – single-axis, symmetric, open, both straight and soft shapes, crossing lines – then hit SEARCH SIGNS. An array of symbols appeared. I clicked on one that matched one of the signs on the cloth – an upside-down half circle topped with a vertical straight line that was crossed by two horizontal lines – and got this description: 'One of the signs for amalgam used in alchemy and early chemistry. Amalgams are alloys made by combining mercury with other metals, preferably silver.'

Of course. I'd seen the symbol in one of my metallurgy classes. I typed in *alchemy* on Google and then clicked on the Wikipedia page. There I read that *alchemy* was derived from an Arabic word meaning the 'art of trans-formation,' that the word *chemist* came from it, and that historically it was best known as the pursuit of transform-ing metals into gold. I scrolled through a list of famous alchemists, then clicked on a link to a list of alchemical symbols. Looking back and forth between the screen and the cloth, I identified the symbols for silver, gold, copper, and lead, several of the planets, seasons, and the four elements: earth, air, fire, and water.

Was the white-haired jeweler a closet alchemist then? I wouldn't be too surprised. The jewelry business was full of eccentrics and romantics. I'd met more than a few in my classes at FIT – professors and students – who were intrigued by the ancient mystic study of natural elements. Its devotees were fond of pointing out that some of its pro-cesses were still used in modern metallurgy. And who in these times wouldn't find appealing a system that pro-fessed to know the secret of turning lead into gold?

But unless I developed that skill soon, I'd need every penny I could bring in. I'd promised the jeweler to deliver the opened box tomorrow. Hopefully he'd get in touch

when he realized he hadn't given me his contact information. And if not, I'd just have to comb the West Village and
Tribeca until I found the store. In the meantime, I might as
well get the job done.

I went into my bedroom – a tiny room tucked under the
sharply sloping roof – and quickly changed out of the skirt
and blouse I'd worn to the lawyer's office into old jeans, a
sweatshirt, and thick leather boots. I'd learned early on in
my jewelry and welding classes that a stray spark could
ruin a favorite shirt and burn through delicate fabrics to
the skin. My soldering clothes were dotted with burn holes
and smelled like gas and metal and ash. I felt instantly
more like myself in them.

I scraped my hair back into a ponytail, went into the
studio, and switched on the radio, which was always set to
WROX, the alternative-rock station I liked to listen to when
I worked. The night DJ's silky voice – her show was called
The Night Flight with Ariel Earhart – always relaxed me. I
smiled as a song by London Dispersion Force came on. My
two best friends were in the band and I was happy they
were getting the airtime. This was a new song, called
'Troubadour': 'The troubadours wrote songs to salve heartbreak,' the lead singer Fiona sang, 'to let their loves know
all their endless pain.' I set up my soldering torch while
swaying to the tune, feeling a calm settle over me that I
hadn't felt all day. *Thank God for work,* I thought, pulling
on heavy gloves and drawing the box toward me. *Now how
the hell am I going to open this thing without damaging it?*

I reexamined the seam of metal that sealed the box.
Since the edges of the box were unharmed, I had to

assume that the metal of the seam was softer than the silver of the box – otherwise, the silver would have melted when the box was sealed. The same went for the seal that had been placed over the clasp. So if I could heat the sealant up, I should be able to slide a blade along the seam and under the seal. I picked out a steel blade and the finest nozzle for the soldering torch and adjusted the levels of acetylene and oxygen. When I had everything in place, I lowered a visor over my eyes and aimed the torch at the metal seam. At first there was no discernible change. If the box seal were composed of lead, it should have begun to melt already. It must be some other compound. I adjusted the level of the flame.

There was still no change.

'Come on,' I whispered to the metal, my breath steaming my visor. 'Don't be a bitch.'

As if responding to my voice, the metal seam beneath the torch point silkened and gleamed like a bright ribbon. It was beginning to melt.

'There's a good girl,' I cooed. I ran the torch along the seam of the box until the metal seal began to bubble. With my other hand I inserted the steel blade in between the lid and the base and ran it all the way around the three sides of the box and then underneath the round insignia. The metal around the seal began to glow, then the whole lozenge glowed white – all except for the figure of the rearing swan in the center. It remained black against the glowing white, like the silhouette of a black swan rising out of a shimmering sunlit pool. For a moment, I could have sworn I heard the sound of wings beating the air, then something popped and the white light enveloped and blinded me.

It was a light I could almost *feel*. An energy that made my bones vibrate, my blood tingle, and every hair on my body stand on end. It was like jumping into an ice-cold lake on a summer day or stepping into a hot bath full of fizzing bath salts or . . . no, it was like *nothing* I had ever felt before. It was like being truly alive for the first time. I knew instantly that if I lived through it I would spend the rest of my life trying to duplicate the sensation.

When the light faded, I looked down at my arms and legs almost expecting to see burnt stubs, but nothing was even singed.

You're okay, you're okay, I said over and over as I patted myself down. I heard the ghost of my mother's voice in the words. It's what she said when I fell down or banged my head on something. *You're okay,* I repeated, trying to slow my racing heart. Nothing was hurt, not even . . . I looked at the box and my heart shuddered to a halt.

It was open. A plume of blue smoke rose up from inside it, drifted toward the ceiling, and coiled around the metal dragon like a second airborne serpent. Mixed in with the smoke were flakes of soot fluttering in the air. But what stopped my heart was what I saw *inside* the box on the underside of the lid. Blue shapes glowed against the molten white of the silver, shapes that moved like icons scrolling across a computer screen.

I stepped closer and reached out a trembling gloved hand to touch the inside of the lid. A blue crescent moon morphed into a circle doubly bisected with two crossed lines and then changed into a triangle with a dot in its center. An upside-down eye turned into the letter Z, then the number 7, then into something that looked like a paramecium.

I closed my eyes, desperately hoping that when I opened them the illusion would be gone. When I had developed the symptoms of ocular migraines at sixteen, I thought at first that I was going crazy. Growing up in a house frequented by artists, I couldn't help hearing about those who had *gone over the edge*. Living on that edge had seemed to be both the gift and the burden of being an artist. And wasn't my mother always telling me how talented I was? Did that mean that I, too, had the potential of slipping over the edge of the rational world into madness? It had been a colossal relief when the eye doctor told me that the flashes of light, jagged-edged blind spots, and blurry coronas were normal. But what if he'd been wrong? What if those symptoms were only the beginning and now I really *was* going crazy?

I opened my eyes. The symbols were gone. The box had turned from white back to silver. *Polished* silver. There wasn't a trace of tarnish on it. *Okay,* I thought, *the lid had been treated with some kind of chemical. The symbols were scratched into each layer so that they appeared as the box heated and then cooled – the way lemon juice becomes visible on paper when held to a flame.* Feeling a little better at the explanation, I took off my visor and gloves and touched the metal. It was slightly warm, but not too hot to touch. I lifted it and looked inside.

The box was empty.

I looked again at the flakes floating down through the

air. They weren't soot, as I had first thought, they were
charred scraps of paper. The papers that had been in the
box had ignited when it flew open (*How had it opened?*).
One fragment, which had landed by the side of the box,
contained an ornate archaic script that I couldn't begin to
read right now with my vision this blurred and my hands
still shaking so hard. The only part I could make out was
the signature – *Will Hughes,* writ large with an elaborate
flourish just under the wax seal imprint of the swan
insignia. The rest of whatever papers had been in the box
had been reduced to confetti, feathery flakes in pale
shades of white and mauve, turning my worktable into that
snowy field in France Pissarro had painted over a century
ago.

Shadowmen

After I cleaned up the paper confetti and stored it away in the box so I could show the jeweler tomorrow what had become of its contents, I closed the lid and left it on the worktable. I considered putting it in the safe where I kept my gold and silver supplies, but the whole house was alarmed. There was no reason to put it away unless my real motive was to keep me safe from *it* . . . and that was just silly.

I took the one large scrap of paper and the silver seal that I had pried off the box with me into my bedroom though, because I wanted to look at them again when my vision cleared. I put them on my night table while I got undressed. The visual hallucinations were dissipating and I hadn't burned myself, I thought as I crawled under the covers and wrapped my arms around myself to stop my shivering. That strange sensation I'd felt when the light flashed . . . well, that was some sort of electrical charge – a shock, nothing more. And the tremors I felt now were from fatigue. It had been a long day. Before I turned off the bedside lamp, though, I took off the medallion I had made when I was sixteen (I usually slept with it on) and picked up the seal that had come off the box so that I could look at them side by side. Yes, they were almost identical, but there must have been many rings made with this seal. It didn't *mean* anything. It *was* nice to have found a token that reminded me of my mother. Almost like a message from her. I fell asleep with the seal in my hand, my fingers tracing the shape of the swan beating its wings.

In my dream I stood on the edge of a round pool. The sun was low on the opposite shore, setting behind an old stone tower and turning the water into a glittering sheet of molten gold upon which swam a black swan. The scene was tranquil, but somehow I knew that something awful was about to happen. The bird sensed it too. The black swan craned its long neck forward, spread its wings, and began to take off. I noticed as the swan stretched its neck that a silver chain with a heavy pendant lay on its breast feathers. Then, just as the swan's wing tips cleared the surface of the water, I felt something whiz past my ear, and then an anguished cry rent the still golden surface of the lake. The air turned dark with black feathers as one minute I was watching from the shore, the next I was in the water . . . and then I was no longer even myself. I was, to my horror, the wounded swan. And I was making that horrible cry, a sound like the trumpets of Judgment Day.

It was the trumpet blare that woke me.

It took me only a second to identify the actual sound as the gallery alarm two floors below – a sound that made my blood freeze. Another second had me up, pulling on the jeans, sweatshirt, and workboots I had discarded beside the bed. One more and I was on the landing looking down through the stairwell. I heard the door on the floor below open and saw my father's bald scalp appear at the banister.

'Dad!' I shouted over the insistent blat of the alarm. 'It's probably just a false alarm. Wait for the police to come.' But he couldn't hear me – or chose not to. He ran down the stairs, his red paisley robe billowing loosely in the updraft from the first floor.

Which meant the front door was open.

I took off after him, my heart pounding with fear as I took the steps two at a time. Roman kept a gun in his night table – a souvenir from World War II. Had he been foolish enough to grab it?

Halfway down the second flight I heard a shout – my father's voice – and then a gunshot. I took the last flight in two leaps and landed on the first floor on my knees. Ignoring the pain, I continued toward the kitchen door, which stood wide-open at the end of the corridor. I reached the doorway in two long, awkward leaps . . . and then froze on the threshold. The scene inside was so bizarre I thought for a moment I had finally achieved my childhood dream of slipping into a painting: a surrealist work by Dalí or de Chirico.

There were three men, each dressed in identical black turtlenecks, black pants, black gloves, and black ski masks. They could have been shadows of men instead of men. One was kneeling next to a bundle of red cloth in the open doorway of the safe, using a box cutter to cut the canvas out of a picture frame. When he was done, he handed it to the second man, who rolled it into a tight tube and who then handed it to the third man, who put it in a long oblong bag, which, I noticed with a queasy sense of the absurd, was a yoga-mat bag. I could almost have laughed. Except then I looked down and saw that the bundle of red cloth on the floor beside the safe door was in fact my father, his red robe spread out around him and blood staining the white collar of his pajama top.

I made some kind of a sound then and they all looked up. They each turned their head up toward me at the exact same moment. They kept their eyes on me for what seemed like an eternity, long enough for a dozen thoughts to run through my head. *Should I run? But how could I leave my father? Was my father dead? Would they kill me?* And, I'm embarrassed to say, *how will we ever get out of debt now if they take all our paintings?*

They all turned away at the same moment. The man who had been cutting free the canvases closed the box cutter and stood up. The second man closed the safe door and the third zipped up the yoga-mat bag. Then they walked toward me.

I pressed myself against the wall of the hallway, repulsed at the thought of one of them touching me, but I couldn't run; I had to get to my father. The shadowmen filed past me as if I weren't there. A pungent odor filled the hall as they passed – rotten eggs and ash – and snaked into my nose and mouth, filling my lungs. The hallway darkened as they passed, as if the shadows in the corners stretched out to meet them, and then they turned at the stair post and started up the stairs.

As soon as they were past me, I ran to my father and knelt by his side, feeling for a pulse in his neck and stripping away the robe to find the bullet hole.

It was below his left collarbone, an inch above his heart. At least I *hoped* it was above his heart. I felt a faint fluttery pulse against my fingers. I got up just long enough to grab the cordless phone from its charger on the wall and yank the tea cloth out from under the teapot I had left on the table. I felt a tug of regret as the blown-glazed pot rolled onto the floor and shattered – it had been my mother's – but dismissed it as I pressed the cloth against the wound and dialed 911. They told me the police and an ambulance were on the way. When I hung up, I listened for the sound of the burglars' footsteps on the stairs, but with the wail of the alarm I couldn't tell if they were coming back or not. *Would they come back and shoot us? Should I try to drag my father out of the house? But how far could I get with him? Would I hurt him if I moved him?* Finally, after what felt like an eternity, I heard the front door banging open and heavily shod feet running down the hall. I lifted my head to see two uniformed officers pointing guns at me.

'The burglars went upstairs,' I shouted over the alarm. 'There are three of them. At least one must have had a gun because they shot my father.' As I said it, I tried to remember if I had actually *seen* any of the burglars holding a gun, but the officers had already turned and left. I could hear them running up the stairs.

I turned back to my father. His face was a sickly gray. 'Dad?' I called. 'Roman? Can you hear me?'

His eyes flickered open, but they couldn't focus on me. He said something I didn't understand. I leaned closer, angling my ear to his mouth.

'Die . . . die . . . ,' he croaked.

'No, Dad, you're not going to die. I promise. The bullet missed your heart.' I tried to make my father look at me but his eyes were skittering back and forth around the room as if looking for something. I followed his gaze and saw my father's old service revolver lying under the kitchen table. He had probably dropped it when the burglars shot him.

'Oh, Dad,' I said, stroking his head. 'You should have left the gun upstairs. Maybe they wouldn't have hurt you.'

My father shook his head again, his mouth working to tell me something. I leaned down closer so he wouldn't have to work so hard.

'*Dybbuk,*' he said at last. It seemed to take all his energy to spit out the word. His eyes rolled back in his head and he lost consciousness. I felt his pulse stutter under my fingertips. Frantically, I moved my hands from his wound to his heart and pressed all my weight down – once, twice, three times – trying to remember what CPR looked like in the movies. I kept it up until an EMT knelt beside me and peeled my hands away. I hadn't seen him come in, and yet the kitchen was suddenly full of people. Uniformed police officers, EMTs, a man in a gray trench coat dripping rain on the hardwood floors. They formed a moat around my father, pushing me back. I felt as I had in my dream when I stood on the shore of the lake watching the swan gliding toward its death, as if I were somehow floating above everything. The man in the trench coat was next to me, saying something, but I couldn't hear him over the beating of the swan's wings.

'What?' I said, turning to him and looking into his eyes.

'I said you look pale. You should sit down.'

I nodded, acceding to the man's good sense, but as in my dream I could already feel myself falling into the lake, the shining water enveloping me in a blast of white light that felt – I had just time enough to think – oddly familiar.

I awoke in the ambulance.

'You passed out,' the EMT told me when I sat up. 'So we put you in here with your father.'

'How is he?' My father's face was covered with an oxygen mask and his eyes were closed.

'He's lost a lot of blood and his BP's low. Does he have a history of heart problems?'

'Angina. He had an angioplasty a year ago. Will he . . . is he . . . ?'

'He has a good shot . . . no pun intended. The bullet went in just above the heart, but there's an exit wound a few inches higher in his shoulder. I think it missed the heart, so you could say he was lucky. The shooter must have been lower down . . . crouching or something. Did he surprise the burglars?'

'I suppose so. I came in after he was shot. One of the burglars was kneeling on the floor . . . he could have been the one who shot him.' *Then where was the gun?* The only gun I'd seen had been my father's. 'He was running down the stairs. He nearly ran into them.'

'The running and the shock have put a lot of stress on his heart, and he hit his head when he fell, but he sounds like a tough old guy – chasing after the bad guys!' The

EMT looked up, a grin on his face that faded when he saw my face. 'You don't look so good, though. You'd better lie down. I don't want you falling and hurting yourself. You would've banged your head hard if that detective didn't catch you.'

I followed the EMT's advice. I still felt, as I had right before I fainted, as if I weren't completely tethered to my own body, as if I were floating above myself watching the ambulance speed toward St. Vincent's Hospital, watching myself following my father's supine body into the emergency room and holding his limp hand while his shoulder was stitched and he was hooked up to an IV. *Who is that calm woman?* I wanted to shout aloud. It couldn't be me because inside my nerves were sizzling like firecrackers and my heart was beating to a wild drumbeat. Apparently the calm façade didn't fool everyone; when the nurse noticed my color, he sent an orderly to get me a chair.

'I don't want you passing out on my watch,' he scolded in a lilting West Indies accent that felt like a warm breeze wafting through the antiseptic ER. His skin was the color of oolong tea, his long, tightly coiled hair was held back with a bright orange bandanna. His name tag read O. Smith.

'Is he likely to regain consciousness, Mr. Smith?' I asked.

'Not with all the painkillers I just gave him, darling. And if he does, he won't be making much sense. You might as well get some rest.' He spoke as if he were used to people doing what he said, but I shook my head.

'I'll stay here,' I said. 'I don't want him waking up alone.'

After an hour or so my father was admitted to a room. There was an empty bed that O. Smith said I was welcome to lie down in, but I was afraid to go to sleep, afraid that if I didn't keep watch over my father, he might slip away. So I sat in the straight-backed chair between my father's bed and a window that faced Seventh Avenue. The sky was dark over the buildings across the street, but their topmost windows reflected the pearl gray light of dawn in the east. Yesterday's rain had finally stopped. The air looked clear and cold. Steam rose from the grates in the street in sinuous plumes. I had grown up thinking that every city was festooned with the floating white puffs until my father explained that New York had an unusual system of steam pipes beneath the streets that predated the use of electricity.

'I thought the city was floating on a cloud the first time I saw it,' Roman had told me when he described sailing into New York Harbor in the late 1940s. 'I thought I was dreaming.'

I had felt as a child that the steam rising from the grates and manholes was proof that there was another world below the surface of this one. Perhaps it was the world my mother talked about when she told me bedtime stories – the Summer Country, she called it, or the Fair Land, a place where it was always high summer but every flower that bloomed from early spring to late fall bloomed there all year long. A place where pure springs bubbled up from deep within the earth and spread over the green meadows like white lace and then gathered in a pool on which swans glided. Sometimes you caught a glimpse of the Summer Country in the green shimmer at the end of a wooded path, she told me, or in the reflection of a mountain pool, or even, sometimes, through an open door on a city street where there had been no door before and nothing but smooth stone when you went back for a second look. Because the door to the Summer Country opened only in a glimpse, never in a second look. You could never look for it, but you might slip into it unawares. And then you might spend a day there only to come back and find a score of years had passed in this world and all your friends and family had aged while you remained unchanged.

'Is that why you never seem to age a day?' my father would say when he heard her telling me this story.

My mother would laugh, but I believed when I was young that she held the key to that magical place. And I believed that if you watched the shapes the steam made on early winter mornings, you might catch a glimpse of that world – of white-breasted swans gliding on crystal lakes and enchanted steeds stepping out of foamy waves. This morning, though, the wraithlike shapes massing in the shadows of the hospital did not suggest beneficent emissaries from a fairy-tale kingdom. They made me think instead of the shades of the damned rising up out of hell on Judgment Day. I don't think I'd ever had that reaction to the steam before. It made me wonder if something had changed in the city overnight – or in me.

'Miss James?' The voice startled me out of my gloomy fantasy. I turned and saw at the foot of my father's bed the detective who had been at the town house. I hadn't heard him come in and I wondered if he'd deliberately snuck up on me, but then I dismissed the idea as ridiculous. The man was a New York City police detective, not a Native American pathfinder.

'Detective Joseph Kiernan, NYPD Art Crime Division,' he said, handing me his card. 'I didn't want to wake your father. I'm sure he needs his rest. The doctor said he's in stable condition.'

'But he hasn't regained consciousness,' I said. 'I don't think that can be good.'

'So he hasn't been able to tell you what happened?'

'No, but I think that should be obvious. He surprised the burglars and they shot him.'

'Did you see them shoot him?'

'No. I was behind him on the stairs. By the time I reached the kitchen he was lying on the floor.'

'And was one of the burglars holding a gun?'

'No, he could have dropped it. They were packing away the canvases. They'd cut all but one out of their frames. They seemed to want to get out of there quickly once the alarm was triggered.'

'Yes, that's another thing I'm confused about.' The detective tossed his trench coat on the spare bed and pulled up a chair. He looked as if he was getting comfortable for a long talk. 'The safe alarm was triggered, but the front-door alarm wasn't. Did anyone else but you and your father know the front-door alarm code?'

'Several people. Our housekeeper, the receptionist . . . we always kept anything valuable in the safe, so . . .'

'And who knew that combination?'

'No one but my father and me. The burglars must have used an explosive . . .' I paused, recalling the moment when the men passed me in the hallway. It wasn't something I wanted to remember. It made me feel as if something were pressing against my chest. 'I smelled something when they walked by. Sulfur . . . and something *burnt*.'

'There was no sign of an explosion,' the detective said. 'They either knew the combination or . . .'

'Or what?' I snapped.

He tilted his head and smiled. He was handsome in a boyish, clean-cut manner, I noted in the same numb detachment I'd felt since finding my father shot on the kitchen floor: curly dark hair, square jaw, cleft chin, broad shoulders, deep brown eyes. He was no doubt used to charming women with his looks. But why was he trying to charm *me*? I was the victim here, wasn't I? 'I don't know,' he said. 'You tell me.'

'I have no idea,' I said truthfully.

'Could your father have given them the combination?'

'Only if they forced him at gunpoint.'

'But you said you were right behind your father on the stairs and they had already cut all but one of the canvases out of their frames. So there wouldn't have been time for your father to give them the combination. At least not then.'

It took a moment for his words to sink in, but when they did I was furious. 'Are you implying that my father was somehow *in* on the burglary?'

Detective Kiernan shrugged. 'I'm just trying to figure

out what happened. Are you sure the safe was locked?'

'Yes, I went back to the office to do it myself . . .' But I stopped, recalling that after I had walked Zach Reese to the door and come back to the kitchen, my father had already put away the Pissarros and locked the safe door. At least I'd assumed he had. 'Actually my father closed the safe when I was seeing a friend to the door—'

'A friend?'

'An old friend of my father's, Zach Reese.'

'The painter?' Kiernan took a notebook out of his suit jacket pocket. The motion revealed a flash of gun.

'Yes,' I said, my mouth dry. 'So you have to study art to be on the Art Crime squad?'

'It helps,' he said, his lips curving into a brief, perfunctory smile. 'But you wouldn't have to be an art expert to know Zach Reese's name. His exploits in the eighties made him pretty famous. There was that car accident out in the Hamptons. A young girl drowned.'

'Yes, that was awful. I was only a kid at the time, but my mother told me Zach was never the same. He became a heavy drinker – not that he'd been a light drinker before.'

'And he stopped painting. He ran into some trouble with gambling debts a few years later.'

'Yes, I heard something about that.' I had a cloudy memory of my parents arguing because Roman had bailed Zach out again, but I shook it away, anxious to deflect Kiernan from the direction he was headed in. 'You can't think Zach had anything to do with the burglary? He's one of my father's oldest friends.'

'We have to examine *all* possibilities, Miss James. I'm

sure you want us to find whoever is responsible for doing this to your father.' He tilted his chin in Roman's direction and stopped. Following his gaze I saw that my father's eyes were flickering open. I got up and moved quickly to his side.

'Dad? Can you hear me?' Roman's eyes opened and focused on me. His lips stretched apart – an attempted smile that turned into a grimace of pain. 'Dad, it's okay. You're in St. Vincent's. You were shot but you're going to be okay.' I looked up at Detective Kiernan, who had moved to the other side of the bed and was studying Roman's face. 'Please get the nurse!' I said. Kiernan hesitated a fraction of an instant, then turned and strode quickly from the room. When I was sure he was out of the room, I looked back down at my father and took his hand.

'There was a burglary, Dad. Three men broke in and stole the paintings in the safe. Do you remember if you locked the safe after Zach left?' Then, lowering my voice to a whisper: 'Did you give the safe combination to Zach?'

'It's okay, dear,' Roman said. I felt his fingers moving; he was trying to pat my hand but barely had the strength. 'They were insured. As long as you're all right, Margot, everything . . . everything . . .'

'It's me, Dad,' I said wincing at the sound of my mother's name on my father's lips. 'It's Garet. Mom's . . . mom's not here.'

My father tried to smile again, but another pain contorted his face. 'Garet,' he said. 'You look more and more like your mother every day . . .' Then his eyelids fluttered closed. The detective returned with the nurse and a doctor, who examined Roman and said his vital signs were strong.

'So there's probably no danger in Miss James leaving for an hour?' Kiernan said to the doctor. 'She lives just a few blocks away and I need her to go over the crime scene with me.'

The doctor not only concurred, but urged me to go out and get some air. He assured me that the floor nurse would call my cell phone if there was any change. Within minutes Detective Kiernan and I were on the street walking west toward the town house. It did feel good to be out in the air. Yesterday's storm had passed leaving a blue sky and crisp, cold air; the morning sun had banished the ominous shadows from the avenue. Detective Kiernan didn't bring up Zach Reese again during our walk. Instead he asked about the paintings that had been in the safe.

'I'll have to look at the inventory, of course,' I told him. 'But I remember them.' I listed each painting and its estimated value, ending with the Pissarros.

'Of course value's a relative term in the art market, isn't it?' Detective Kiernan asked. 'Those Pissarros didn't sell at auction. That must bring down their value.'

'I'm just giving you the valuation the insurance company assigned when the current policy was renewed several months ago.'

'So that was prior to the current downturn in the market. Conceivably the paintings might be insured for more than they're worth in this market, couldn't they be?'

We'd reached the steps to the brownstone, but the detective's question brought me up short. *The insurance.* My father had just reassured me that the paintings were insured. And last night before he went to bed he had said,

Something will turn up. But he wouldn't have . . . ? Detective Kiernan *couldn't* think that my father had arranged the theft and being shot to collect the insurance? He was smiling at me, his face as bland and mild as the morning sunshine.

I turned away without answering his question and climbed the steps. I wanted to be inside my home – the one place I had always felt safest – and yet, just yesterday I had learned that it didn't even really belong to us anymore. I stepped inside . . . and immediately began to shake. The presence of those three black-clad men was so palpable I could feel it like a heaviness in the air. Detective Kiernan passed me in the hallway and went into the kitchen. 'The forensic lab has finished in here, so you're welcome to clean up the rest,' he was saying. I started to follow him, but stopped in the doorway; I wasn't yet ready to step into the room where my father had been shot. Kiernan came back, holding an object in a plastic evidence bag.

'We found this on the floor. Do you recognize it?'

'Yes,' I told him, 'it's my father's service revolver from World War Two. And no, I don't suppose it's licensed. Frankly, I can't imagine it even works.'

'Uh-huh,' he said as if nothing surprised him anymore. 'There's one more thing. You said you were standing in this hallway when they passed you?'

'Yes.'

'So you weren't blocking the front door?'

'No. I don't think they would have cared if I had been. They didn't seem to take any notice of me. It was almost like they didn't see me.' I stopped, trying to remember something. 'There was something weird about their eyes.'

But Detective Kiernan wasn't interested in the burglars' eyes. 'Hm . . . so why do *you* think they didn't go out the front door?'

I shook my head. 'I don't know . . . maybe they were afraid the police were on the way . . . or maybe there was something they wanted upstairs.'

'Is there anything of value up there?'

'Some keepsakes of my father's . . .'

'He lives on the second floor, right? The burglars don't appear to have gone into his apartment. But the third floor . . .'

I was on the stairs before Detective Kiernan could finish his sentence. The thought of those creepy burglars trespassing in my studio and bedroom made me feel sick. I sprinted up the two flights of stairs, Kiernan a few steps behind me. What had they done in my studio? When I reached the open door, I thought for a moment that a snowstorm had swept through the room. The floor was covered in white.

I knelt on the floor and touched one of the flakes. It was dry to the touch and left a grayish streak on my hands. Of course. It was the paper that had come out of the silver box last night . . . only I was sure that I had swept all the paper debris up and put it back in the box. Then I had closed the box and left it on my worktable.

I crossed the room in three long strides, the paper confetti crunching underfoot. My soldering torch lay where I had left it last night, but the silver box was gone.

air & mist

'What's wrong? Is something missing?'

I looked up from the table to Detective Kiernan. I noticed that a flake of paper was stuck in a curl of hair that fell over his forehead. The paper was drifting around the room, buoyed by a draft from somewhere.

'A silver box,' I answered, looking around for the source of the draft. 'Something I was working on last night.'

'Was it valuable?'

'I don't really know. It wasn't mine.' I described how I had come by the box, as briefly as I could.

'It doesn't sound that valuable if the jeweler would just let you walk out with it.'

'No, I suppose not.' I thought of the blue symbols I had seen scrolling across the inside of the lid last night, but I certainly wasn't going to tell the police detective about *that*. It had been an ocular illusion, that was all, a new twist in my ocular migraine symptoms.

'They probably just grabbed it on their way out.' Kiernan pointed up with one finger. I stared at him, confused. One might use that gesture to indicate a person had ascended to heaven, but the burglars hadn't died. Then I looked up and saw what he meant. The skylight above our heads had been shattered. The metal bookcase against the wall was tilted slightly out of line and pieces of scrap metal had been shoved aside. The burglars must have used it as a ladder up to the skylight and the roof above. 'But you will have to add it to the list of stolen items,' he continued. 'You should let the owner know as soon as possible.'

'I would, only I don't have his name or address.' I was instantly sorry I had admitted to this. I could just have said I'd contact the man later. The detective was staring at me now as if I were crazy.

'I know, it sounds nuts, but you have to understand that I was distracted. I'd just gotten some bad news at our lawyer's office.'

'Really?' Detective Kiernan took out his notebook and sat on the edge of the worktable. 'Why don't you tell me about *that*?'

An hour later I finally managed to get away from Detective Kiernan, but only because the hospital called to tell me that my father was awake and asking for me. I told Kiernan I really needed a few minutes to myself before returning to the hospital, and so he reluctantly left the town house as I practically shoved him out the door. Then after he'd turned the nearest corner, I walked the few blocks to St. Vincent's, cursing myself for letting the police detective lure me into a full disclosure of our financial troubles. True, he would eventually have found out about the loan being called, but now it would color the whole investigation into the burglary. He'd focused on how *convenient,* as he kept saying, it was that the insurance money could be used to pay off the loan, or some of it. It was clear he suspected my father had arranged the burglary to collect on the insurance. All he needed now was to find out that Roman had been arrested for insurance fraud once before.

It had happened eleven years ago when I was fifteen. I knew that money was tight because I'd had to switch from private school to public the year before. I hadn't minded that – I'd gotten into LaGuardia and loved the art program there – but I hated hearing my parents arguing about money. Especially when I heard my mother complain that Roman had used money set aside for my college to buy a Warhol silk screen from one of Zach Reese's friends.

'I'll sell it for twice what I paid for it,' I heard my father say one night. 'And Garet will go to Harvard if she wants to.'

But then the Warhol Board had denied authentication to the silk screen. They claimed that Zach Reese had run off copies of the silk screen without Warhol's permission. Without the Board's seal of approval the piece was almost worthless. Three days after Roman received the news from the Warhol Board the gallery was robbed. A few paintings by minor artists were taken, but the only item of 'value' taken was the Warhol, which had been insured for the purchase price. When the same friend of Zach Reese's who had sold the painting to Roman was arrested while trying to sell the same painting to a Japanese art collector, Roman was also arrested for conspiring to defraud the insurance company. The case had dragged on for a year, during which time the gallery's reputation was nearly destroyed and my mother died in a car accident. Her obituary ran in the *Times* the same day that the case against Roman James was dropped due to lack of evidence. It wouldn't take long for Detective Kiernan to dig up that information. In fact it was weird he didn't know about it already.

Unless he did know and had only been waiting for me to mention it. Had I looked more suspicious *not* bringing up the other case? But then why should I mention it? The cases were completely different. After all, Roman had been *shot* in this burglary. If he'd hired the burglars – and the idea of my father having anything to do with those *thugs* was unthinkable – surely they wouldn't have shot him.

You could almost say he was lucky he had been shot.

I admonished myself for the thought as I entered my father's room. He looked shrunken and ancient in the hospital bed, his skin a sickly yellow against the white bandages on his shoulder, the bruises on his bald scalp livid under the hospital's fluorescent lighting. His eyes were open, but he was looking toward the window so he didn't notice me until I bent down and kissed his forehead.

'There you are!' he exclaimed, as if we'd been playing hide-and-seek and he'd just discovered me crouched behind the couch. 'I told that nurse you'd be back any minute. My Margaret wouldn't abandon her old father.'

'I'm sorry I took so long, Dad,' I said, drawing a chair closer to his side. 'I had to talk to the police at the gallery, give them the inventory list—'

'Our beautiful Pissarros!' he wailed, pressing his hands

together as if in prayer. 'That must be what they were after.' Then, lowering his voice to a hoarse whisper, he added, 'I bet it was someone at Sotheby's that tipped them off. How else would those *ganovim* know the paintings had just arrived back?'

I smiled at the Yiddish word for thieves. Roman had called them something else in Yiddish just after the shooting, but I couldn't recall what now. 'Maybe, Dad. You shouldn't have tried to stop them. You could have gotten yourself killed. Do you remember which one of the men shot you?'

Roman's brow creased and his hands fluttered shakily above the folded bedsheet. 'They all looked alike. In black . . . like Nazis . . .' He laced his fingers together and relaced them, as if trying to get a grip on some half-remembered impression. I placed my hand over both of his. I should have known that the burglars would remind him of the German soldiers who had rounded up his family and driven him from his home in Poland. 'Don't worry about it, Dad. It doesn't matter which one shot you—'

'And their eyes! Did you see their eyes? There was nothing there. It was like looking into a black pit . . . the pit of hell!'

That's what had been strange about their eyes. They had been completely black; no whites showing at all. I shuddered. 'I know, Dad, they were really creepy. I'm sure the police will catch them.'

My father's eyes widened and then darted around the room as if he were afraid that the black-clad burglars were hiding in the shadows. 'No, no, they won't find them . . . or they'll only find their shells.'

'Their shells?'

Roman's head bobbed up and down and his restless hands twisted and seized my hands so hard that I almost cried out. I wrested one hand away to press the nurse's call button. He might be having a bad reaction to whatever medication he was on. He certainly wasn't making any sense.

'The dybbuk latch on to weak men and possess them.'

'The dybbuk?' It was the word Roman had used when he first regained consciousness in the house. 'What does that mean, Dad?'

'*Demons*,' he answered, his eyes skittering into the corners of the room. 'I could feel them trying to get inside of me, trying to control me . . .'

'It was a terrible shock coming upon those men. Of course you were frightened. And then you were shot and you hit your head when you fell. Try not to think about it anymore.'

I looked up, relieved to see a nurse coming through the door. It wasn't the kind nurse from last night, but a middle-aged woman with dishwater blond-gray hair and a harried look on her face. She was carrying a tray with a syringe. 'Sounds like someone's getting himself all worked up,' she said, but it was me, not Roman, whom she looked at reprovingly. 'We can't have that.' She injected the syringe into the IV line. Roman's eyes were still skittering back and forth, but in an ever shortening arc until they settled back on me.

'I made sure they couldn't get inside me,' he said, smiling slyly as his eyelids began to close. 'I tricked . . .' He lost consciousness before he could finish his sentence.

'There,' the nurse said. 'That's enough of that nonsense. He was rambling something awful before.'

'My father is usually quite sharp.' I understood that the nurse was just tired and overworked, but I didn't like her giving him medication just to shut him up. 'Is it possible he has brain damage from the fall? Or that the medication you're giving him is causing hallucinations?'

The nurse clucked her tongue and snapped the bed-sheet tight over Roman's narrow, sunken chest. 'Your father's eighty-four years old. Even the sharpest octogenarian can become a bit unhinged after a shock like the one he's had. Thing to do is keep him calm, not get him all excited.'

'I'll remember that,' I said. 'Still, I'd like to talk to his doctor about his medication.'

'Dr. Monroe is in his office right now talking to that police officer. I believe they're old friends from when the doctor used to work in the ER. Why don't you poke your head in the office door?'

With a mounting sense of dread I followed the nurse's directions to Dr. Monroe's office, along a serpentine path that seemed designed to keep the relatives of the sick and injured from tracking down their loved ones' doctors. Detective Kiernan and Dr. Monroe might be 'old friends,' but if the case came up, that might not stop the doctor from passing on to the detective something outrageous Roman had said to him. God knew what my father might say in his current mental state. While I still couldn't believe that my father had engineered the theft, I could imagine him commenting on how lucky he was that the paintings were insured. I could only hope he hadn't broadcast his belief that the burglars had been possessed by demons.

When I reached Dr. Monroe's office, I paused outside to see if I could get an advance hint of what my father might have said. The doctor and the detective weren't talking about Roman's case, though; they were discussing Sunday's Jets game.

'It's a sign of things to come,' Kiernan was saying. 'Once Favre gets fully used to the new system, it'll be "bombs away" every Sunday. Great to watch.'

'I don't know,' the doctor countered. 'Favre has a knack for an interception at the worst time.'

'I hope I'm not interrupting any medically crucial discussion,' I said as I poked my head in the doorway.

Dr. Monroe, who looked about my age, smiled at me. The detective invited me in.

'Not a sports fan I take it,' Kiernan commented.

'I'm just concerned about my father,' I said, directing my gaze exclusively at the doctor. 'He seems disoriented. Is his head injury serious?'

'I should go,' Detective Kiernan said, starting to get up in an offer of privacy.

'You can stay,' I responded. It was a debatable decision, but I felt that I should bend over backward to look as if we had nothing to hide.

'The X-ray of his brain looks fine,' Dr. Monroe said,

tapping one of the X-rays clipped to the light board behind his desk. 'The disorientation is probably a result of the morphine he's on – a very common side effect, especially in elderly patients. Had you noticed any cognitive impairment before this incident?'

'None at all,' I said with conviction. 'My father does the Sunday *Times* crossword puzzle in twenty minutes and remembers the name of every customer and artist who's passed through the gallery in the last forty years.'

'And you haven't noticed any depression or suicidal thoughts?' The question came from Detective Kiernan.

I felt a prickle of unease travel up my spine but couldn't imagine what he was after. 'No. My father is not prone to depression. Of course he grieved when my mother died ten years ago, but my father is a survivor. He saw his entire family die in the Holocaust.'

'A lot of Holocaust survivors suffer depression—' Dr. Monroe began.

'Not my father. He's always believed that it was his duty to live for those who perished. What is this about anyway? What does my father's mental state have to do with getting shot by a burglar?'

Neither the doctor nor the detective said anything for a minute. I saw the two men exchange a look and then, at a nod from Kiernan, Monroe pointed at another X-ray clipped to the light board behind his desk.

'This is an X-ray of your father's shoulder. You can see where the bullet entered your father's chest just above his heart and here' – he tapped another X-ray – 'where the bullet exited just below his trapezius muscle in his back.

From the angle of the bullet's trajectory and the powder residue on his chest and hand—'

'His hand?'

'Yes, *his* hand.'

'The bullet came from the service revolver we found on the floor,' Detective Kiernan interrupted. 'The one you identified as your father's. There's really only one likely conclusion. Your father's wound was self-inflicted. He shot himself.'

Twenty minutes later I left the hospital, crossed Seventh Avenue, and started walking west on Greenwich as fast as I could go. I was too shocked and upset to go back to the gallery. I couldn't bring myself to face Maia or any of our concerned clientele or neighbors who might drop by the gallery when they heard about the burglary. Once the rumor got out that Roman James had orchestrated the theft himself, they'd resent their own expressions of sympathy made now. And what other conclusion would anyone reach but that Roman James had shot himself to make it look as if he were the victim of the burglars? Still, every time I tried to imagine my father aiming a gun at himself I just couldn't picture it.

'The body is the sanctuary of the soul,' Roman had said to me when he'd learned I was thinking of getting a tattoo when I was in college. 'You wouldn't spray-paint graffiti on the synagogue wall, would you? So why do it to your soul's house?' How could he have fired a gun into his own flesh? There had to be some other explanation.

I crossed Eighth Avenue and continued west on Horatio

Street. I could see the Hudson gleaming at the end of the street. I could cross the West Side Highway and walk on the Hudson River Greenway for miles . . . walk until I was too exhausted to think or . . . I stopped and looked south on Hudson Street. The jeweler had to be on one of these streets near the river. I could work my way back and forth until I found him. Then I could tell the jeweler that the box had been stolen and I could also tell Detective Kiernan the address of the shop. He'd acted as if he didn't believe the silver box or its owner existed. As if I were crazy.

I started working my way south along the narrow, cobblestoned streets that lay between Hudson Street and the West Side Highway. As I ticked off each street – Horatio, Jane, Bethune – failing to find the antiques shop, I felt a mounting sense of panic over my father's situation. What if Detective Kiernan was right? What if my father had shot himself and had arranged the burglary to collect on the insurance? Although he'd not been charged in the Warhol case, I couldn't help but remember the arguments about money he and my mother had had right before that theft. And now, just when I'd told him how dire our financial situation was, there'd been another burglary, albeit one that occurred only a few hours after he'd received the information. It was inconceivable that there had been enough time for him to plan anything. I hated myself for thinking it, but doubt had seeped into my mind. *And,* an insidious voice inside me insisted, *if he is guilty, he'll go to jail and you'll be all alone.*

I stopped in the middle of Cordelia Street, my eyes

filling with tears, my vision swimming. *You're okay*, I said to myself, trying to substitute the reassuring voice of my mother for that of the nasty pessimist who seemed to have taken control of my brain. *You're okay*.

I wiped my eyes, blinked away the tears . . . and saw that I was facing a glass door that sparkled with gilt in the sunlight. It looked familiar. I stepped into the doorway and drew my fingers along the fragment of gold lettering and read *mist* . . . I'd noticed it yesterday and guessed that it was the remainder of the word *chemist*. Now I wondered if it could also be the remainder of the word *alchemist*. In any event, this was the place.

I tried to look through the glass, but it had somehow acquired a layer of grime overnight. I rubbed at it, uncovering a few more golden letters. An *a*, an *i*, and an *r* together, then below them an ampersand. *Air & Mist*. Nothing and nothing. The words seemed almost mocking. When I'd cleared a clean circle I peered through the glass, but everything was still gray. It took me a moment to realize that that was because everything inside the shop *was* gray. There was the same counter with its art-nouveau curves and the glass shelves, only they were broken and covered with a thick layer of gray dust. The damask curtain behind the counter hung in mildewed shreds festooned with cobwebs. The floor was dusted with a perfect silt of gray unbroken by footprints. It looked as if no one had set foot in the shop for years.

Tea and Scones

I stared through the glass until a voice from the street drew my attention. '. . . and then we'll have our tea and scones and *then* we'll go look at the puppies in the window and *then* we'll go pick up Daddy's dry cleaning . . .'

The voice was coming from a young woman pushing a toddler in a stroller. The little girl – she was somewhere between two and three I guessed – was wearing an olive-and-mauve, crocheted sweater over a plaid jumper and bright pink tights. She was waving a doll crocheted out of the same color yarns as her sweater.

'Excuse me,' I called, but the mother didn't seem to hear me.

'. . . and then we'll go back home and have our naps . . .'

I stepped out into the street nearly colliding with the stroller. The woman gasped and looked at me as if I were planning to snatch her child. 'Sorry,' I said. 'I didn't mean to startle you. I just wanted to know if you knew anything about this store. Did it just go out of business?'

'What store?' the woman asked, leaning down to adjust her daughter's perfectly aligned sweater.

'*This* store.' I jabbed my finger at the grime-covered

window that yesterday had sparkled with gold and silver. The mother glanced cursorily toward the window but her eyes didn't seem to focus. Her child waved her doll toward the door and made a gurgling sound.

'It was an antique-jewelry store yesterday,' I told her.

The woman shook her head. 'We've lived on this block for over a year and I never noticed it,' she said, shrugging. 'Sorry.'

I watched her push the stroller down the street. At the corner she went into a doorway under a painted wood sign that read PUCK. As I watched, another woman piloting a stroller approached, her little boy enthusiastically waving a toy truck at the store. A neighborhood spot for local moms, then.

I glanced over my shoulder at the abandoned storefront. I should at least get the address. There was no number on the door so I checked the number on the building west of it: 123. Then I walked to the building east of it. It was 121. Could there be odd and even numbers on the same side? But when I crossed the street I found 122 there, slightly to the west. Okay, then, 121½. It wasn't as if it were the *only* half address in the city.

I paused outside the glass door of Puck looking in at a long narrow room under an old stamped-tin ceiling, full of mismatched chairs and unpainted picnic tables. There were metal lawn chairs painted in faded pastel colors, weathered Adirondack chairs, overstuffed easy chairs, and chairs that looked as if they had been made from bent branches still covered with bark. The tables were crowded with teapots, china plates, and three-tiered platters holding scones, sandwiches, and cookies. A tearoom, however rustic the décor. They were certainly getting popular in the city.

When I opened the door, the aroma of warm butter and sugar made me remember that I hadn't eaten in over twenty-four hours. I'd get something, then. It would give me an excuse to chat with the patrons, one of whom *must* have noticed the antiques store down the block. I sank into an Adirondack chair, which I suspected was going to be too low to the ground for comfort, but turned out to be surprisingly comfortable. The woman I'd accosted on the street looked at me and whispered something to another mother. I decided I might as well jump right in before they concluded I was a pedophile.

'I'm sorry I startled you before,' I said. 'I'm trying to locate a jeweler who had a shop on Cordelia Street. You see he was fixing my father's watch and now the store seems to have moved.'

The notion of losing a family heirloom instantly galvanized the crowd of mothers. 'That's awful,' the mother of a little boy in a red fleece hoodie said. 'There's no forwarding address on the storefront?'

'No. And I don't even have the man's name. Have any of you ever been in the store? It's halfway down the block on the south side.'

The women conferred and discussed and resolved that no, no one had ever noticed a jewelry store or an antiques store or a watch-repair store on the block even though they all regularly traversed Cordelia Street between their homes and preschools and parks and shops. A woman whose little boy she addressed as Buster summed it up for the rest of them: 'It's strange there'd be a store there that none of us ever saw.'

I concurred. It was strange.

'But you should ask Fen,' another woman said. 'After all, she works here.'

Realizing they meant the baker behind the counter, and also noticing that there was no table service, I thanked the women and heaved myself up from the Adirondack chair. The woman behind the counter was just pulling a tray of scones out of a small convection oven. She was wearing a brown corduroy jumper over a cream turtleneck and a matching brown corduroy tam with green trim that sat straight on top of her light brown hair. She wore small round-framed glasses balanced on a diminutive nose. She looked as if she'd escaped from a Beatrix Potter illustration. If she had turned to reveal a bushy gray tail, I wouldn't have been too surprised.

'The reason none of them remember the shop is that it was hidden by the mist yesterday,' she said before I could ask my question; clearly she'd been listening in on my conversation with the customers. 'How did you find it?'

'I ducked into its doorway to get out of the rain,' I said.

'Ah.' Fen the baker pushed her glasses up her nose to look at me more closely. 'You see, *they* all had umbrellas and raincoats and stroller canopies to keep the rain from chasing them into doorways. But you didn't, did you?' Her gaze traveled from my face down to my hands and fastened there.

'No, I didn't. The forecast didn't say rain.' I wasn't sure

why I felt that I had to defend myself against the baker.

'No, it didn't.' She looked up from my hands and into my face. 'It didn't say fog or mist either, did it? When I saw the fog rolling in from the river, I knew that something was up and now I see that it was you. Dr. John Dee's Watch Repair and Alchemist hasn't been at that address for quite some time.'

'John Dee, is that his name?' I asked grasping at the one solid piece of information to come out of the baker's serpentine rambles. The name was familiar, somehow, but I couldn't place it right away.

'One of them,' she replied. 'Oh! My scones are done. You look half-famished, by the way. I'll pack up something for you to take home for you and your friends.'

'I don't need—' I began to explain that I didn't need food for anyone but myself, but the baker had already disappeared into the back room. A man's voice – a rich bass that sounded as if it belonged to a golden-age radio announcer – asked, 'Is she the one who went into Dee's yesterday?'

The baker's murmured reply was impossible to make out, but whatever it was seemed to startle the man. 'The swan?' he boomed. 'The black swan?'

I looked down at the swan signet ring on my right hand. That's what the baker had been looking at. It was also what the jeweler – *John Dee, where had I heard that name before?* – had noticed yesterday. But what could an old signet ring my mother gave me have to do with anything?

The baker returned with two large brown bags. I reached into my coat pocket for my wallet but the baker shook her head. 'It's on the house. Savory tea pies,' she said, holding up the bag in her right hand, 'and scones,' holding up the one in her left. Before I could object, she pressed both bags into my arms. They were warm and deliciously fragrant.

'Thank you, it's awfully kind of you . . .' I fell silent because I was afraid I might start to cry.

'No, no, no!' she said, waving her arms. 'Please don't thank me. You need some sustenance after what you've been through.'

I was about to ask her how she knew that I'd been *through* anything, but the *ting* of an oven timer summoned her away. No doubt I looked as if I'd been through hell, I told myself, and really, I had been. Now, though, I just felt drained and exhausted . . . and hungry. I needed to go home and try to make sense of what I'd learned and then figure out a way to track down this John Dee fellow. As I turned to go, I remembered where I'd seen the name John Dee before. It had been on the Wikipedia list of famous alchemists I'd looked up when I brought home the silver box. John Dee was a famous alchemist and astronomer. *An Elizabethan alchemist and astronomer.* The original John Dee had been dead for nearly four hundred years.

I walked back to the town house, cradling the warm bags in my arms. I was so weak with hunger that I almost sat down on a curb to eat the contents right there, but I was only a few blocks away. When I got to the town house, I was relieved to see that Maia, whom I had called earlier, had put a notice on the gallery door informing our patrons that the gallery was temporarily closed for repairs. I let myself into the house and started back toward the kitchen . . . but froze when I heard a loud crash from the back of the house. An image of the black-clad shadow-men came back to me. It was all I could do to force myself down the hall, clutching the warm bakery bags to my chest as if they could protect me.

Instead of burglars, though, I found Becky Jones and Jay Fine, my two best friends since high school. Jay was on his knees by the safe door scrubbing the floor. Becky was sweeping up broken pottery. The back door to the garden was propped open by a kitchen chair, which had toppled over – no doubt the source of the crash I'd heard. As soon as she saw me, Becky dropped the broom and held out her arms. I barely had time to put the bags on the table before Becky wrapped her arms around me, her chin hitting my armpit. She squeezed tight and then took a step back and swatted me hard on the arm.

'Why didn't you call us?' she asked. 'And why don't you have your cell phone on?' Like most of our generation Becky couldn't imagine going five minutes without check-ing her cell phone. Maybe because I had grown up with older parents who had a more old-world sensibility in a house with windup clocks and record-playing phono-graphs, I wasn't quite as attached to the new technology. Becky accused me of being a Luddite; Jay thought it was kind of cool and steampunk.

'I forgot my phone when I went back to the hospital,' I said. 'And I was going to call, but one thing happened after another. How did you find out?'

'Maia called us.' Jay sat back on his heels and dropped the sponge into a bucket of water. Red water. 'We came right over, but then we didn't know where you were. Maia let us in. She said that the police said it was okay to clean up.'

'Where were you?' Becky demanded, punching my arm again. For a tiny girl – she claimed five feet but I knew she was really four feet eleven and a half – Becky's punch packed a wallop. She had so much bottled energy inside her that it seemed to crackle from the ends of her tightly curled brown hair. When she played drums onstage, she sometimes seemed to hover midair above her drum set. Jay, on the other hand, was slow and deliberate. I often wondered how they played music together, but their band, London Dispersion Force, had been going nonstop since college. They'd just come back from a tour of England and they were recording their first album on a small indie label.

'I took a walk after visiting my father in the hospital . . . and got some food.' I gestured toward the bags. 'Aren't you guys playing at Irving Plaza tonight? I'm surprised Fiona let you out.' Fiona was the lead vocalist and business manager of London Dispersion Force and a stickler for rehearsal times.

'Fiona said to tell you that if you find out what a-holes did this to you and Roman, she'll take care of them,' Becky said.

For the second time today I felt my eyes filling up with tears. Apparently baked goods and threats of vengeance made me sentimental.

'Why don't you sit down,' Jay said, pulling a chair out for

me. Jay was the one who always noticed when someone was skating on thin ice. Beneath his laid-back exterior, he was the sensitive one in the band – the one who wrote the song lyrics and made sure everyone was okay. 'And tell us all about it.'

'I'll make some tea.' Becky was already at the sink, filling the kettle. The sight of tears always made her get busy.

'Okay. I've got some food.' I pointed to the bags on the table. 'There's plenty for all of us . . .' I stared at the bags and felt a sudden lurch in my empty stomach. How had the baker at Puck known I would need extra for my friends?

'I simply refuse to believe your father arranged the burglary.' Becky swept away any possibility of Roman James's culpability as neatly as she swept the pastry crumbs off the table. Crumbs were practically all that was left of the two bags of savory tea pies and scones. They were so delicious – the pies had held an assortment of mincemeat, eggs, cheese, leeks, and something with curry; the scones had come with clotted cream and raspberry jam – that I had to resist the urge to lick the buttery flakes not just from my fingers, but from Becky's and Jay's fingers and chins as well. A feeling of warmth and contentment spread out from my stomach to the tips of my fingers and toes. My friends' steadfast belief in my father's innocence was no small part of the pleasure I felt.

'No way,' Jay said, leaning back and rubbing his swollen belly. 'He wouldn't let those thugs into the house with you here. I say this Dee guy you met at the jewelry store is behind the whole thing. If he was legit, then why would he have packed up shop so suddenly and gone to such lengths to make it look like the shop hadn't been occupied in years? And why would he use the name of a dead alchemist? It's obviously an alias. It all smells like a con game. I bet he put some kind of drug in that box that knocked you out.'

I smiled at Jay. He was a big fan of pulp fiction – Doc Savage and The Shadow – and loved elaborate explanations for everyday occurrences. 'But even if that were possible, Jay, I wandered into his store randomly.' In my head, though, I heard the baker at Puck saying that the rain had pushed me into Dee's doorway, the rain that hadn't been in the weather forecast, but I dismissed the idea. I was grateful that neither of my friends had suggested I had the wrong store – or that I'd made the whole thing up; I wasn't going to impose on their credulity any further by talking about supernatural weather or dybbuks or the blue symbols I'd hallucinated inside the silver box. 'How could Dee really have set up such an elaborate scheme on such short notice?'

'Clearly he was organized enough to vacate his store and make it look like it hadn't been used in years,' Becky said. 'I say you're dealing with a clever mastermind.'

'An evil genius!' Jay added in an ominous low voice.

'Thank you, Orson Welles.' Becky swatted Jay with a dish towel. 'You have to give Detective Kiernan John Dee's name and the address of the store. Maybe he's a known con man.'

'Sure. I'll just tell him that the baker at Puck's told me that John Dee, Elizabethan alchemist, who resides at 121½

Cordelia Street, an abandoned storefront, has our Pissarros. I'm sure he'll drop the investigation of my father immediately.'

As Becky and Jay exchanged a look, I was sorry I'd let myself sound as bitter and discouraged as I felt. Especially around Jay. I knew he picked up on people's unhappiness and took it on himself.

'You need some rest, James,' Becky said. 'We'll stay and keep you company. You shouldn't be alone here. What if those thugs come back?'

'No way! You have that gig at Irving Plaza tonight, which – shit!' I looked at the clock over the stove and got to my feet. 'Which you're going to be late for. And I have to get back to the hospital to check on Roman. I promise I'll be fine.'

Becky looked as if she were going to launch into a speech, but Jay silenced her with a look – no mean feat. 'We'll walk you to St. Vincent's then,' he said. 'And we'll come back here after the last set. It's easier than hauling the equipment back to Williamsburg anyway.'

I couldn't argue with Jay's plan. The truth was I didn't relish the idea of being alone in the town house with the thought that those hollow-eyed men might come back.

Jaws

My father was sleeping when I checked in on him at St. Vincent's, and my favorite nurse – whose first name, I learned, was Obie – assured me that he was doing fine. 'Don't you worry; I'll watch out for him tonight. You hurry on home.' He glanced out the window beside my father's bed. 'Looks like some weather's coming up from the south.'

Obie Smith was right. A cold, needle-sharp rain was falling when I left the hospital. I turned my coat collar up and bowed my head, wishing I'd brought a hat or an umbrella. But the air had been dry and crisp when I'd left the house. On the corner of Seventh Avenue and Twelfth Street I looked north toward midtown. The lights of the avenue shone clear white against a cobalt sky. But when I looked south, I couldn't make out the opposite street corner for the fog. It was as if the southern tip of Manhattan had been swallowed by a cloud.

Weird weather, I thought crossing the avenue, perhaps another sign of global warming. But it wasn't anything to get nervous about. There were plenty of people on Greenwich Avenue walking toward me . . .

I stopped on the corner of Jane and looked around me.

All the pedestrians on Greenwich were walking toward Seventh Avenue, *none* were walking toward Eighth. Could there be a parade or an event I didn't know about? But what parade fell in the middle of December? Maybe they were all heading over to Irving Plaza to hear London Dispersion Force, I thought, determined to think *positively*.

The fog was worse on Jane Street: a viscous clot of curdled cream, tinged yellow and faintly redolent of rotten eggs, sort of the same odor the shadowmen had given off. *This* couldn't be freak weather – it had to be a water-main break or a gas leak. Maybe I should go back . . . but back where? I was exhausted. All I wanted was to be in my own home in my own bed. The banister of my stoop loomed up out of the fog. I'd go inside and watch the TV news to find out what was going on.

After I unlocked the door, entered, and punched in the alarm code, I leaned my back against the door as if to keep the fog outside. Only the fog seemed to already *be* inside. The hallway was murky, the shadowed corners smeary and blurred. I must be getting one of my migraines. The distinctive jagged-edged blind spot that always heralded the headaches, which I'd grown to think of as an evil air-borne sprite, was bobbing across my line of vision. It was no wonder after all I'd been through. I needed to take two Advils and lie in a dark room for ten hours. That was all.

I trudged up the two flights of stairs recalling how my mother used to say that we'd need to install an elevator when she was an old lady.

'You'll never be an old lady,' Roman would always quip,

meaning, of course, that my beautiful mother would never look old, not that she would die in a car crash at sixty-one. Roman had been right about one thing: Margot James had still looked like a woman in her thirties when she died.

When I opened my apartment door, I found that Becky and Jay had been up there too. Someone had swept up the paper confetti and dusted away the fingerprint powder and someone (Becky, probably, whose carpentry skills had been honed during a summer working for Habitat for Humanity) had nailed a board over the broken skylight. I could see a sliver of sky between the board and the frame, though; I hoped Becky had been a little more thorough in those homes in Ecuador. It even looked as if Becky had gotten to do what she'd been threatening to do for years: she'd dusted and polished my shelves of jewelry supplies and scrap metal. The bent street signs, discarded bicycle wheels, lengths of chain, and junk car parts that I had culled from city streets and abandoned warehouses gleamed like brand-new toys. Even the tanks of acetylene and oxygen looked as if they'd been wiped down with a rag. The one object that hadn't been dusted was the dragon sculpture that hung over the worktable. Becky thought it was creepy. I couldn't blame her.

The head was a hydraulic spreader and cutter that I'd found in a dump out in Greenpoint. Even lying in a heap of garbage it had looked like the snout of a reptilian monster. It was the monster I saw every night in my dreams. The last time I had seen it in real life had been when my mother died.

I was sixteen. My mother had rented a car to drive me

to a college interview at the Rhode Island School of Design. We'd argued the whole way back, driving through a snowstorm, over where I wanted to go to school. I was so angry at her that I moved to the backseat when we stopped for gas. I had decided I would rather stay in the city and go to FIT. It was a fraction of the cost of a private school such as RISD and way less pretentious. My mother kept insisting that she'd find resources to send me to RISD. 'You can be anything you want to be, Garet. You have to be free to choose . . . you'll be better off out of the house.'

'So I don't have to listen to you and Dad fighting?' I'd asked, putting on my Walkman headphones and turning my head to the window, which was fogged over by the falling snow. I was still staring out the right rear-seat window when the driver of a red Ford Expedition changed lanes without checking her blind spot and rammed into our rental, flipping it over and sending it skidding across three lanes of traffic. A second SUV hit the upended left rear fender at an angle, sending our car spinning into a low concrete wall against which it came to rest. I found myself pinned between two walls of metal, the passenger-side door and an accordioned version of the door on the other side. I could see the back of my mother's head and hear my name being said over and over.

'Garet, can you hear me? Are you okay? Garet?'

'I'm here, Mom. I'm okay, but I can't move. Are you okay?'

My mother hadn't answered at first and then she told me that she was fine. She told me that she was sorry we'd argued about college. She trusted me to make the right decision for myself. 'Marguerite,' she said, using the French version of my name, which she always pronounced like an endearment, 'always trust your own instincts. You're a rare bird . . . unique . . . think for yourself . . .'

She'd said something else that I lost in the blare of sirens that suddenly surrounded us. The face of a man in a fire helmet appeared at the driver's-side window and my mother said something to him that I couldn't hear. Then the man was at my window, his face a menacing red from the emergency lights pulsing behind him.

'There's something else I need to tell you,' my mother was shouting over the sirens.

'It's okay, Mom, they're getting us out,' I screamed back at her.

'Yes, yes, but just in case, honey—'

Whatever my mother was about to say was obliterated by the screech of tearing metal. Something rammed into the twisted doorframe. It looked like the snout of a giant beast and as I watched in horrified awe, it spread its jaws and let out an anguished scream.

Later I would understand that the rescue workers were using a hydraulic spreader and cutter – the so-called Jaws of Life – to cut me out of the wrecked car, and the sound I heard was the sound of ripping metal. But to me it would always seem as if the thing itself had opened its jaws and screamed.

When the fireman pulled me out of the car, I was screaming too, yelling at the man to go back and get my mother. We'd only gone ten yards or so when the car exploded into a ball of flames that narrowly missed us.

Later I would learn that my mother had been impaled on the steel rod of the crushed steering wheel. She wouldn't have lived even if they'd gotten her out. Guessing that, my mother had told the fireman to get me out instead. I've always felt, though, as if I had been snatched from my mother by that screaming, snapping *thing*, the Jaws of Life.

A few years later – in my senior year at FIT – I found the one I had now and knew immediately what I wanted to do with it. I had taken it home and using chain links and spare automobile parts welded it into a fire-breathing dragon. I called it Jaws. I thought it would be cathartic to turn my worst nightmare into a piece of art. After all, isn't that what art is all about? Turning chaos and pain into something meaningful? Looking at the creature now, though, all I saw was how scared I'd been in the days right after my mother had died, terrified that if my father were sent to prison, I'd be as good as an orphan. And here I was back in the same place. I'd almost lost my father last night. If Roman was convicted of arranging the robbery, I'd lose him to prison. How long would a man his age survive there? I might have been ten years older than when my mother died, but I was no more ready to be alone.

To be an orphan.

The words were in my head, but they were voiced in a sibilant hiss, which wasn't my own.

It was the voice of the monster. Its red reflector-light eyes were leering at me, its serrated, rust-stained teeth grinning, mocking me for any hope I'd ever had that I was strong enough to make it on my own.

You're a rare bird, my mother had always told me.

You're a lame duck, Jaws quipped.

. . . unique . . .

. . . a freak . . .

. . . you've accomplished so much . . .

. . . you're about to be out on the street, bankrupt, alone . . .

I turned away from the metal monster toward my work-table. I caught a glimpse of myself in the befogged windows, my long black hair wild and scraggly around a pale, gaunt face, my eyes hollow black sockets. *A witch, a hag,* the monster hissed. I picked up the soldering torch that I'd used last night and then put it down. *No, it was too small.* I needed the welding torch. I'd melt the damn thing down to a puddle – a heap of scrap metal and junk. That's all it was – not art. I hadn't wrested meaning from pain, there was no meaning, just chaos.

I put on my visor and gloves and adjusted the acetylene and oxygen levels in the welding torch. Then I climbed up onto the table, unhooked the sculpture from the wires that held it up, and dumped all six feet of the metal monster down onto the worktable. Its head bobbed on its chain-link neck, those sharp, serrated teeth brushing at my leather gloves, and it made an awful noise as it fell to the metal table. As I clambered down to the floor, part of my brain knew I shouldn't be handling a welding torch in my current exhaustion and despair, but that part of my brain was curiously muffled, as if it had been swamped by the fog that pressed on the windowpanes and which, even now, was beginning to creep under the edges of the board Becky had nailed over the skylight. The part of my brain that wasn't muffled wanted to destroy the leering metal monster. I clamped a pair of pliers on to the monster's jaws and aimed the torch at the chain link at the base of its head. I'd break the damned thing's neck first. Sparks flew up from the heating metal, cascading over its head, smoldering on its glass eyes and glowing bloodred on its needle-sharp teeth. Fog spewed out of its mouth like smoke. Just before I cut the chain link in two, something flashed in its eyes. It almost looked as if it were laughing.

The length of the chain that formed the monster's neck, now cut from its head, unspooled to the floor.

Damn! I screamed as twenty pounds of stainless steel hit my workboot. I took a step back and caught my ankle on the chain. I fell backward, the torch following me down like a serpent slithering over the table. It wriggled on the floor, spitting flame. Kicking my foot free of the chain, I scuttled backward. On the table the monster's head turned.

It can't, I thought in that dim corner of my brain not paralyzed with fear, it's not connected to the chain anymore. But that's what it was doing. The head turned toward me, its eyes burning, and it opened wide its terrible jaws.

My back hit the oxygen and acetylene tanks. I pushed myself upright against them and turned – hating to turn my back on that *thing* – and turned off both tanks of gas.

Something hissed behind me. When I turned around, the extinguished torch was lying on the floor a few feet from the pile of chain. The Jaws of Life was hanging over the edge of the table. Flakes of black ash were falling through the air, which is what happened when the acetylene was too high.

Outside the fog pulsed against the window as if it would break the glass, but then it rolled back into the night, like a hurt animal slinking back to its lair.

Saint Lion

When I woke up the next morning, I felt hungover, as if I'd gone out and done a dozen tequila shots. When I stumbled out into my studio, I was greeted by the malevolent eye of Jaws staring up at me from my scorched worktable. What had possessed me?

What had possessed me?

Roman had said that the burglars were possessed by demons. Last night I had felt as if I'd been possessed by the demons of despair and self-loathing, and then Jaws had come to life and attacked me. Or at least it felt as though he'd come to life. It could have been my imagination, just as the figures on the box could have been a trick of the eye. Maybe something was wrong with my eyes . . . or my head. What if I had a brain tumor? Should I check myself into St. Vincent's for a CAT scan? I had a feeling, though, that if I told a doctor about the things I had seen in the last few days, it might not be so easy to check myself *out* of the hospital.

I went downstairs, hoping to fight off the creeping feelings of despair with a pot of strong tea. I found Becky sitting at the table reading the *Times*. She was so immersed in whatever article she was reading that I was two inches from her before she noticed me. Then she jumped and wadded the paper into a ball, which she attempted to shove into her lap under the table.

'What?' I asked. 'Did you get a bad review? Those bastards. Let me see.'

'No, it's not a review. In fact we had a great night – there was this guy from a major record label who said he was going to bring a producer to our show at the Apollo tonight. So no, no bad review. Really.'

'That's great.' I gave Becky a hard stare. I hadn't seen her this twitchy since she took the LSAT, back when she was still going to fulfill her mother's dreams of becoming a lawyer.

'Yeah . . . well, I just put some of those scones in the oven and made a pot of tea. You should have some tea, you look awful.'

'Thanks, Beck. I will.' I moved to open the oven door without an oven mitt and Becky jumped up to stop me from burning myself. The paper fell to the floor and I grabbed it to open it to the page she'd been reading. It was in the Metro section. The story was on the burglary of the James Gallery. 'Second Theft in Decade at Village Gallery.'

'"*Second Theft*,"' I read out loud. 'As if we're the only business in New York City to be burglarized more than once in a decade.'

'Those bastards,' Becky swore as she took the scones out of the oven. 'Don't let them get you down, kid. They don't know what they're talking about.'

I read the rest of the story with a sinking heart. The

reporter had dug up the ten-year-old fraud case against my father. Of course, the story made no claims that there was anything suspicious about this theft, but it was hard to avoid the implication. It ended with the line 'Repeated calls to the gallery were not returned.'

'Like I have nothing better to do with my father in the hospital than return phone calls to the newspaper,' I said, guiltily glancing at the blinking light on the answering machine. I'd have to listen to messages sooner or later.

'Those bastards,' Becky repeated, pushing the plate of scones in my direction.

'Um,' I said, reaching for a scone, 'I didn't think we left this many scones last night. I didn't think we left *any*.'

'Me, neither, but the bag was nearly full when I came down this morning.' She took a bite, closed her eyes, and let out a little moan.

'God, Becky, get a room.' Then I took a bite and closed my eyes and swooned a little, too. I felt instantly better. The article wasn't such a big deal. If I could find John Dee, I might be able to redirect the police investigation. The only problem was I had no idea how to find John Dee.

I opened my eyes and reached for a wayward scone crumb that had fallen on the paper. My finger landed on a name. It was a name I had recently seen but for a second I couldn't remember where.

Will Hughes: a hedge fund manager for hard times, the story read. *Will Hughes reports that his fund, Black Swan Partners LP, is up +14% ytd despite the dramatic declines in all market indices this year.*

'Will Hughes,' I said out loud. 'That's the guy whose

name was on the paper in the box. Weird that his fund is called Black Swan . . .' I turned the page to where the story was continued. Will Hughes was pictured standing in the arched doorway of a Tudor-style building.

'Hm, he's good-looking,' Becky said.

He *was* good-looking – wavy, light brown hair framing wide cheekbones, pale eyes framed with dark lashes, and a full, sensuous mouth – but I wasn't looking at him. I was looking at the crest on the arch above his head. It was the same device as the one on my ring and the one on the box.

Becky was skeptical that I'd be able to just call up a billionaire hedge fund manager and get an appointment. 'I mean, how are you even going to get his number?'

'From Chuck Chennery,' I told her.

I called Chuck and after listening to his polite expressions of concern for Roman's health – God bless his upper-crust reserve, he never once let on there might be something fishy about the burglary although he certainly knew my father's history – I asked if he could get me Will Hughes's phone number.

'Will Hughes of Black Swan Partners?' Chuck asked. 'May I ask what for?'

'I recognized the coat of arms he's standing under in today's *Times* photo,' I said truthfully. 'I've got a crest like it and I thought he might buy a medallion.'

'Ha! Make him buy a round hundred, Garet. He can give them out as Christmas presents to the partners in his fund.'

He had me hold on while he asked his secretary to look

up the number. I gave Becky a thumbs-up sign and waved at Jay as he stumbled into the kitchen, bleary-eyed and unshaven. I wrote down the number while Becky explained to Jay what was going on.

'So,' Becky said when I ended the call with Chuck. 'Let's brainstorm how you're going to approach Will Hughes.' But I'd already dialed the number. I got voice mail.

'Mr. Hughes,' I said to the recorder, 'my name is Garet James and I believe I have your ancestor's signet ring.' Then I gave my cell phone number and hung up.

'That's it?' Becky asked, squirming in her seat.

'Yup.' I handed her my cell phone. 'I'm going to go shower. Let me know if he calls back.'

I took a long shower. I shampooed and rinsed my hair twice and applied a lavender cream rinse. The scent always reminded me of my mother. It was the thing she missed most about the village in France where she'd grown up – the fields of lavender. She grew pots of lavender in our tiny backyard garden, tied bunches in purple ribbons, and hung them from hooks in the kitchen to dry. Then she sewed the dried flowers into sachets that she put in the linen closets and clothing drawers. Just breathing in the scent made me feel clean and calm.

I got dressed in black slacks, a crisp white cotton shirt, and a green cashmere sweater – comfortable clothes that looked smart enough in case I had to talk to the police or reporters at the hospital. Before I went back downstairs I sat on my bed and read the whole article about Will Hughes.

Will Hughes reports that his fund, Black Swan Partners LP, is up +14% ytd despite the dramatic declines in all market indices this year. 'My strategy is based on historical equity patterns,' Hughes told this reporter, 'and I suspect I go back further and in more detail through stock market records than most managers do.' When asked to elaborate Hughes said only that he has a long family history in the stock market, and thus access to private financial records that are not available to the investing public. Hughes's favorable results have resulted in an influx of capital this year; Hughes would not give specifics but he is reputed to manage in excess of five billion dollars and he said the additional funds are 'significant.' 'I'm being contacted by so many investors that I'm giving thought to starting a second fund, Green Hills Partners, which would have a socially conscious, environmental orientation that Black Swan lacks,' Hughes revealed. 'Maybe some concern for animal protection issues too. That's long been a dream of mine.' Asked about the frequent criticism of socially conscious investing for being less lucrative than the mainstream variety, Hughes responded wryly that he wouldn't call investing in today's market 'lucrative.' 'An investor needs a quality manager who learns from the past and studies the future, not one who fantasizes about it by taking foolish risks. That's all that matters.'

I put the newspaper article down and reached for my pendant, which I'd left on my night table last night. Instead of finding the pendant, though, I picked up the silver seal that had come off the box. I'd left it on my night table two nights ago after I opened the silver box, along with the one sizable scrap of paper with Will Hughes's name on it. I picked that up now and tried to read the lines above the signature and the seal, but the letters were so tiny I couldn't make them out. It was as if the writer had wanted to encode his message.

I took the paper out into the studio, retrieved my jeweler's loupe from my bag, and, laying the paper on the worktable in a pool of bright sunlight, looked through the magnifying glass. The words were larger, but they still didn't make any sense. I picked up the fragment and the delicate paper turned transparent in the sunlight, the black writing hovering in the air like winged words. Still indecipherable, but ... I turned the paper over and the enigmatic script resolved itself into English words. Holding the reversed paper up to the loupe, I read what appeared to be two lines of poetry.

Then swan in sudden flight startles, distracts,
And dominates the sky with wings of black.

The image was eerily like the one in my dreams, the black swan rising from the silver lake. For a moment I seemed to hear the sound of those wings again, but I shook my head and the sound vanished. Instead I heard the beating of my own heart. Could it be that this man, Will

Hughes, who ran a hedge fund called Black Swan Partners and posed under a coat of arms identical to the seal on the box, was somehow connected to whoever wrote these lines? I shook my head again, this time because I had a strange and claustrophobic sense of things closing in on me. There were too many coincidences . . . too many connections. And yet . . . if Will Hughes was connected to the box, he might be able to help me find it again.

I went downstairs feeling curiously buoyed. The sun was shining, my father was going to be all right, and I had a lead that could possibly prove his innocence. When I saw the shocked looks on Jay's and Becky's faces, though, I was afraid that something awful had happened, but it wasn't awful, just surprising.

'Will Hughes called ten minutes ago—' Jay began, but Becky, writhing in her seat, cut in.

'He's sending a car for you at three. He said to bring the ring.'

My good mood lasted through the walk to the hospital. The day was crisp and clear, mild for mid-December – all signs of last night's malodorous rain and fog swept from the clean blue sky. The only remnants of last night's freakish weather were the puddles of dirty water that the shopkeepers on Greenwich were sweeping out into the streets. I waved at the couple who ran Tea & Sympathy and said good morning just for the joy of hearing their British accents and getting called 'love.' I gave a couple of dollars to a homeless woman who was sitting cross-legged on the curb conversing intently with a plume of steam rising from a manhole cover. She raised her nut-brown face to me, then lowered it, spit in her hand, and waved to me as I continued up Greenwich. I passed the hospital on Seventh and continued on Greenwich to the Lafayette French bakery, which made an apple strudel my father said reminded him of one his mother used to make.

On the way to the bakery I passed Tibet Kailash, a Tibetan clothing store where I often bought gifts. The window was full of bright silks that reminded me of the head-scarf Obie Smith had been wearing last night. The store didn't usually open this early, but when he saw me peering through the window, the owner buzzed me in. The shop smelled deliciously of sandalwood and rose water. I picked out a multicolored silk scarf with silver and gold threads running through it and brought it up to the counter.

'I don't think I've smelled this incense before,' I commented as the owner wrapped the scarf in purple paper and slipped it into a small orange bag (one of the reasons I loved buying gifts here was for the pretty packaging, which often came with a poem from the Dalai Lama).

'The street had a peculiar smell this morning,' he said. 'This takes it away. Here.' He added a few cones of incense to the bag. 'Burn these if there's another fog like that.'

'Sure, thanks. I hope we don't have weather like that again, though. It gave me a migraine.'

He shook his head. 'I think we're in for a lot more like that – and worse.' He added three prayer cards to my package.

I left, trying to shake off the Tibetan man's words, my mood beginning to dampen. The smells of the bakery revived me a little and I felt better when I entered my father's room and found him sitting upright in bed, his color good, his eyes alert.

'Margaret,' he crooned when he saw me. 'You'll never guess who visited me last night!'

'Last night? I was here until the end of visiting hours.'

He waved away the strudel I offered him and grabbed my hand. 'Santé Leone!'

'Santé Leone?' I repeated the name, sitting down on the edge of his bed.

'You remember him, don't you? He was from Haiti and he did those enormous canvases full of tropical colors . . .'

'Yes, I remember him, Dad. It's just—'

'It was wonderful to see him again! And the best thing of all' – he drew me toward him and whispered – 'he's painting again! His clothes were splattered with fresh paint in every color of the rainbow. He told me he had a dozen new paintings for me. You know what people would pay for a new Santé Leone?'

'Millions, Dad. I'm sure they'd pay millions.'

'You bet! See, I told you something would turn up. Our financial troubles are over.' He released my hand and fell back against his pillows.

'Okay, Dad,' I said, running my hand over his forehead. His brow was a little warm to the touch but not feverish. 'That's great. You just lie back for a moment. I'm going to go find your doctor.'

He closed his eyes and fell immediately to sleep, snoring softly.

'He's been waiting up since four in the morning to tell

you about his visit from Saint Lion.' The voice came from a man leaning in the doorway. It took me a moment to recognize Obie Smith out of his nurse scrubs. He was wearing a long black leather coat over black jeans and an orange silk shirt. His long dreadlocks, which had been covered by a bandanna last night, hung loose down his back.

'Saint Lion,' I repeated. 'I haven't heard anyone call him that in years.' Santé Leone – Saint Lion – had come from Haiti in the early eighties on a scholarship to Pratt. He'd dropped out and started painting luminous murals all over Manhattan, always signed with his trademark: a stylized lion with one raised paw and a halo above his head. Saint Lion. My father had tracked him down to the burned-out tenement building on the Lower East Side where he was living – camping out, really – and bought six of his paintings. He'd nurtured his career, brought him to the town house for meals, introduced him to the art world, and gave him his first show. The night before his work was to appear at the Whitney Biennial, Santé died of a heroin overdose.

'My dad always thought he could have done something to save him,' I said, getting up and joining Obie Smith in the doorway. 'I hope that thinking about him now doesn't mean he's reliving that guilt.'

Obie Smith shook his head. 'He said Santé came to show him there were no hard feelings.'

I ducked my head to hide the tears that had sprung to my eyes. 'Here.' I held out the orange bag for him. It matched his shirt. 'You've been so kind, I wanted to—'

'Don't thank me,' he said, taking the bag from me. 'I'm just doing what I do.' He opened the package and smiled at the multicolored scarf, then whisked it out of its wrapping paper so that it floated on the air like an exotic butterfly, then settled around his neck.

'It suits you.'

'I do believe it does,' he said, grinning at me. Then he gave me a courtly bow and swirled around, his black coat billowing around him like a cape, and walked away. He had a spring in his step that made me feel he was listening to music only he could hear. I watched him all the way down the long hall, and then just before he reached the corner, he turned back to face me and gave me another huge smile.

I blushed to be caught watching him and quickly turned away . . . only to run into Detective Joe Kiernan.

'Oh good, I'm glad you're here,' he said, taking my elbow and steering me toward the waiting room.

'I'm here to see my father, Detective.' I shook my arm free of his and started back toward my father's room, but Kiernan caught up with me and blocked the doorway. 'What? Is it about something my father said? You know I don't think anything he says under the influence of the drugs he's taking is admissible—'

'It's not something your father said. It's what the men who robbed your house are saying.'

'Really? You caught them?' I asked genuinely surprised and delighted at this turn of events. Now there'd be no question of my father having been involved in the burglary and we'd get our paintings back. 'That's great! Did they have the silver box?'

Kiernan gave me a strange look. 'They had your Pissarros, Miss James. No sign of a silver box.'

'Oh . . . that's too bad . . . but, thank God the Pissarros have been recovered. That's really good news.'

'I'm afraid it's not all good news. The two men have both confessed, separately, that your father hired them to commit the burglary.'

You're not allowed to use cell phones in St. Vincent's, so after I finished talking to Detective Kiernan, I went out-side to call Chuck Chennery.

'I simply cannot believe that of your father,' Chuck said in his reassuringly plummy drawl. 'Someone is setting him up. I'm going to have a talk with Dave Reiss in our criminal division and then we'll be down to see you at the hospital later this morning.'

I thanked him and went back inside to see my father. He had woken up and was arguing with the nurse about eating his breakfast.

'I'll take it from here,' I told the nurse.

When she was gone, I took away the tray of congealing eggs and runny Jell-O and presented him with the apple strudel from Lafayette's. He didn't seem to have any memory of me bringing it earlier – or, in fact, of seeing me earlier – so I didn't bring up his 'visit' from Santé Leone. Instead, when he had finished the strudel and I had brushed the crumbs from his bedsheet, I told him I had to ask him a question.

'I want you to promise me not to get upset,' I said. 'I'll only ask it this one time and I'll accept whatever you tell me.' I took a deep breath. 'The police have caught the men who robbed the gallery—'

'That's great news—'

'—and they're saying you hired them to do it.'

All the color drained from my father's face and his hands knotted the hem of his bedsheet. I regretted having to tell him this, but it was better he heard it from me and not from a police officer. 'Margaret,' he said – he only ever used my full name when something serious or momentous had happened – 'do you think I would bring . . . *ghouls* like that into our home?'

'I'll believe whatever you tell me, Dad. Did you?'

'On your mother's memory, I swear I had nothing to do with it.'

I squeezed his hand, easing his grip off the crumpled sheets. 'Okay, Dad, that's good enough for me. Chuck Chennery is coming over here and he's bringing a criminal defense lawyer from the firm. We'll take care of this. You're not to talk to anyone about it but me and Chuck and the other lawyer. Okay?'

My father held up one finger, a gesture he made when he had a point to make. 'And your mother, of course.'

'What about Mom?'

'I can talk to her about it, can't I?'

I patted his hand. At least he hadn't asked if he could talk to Santé Leone about it. 'Sure, Dad. You can talk to Mom.' Then I smoothed down his sheets and tucked the ends back under the mattress. My hands brushed something rough on the fabric, as if something had spilled on the bed. I looked down and saw a spray of paint on the sheets – lime green, coral, sun-washed yellow, and aquamarine. The colors Santé Leone had favored.

The Watchtower

I spent the rest of the morning and early afternoon at the
hospital. Charles Chennery came at noon with a young,
clean-cut lawyer in a Hugo Boss suit and shiny shoes that
squeaked on the hospital floors. They talked to my father
for half an hour, then Chuck took me aside and told me he
was filing for an injunction to keep the police from
questioning my father any further as a 'witness' while he was
taking pain medication in the hospital. I didn't ask him if my
father had mentioned talking to Santé Leone or my mother,
but he patted my shoulder and told me that when his eighty-
six-year-old mother was in the hospital for her hip
replacement, she had a long talk with Mamie Eisenhower.

After Chuck left I filled out insurance forms and tried to
find out whether Medicare would cover home nurse visits
when my father was discharged. Zach Reese came around
one with a take-out bag from Sammy's Noodle Shop. 'I'll
keep an eye on him,' he promised me, taking a container of
hot soup out of the bag. I was glad to know that my father
would have company – of a less ethereal kind than deceased
painters, but before I left I checked the take-out bags for
liquor bottles when Zach wasn't looking.

It was two-thirty before I could get out of the hospital. Barely enough time to get home and change into a slim black skirt, burgundy cashmere sweater, silk scarf, and high-heeled boots for my meeting with Will Hughes. I put on an old Jaeger raincoat that my mother had bought in London twenty years ago and took an umbrella. The forecast didn't say rain, but that didn't seem to mean much these days.

It was clear out, though, when I stepped outside my door to find a Rolls-Royce Silver Cloud waiting in front of the town house. As the driver held open the door for me, I had a fleeting urge to turn around and flee. I knew nothing about Will Hughes. I was going to him because I thought he might be able to tell me where to find John Dee, but what if he was working with John Dee? What if he had something to do with the robbery? But then I saw how ridiculous I was being. Why would a billionaire hedge fund manager want to steal a couple of Pissarros and an old silver box? I slid into the backseat, telling myself to get a grip.

The car drove west on Jane Street and then turned north onto the West Side Highway.

'Are we going to Mr. Hughes's office?' I asked.

'Mr. Hughes works out of his residence,' the driver replied.

'Oh,' I said, beginning to feel nervous again. 'And where does Mr. Hughes live?'

'Uptown.' The driver glanced in the rearview mirror. His eyes were dark and – I was relieved to see – perfectly normal.

I settled back against the plush upholstery and looked out the window toward the Hudson River, which glittered in the late-afternoon sunlight. People were walking and biking on the Hudson River Greenway, enjoying the unusually mild December weather. It was a perfectly normal day in New York City. I leaned back and tried to enjoy the ride.

When the car appeared to be getting off at the exit for the George Washington Bridge, however, I grew alarmed. 'Are we going to New Jersey?' I asked, my voice shriller than I'd meant it to be. I had a brief, vivid picture of my body being dumped in the New Jersey Meadowlands, but then we switched lanes and continued north onto the Henry Hudson Parkway instead. We got off at the exit for the Cloisters.

'Don't tell me,' I said. 'Mr. Hughes lives in the Cloisters. I knew he was rich, but I didn't think he lived in a castle.'

I saw the driver's eyes glance at me in the rearview mirror, but he didn't respond. We drove up and around the silent park, past the stone medieval towers of the Cloisters. My mother and I had spent many Saturdays of my youth exploring the echoing halls and colonnaded gardens of the museum. She often did research there when she was getting her master's degree in French medieval literature, and like the lavender she grew, the place reminded her of her native France. She would point to a sign sometimes and say, 'These old stones came over the ocean just as I did.' When I was in college, I often came up here to look at their collection of medieval jewelry for inspiration. I'd become friendly with one of the librarians my mother had known when I was researching my senior thesis.

The car exited the park at Fort Washington Avenue, made a right turn on 181st Street, another right on Cabrini Boulevard, and pulled up in front of the Tudor Castle Apartments.

'So he *does* live in a castle,' I remarked to the still taciturn driver as I surveyed the twelve-story redbrick apartment building trimmed in white granite stonework that gave it the look of a medieval English castle. I'd read about it in a *Times* real estate article once and knew that it had replaced an actual castle that had been built by a British financier at the turn of the last century and had burnt to the ground in the 1930s. The apartments were reputedly large and airy, contained working fireplaces, and enjoyed magnificent views of the river. Still, I was surprised that this was where Will Hughes lived. 'I thought hedge fund managers lived on Park Avenue,' I said as the driver opened my door and offered a hand to help me out. 'Not that this isn't a great building. It's so wonderfully romantic.'

'Mr. Hughes will be delighted to hear you think so. He's rather sentimentally attached to the building, seeing as he owns it.'

The driver escorted me under the stone portico emblazoned with the heraldic shield I'd seen in the paper, and through the lobby, exchanging a nod with the liveried doorman. Apparently I was expected. Instead of taking me to the central bank of elevators, he showed me to one marked PRIVATE, waved me in, and bowed as the doors began to close.

'Wait, what floor?' I shouted. But then I saw that there were no buttons to push. As soon as the doors closed the elevator began its ascent to what I assumed must be the penthouse. I closed my eyes and took deep *ujjayi* breaths – what my yoga teacher called *ocean breathing* – to calm myself down. Surprisingly, it worked. When the elevator came to rest, I felt calm. I opened my eyes as the doors opened and I stepped directly into a palatial living room surrounded on three sides by floor-to-ceiling glass windows. It was like standing on the top of a high tower. In front of me was the Hudson River and the New Jersey Palisades, to the south the skyscrapers of Manhattan, and to the north the square stone tower of the Cloisters. The glass appeared to be tinted, perhaps to cut down on glare. I took a step toward the north-facing windows, but then halted by a painting that hung on the wall near the elevator.

The full-length portrait was of a young man in Elizabethan dress. Something in his wide, silver-gray eyes held me motionless before him. He had long, ringleted blond hair and a cupid-bow mouth twisted into a cruel smile. His throat was white against the black collar of his velvet doublet, as was the hand that lay on top of an opened book atop a marble pedestal. Stepping closer I saw the swan signet ring. *My ring.* Could it really be the same one I wore on my finger? I held my hand up in front of the painting so that the ring was level with the one in the portrait.

'Remarkable,' came a voice from behind me, 'it *is* the same ring.'

I turned around and found myself looking into luminous silver eyes identical to those in the painting. This man was dressed in modern clothes – a tailored, white dress shirt and faded black jeans – and his hair was a shade or two darker and cut short. His mouth was the same shape, and in the first instant as I turned, I thought I detected the same potential for cruelty that I saw in the painted face. But then the polite smile he'd prepared for me faltered and I saw something that looked like surprise or vulnerability.

'What's more remarkable is that you look just like him,' I said, wondering why he looked so startled at my appearance. Had he expected someone else?

'The Hughes family curse,' he said, recovering himself and holding out his right hand.

His eyes locked on mine with an unsettling intensity. Then I felt my ring clink against one he wore, and I looked down to break the force I felt in those eyes. I thought he might have a copy of the swan signet ring, but he wore instead a gold ring set with a flat, black stone.

'Please, come sit down.' He gestured toward a low velvet couch in front of the west windows. All the furniture in the room was low and unobtrusive, allowing the views to take precedence. The only objects on the glass table in front of the couch were a crystal decanter, two glasses, and an open laptop. Numbers and signs scrolled across the computer's luminous screen. Stock-trading symbols, I assumed, but they were as arcane to me as the symbols I'd seen inside the silver box. Hughes closed the screen, poured two glasses of the amber-colored liquid, then sat in a leather-and-chrome Eames chair directly across from me. Then he leaned forward and took my hand. The intimacy of the gesture almost took my breath away, but then I realized that he was looking at the ring. I noticed, though, that I hadn't tried to take my hand away.

'It does look exactly like my ancestor's ring,' he said. 'Where did you find it?'

'My mother gave it to me.'

He looked up, but he still didn't let my hand go and I didn't take it away from him. I had the odd feeling that I couldn't until he let me. I felt as powerless as I had when the thieves passed me in the hallway, but where that had been a repugnant sensation, this was . . . *seductive*. I wasn't sure which was more dangerous.

'What was your mother's name?'

'Margot James,' I replied. 'Her maiden name was D'Arques.'

'She was French?'

'Yes. Her parents were killed in World War Two and she was taken in by an English family. She met my father there after the war.'

'And she gave you her name – Garet is short for Margaret, isn't it?'

'Yes, but she called me Garet from the beginning.'

'Did she tell you what it means?'

'*Margaret* means "pearl,"' I said, wondering what this had to do with anything. I'd come to get information from him, but he was the one asking the questions. With an effort I wrenched my hand away from his – although in reality he'd held it lightly – and reached into my bag. I took out a small flannel jewelry bag and tipped it over. The silver seal that had been affixed to the box spilled out onto the glass and spun on its edge for a moment before landing faceup.

Will Hughes looked up from it, his eyes flashing as silver as the seal. 'Where did you get this?' he asked.

'From a silver box that had been sealed.' I told him the whole story – from wandering into the jewelry store on Cordelia Street to opening the box (I left out the moving symbols) to the robbery and finding the abandoned storefront. 'And now my father is being accused of insurance fraud. I know it might sound far-fetched that this John Dee fellow—'

'Who told you that name?'

I stared at him. I hadn't mentioned not getting the name from the man himself. 'From someone in a bakery at the corner . . .'

'Puck? Did Puck himself tell you?'

I laughed. 'I didn't know there was a *Puck himself*. I spoke to a baker named Fen—'

'Fenodoree,' he said, smiling. 'How is she?'

'Uh . . . she looked fine,' I said, surprised he would know the baker. 'Anyway, I know it probably seems crazy that this John Dee fellow had anything to do with the robbery—'

'Not at all.' Hughes got abruptly to his feet and paced to the west window and turned to face me. The sun, beginning its descent over the Palisades, turned the river into a sheet of sparkling gold. Even though the glass was tinted, the light was so bright I had to close my eyes against the glare . . . Immediately I saw myself in my dream standing on the shore watching the black swan gliding on the water. When I opened my eyes the only thing riding the Hudson was the reflection of the sun, but I had the same sensation of impending disaster.

'When you opened the box, what happened?' he asked. He came over to the chair he had vacated, but remained standing. With the glare of the sun behind him he was only a silhouette, the only feature of his face visible, those oddly magnetic eyes.

I had no intention of telling him about the blue figures . . . but then, looking into those hypnotic silver eyes, I did. The words seemed to spill out as if he were sucking them out of me. I told him about the symbols that changed in front of my eyes and the blue smoke that rose from the box. Then I told him about the blank eyes of the robbers, the smell of sulfur that trailed behind them, the fog that followed me home last night, the way my metal sculpture had seemed to come to life, and, finally, about my father's visit from Santé Leone, who died in 1987.

When I finished, Will Hughes bent down until I could see his face and his silver eyes flashing like coins. 'My dear Garet, after all that, do you have any doubt that something out of the ordinary is happening?'

'I don't know what you mean by out of the ordinary,' I said carefully.

He sighed and sat down in the chair. He reached for my hand again. 'Your mother gave you the ring, but she didn't tell you where she got it or what it meant?'

'She died soon after,' I said, embarrassed to feel my eyes

instantly fill with tears. I looked away, toward the north window and the Cloisters.

'That explains it,' Hughes said. 'She didn't have the time. Assuming her mother had been able to tell her. You say her mother died young as well . . . in the war?'

'Yes, she was caught hiding Jewish refugees and was executed.'

'That's terrible. So perhaps your mother didn't know either.'

'Know what?' I looked back to face Will Hughes. The minutes gazing away from him had given me the nerve to question him. 'What does this have to do with my mother?'

'Everything. Your mother comes from a long line of women who have a very important role. Here, look at my ring.' He took off his gold ring and handed it to me. When I looked at it more closely, I saw that the stone was actually an intaglio inscribed with a coat of arms. I took my jeweler's loupe, which I always carried with me, out of my bag and held the ring up to it. The design sprang to life: a stone tower surmounted by a disembodied eye, rays coming out from it. Latin words surrounded the tower but they were backward so I couldn't make them out.

'The inscription reads, *Quis custodiet ipsos custodes?*' he said.

'"Who watches the watchmen?"' I translated. He tilted his head at me and smiled. 'I've made a study of heraldic mottoes,' I explained, holding up my pendant for him to see. 'I feel like I've seen this one before.'

'Perhaps your mother showed you a picture of it. Are you sure she told you nothing about the Watchtower?'

'No . . . what's that? It sounds like Jehovah's Witnesses.'

'Same symbol, different purpose,' he said, sitting back. 'The watchtower is an ancient symbol of protection against evil. It stands on the border between the seen and the unseen, between the natural world and the unnatural world, between good and evil.'

'That's a pretty tall order,' I said. 'But I still don't understand. What is it?'

'Not *what; who*. You're the Watchtower, Garet James.'

I tried to laugh – the sentence was so portentous! – but my throat was dry so I coughed instead. He handed me my glass of sherry and waited while I took a sip.

'What in the world do you mean?' I asked when I could speak again.

'It's what your name means, for one thing. From the Old French *garite*, which means *watchtower*. It means that you're the appointed guardian—'

'The guardian of *what*?' I asked, unable to restrain my impatience.

He stared at me – I'd have bet he wasn't used to people interrupting him – then he sighed. 'It's difficult to explain. A guardian against evil, I suppose you could say. It's a role handed down from mother to mother.'

'Like some sort of secret society?' I asked, incredulous. It was like something from one of Jay's books, the Central Council of Anarchists, or the League of Extraordinary Gentlemen. 'Do you know how ridiculous that sounds?' I started to get up, but he was suddenly beside me, a restraining hand on my arm. The quickness of his movement made my head spin. I sat back down, afraid to move until I stopped feeling dizzy.

'I know this all must sound crazy to you, but why don't you just listen? Pretend it's a legend you're reading about in a book, why don't you?'

'A legend?'

'Yes, a legend that began very early in the seventeenth century when your ancestor met my' – he tilted his head toward the portrait on the wall – 'predecessor and exchanged rings with him. That's why you have the swan ring and I have the tower ring. Will Hughes . . . my ancestor . . . wrote a detailed account of his encounter with a French woman by the name of Marguerite. Marguerite possessed a silver box which contained . . . well, let's say it contained some valuable information . . . especially valuable to the alchemist John Dee. It was very important that John Dee not get the information inside the box, so Marguerite and Will Hughes sealed it using this ring.' He touched the ring on my hand.

'That's quite a story, Mr. Hughes, but even if the jeweler I met yesterday was a descendant of the original John Dee, how could he have known that I was going to wander into his shop? And why would he need me to open the box? And then why steal it? I'm sorry, but none of this makes any sense. Why would a complete stranger do all this to me?' For the second time since I'd come into this apartment I was close to tears. I didn't want Will Hughes to see me cry. With a great effort, I got to my feet.

'Your whole story about guardians and watchtowers and alchemists, it's just too much. I can't believe it. And even if

I did, what good does it do me? All I want to know is if you can help me find this man who calls himself John Dee so I can find out if he had anything to do with the burglary, so I can prove that my father *didn't* have anything to do with it. Can you do that? Can you help me?'

The shimmering light in his eyes seemed to flare for a moment. It lit his whole face up and it nearly took my breath away. He looked younger – he looked like the man in the painting – but then the light faded from his face, extinguished like a dying ember.

'No,' he said. 'I can't help you find Dee.'

'That's it?' I asked, my voice rising shrilly. 'You tell me this wild story about guardians and watchtowers and alchemists and then you tell me you can't help me?'

'I'm sorry.' He wasn't looking at me. He was looking out the north window, to the Cloisters, where a red light had just come on atop the tower. I stared at it too, drawn to the beacon much as I had been drawn to Will Hughes's eyes a few moments ago. When I looked back, I saw that he had gotten to his feet. I was being dismissed.

'I really am sorry that I can't help you,' he said at the door to the elevator.

'Not as sorry as I am,' I said looking into his eyes – I'd be damned if I'd shrink away afraid to meet his gaze. But I must have been looking at the red light on top of the Cloisters too long because I saw it again, twinned and flickering, at the centers of Will Hughes's pupils.

The Manticore

—

In the lobby the driver stopped me and told me he had instructions from Mr. Hughes to take me wherever I wanted to go.

'No, thank you,' I told him. 'I'll walk to the subway.'

I went briskly up Cabrini Boulevard, past Mother Cabrini High School and the chapel where Mother Cabrini was buried, to Margaret Corbin Circle and the subway station at 190th Street, which was near the entrance to Fort Tryon Park. Although the sun was low in the sky and would soon set, plenty of people were still enjoying the unusually mild weather. The same normal scene I'd seen from Hughes's car coming uptown, but now it all appeared surreal. Had I really just been listening to a story about four-hundred-year-old guardians and alchemists? I was too upset and confused to sit in a subway for thirty minutes. I had to keep moving. I joined the tide of late-afternoon strollers, nannies with their charges, courting couples, and joggers all heading into the park.

I wandered for a while through the Heather Garden, where a few late-blooming flowers glowed purple and blue in the ruddy light of the setting sun, trying to absorb some calm from the peaceful setting. My mother had loved this garden, probably because the purple heather had reminded her of those lavender fields of her childhood, and I had come here often when I was doing research at the Cloisters. It was a place where I had felt close to her, but it didn't give me any peace right now.

As crazy as Will Hughes's story was – and it was definitely crazy – the part that most upset me was the idea that if there was a kernel of truth in it, and my mother had known about this history, she hadn't told me. How could she keep something so important from me? It was as if she had hidden away her real self. So, it couldn't be true. But then why would Will Hughes make up such a story? Could it have *any* basis in reality?

I climbed up to the flagpole above Linden Terrace, the highest natural spot in the city, where a few teenagers in sweatshirts and low-slung jeans were skateboarding. They politely made way for me as I approached the stone wall overlooking the city. To the south I saw storm clouds gathering over the skyscrapers of Manhattan; to the north was the fortress of the Cloisters, the red light on its tower shining like a beacon.

'I'll always watch over you, Marguerite,' my mother would sometimes say. And she always used the French version of my name when she said it . . . unless she wasn't saying *Marguerite* at all, but was actually saying *Ma garite:* my watchtower. Had my mother known this story about her family? And if she did, had she meant to tell it to me before she died?

I stared at the tower as if it could tell me . . . *maybe it could.* My mother had done her own research at the Cloisters for years when she was studying for her master's in French medieval literature at Barnard, and she'd made friends with many of the curators and librarians there. When I'd gone there to research jewelry designs, one of the librarians who'd been friends with my mother was especially helpful to me – Dr. Edgar Tolbert, a specialist in French medieval iconology. I didn't know if he still worked there, but if he did maybe he'd be able to tell me if my mother had been particularly interested in any tradition surrounding a watchtower.

I knew that even if I found some historical basis for Will Hughes's crazy story, I still wouldn't be any closer to helping my father, but something compelled me to head down toward the path that led to the Cloisters. Maybe it was having had my faith in *both* parents challenged in one day.

As I turned to leave the flagpole circle, I noticed that although the skateboarders had left, there was a man in a red hooded sweatshirt watching me. Or at least he was facing in my direction. His hood was pulled so far forward that I couldn't really see his eyes. He was probably harmless, I told myself, but still, I should find an area with more people.

The path to the Cloisters, though, was nearly deserted. I considered turning back and exiting the park at Margaret Corbin Circle, but then I'd miss my chance to talk to Dr. Tolbert at the Cloisters today. I glanced back . . . and saw the man in the red sweatshirt about twenty feet behind me.

I sped up, practically running toward the lawns

surrounding the Cloisters where I could see a few late-afternoon strollers. When I got closer, I noticed that the people were all coming out of the museum and walking away from it. Where would I go if the museum was closed? And how would I get rid of the man following me? When I reached the downstairs entrance, the guard at the door told me that the museum was closing in fifteen minutes.

'I'm a friend of Dr. Edgar Tolbert, one of the librarians,' I said, my voice coming out in breathless gasps. 'I just wanted to talk to him for a minute. Do you know if he's still here?'

The guard smiled. 'Dr. Tolbert is always the last to go home. I think he's giving a lecture in one of the cloisters. Go on in.'

Before I went in, I turned around to look for the man in the red sweatshirt, but I didn't see him.

I walked up the long vaulted passage to the Entrance Hall and told the guard at the desk that I was looking for Dr. Tolbert, and he directed me to the Cuxa Cloister. I went through the Romanesque Hall and entered the cloister through an arched doorway flanked on either side by two crouching-lion statues. I saw Dr. Tolbert right away, his shock of snow-white hair atop a regal leonine face making him instantly recognizable across the courtyard. He was lecturing to a small group, pointing up at a figure carved into the capital of one of the columns supporting the arcade around the central courtyard. I took a seat on a low marble wall that rimmed the enclosed garden, thankful for a moment to catch my breath and recover from the fright of being followed in the park. It had been stupid to walk by myself in a city park at dusk, but that was all it was, I told myself, a mugger looking for an opportunity to rob a solitary woman who looked distracted. Surely he'd give up now that I was inside the museum.

I took a deep breath and looked around the cloister, trying to draw calm from my surroundings. After all, monks had come to this place to meditate. The cloister had originally been part of a twelfth-century Benedictine monastery. Even now, when it rested inside a New York City museum, it retained the quiet of centuries within its pink marble walls. The last of the late-afternoon sunlight filled the courtyard like honey spilling into a stone box. A sheet of glass separated the arcade from the central garden, but the sun had still warmed the wall. I leaned against it and looked up at the figures carved into the columns. Fantastic beasts swallowed other animals and men. I remembered learning in art history that the motifs represented the struggle between good and evil, reminders to the monks to remain ever vigilant against the forces of darkness. It certainly seemed that the wrong side had the upper hand in the battles waged by the marble creatures.

'The most impressive collection of deadly beasts adorns this twelfth-century arch from Narbonne, France,' I heard Dr. Tolbert say as he approached my corner. The group gathered under the arch I had come through while Dr. Tolbert described the array of mythical beasts featured on it. When he'd finished describing the griffin, harpy, and centaur, his cane came to rest on the first figure on the left side of the arch. A small boy had begun to drift away from the group; Dr. Tolbert pitched his voice in his direction. 'And here is a monster straight out of your worst nightmares!' The boy turned and looked up at the figure on the arch.

'This is the manticore – a beast with the face of a man, gleaming red eyes, three rows of teeth, and a tail that stings like a deadly scorpion's. It can leap like a lion and its claws are as sharp.' Dr. Tolbert bent down toward the boy, whose face was rapt with attention now. 'The only thing good to say about the manticore is that it has a beautiful voice – like a fine flute. But don't allow yourself to be lulled by its song, because it also has a taste for human flesh.'

'Like a zombie!' the boy declared, shivering with delight and horror. The group laughed and Tolbert dismissed them. I waited until the last one had left before approaching him.

'Margaret James!' he crooned, swooping his arm around my shoulder and drawing me in for a kiss on the cheek. When he held me out at arm's length to look at me, I saw that his blue eyes were watery. 'Ah, you look more like your mother every day. I was just thinking about her today . . . now what was it that reminded me of her?'

'The article in the *Times* about the gallery being robbed?' I suggested.

His face darkened. 'No! The gallery was robbed? I had no idea. I'm terribly sorry. Was anyone hurt?'

'My father was shot, but he's going to be okay . . .' I couldn't bear to tell him that Roman was suspected of shooting himself. 'But if you didn't see the article about the robbery, what was it that reminded you of my mother?'

The question distracted him from asking more questions about the robbery. He closed his eyes and tapped two fingers to his forehead in much the same way I tapped my laptop touch pad to wake up the hard drive. 'It was an article in a journal,' he said at last, opening his eyes. 'It's in the library upstairs. Do you have time to come up and see it?'

'Yes, of course. Actually . . . I came to see you. I had some questions about my mother and the research she did here.'

'Well, we're in luck then. The article was on one of her favorite subjects – the watchtower in medieval imagery.'

As Dr. Tolbert escorted me back through the Entrance Hall, I explained that I wanted to see any material concerning medieval watchtowers that my mother had used in her research.

'Yes, I think I have a book she used that mentions a watchtower,' he said while waving good-night to the guard on duty. The guard was ushering the last visitors out; the museum was closing for the night, but I gathered they were used to Dr. Tolbert staying after hours. He unlocked a spiked metal gate and took me up two flights of stairs. Several of his colleagues passed us on their way down saying their good-nights. He ushered me into a square, barrel-vaulted room lined on four sides with floor-to-ceiling bookshelves. Long wooden tables filled the room. A round leaded-glass window high up on the arched wall at the end of the room glowed dimly, lit by the last fading light of the day. At its center was a stained-glass roundel containing the figure of a winged angel holding a trumpet – one of the angels of the Apocalypse blowing his horn on Judgment Day.

'Have a seat while I find the article,' Dr. Tolbert said. 'I think it was in *Comitatus* . . . or was it *Medieval Studies* . . . hm . . . maybe I left it in my office . . .'

His voice drifted off as he wandered out of the library and down the hall. I sat at the end of one of the long tables and turned on the last of a row of green-shaded lamps. The chairs were the same as I remembered – wide, wooden, U-shaped frames upholstered in faded green velvet, bolted down with decorative brass tacks. They always reminded me of the chair that Laurence Olivier brooded in when he played Hamlet. If it was as un-comfortable as these, I could see why Hamlet was always getting up to stalk around the castle of Elsinore.

Dr. Tolbert came back with the journal and a thick, clothbound book.

'This was one of the books your mother used in her research on watchtower imagery. I'm afraid I can't let it out of the library, but you're welcome to browse through it here.'

'I don't want to keep you, though,' I told him, taking the heavy book from him.

'Oh, you're not keeping me. I was going to do a little writing down in the Cuxa Cloister.'

'You write in the cloisters?'

'Yes. I find it peaceful after the visitors have gone. The guards are tolerant of my little eccentricities. When you're done, just leave the books here and come down and find me. If you like, we could go for a drink. There's a delightful new place in Inwood called the Indian Road Café.'

'I'd love to. I'll be down within the hour.'

'No hurry, no hurry,' he sang as he left the library.

His voice faded as he went down the steps and I turned to the materials he'd brought me. The journal article flagged with a Post-it note was on the role of the watchman in Provençal poetry. It included a twelfth-century alba – a traditional form of troubadour poetry in which a lover expresses regret at the coming of dawn.

> *While the nightingale sings*
> *I am with my beloved*
> *through the perfumed night,*
> *until our sentry from the tower*
> *cries: 'Lovers, get up!*
> *The nightingale sings no more;*
> *it is the lark*
> *greeting the break of day.'*

The poem was illustrated by a woodcut of a watchtower under which two lovers clung to one another while a sentry leaned out a window and shouted at them. The article itself was interesting, and I could see why it had reminded Dr. Tolbert of my mother, who had spent her summers in a village in southern France, but it didn't tell me a thing about ancestral orders of guardians.

I put the journal aside and turned to the book . . . and turned cold when I read the title: *John Dee and the Four*

Watchtowers. I had to remind myself that it only *felt* like a strange coincidence to find that the Elizabethan alchemist was connected to the symbol that Hughes claimed was part of my mother's history. After all, Hughes was the one who had linked the two together in the first place.

Before turning to the page that Dr. Tolbert had book-marked, I skimmed through the first few chapters to find out a little more about John Dee. The Wikipedia entry I'd read about him had told me little more than that he had been the official astronomer to Queen Elizabeth I. Now I discovered that he had amassed the largest library in Europe in his age, lectured on algebra at the University of Paris, and coined the term *British Empire.* Late in his life he had turned to the supernatural, attempting to contact angels with the help of a medium named Edward Kelley. Dee later fell out favor under King James I and reputedly died in poverty at his home in Mortlake (although there was no record of his death and no gravestone bearing his name in Mortlake's cemetery).

I turned to the bookmarked page and found an illustration of the four watchtowers, which Dee had learned about through the teachings of the 'angels' con-tacted by Edward Kelley. Each one corresponded to one of the elements: earth, water, air, and fire. I read through the whole chapter, growing impatient with the flowery language and elaborate constructions invented by Edward Kelley, but could find nothing about a line of woman guardians. I was about to put the book aside when a yellowed index card slipped loose from one of the pages and fluttered to the floor. I leaned down to pick it up . . .

and heard a faint sound coming from downstairs. I paused to listen, wondering if it could be Dr. Tolbert calling for me, but it wasn't a voice, it was music. A flute playing a haunting melody. Perhaps there was a concert planned for tonight.

I picked up the file card. It contained a drawing of a watchtower surmounted by an eye and, underneath, the words *Quis custodiet ipsos custodes?* Exactly the same image as the one on Will Hughes's ring – the ring he claimed had once belonged to my ancestor. What startled me even more, though, was the handwriting. It looked like my mother's.

I turned the card over. In the top right-hand corner was a number, 303, which I guessed corresponded to a page in the book I was holding. I turned to page 303 and saw a ghostly white square on the yellowed page – a square the same size as the card I was holding. Knowing my mother's research habits, she would have placed the card under the lines she was interested in, so I read the passage directly above the white square.

The watchers watched over humanity from the four watchtowers at the corners of creation, but they were beguiled by the beauty of human women and descended to earth to consort with them. In exchange for their company the watchers taught their consorts enchantments and spells and all manner of esoteric arts.

I looked back at the index card. Under the page number my mother had written, *Despite the erroneous identification as consort, perhaps an echo of our people's tradition of the watchtower.* The word that stunned me was *our.* My mother *had* been aware of some tradition associated with a watchtower – and not just in a scholarly way (and she would have hated any ancestor of hers being called a consort!). It was part of her family (I assumed that's what she meant by *our people*) tradition, but she had never told me about it. I recalled all the nights she had read me bedtime stories – the old classic French fairy tales, like 'Beauty and the Beast' and 'Cinderella,' but also strange Celtic tales about seals who turned into maidens and maidens who turned into swans who lived in a magical land that she called the Summer Country or the Fair Land, where it was always summer and no one who dwelled there ever aged. Why had she never told me this story? I couldn't help but feel betrayed by the omission.

I looked through the rest of the book for any other file cards, but found nothing. I took out my notebook and copied the passage on page 303. Then I stuck my mother's index card in my notebook. I didn't think Dr. Tolbert would mind me taking it. After all, it had belonged to my mother. I would show it to him and ask if he knew anything else about the watchtower story and if he knew anything else about my mother. Maybe my mother had never told me the story for a reason – some shameful secret about her family that she had felt she had to keep from me.

I shouldn't keep Dr. Tolbert waiting any longer, though. Even if he had work to do, I didn't imagine that it was good for a man his age to sit on a cold stone wall in a drafty cloister for too long. And it *was* cold. They must turn off the central heating after the museum closes, I thought, putting on my jacket, slipping the strap of my bag over my head, and adjusting it across my chest. Then I neatly aligned the book and journal with a ray of red light that lay upon the table. I looked up and saw that the light came from the angel's halo in the stained-glass window ... but how? I checked my watch. It was five thirty, a good hour after sunset. What light was shining through the window?

It must be an outside security light, I told myself, turning away from the room. In the hall I looked out a window to see if I could see any outside lights, but I couldn't see anything at all; the building was surrounded by fog. More freakish weather? I started down the stairs, reminding myself that I wasn't alone. There were guards and Dr. Tolbert ... and musicians, I recalled as the flute music resumed. In the Entrance Hall I looked for the guard who'd been there earlier, but the desk was empty. I turned and went toward the Cuxa Cloister, where the music was coming from.

As I stepped under the Narbonne arch, I could see that the walkway around the cloister was dark, but behind the glass – now opaque with condensed moisture – the enclosed garden was lit by a strange yellow glow. Silhouetted against the glass sat Dr. Tolbert. I couldn't see his face, but I could see that his head was tilted up toward the arch above my head.

'Still studying your mythological beasts, Dr. Tolbert?' I asked, stepping through the arch.

He neither answered nor moved his head in my direction.

I took another step forward and saw the expression of horror frozen on his face.

'Dr. Tolbert!' I cried as I crossed to him quickly and put my hand to his neck. There was no pulse . . . and his skin was already cool. I touched his hand, which still gripped his cane. His fingers were supple yet and loosened their grip at my touch. The cane would have fallen if I hadn't caught it.

He's evidently had a heart attack or a stroke, but why? He'd been perfectly fine an hour ago. He looked as if something had shocked him, but what could have frightened him in this peaceful place? It looked as if he had positioned himself to contemplate his favorite sculptures . . . I turned around and followed his gaze to the Narbonne arch.

On the left side, where the manticore had been, was a blank spot, as if the figure had been chiseled loose or . . .

From behind me I heard the trilling of a flute.

As I turned around, I recalled Dr. Tolbert's words from his lecture. *And here is a monster out of your worst nightmares!* I must have entered the world of nightmare. A small winged creature – about the size of a well-fed rat – hurtled toward me through the air, three sets of teeth bared. I brought the cane up just in time to strike it. It hit the glass wall so hard that the glass shattered, letting a wave of fog roll in. I heard the creature's horrible high-pitched squeal as I turned and ran into the Romanesque Hall, through the Entrance Hall, and down the long vaulted passage. Halfway down I tripped over the body of the guard who had let me in earlier. As I landed on my knees, I felt the manticore's claws graze the top of my head. If I hadn't fallen, it would have been on me already. It spun around at the bottom of the stairs, hissing and lashing its scorpion-tipped tail like an angry house cat. But this was no house cat. I could see the sinewy muscles of its hind legs preparing to bound. I gripped the cane in both hands and swung when it leapt, catching it in its mouth. Needle-sharp teeth rained into my hair. I took the last stairs in one bound and hit the door at the bottom with my shoulder. I fell out into the fog, stumbled, and scrambled to my feet just as the manticore slammed into my back, tackling me onto the ground. I heard one impossibly sweet note trill in my ear as its teeth sunk into my neck.

It Is the Lark

My hands flailed at the creature to pull it off and fastened around the tip of one scaly wing, but then something yanked it out of my grasp. I rolled over, raising my arms against another attack, but none came. A tall man in dark clothes held the manticore by its neck. I couldn't see the man's face because the manticore's wings were beating the air in front of him. The scorpion tail lashed toward the man's hand trying to sting him, but the man wore gauntleted leather gloves. He brought his other hand up and with a quick wringing motion snapped the manticore's neck. Its wings beat twice more and went limp, but the scorpion tail still writhed. He dropped the creature to the ground and smashed the scorpion beneath his bootheel.

When he looked up, I saw that it was Will Hughes. His face was splattered with so much blood that even his eyes appeared to be red. His whole face was contorted, his lips pulled back in a grimace that bared his teeth . . . I stared at his teeth, hardly believing what I saw. Where his canines should have been were two sharp fangs. I recoiled in horror even as a voice inside my head said, *Of course, it would take a monster to destroy a monster.*

Frantic, I tried to get to my feet but my legs had gone numb. Hughes raised his eyes from the body of the manticore and looked at me, but I wasn't sure he really saw me. His eyes were flooded with blood. I somehow knew that all he would see through those eyes was blood: the blood pulsing through my veins. His eyes were fastened on my neck where I could feel blood trickling from the manticore's bite down onto my collarbone.

I tried to scramble backward but now my arms were numb. Will Hughes blinked and a single tear of blood spilled from his eye and ran down his cheek. The red haze began to clear, replaced by a silver gleam. I tried to scream but it came out as a hoarse choking sound. The numbness had spread to my throat.

'The manticore's bite is poison,' he said. 'You'll die unless I get it out.' He knelt down by my side, keeping his eyes on me. 'But I need your permission.'

I tried to scream again but this time no sound came out at all.

'Nod your head if you give me your permission, but quickly. Once the poison travels to your brain—'

I didn't need him to finish his sentence. With a great effort of will I jerked my chin up and down. It must have been enough because he was on me immediately, his chest leaning against mine, his mouth at my throat. I couldn't feel the pressure of his body against mine, but I *could* feel his teeth sinking into my flesh. After one sharp painful sting, the pain turned into something else – a warmth that spread outward, down through my chest and into my belly, out into my arms and legs, like a hot liquid moving through my veins. It burned away the numbness. Slowly I became aware of his body pressing against mine, the tug of his lips and tongue on my neck pulling a silver thread that ran into the very core of my being.

I moaned as my throat muscles loosened. His mouth left my skin and he exhaled softly over the wound, sending a ripple of shivers through my whole body. When he moved away, I could see a shimmer of silver light filling the space between us. It lit up his eyes and made his skin glow.

Then he knelt back on his heels and wiped his mouth with the back of his hand. 'You'll be all right now. I think I've gotten all the poison—'

Before he could finish his sentence, he began to shake. He fell back and I reached for him, but he held up a hand to keep me away.

His skin, already pale, turned a shade of milky blue, against which his veins stood out a darker blue. I could have left while Will Hughes writhed on the ground. I *should* have left. I was terrified. Although he was helpless now, I'd seen what strength he had when he broke the manticore's neck. I'd seen his lust for blood. I let myself say the name to myself. *Vampire.* Just thinking the name made me want to run away and pretend that none of this had ever happened. But I didn't. No matter what kind of monster he was (*vampire,* the voice inside my head said again, *he's a vampire*) he had saved my life by sucking the manticore's poison out of my veins, and now that poison was inside him. I wouldn't just leave him while he suffered because of me. Nor would I tell myself that I had imagined that statue coming to life. The manticore *had* come to life and it *had* killed poor, innocent Dr. Tolbert. Will Hughes *was* a vampire *and* he had saved my life. Everything that had happened to me over the last two days since I'd walked into that shop on Cordelia Street was real. The silver box had flown open in a flash of otherworldly white light, blue alchemical symbols had moved across its lid, possessed shadowmen had broken into my house to steal the box, my metal sculpture had come to life and attacked me, and my father had talked to a dead man who had spilled paint on his bedsheets. It had all happened. I wasn't crazy. I hadn't gone over the edge – the world had. I may not have understood it and I might have been terrified, but I would wait beside the vampire who had saved my life until he was well enough to explain it all to me.

When the shaking had stopped, he sat up and wrapped his arms around his knees. He drew in a long breath. 'Thank you for staying,' he said.

'Thank you for saving my life,' I countered, 'from that . . . thing.' I looked over to where the manticore's body had lain, but all that was there was a heap of marble debris.

'Air and mist,' Hughes said, lifting a handful of stones and letting them sift through his fingers. 'Dee sent the fog to animate this thing. I saw the fog come up as you left, but I had to wait for nightfall to leave my apartment.' He grimaced. 'I would have been here sooner but Dee had sent an emissary I had to deal with first.'

'A man in a red sweatshirt?'

Hughes nodded. 'You saw him?'

'He followed me from the other side of the park. Is he . . . ? Did you . . . ?'

'He's alive. When he wakes, he won't even remember what happened. He was only half-enspelled; Dee must have been in a hurry. He'd been implanted with the notion that he had to follow you and little else.'

'You can read minds?' I asked, wondering if anything should surprise me anymore.

'Only when I drink someone's blood.' I lifted my hand to the wound at my neck and he smiled. 'Don't worry. All I got from you was your fear of the manticore . . . and sadness at your friend's death. I'm sorry that I wasn't able to save him.'

'Dr. Tolbert. Edgar Tolbert. He was a friend of my mother's.' An image of the librarian's face – his expression of horror – passed painfully before my eyes and I looked up at the looming bulk of the Cloisters. 'We have to tell the police what's happened . . . so they can remove his body.' I started to get to my feet, but even though I could feel my arms and legs now, they were weak and my head swam when I tried to stand upright. I started to sway and Hughes, who had been a good six feet away, was at my side in a heartbeat to hold me up.

'We can't do that,' he said. His voice seemed to echo in my head, filling me up, driving out every other thought. 'There's nothing more that you can do for him. Involving yourself with the police will only place more obstacles in your way in the days to come and believe me, you have your hands full already.'

He started leading me away from the Cloisters and

across the lawn, his arm clamped tight around my shoulders, his voice silky and insistent in my ear. I felt that pull again, just as when his mouth was at my throat. . . . We had already crossed the lawn that separated the Cloisters from the woods. We were on the edge of the lawn beside a wooded path. How had we gotten so far away from the building so quickly? He was doing something to make me do what he told me to do, exerting some kind of power.

'Stop!' I cried, planting my feet firmly on the ground. 'Stop whatever it is you're doing . . . forcing me . . .'

Will Hughes turned around to face me. He was so close that I could see a blue vein at his temple pulse . . . *but how?* Wasn't a vampire supposed to be *dead*? Then I understood. It was *my* blood moving through his veins. I started to feel faint again, but his arm held me up.

'All right,' he said. 'I won't force you, but then you have to listen to reason. We have to leave. How would you explain all this to the police?'

He waited for my answer. I still felt the pull of him, but I no longer felt a compulsion to do whatever he said. The power he'd been exerting over me a moment ago was gone. He had let it go. He was giving me the opportunity to discuss the matter. *Awfully civilized for a vampire,* that cooler voice inside my head remarked. It was up to me to make my argument.

'The police will know that I was in there. It will look bad that I left the scene,' I said, willing my voice to sound calm and rational. 'The guard saw me come in.'

'There's no one left alive in there,' he said, his eyes steady on mine. 'The manticore killed them all.' He slid his right hand down my arm. His touch made me tremble, but I didn't pull away . . . then I saw he was only pointing to my messenger bag, which was still slung across my chest. I recalled, as though from another lifetime, slipping it over my head in the library and fastening the clasp.

'You've got your bag. Did you leave anything else?'

I shook my head. 'No, but . . . Dr. Tolbert's cane . . . I grabbed it and used it against the manticore.'

Hughes lifted his arm. The handle of Dr. Tolbert's cane was hooked over his forearm. 'I thought of that. There's nothing in there to link you to your friend's death. I know it feels like a betrayal to leave him, but if you want to bring his murderer to justice, you have to leave now.' He waved his hand toward the wooded path. If there were streetlamps to light it, they weren't working; the path lay in deep shadow. I had the feeling that the moment I stepped off the lit lawn and into the dark woods, I was committing myself to . . . *something*. A few moments ago, when I had watched Will Hughes writhe in agony, I had thought I'd gotten over the hardest part. I'd accepted that the supernatural was real. But now I realized that was only the beginning. The supernatural was asking me to take his hand and step into the dark with him. I looked at Will Hughes. His eyes flashed back at me, silver in the darkness, twin beacons. The dark would never be impenetrable with those eyes to lead me. I stepped out of the light and into the shadows, only realizing as I did so that I would be completely dependent on him once we were in the dark.

❊   ❊   ❊

I was wrong, though. After we'd gone a few yards down the dark path, I could see perfectly well. It was not, though, as if my eyes had grown accustomed to the dark; it was rather as if the dark had grown accustomed to *me*. With each step the dark opened itself up to me, letting me into its secrets. Colors I had never before seen unfolded in the darkest shadows: deep indigos and violets, hidden cores of tender lilac and pale pink. As we walked deeper into the park, the shadows unfurled like buds opening in the sunlight, only here they were reaching for the dark. Out of these knots of inky black unrolled cascades of gold and silver that grew to waves of light swirling around us that seemed to push us forward like gusts of wind. And yet I felt no cold and no fear, only an overwhelming sense of wonder. I looked at Will Hughes and saw that his eyes glowed like twin silver stars in the roiling darkness.

'How am I seeing this?' I asked. 'Have you done this to me?'

'When I drank your blood, some of my blood entered your bloodstream. It gave you some of my ability to see in the darkness.'

I pulled up short and whirled around to face him, all that wonder becoming fear again. 'Does that mean I'm going to become like you? Am I going to turn into a vampire?'

He gazed at me, taking in my horror, not answering right away. Then he looked away, his eyes flashing red again. 'No. I didn't take enough of your blood. I'd have to drain you of all your blood and then give you some of mine to drink—'

I made an involuntary sound that made him pause. 'That disgusts you, doesn't it? And yet it's the little bit of my blood that mixed in with yours that has enabled you to see all this.' He opened his arms wide as if to embrace all the colors swirling around us, and I felt a little sorry that I had maligned his gift.

'Does this happen to everyone you bite?' I asked, moving on ahead of him so he wouldn't see me wince at the word *bite*.

'No, not everyone. You have to have a touch of the fey to see what you see. You have it . . . many artists do . . . poets, painters . . .'

'I'm not an artist,' I said reflexively, 'but this does remind me of a painting: van Gogh's *Starry Night*. This must be how van Gogh saw the night.'

'Poor Vincent. He fell in love with the colors of the night. They were like a drug to him. He grew addicted to the night. It drove him mad at last.'

I started to ask him if he'd actually known the artist, but then something else struck me. 'What did you mean *a touch of the fey*? *Fey* as in *fairy*?'

He laughed, a sound that sent sparks of light shooting from his fingertips. 'Don't tell me that after encountering a manticore and a vampire tonight you're going to balk at fairies? Look again. They're all around us.'

We'd reached the Heather Garden, where I'd started my walk earlier tonight – or was it yesterday evening? I'd lost all track of time as we wandered through the park – and at first all I saw were dazzling swirls of color and light among the last of the late-blooming flowers. But then I saw that there were shapes in the light, moving so quickly I could only catch glimpses of them: the sinuous curve of a smile, the rounded haunch of a hip, the sudden flash of wings beating the air.

'They're moving too fast!' I complained.

'No, it's you who are moving too fast. You have to slow your heartbeat.' He came close behind me and slipped his arm over my shoulders and his hand under my sweater. He lay his hand over my heart. I felt the pulse in his wrist beat against my skin and an answering beat in my heart. *My blood,* I remembered again, *it's my blood beating in his veins.* 'Take long, slow breaths,' he whispered in my ear, his breath purling over the back of my neck, over the still open wounds made by his teeth. I started to close my eyes, but then I saw *one.* A creature spun out of the colors of the night – indigo, violet, silver – it slipped among the heather bushes on blue-veined wings, absorbing the colors of whatever it landed on, bending its tiny, foxlike face toward each tiny, bell-shaped blossom. I thought at first that it was sipping nectar from the flowers, like a bee or a humming-bird, but then I saw that it was drinking light and color instead. As it dipped its face into a bloom, its diaphanous body vibrated with the flower's color.

I turned to Will Hughes. 'Is this real? Are you making me see these things?'

'They're real. They're called light sylphs because they drink the light. They can only come out at night, though; they'd drown in the daylight.'

The creature looked up from a flower, its mouth stained purple, and met my startled gaze. It cocked its little head and moved its lips as if to smile, but the smile turned into a snarl revealing a row of tiny, needle-sharp teeth and then it flitted away.

'Why . . . ?'

'Don't worry,' Will said, drawing me away. 'It's not you it's scared of; it's me. The light sylphs aren't too fond of vampires, but since we share the night, we mostly keep out of each other's way.'

He drew me down the hill. Knowing things with teeth were riding the night, I stayed close to him – the *bigger* thing with teeth.

'You said before that only someone with a touch of the fey could see this,' I said. 'How did you know I had it?'

'Because you're descended from Marguerite D'Arques. And she was one of *them*.' He shivered as he said *them*. What scares a vampire? I wondered. Then I thought of something else – vampires could live forever, couldn't they? And he'd already spoken of knowing Vincent van Gogh . . .

'Did you know the first Marguerite then?'

We'd come to a stone wall overlooking the Henry Hudson Parkway and the river. He leaned against the wall and faced me. The silver light in his eyes dimmed, then gleamed dully like tarnished plate, then like the sky before a storm. I felt something gathering in him, something that could lash out against me.

'Yes, I knew her. Knew her and loved her and lost her. She is why I am what I am today.' He laughed. 'Well, I should say what I am *tonight*.' He hoisted himself up on the stone wall and swung his legs around to face the river. If he had spread his arms and taken flight, I wouldn't have been too surprised, but instead he patted the wall beside him. 'Come sit here and I'll tell you all about it. After all, it's your story as well.'

'When I was a young man I was, I am sorry to say, exceedingly vain of my good looks and exceedingly shallow.' He spoke facing the river so that all I saw was his profile outlined against the night sky, like a white cameo set in onyx. I could see how he might be excused for being a little vain. But shallow? If he had once been, the centuries had given him depth. 'So vain that although many beautiful young women fell in love with me, and my father begged me to marry and produce an heir, I would not tie myself to one lest I lose the adulation of the many. My father was so desperate to have an heir that he commissioned a poet to write verses imploring me to procreate in order to assure my immortality. The poet came regularly to tutor me in poetry, love, and the responsibilities of my station . . . and then the poet fell in love with me.'

'Wait,' I said, 'this sounds familiar.'

He smiled and went on with his story. 'No longer did the poet tell me I must beget a son to gain eternal life, rather I should look to *him* to ensure my immortality through his verses. Vain as I was, I became enamored of that notion, and when the poet was sent away I followed him to London and joined his acting company.'

'Don't tell me. Your poet was William Shakespeare.'

He turned to me, his eyes glowing with mischief. 'Don't tell *me,* you see a manticore, a vampire, a fairy, but you balk at William Shakespeare?'

'Yes!' I declared. 'It's like those séances where all the spirits turn out to be Cleopatra or Napoléon.'

'I see your point. Shall I go on calling him *the poet* so as not to strain your credulity?'

'Oh, call him whatever you like!' I cried, throwing my hands up in defeat. What was the point of questioning the details when I'd already accepted the premise? Besides, there was too much I was curious about. 'Was it really William Shakespeare? What was he like?'

'Possessed. Mad. Talk about touched by the fey! Sometimes I thought *he* was a wizard the way he cast spells with his words. He had a fire burning in him that made this' – he swept his hand toward the million lights of Manhattan – 'look like a swarm of fireflies. How could I not fall under his spell, even after I found out that there was a rival for his affections back in London?'

'Don't you mean in Stratford-upon-Avon?'

He tilted his head up and raised one eyebrow almost mockingly. For a moment I saw the cruel young man he had been and felt sorry for those Elizabethan girls who had lost their hearts to him. 'No, I don't. The woman who captured his heart had to have more than a round bottom and a prosperous father. She had to offer him *inspiration* – the magic to spin words into pictures.'

'A muse then?'

'Yes, you could call her that. The poet called her that many times. She was a mysterious dark-haired woman. No one knew her full name or where she came from. She so rarely presented herself in public. And even when she did, she seemed to blend into the shadows somehow.'

'The Dark Lady?'

'Yes. I always thought it was fitting that posterity gave her that name. It was close to her real name – Marguerite D'Arques.'

'My mother's name? *This* was the Marguerite who you say is my ancestor? But you said no one knew her full name.'

'No one but me, and I learned it because I fell in love with her.' He paused for so long I thought he might not go on, but at last he drew in a long breath – it sounded like the sigh of the wind rustling the heather behind us – and went on, 'And she with me. William was, of course, furious. He turned on her and wrote those nasty poems condemning her. All the hard things he ever wrote about women I believe stem from his anger at Marguerite. She never blamed him for his attacks on her, though. She never took away the gift of fey sight she had given him. How do you think he wrote those fairy scenes in *A Midsummer Night's Dream*? Or wrote about Caliban and Ariel in *The Tempest*?

'At first we were happy together . . . until I discovered that the reason she had the power to inspire Shakespeare to write about fairies was because she was one of them. She was one of the fey. Immortal. She would never grow old, never change. She had what I had dreamed of, what Shakespeare in his poems had promised me – eternal youth and immortality. I begged her to make me immortal too, but she refused. She was happy to spend *my* life with me, but I, in my vanity, couldn't bear the thought that *I* would grow old while *she* remained young. She told me I didn't know what a burden it was to live forever. We fought. And she left.'

A tremor passed over his face and he turned away for a moment. When he turned back toward the river, his face was once again as immobile as carved stone against the blackness. Beautiful, but oddly cold, inert.

'I was angry with her and yet desperate to be with her, and to prove her wrong. I sought out every magician and alchemist I'd ever heard of. Shakespeare had known them all, but these were different days now that King James the First had come to the throne. It was dangerous to be suspected of wizardry, and they had all gone into hiding. But I tracked down the most famous of them all.'

'John Dee?' Just saying the man's name made me tremble, as if the sound of his name might summon him here.

'Yes. I knew that he and Edward Kelley had trafficked with spirits. I knew that he had sought the secret to eternal youth. When I told him why I wanted it – and what Marguerite was – he told me that I had to follow her to France and steal a silver box she kept with her at all times, and her ring, and bring them to him. With those two things, he told me, he could make me immortal.' He smiled ruefully. 'You must wonder why I believed him, but I was desperate . . . and Dee can be very persuasive. I followed Marguerite to Paris . . . and from there I tracked her across France until I found her. I stole the box and the ring from her—'

'You told me that you and Marguerite *exchanged* rings.'

'A little lie. Forgive me. It *was* an exchange of sorts. I left her my ring with a note that said I would return soon and that then we could be together for all eternity. Meanwhile, I'd gotten word that John Dee had followed me to France. I met him and gave him the ring and the box. He used them to summon a demon from the shadows – a vampire who attacked me and made me *this*. When I awoke, John Dee laughed at me. "Now you'll live forever," he said, "that is, as long as you drink blood every night and hide your face from the sun during the day."

'I tried to kill him, but he'd taken precautions and was able to escape. I wound up wandering the streets of Paris . . . half-mad with bloodlust and despair. I even crawled into the catacombs . . .' He broke off and smiled a rueful smile. 'But you don't want to hear about that. Eventually, Marguerite found me. I was afraid that she would be repulsed by the monster I had become.' He stopped again. This time for so long I was afraid he wouldn't go on. I laid my hand on his.

'Did she turn her back on you?'

He shook his head. 'No. Not exactly. She wasn't repulsed by me, she wasn't frightened of me, she was only sad . . . she sat me down to tell me a story.' He smiled and glanced at me. 'Much as I have sat you down to tell you this story, only we sat beside the Seine, not the Hudson. She told me that she had found a way to become mortal, but because it was not permitted for one of her kind to become mortal, she made a deal with her rulers. In exchange for mortality she pledged herself and her descendants to guard the borders between the worlds and to protect humans from the demons of the night. Then she patiently explained that one of the creatures of the night she was pledged to protect mortals from was *me*. As you can imagine, that put a crimp in our . . . relationship.'

He laughed, but it was a joyless sound. I shifted my legs on the stone wall, realizing I had grown stiff. How long had we been sitting here? I wondered. How long had we wandered the park before coming here? How long before dawn? I felt as if I were under a spell. Would all this evaporate with the sunlight?

'Did you ever see her again?' I asked.

He shook his head, opened his mouth to say something, and closed it. He picked up a stone from the wall, stretched his arm back, and threw it toward the river. I watched it sail through the air with my heightened sight – *fey sight*, he'd called it – for farther than any *human* could have thrown it, until it landed in the water. I remembered the strength in his hands as he wrestled with the manticore. I remembered his teeth at my neck. And *I* was supposed to be pledged to protect the human race against *him*? How was I supposed to do *that*?

'And did you ever meet any of her descendants again . . . I mean, before me?'

'My path has crossed with some before, but only briefly. I have not come this close to one before. I can't tell you how shocked I was when you walked into my apartment . . . and when you asked for my help. You see now why I had to say no.'

'But you came to the Cloisters to help me.'

'When I saw the fog rising, I knew Dee was sending something to kill you. That's how he works. He can send his spells through the fog.' I thought of the fog that had risen last night when Jaws had come to life, and the fog that had closed around the Cloisters just before the manticore came to life. Air and mist, Will had said before. How could anyone defend herself against that? '. . . and I knew that without any training you would be helpless against him. I couldn't just let you die . . . I didn't plan though to . . .' He touched my neck and I had to bite my lip to keep from moaning out loud.

'What have you done to me?' I asked.

He stroked my neck, my hair, then lifted my chin with one finger. 'I've done it to myself as well. Now that I've drunk your blood we're connected. I can't help that. The one good thing is that it's awakened your sight. You'll need that when Dee comes after you again—'

'Again?' I asked, horrified. What other monsters might he send against me?

'Yes. He won't stop now. He knows you'll try to get the box back from him.'

'But what if I don't want to get it back? What if I just let him keep it?'

He gave me a long searching look. 'I don't think you want to live in the world that Dee will make with the power that the box gives him. Even without the ability to open the box Dee has wreaked havoc over the centuries – he was with Cromwell in 1649 and he blighted the Irish potatoes in the 1840s. It was one of his shadowmen who shot Archduke Franz Ferdinand, and he sat beside Hitler whispering in his ear.'

'But why? What does he get from creating so much horror in the world?'

Will shook his head. 'I've never been entirely sure. He seems to feed off chaos and horror. He grows more powerful with each war, each genocide, each atrocity . . . and now that the box has been opened, he'll be more powerful than ever. He'll use it to summon the demons of Despair and Discord.'

'Maybe it's too late already,' I said.

'That's your despair talking. No. Opening the box was only the first step for Dee. He couldn't do it himself, he needed a descendant of Marguerite to do it for him. He waited centuries for one who didn't know that the box must stay closed and then he tricked you into opening it away from him. You remember the light that came out of the box? That would have destroyed Dee. He had to use his mindless minions to retrieve the box. Even now it's very dangerous for him to be near the box when it's open, but he must keep it open for seven days in order to bring the demons of Despair and Discord into this world. You opened the box two nights ago – so you only have five days to find him and close the box, or Despair and Discord will gain control of the city.'

I gaped at him, trying to absorb all this fantastic information. It was one thing to accept the existence of a supernatural world, it was quite another to believe I had such an important role in it.

'But as you've pointed out, I'm untrained. My mother died before she could teach me what to do—' I felt my eyes filling up with tears. The shadows around us seemed to creep nearer. I smelled copper in the air and heard something hiss in the bushes. *Poor orphan,* it seemed to say, *poor motherless orphan.*

Will took me by the shoulders and turned me to face him. 'You can't let yourself give in to despair. That's what he *does*. There are others who can teach you, *guides*. They're all around you. You just have to open your eyes and you'll see them.'

'But can't you help me?' I asked, instantly hating the whiny tone of my voice. I wouldn't blame him if he turned from me in disgust.

'I've done as much as I can in opening your eyes. I've done more than I should. You'll have to find other teachers. I promise you, though, that I'll protect you when I can . . .' He stopped and tilted his head, listening. I listened too, but all I heard was a bird singing – a pure sweet sound that reminded me of that French poem I'd read in the Cloisters library only a few hours ago. So much had passed since then – so many horrors and wonders – that it felt like years since I'd read those lines: *The nightingale sings no more; it is the lark greeting the break of day.*

I turned around to look toward the eastern sky and saw that it was beginning to pale. When I turned back, I was alone on the stone wall. Will Hughes had vanished as swiftly as the night.

King of Moonshine, Prince of Dreams

Walking back to the 190th Street station, I noticed that the last of the heather, which had glowed indigo and violet last night, had faded to pearly gray and mauve, blighted by frost. I looked around for the light sylphs, but they were gone. Drunk on color and light, no doubt. But where did they go in the daytime? And what did they live on when they'd drunk all the colors, and winter turned the landscape barren and pale?

I paused at the park entrance and turned back to look at the gardens, struck that *these* were the questions preoccupying my mind, not whether all that had happened last night was real. My hand slipped underneath my scarf, which I'd tied tightly around my throat to hide the marks of Will Hughes's teeth. When I touched the torn flesh, I felt a tremor throughout my body. No, I hadn't imagined what had happened. I readjusted the scarf. Will Hughes had said I would find guides. But how? Where?

Not here, a voice inside my head said. A supernatural voice? I wondered. Or just the voice of reason reminding me that I was tired and hungry and cold and that it was time to go home? I couldn't tell – and if I couldn't tell *that,* how was I ever going to find the guides to teach me what I needed to know?

I left the park feeling as if the minute I stepped outside its gates I might never again find entrance into the world I had glimpsed last night. Certainly nothing could have felt more mundane than descending into the subway station and waiting on the platform with early-morning commuters for the A. Plugged into iPods, clutching their paper coffee cups, eyes fixed on the track for the approaching train, which one of them would believe me if I told them what had happened to me in the last forty-eight hours? Certainly not the woman in a gray suit texting on her iPhone, or the yawning high school student trying to focus on her AP chemistry book. And how could I tell anyone about being in the Cloisters when Edgar Tolbert was killed? They'd think I was as crazy as the man wearing the Daniel Boone cap muttering to himself as he went from person to person holding out a worn paper cup asking for spare change. He was dressed in layers of tattered clothing in a rainbow of faded plaids and prints that hung loosely from his slight frame and shook like quaking aspen leaves as he shambled along the platform. As he got closer to me, I heard a bit of his patter.

'You're looking as lovely as the queen of Egypt,' he said to the woman in the gray business suit. 'Purple the sails,' he cried out, 'and so perfumed that the winds were lovesick with them.' He performed a pirouette, his loose clothing billowing out like Shakespeare's perfumed sails and turning into a blur of color as he spun. When he came to a stop, the blur remained – trembling bars of color like a rainbow caught in a sprinkler on a summer day. I almost cried out in delight at his trick, until I realized that the woman in the gray suit clearly didn't see what I saw. She was staring right at the beggar, but her face was empty of emotion and as gray as her suit . . . or . . . I looked at her more closely. The gray didn't end where her clothes ended. A shimmer of gray, about an inch thick, surrounded her like a second skin.

The beggar performed another pirouette and this time the woman relented and smiled. The gray changed to sky blue. She dug in her purse and found a handful of coins to drop in the beggar's cup. He swept his hat off and bowed low, plumes of color sparking the air around both of them. I looked around to see if anyone else on the platform was witnessing this light show, but everyone else was studiously ignoring the exchange. I saw now, though, that each person was surrounded by a faint glow – a corona – each a different color. For many the glow was low and muted, for some it was muddied. I had seen these coronas before, only I had dismissed them as symptoms of ocular migraine.

My yoga teacher was always going on about auras, about how to see your own aura and others', about how to recognize from a person's aura if he or she was balanced and happy or depressed or sick. I'd always thought it was a bunch of New Age hooey, but once when I was sitting in TekServe waiting to get my laptop fixed, a man sat down next to me and after a few minutes turned to me and asked, 'Are you an artist?'

I knew it was probably just a pickup line, but what

struck me was that I happened to be dressed very conservatively that day because I was going to an auction at Sotheby's with my father later. Nothing about my clothes or accessories looked particularly artistic.

I told him no, but that I designed jewelry and used to draw and sculpt.

'You're an artist,' he had said. 'I can tell from your aura.'

We chatted a few more minutes – he made no attempt to pick me up or ask me for a handout – and then my number was called. My good mood lasted through learning it would cost $800 to repair the damage to my hard drive incurred by spilling a glass of white wine on it the previous night.

Now as I got on the subway and sat down, I wondered what he'd seen. The green glow that surrounded a young Latina woman in scrubs and thick-soled sneakers sitting across from me? The yellow flares that emanated from a pretty, dark-haired girl whose head bobbed to the music from her iPod? I hoped he hadn't seen the murky gray miasma that seeped from the elderly man hunched into his overcoat and matched his skin tone, or the mustardy yellow that hovered over the head of an elderly woman who winced in pain and touched her right temple each time the brakes screeched. It wasn't hard to see who was well and who was sick, who was happy and who was sunk in despair. What I noticed, too, is that sometimes one person's aura touched another's and each changed.

I saw it first at the 175th Street stop. The train was beginning to get crowded, so that when a middle-aged man in a brown raincoat got on, there were no seats. When he reached his arm up to hold on to the overhead bar, he winced. He wasn't so old that anyone would automatically give up his or her seat for him, but he was clearly in some discomfort. He was surrounded by a dark red cloud – a bloody haze that seemed to envelop him. I noticed that several people who came close to him moved away, as if aware of some contagion. I was just getting up to offer him my seat when the Latina woman in scrubs got to her feet and gently touched him on the arm. He glared at her so angrily that I was afraid he was going to hit her, but then she lay her hand more firmly on his arm and gestured with her hand to her vacated seat. He muttered something under his breath, still scowling, but he took the seat anyway and as he leaned back, I saw the angry red glow subside to a pale pink. The woman who'd given up her seat still had the green glow around her, but now it shone brighter and extended farther out around her. It touched the elderly woman with the headache, turning her mustard yellow into a clear daffodil gold. The girl who'd started out with the yellow aura sang a line from a song on her iPod, which made the old man with the gray aura laugh out loud. Colors rippled down the car, turning brighter and clearer, as if that one act – the woman in the scrubs touching the sick man's arm and giving him her seat – was a pebble cast into the water radiating out into widening circles. I wondered how far it would go and what, if anything, could stop it. I soon found out.

At 168th Street the woman in scrubs got out – going to New York Presbyterian Hospital, I figured – and the car got more crowded. An overweight man lost his footing and bumped into the knees of the gray man, who muttered a derogatory remark about fat people. The overweight man blushed, his aura flaring magenta, and he pushed his way farther along the car, knocking his elbow into a well-dressed woman, who scowled and sent out sparks of sulfurous yellow that filled the air with a murky smoke. I could feel the tension rising in the car and considered getting off at the next stop and catching a cab, but at this time in the morning it would take forever to get downtown and cost a fortune. At the thought of the expense of a cab ride, all my money worries came rising up. The events of the last two days had eclipsed such mundane worries, but when the dust settled, we'd still be left with colossal debt. And it certainly wouldn't help the gallery any if my father was suspected of insurance fraud. I wondered too, what would happen to the paintings that the police had confiscated from the burglars. Would they be held as evidence? Would we be able to sell them if we had an offer on them?

My mind reeled with all the complications. The idea that I was supposed to be saving the world from the evil John Dee seemed absurd – even more absurd than believing in the existence of manticores, vampires, and fairies. I couldn't save my father and myself from financial ruin. I hadn't been able to save Edgar Tolbert. A great tide of shame washed over me at the memory of Edgar Tolbert. Here I was being entertained by fairies and auras and a man was dead because of me. What kind of monster was I? And how could someone as puny and selfish as me possibly do anything against someone as powerful as John Dee?

By the time the train reached the Fourteenth Street stop I felt mired in the same muddy gloom that I saw all around me. My mood didn't improve when I'd climbed to street level. The day that had dawned so brightly had turned gray and overcast. The people I passed on the street were huddled into their coats, heads bowed, eyes on the pavement, a wreath of gray or brown fug hovering over their heads.

It was even worse in the hospital. When I reached the front door of St. Vincent's a woman stepped out, her skin white and drawn. She covered her face with her hands and turned toward the wall beside the door. The man following her stood helpless by her side, one arm lifted to stroke her back, but arrested midair. I had no idea what horrible news they had just received but I could taste their grief in my mouth – a taste like pennies and blood.

The whole hospital had that smell. Crossing through the lobby, I felt such waves of fear and despair that I could barely stand. The people sitting in the waiting room were sunk into pools of dark muddy red and brown. Here and there, though, a flash of brighter color and light appeared. A man who held his elderly wife's hand glowed violet, a child who held up her doll while reciting her ABC's to her mother was surrounded by a halo of pink. And when I reached the floor my father was on, I immediately felt a lightening in the air.

There shouldn't have been one. Patients in critical condition were on this floor, but there was a feeling of calm here that I hadn't felt on the other floors. I took a deep breath, realizing it was the first really full breath I'd taken since getting off the subway. The air still smelled like stale disinfectant, but beneath that smell – or maybe it was *above* that smell or *all around* the smell – ran a fresher current, as if air that had moved through pine trees and fresh water. It grew stronger as I neared my father's room. I could see it – a green glow emanating from his room. I stopped for a moment and just breathed it in. I felt myself grow calm and hopeful once more. What did all the money problems in the world matter as long as my father was still alive and I was still alive? One of my favorite Latin mottoes – which I'd found on an old signet ring I'd used to make one of my medallions – ran through my head. *Dum spiro, spero.* 'As long as I have breath, I have hope.' I'd find a way out of our problems and I'd do what I could to stop Dee. But first I'd find out who was spreading this healing aura.

I walked into the room and found Obie Smith sitting on a chair beside my father's bed playing a hand of cards with my father and Zach Reese. Zach and my father were laughing at something the nurse had just said. They didn't notice that I'd come in. But Obie Smith did. He raised his face to me and I saw sparks of green fire coming from his eyes and his fingertips as he dealt another hand. Flashes of gold lit the air around him. I would once have identified those flashes as scintillations – another of the symptoms of ocular migraine – but I'd never seen those scintillations take the shape of fairy wings before.

'Garet,' my father crooned when he noticed me standing in the doorway, 'why are you standing in the door with your mouth open? Come in! It turns out this young man . . . what did you say your name was again?'

'Oberon.' He had his eyes on me as he answered my father's question. 'Oberon Smith.'

Oberon. The king of the fairies, I thought, amazed that anything still had the power to amaze me. But the sight of this creature out of Shakespeare's *A Midsummer Night's Dream* did.

'Oberon here knew Santé Leone in Haiti,' my father said.

I looked at my father. Was it possible to be in the presence of this . . . creature, this *luminous* creature . . . and not know what he was? But then I had met him three times before and not suspected that he was anything other than an effective nurse and decent human being. But he wasn't a human being at all. That was clear to me now as I entered the room and he stood up. The semitransparent green and gold wings spread out behind him like a peacock's tail unfolding. I felt as if I were supposed to curtsy, but instead he bowed to me first, sweeping his arm toward the chair he had just vacated.

'Please, Miss James, take my seat. You look like you've had a long night.'

His eyes were on my throat. I'd wrapped my scarf around my neck, but I could feel the force of his gaze on the two puncture wounds there and I felt the blood rise to my face.

'You do look tired, Garet. You mustn't let yourself get run-down while I'm not at home to look after you.'

I almost laughed out loud at the look of solicitation on my father's face. When was the last time I had felt *looked after*? Not since my mother had died. I remembered that when we came home from her funeral my father had sat down in my mother's rocking chair – a favorite chair that they had bought in an antiques shop on Fourth Avenue when she was pregnant with me – and the chair had collapsed beneath him. He'd wept then, as he hadn't at the funeral, but I hadn't. I'd known with a certainty that if we both cried, we'd never stop. I'd been looking after him ever since. Had he thought all this time that he'd been looking after me?

'Have you been fussing too much over the gallery with me not there?' he asked.

'Maia's been filling in admirably for both of us,' I reassured him. 'But we really do need to think about scraping together some money to pay her more now with all the extra hours she's putting in.' I winced at having brought up money when Roman was recovering, but Maia had been going well beyond the call of duty.

My father nodded his agreement as I took the chair Oberon offered to me. Oberon moved a few inches away and leaned against the wall, his wings folded and pinned behind his back. How had I missed the signs? His almond-shaped eyes tilted up at the corners like a cat's, the color wasn't just green – they were emerald flecked with gold. The tips of his ears were slightly pointed and his skin had a golden sheen. Even in hospital scrubs he looked like a king. I recalled a line of poetry – not Shakespeare, but some other poet describing Oberon: *King of moonshine, prince of dreams*. The lines fit. This creature seemed to be made out of moonshine and dreams.

'So you're from Haiti?' I asked, looking him straight in the eye. I remembered from the fairy tales that my mother read me that fairies couldn't lie to a direct question.

'My people came to the islands from abroad,' he said, smiling slyly.

'But you really knew Santé Leone? You look young to have been much more than a kid in the seventies when Santé lived in Haiti.'

'I'm older than I look. I came to New York right around the time Santé did. In fact, I was just telling your father that Santé stayed at my place for a while. Just before he died he left a painting in my apartment. It's of a beautiful dark-haired woman standing in front of a stone tower. It's called *Marguerite.*'

'It must be of your mother,' Zach said. 'Santé thought the world of her . . . of course we all did.'

I looked over at Zach. He had swept up the playing cards, his big rawboned hands deftly shuffling them. There was something different about him. I hadn't noticed my father's or Zach's aura since I'd walked in because Oberon's green glow overwhelmed every other color in the room, but now I noticed that there was a lighter green glow around Zach. It was the color of new leaves in the spring and was only about a quarter inch thick, but even though I'd never consciously seen Zach's aura before, I was sure this hadn't been its color . . . at least not for a long time.

The other thing I noticed was that Zach's hands weren't shaking. I don't think I had ever seen them this steady. Certainly not when he talked about my mother.

'Of course it's of Margot,' my father said. 'He always

called her Marguerite. "Marguerite, my tower of strength," he'd say, "watch over me." It does me good to think he painted her near the end, that he hadn't forgotten her.' I looked at my father, surprised that he'd remembered that Santé was dead. He didn't seem upset, though.

'I'd like to see that painting,' I said, looking up at Oberon Smith.

'I told your father that I would bring it to him, but perhaps you'll come with me and bring it back yourself. I'm going off my shift now. If you're not busy, you could come with me. I don't live far.'

'I only just got here, I want to spend some time with my father . . .' But before I could finish my sentence I heard a low gurgling sound. I glanced at my father and saw that he had fallen asleep and was snoring peacefully.

'I'm afraid we've tired him out telling stories all night,' Oberon said in a low, musical voice. He laid a hand on Zach's shoulder, and the big man slumped down in his chair and instantly fell asleep. The leaf-green glow around Zach's skin pulsed and thickened another quarter inch. 'Why don't you come with me. We've got much to talk about.'

I got up and followed Oberon out of the room. There were a million things I wanted to ask. Were there more creatures like him? Was he really the same Oberon that Shakespeare wrote about in *A Midsummer Night's Dream*? Could he fly with those wings? Or were they an illusion, a trick? Was it all a trick? Was I going crazy? But instead I found myself asking a rather mundane question about his profession. 'So,' I asked when we were in the hallway, 'what's the King of Moonshine, Prince of Dreams, doing working in a hospital?'

He tilted his head back and deep, rumbling laughter flowed out into the hospital corridor. A wave of green-gold light cascaded in front of him washing over an orderly and a shrunken, desiccated man in a wheelchair, who looked up and lifted a trembling hand to his own face as if he'd just remembered who he was.

'That old scoundrel Horace Walpole! I told him his flowery praise would embarrass me someday. Well, to answer your question, darling, things are rough all over. And they're about to get rougher.'

gone to earth

I followed Oberon to the nurses' fifth-floor locker room so he could get his coat and watched as he swung it over his shoulders. It slid between his shoulder blades and wings without ruffling his wings at all.

'The first thing you have to learn,' he said, taking in where my gaze rested, 'is that magic and reality – what you're used to thinking of as reality – are layered. It's not always so clear where the one leaves off and the other begins.'

'I thought my job as a Watchtower was to guard the door between the two,' I said as we took the elevator down to the lobby.

He gave me a long assessing look, but instead of saying anything he took out a Sharpie pen from one pocket and a pack of multicolored Post-it notes from the other. He scribbled something on the top green note – a sort of spiral doodle – then flipped to the next sheet and scribbled the same mark on that.

We didn't speak for the rest of the ride down or as he strode through the lobby so fast that the tails of his long coat snapped at his heels. Outside, he crossed Twelfth

Street in the middle of the block. I had to dodge a car to keep up with him. Had I said something to make him angry? Maybe I wasn't supposed to talk about being a watchtower.

Halfway down the block he abruptly stopped, his wings beating the air as he turned, grabbed me, and pulled me into a doorway framed by two columns. He pushed me behind him and spread out his arms, a Post-it note affixed to the palm of each hand. The symbols he had drawn began to glow green, then blue, then white – like heating metal – and then began to smoke. The inside of the spiral glowed like an eye. Then he wrapped his hands around the columns on either side of the doorway. I heard a sizzling sound and smelled singed flesh. When he moved his hands away, the spiral eyes were imprinted on the columns, glowing silver. A skein of light, like a spiderweb made up of silver threads, sprung up between the two columns.

I wanted to ask him if it had hurt his hands, but when he turned to me, his eyes were blazing gold and green with anger. He pulled my scarf down away from my throat, revealing the marks on my neck.

'Tell me everything that happened between you and the vampire,' he said, his voice stern, all trace of that lovely West Indies accent gone now. 'And everything he told you about the Watchtower.'

I told him everything that happened from the time Will Hughes's driver picked me up until the moment Will Hughes vanished from the park. While we talked, two people approached the doorway – one a woman with grocery bags in her arms who clearly lived there, the other a UPS deliveryman carrying a package and clipboard. Each time their eyes became cloudy when they approached the doorway. They stopped, appeared to remember something they had forgotten, turned around, and left. The delivery-man had been so close to me that I had looked straight into his eyes, but I couldn't see my own reflection in them, only an empty doorway.

When I was done, Oberon asked one question. 'You say he told you Fenodoree's name?'

I nodded.

'All right,' he said after a moment. 'We'd better go talk to Puck.'

He peeled the two Post-it notes off the doorway. The two spiral eyes blinked and then vanished. The silver web sizzled and dissolved into a shower of sparks, which Oberon stirred with his hands and then walked through. At Seventh Avenue he crossed against the light. A yellow cab screeched to a halt inches from us. Oberon glared at the driver and the man stammered an apology. We continued west on Greenwich Avenue. Oberon's green aura had dwindled to a hard malachite shell, but it glowed with a fiercer light, like a banked fire. People on the street got out of his way. Three car alarms went off as he passed. A Great Dane whimpered and pulled his owner into the gutter.

'I don't understand what's so bad,' I said. 'Will Hughes saved me from the manticore. He told me to seek out a fey guide. He seemed . . . *nice*.'

'That's what's so bad,' Oberon roared, turning on me.

'You thinking a four-hundred-year-old bloodsucking vampire – a creature of the darkness – seems *nice*. You . . . the descendant of the Watchtower.'

'According to the story he told me, the original Marguerite was in love with him. She's the reason he became a vampire in the first place.'

'And did you believe everything he told you?'

I considered the question. I found that when I thought about Will Hughes, I felt a prickling sensation in my neck where he had bitten me. The sensation traveled down my throat, into my chest, made my heart beat faster, then spread lower. I remembered his body pressed against mine, his mouth on my throat, the tug of a silver thread that traveled from his lips to the core of my being. I could feel it now. I lifted my hand in front of my face and saw a silver glow surrounding my fingers. *We're connected,* he'd said. Could he have lied to me after that?

'I believe that he believed everything he told me,' I said.

Oberon reached out and touched my hand. The silver light flared. Sparks flew into the air – silver and gold – then swirled up into the sky like a miniature tornado. 'Okay,' Oberon said, nodding. 'I think you're right about that part – and you're not so far gone that you can't question what he says. I think he tied himself as much to you as he tied you to him . . . and that might come in handy. But don't forget, he's a thing of the dark. He may not be on Dee's side, but he's not on ours either.'

We'd come to the corner of Cordelia and Hudson, to the door of Puck's tea shop. Oberon stopped and looked up Cordelia Street toward the river.

'What did Hughes say about the demons Dee would raise?' he asked me.

I closed my eyes to remember exactly what Will Hughes had said. I could hear his voice so clearly that when I opened my eyes, I half expected to find him standing in front of me. In broad daylight. The thought that he hadn't stood outside in the sunlight for four hundred years brought tears to my eyes.

'He said that Dee would use the box to summon the "demons of Despair and Discord."'

'*Despair and Discord?* Those were his exact words?'

'Yes.'

'I just want to look at something.' He took off down the street. This time I couldn't begin to keep up with him. I found him standing in front of 121½ Cordelia Street, staring at the glass door with its faded gilt lettering. *Air & Mist,* it had read before, I was sure of it. But now other letters had appeared. A *d,* an *e,* and an *s* on the line above the word *air,* and a *d* above the word *mist* – only the *t* in *mist* had disappeared and part of the ampersand had rubbed off, leaving something that looked like a letter *d.* The letters *c o r* and *d* had appeared in the bottom line where you would expect the street address to be. I *knew* they hadn't been there before because I hadn't been able to see an address on the door. I looked at the whole door, sounding out the letters until they made sense.

'"Despair,"' I read out loud. '"Discord."'

Oberon turned to me. 'We're too late. He's summoned the demons already.'

*   *   *

166 • Lee Carroll

'Will Hughes said that the box had to be opened for seven days to summon the demons,' I said as we walked back to Puck's.

Oberon shook his head. 'He's managed to bring the demons into the world in an incorporeal form as a fog. They can still be banished if we close the box before seven days have passed, but in order for him to have done this much Dee must have grown even more powerful than any of us realized – or the box has grown more powerful during the years it remained closed. I told Marguerite at the time that you can't seal up magic without some repercussions.'

'You knew the first Marguerite—?' I began to ask as Oberon opened the door to Puck's, but he put a finger to his lips.

'Shh,' he said. 'Puck is still a trifle jealous of Marguerite. Best not to bring her up.'

'It's too late,' a voice came from the back of the shop. I looked for the baker, but the space behind the counter was empty. In fact, the whole tearoom was empty even though it was packed at exactly the same time yesterday. I wondered what thought had intruded itself into all those mothers' heads to send them off somewhere other than their favorite hangout.

'Puck gave all the children a rash,' the baker said as she straightened up behind the counter holding a tray of pink petits fours in her hands. 'Every pediatrician will be scratching his head. Literally. It doesn't bother the children any, but it makes any adult within two feet itch.'

'That's awful,' I said.

Fen shrugged. 'It's perfectly harmless and will go away by tomorrow. We're lucky he didn't give them nits. I haven't seen him this upset for a while.'

'I hope it's not because of me,' I said. 'Oh, and by the way, thank—'

She held up both hands and Oberon whispered in my ear, 'Brownies don't like to be thanked. And whatever you do, never give one clothes.'

'So you're a brownie?' I asked coming closer. Of all the revelations I'd heard in the last twelve hours, this one was the least surprising. I'd known there was something other-worldly about the baker the minute I'd seen her, and now I could clearly perceive that a warm butter-yellow glow – the color of buttercream frosting – filled the air around her. I could also see that beneath her corduroy tam her ears were pointed.

'A Manx brownie,' she said, 'or rather, a fenodoree, as we're called on the Isle of Man.'

'Garet has regards for you from a friend,' Oberon said, coming up beside me.

'I do?' I asked. 'Oh . . . you mean Will Hughes. He did ask how you were doing.'

Fen turned as pink as the icing on the petits fours. 'Oh, I can't imagine why he'd ask after me,' she said, turning to punch down a lump of dough in a blue bowl. 'Why it must be years since I saw him . . . decades . . .' She turned the dough out onto a floured board and began kneading it vigorously. 'Centuries even.'

'When *exactly* did you see him last?' Oberon asked.

She looked up. Her round glasses flashed green from

the reflection of the light blazing off Oberon. 'Last week,' she answered meekly. 'I happened to run into him at a lecture at the Ninety-second Street Y.'

'What was the lecture on?' Oberon asked.

'"The Mysteries of Science,"' Fen recited, tilting her chin up defiantly as if remembering the exact name of the lecture proved the meeting with Will Hughes had been accidental. '"Nanotechnology in the Twenty-first Century."'

Oberon tilted his head and looked skeptically at her.

'The science lectures get the most men,' she added, now more defensive than defiant. 'You try meeting a nice single man in New York! And I found it quite interesting. All those wee atoms remind me of the *ferrishyn*.'

'And Will Hughes frequents the Ninety-second Street Y?'

'He might have known I'd be there,' she said in a very low voice.

'How long have you been meeting him?'

A bell chimed in the back room before Fen had to answer. 'That's my sponge cake,' she said, scurrying through the doorway.

'Come on,' Oberon told me, lifting the counter up to pass behind it. 'She's gone to earth.'

'Gone to earth?' I repeated. 'What—?' But he was already in the back room, a tiny space dominated by a huge cast-iron oven. A yellow sponge cake sat on a cooling rack, steam rising from it, but there was no sign of Fen. Oberon glanced around the diminutive kitchen – I half expected him to check the oven, but instead he moved a rush mat on the floor, uncovering a round wooden door with a bronze handle set into it. He lifted the door, revealing the top steps of a spiral staircase that twisted down into the gloom. 'Come on,' he said.

'Down there?' I croaked, unable to disguise the fear in my voice as I looked down into the dark hole. In the last twenty-four hours I'd defended myself against a mythological beast and walked through a fairy-ridden park with a vampire, but there was no way I was going into a dark pit below the streets of New York City. Who knew what nightmares out of urban legend might be lurking down there – albino crocodiles, giant rat people, mutant cockroaches . . . the possibilities seemed endless. No, I'd had enough. It was time to put my foot down. 'I'll wait up here. It's too dark down there for me.'

In answer he snapped his fingers and a small yellow-green flame appeared at the tip of his thumb. 'Here,' he said, 'you might as well begin your lessons. You work with fire every day, so it shouldn't be so hard for you to conjure it. Hold your hand up . . . palm facing you.' He turned my hand around so that my palm was about five inches from my face. 'Now, focus on your aura.'

I'd seen the silver glow around my hand earlier on the street, but that had been when I was thinking of Will Hughes. I found myself a little worried about what color my aura would be when I wasn't thinking about him. I'd been through a lot lately. I'd blurted that concern about paying Maia to Roman in the hospital without any real concern for his condition, which was so unlike me—

'Focus!' Oberon's booming voice crashed through what was sure to become yet another self-pity session. I stared at my hand, freeing my mind of everything but the task at hand: seeing my aura. After a few seconds I began to see a bluish white glow limning my hands. The glow came to a point at the end of each fingertip and trailed off into the air like streamers.

'I see it!'

'Good.' Oberon's voice was warm with the lilt of the West Indian islands again, and I felt a warmth in the air that hadn't been there a second ago. I wondered if he was deliberately using his voice to literally *heat things up*. 'Now touch your thumb and middle finger together, concentrating on the heat your aura produces. When you can feel a spark, snap your fingers together.'

I snapped my fingers together. Nothing happened.

'Too soon,' he said. 'You have to wait until you feel the spark.'

I tried again. This time I waited until I felt the spark – a tiny charge like static electricity – but when I snapped my fingers, the spark flew off into the air and sizzled to the ground.

'Hold your thumb straight up after you snap your fingers to keep the flame steady.'

I tried again. This time the spark traveled to my thumb and flared up into a tiny bluish white flame. The sight of my own thumb on fire startled me so badly I shook my hand to make it go out.

Oberon groaned. 'It's your own life force burning,' he said as if lecturing a kindergartener. 'It can't hurt you. Now try it one more time.'

I stared at my hand, summoned my aura, placed thumb

and middle finger together, waited for the spark, snapped my fingers, held my thumb upright . . . and the flame leapt out of my thumb and swayed there like a miniature hula-dancer. Oberon was right; it didn't hurt.

'Good job,' he said.

I glanced away from the flame and grinned at him. 'This is the coolest thing I've ever done. I almost wish I smoked so I could show it off.'

He shook his head and started down the steps with me following him, my fears abated by delight in my new powers . . . until Oberon gave me something else to worry about. 'Just don't try to do it if you're menstruating. Women have a tendency to light themselves on fire at that time of the month.'

I started down the stairs after him, wondering how he had known it *wasn't* that time of the month, but he was already issuing another warning. 'Stay close to me and don't go off into any of the side corridors.'

How many side corridors could there be in a Manhattan basement? I wondered as I followed him. But as we went farther and farther down the spiral stairs, I began to suspect that this wasn't any ordinary Manhattan basement. For one thing, the walls were faced with a glittering pink quartz. When I held my thumb-flame up to the wall, I saw symbols and pictographs etched into the stone. There were carvings of figures – beautiful men and women riding on horseback through a landscape of mountains and woods. There were scenes of people dancing around circles of standing stones and great bonfires. Winged creatures flew through the air – dragons and griffins and, I noticed with a shudder, manticores. Dragons also crouched inside caves deep inside mountains where small, wizened creatures mined gems and minerals. These pictures were adorned with actual gems: diamonds, rubies, sapphires, and emeralds that glittered in the light from my hand. I'd taken enough gemology in college to know they were real, but I couldn't begin to estimate the monetary value of such a hoard.

The largest stones of all were four gemstones, a sapphire, an emerald, a ruby, and a topaz, each carved into the shape of an eye, each set on top of a tower.

'Come on,' Oberon called from a few steps below me. 'We don't want to leave Puck and Fen alone too long—' He stopped when he saw how closely I was looking at the wall and climbed back up to where I stood.

'Are these the watchtowers?' I asked.

'Yes,' he said, his eyes on me, not the pictures. 'They were built to defend humanity against the dark forces. Each one was given a guardian, one of the fey who dedicated her life to guarding the tower.'

'What happened to them?'

'There was a war. The towers were destroyed . . . one of the guardians was killed—'

'I thought you guys were immortal.'

Oberon shook his head. 'We don't age, but we can be killed in a few specific ways and sometimes we . . . *diminish*.' He uttered the last word with such a dire intonation that I didn't dare ask him to elaborate. Instead I asked him what had happened to the other three guardians.

'One went into hiding, one chose to become human – that was your ancestor, Marguerite.'

'And the fourth?'

'We don't speak of her,' he said, turning to go down the stairs. 'She joined the other side. And for that she was consigned to the deepest pit of hell.'

King of Shadows

Just when I was beginning to be afraid that *we* were descending into the deepest pit of hell, we came to a round room at the bottom of the staircase. Four narrow corridors branched off from the circle. I couldn't see that they were marked in any way, but Oberon didn't hesitate before setting off down one. As he went, he touched the flame on his hand to sconces along the wall that instantly flared up, lighting the arched corridor. I tried to guess what direction we were heading in, but going around and around in that spiral staircase had completely turned me around. At any rate, it was hard to imagine that we were still below the streets of Manhattan at all – that subway trains ran over our heads, that people were going to work, eating lunch, working out at gyms, walking their dogs, putting cranky toddlers down for their naps up there in the 'real' world. That felt like an illusion. This felt real – the solid stone walls, the arched ceiling . . . I looked closer at the ceiling. It was paved in a herringbone pattern of ceramic tiles that looked familiar.

'Hey,' I called to Oberon's retreating back, 'this ceiling looks like the one in the Oyster Bar at Grand Central, and like the dome at St. John the Divine.'

'That's because they were made by the same person – Rafael Guastavino,' Oberon answered without turning around. 'He was brought down here in the 1890s. We'd always had trouble with leaks before.'

'Really? You mean a mere mortal was able to do a better job than a bunch of immortal fairies?'

Oberon stopped so abruptly I nearly ran into him. The expression on his face looked pained, but when he spoke his voice was gentle. Sad, even. 'There's nothing *mere* about mortals. There are many things that you can do that we cannot. We may have once been a great people – there were those among us who were revered as gods – but over the centuries we have grown stale and insular. What spark we have left we get from contact with your kind – from the great thinkers and creators among you. It is that spark that keeps us alive. We feed on it.'

'You make yourselves sound like parasites.'

He shook his head. 'The humans we touch bloom in our company. They do their best work while we drink of their dreams. It's a mutually beneficial relationship.'

'And what happens when you leave them?'

Oberon tilted his head. In the light of the torches he looked old. Centuries old. 'What makes you think we ever leave the ones we love?'

'Because I grew up in a house filled night and day with artists. I've listened to the stories about the ones who went mad – like van Gogh – and I've *seen* the ones who burned with so much passion that they seemed to glow . . . and I've seen that glow go out. Why did Ray Johnson jump off the Sag Harbor bridge? Why did Santé Leone overdose on

176 • Lee Carroll

heroin? Why hasn't Zach Reese painted anything in twenty years?'

'It's true,' he said. 'Sometimes our touch is too much for them. The fire burns through them leaving a shell. Sometimes a careless fey moves on with so little warning the human is left searching for that light for the rest of his life. But you shouldn't judge us by our failures. We've also fostered Shakespeares and Beethovens, Tolstoys and Brontës, Picassos and Einsteins. It isn't all up to us. Sometimes the human is more fragile than we thought . . . or sometimes too greedy. Sometimes they leave us and choose a dark companion.' Oberon glared meaningfully at my neck. 'We're not the only players here.'

He turned and strode on in front of me, into a high-ceilinged circular room at the center of which was a large round oak table that gleamed under a chandelier made out of twisted branches that was lit with a hundred sparks of light. More than two dozen chairs ringed the table, but only two people – if I could call them that – sat there: Fen and the rainbow-garbed beggar I'd seen at the 190th Street station. He'd taken off the fur cap so that I could see that his ears were pointed. When he smiled, I saw that his teeth were pointed too.

'Well met by moonlight,' he exclaimed as we came in. 'Welcome, daughter of the Watchtower, fair Marguerite. We are honored to have you grace our company.'

'It's a pleasure to meet you,' I said, returning the bow and taking the chair he pulled out for me. '*Again*. If I'd known who you were, I would have added something to your cup.'

Oberon scowled. 'Puck, have you been panhandling again? Surely I pay you handsomely.'

'It's not for the money, my lord, it's for the spark. When I amuse a weary traveler and they forget their woes, their light warms me to the bottom of my toes.' He lifted his feet and wiggled them in the air. I half expected pointed slippers, but he was wearing red Nike Air Jordans.

'And it was just a coincidence that you ran into Garet?'

Fen answered, 'I told him she would be coming out of Fort Tryon Park. I didn't tell him who told me.'

'It's true,' Puck said, 'I didn't know our Fenodoree was in touch with the vampire until a few moments ago. But you mustn't be too hard on her. Remember, he was our friend before he became a dark one – and beloved of our Marguerite.'

'She asked me to keep an eye on him,' Fen said.

'And so you've been his spy for all these years?' Oberon roared, his shadow, thrown onto the curved stone wall by the light of the chandelier, seeming to grow larger. I noticed other shadows on the wall that ringed the room. Shadows that seemed to be cast by nothing I could see.

'Not a spy!' Fen insisted. 'A caretaker. An observer. And a reminder of what he once was. He never takes life unless he has to, or turns the ones he drinks from to the dark. In truth, he always leaves them happier than when he found them.'

I thought of the way it had felt when Will Hughes drank my blood – the way it felt now when I thought of him – and turned away from the table so they wouldn't see me blush. The shadows ringing the table seemed to have inched closer.

'That's very sweet. I'll remember to nominate him for vampire of the year. I suppose you told him about the reappearance of the Watchtower?'

'No! He called me early this morning – just after dawn – and told me she was leaving the park. He asked me to send someone to watch her home, so I asked Puck. And see? She's come to no harm.'

I was afraid that Oberon was going to rip the scarf from my neck and reveal the fang marks there, but he didn't. He only sighed and sank down into a chair. 'What's past is past. We have to decide what to do going forward. Dee has summoned the demons of Despair and Discord.'

'Already?' Fen asked. 'I thought we had seven days from when the box was opened.'

'We have four days now to be rid of them,' Oberon answered.

'But how will we banish them if they're already taking shape?' Puck asked.

As they went back and forth, I noticed that the shadows around the room were drawing nearer. One by one they detached themselves from the walls, slouched toward the table, and slipped up into the chairs. Once at the table they took shape . . . or, rather, *shapes*. One sprouted horns and a tail, another grew a dozen eyes and claws. Many unfolded wings, slick and black as if they'd just hatched from a cocoon. *Goblins*. The word came unbidden to my mind as if I'd always known such creatures existed . . . and not just in storybooks. I remembered my mother reading me a poem she loved called 'The Goblin Market' and shivering at the descriptions of the creatures in it. *One like a wombat prowled obtuse and furry, One like a ratel tumbled hurry-scurry.* Oberon had called Will Hughes a *dark* one as if distinguishing him from creatures like himself and Puck and Fen, but then what were these grotesque creatures? Dark ones or light ones? Maybe the lines between them couldn't be so sharply drawn. I peered into the shadows to better make out their shapes, but it was hard to get a clear picture of them in the flickering light . . . then I realized that the light was flickering because it too, was on the move. The flames in the sconces hissed and undulated, then divided and flitted through the air to land on the table where each flame became a diminutive person with wings. They looked like the light sylphs I had seen last night only brighter, and instead of being transparent their skin was spotted orange and yellow like a salamander's. Yellow and orange flames licked around their heads instead of hair. Some fluttered around my head before they landed on the table, and I could hear a sound like cicadas buzzing and tree frogs peeping. One hovered so close to me I could feel its wings brushing my face. It took all my willpower not to bat it away.

'Don't worry,' Fen whispered to me when she noticed the frozen expression on my face. 'They're fire fey. They're perfectly harmless.'

One landed on my arm and sat on my elbow. I looked down at it, remembering the way the sylph had snarled at me last night, but this creature only yawned and curled up in the crook of my arm and began to make a low humming noise like a cat purring. When its friends saw I wasn't shooing it away, a dozen more perched on my shoulders, arms, and lap. One landed in my hair.

'It won't set my hair on fire, will it?' I asked Fen.

'No, but you might not like how she does your hair. Lol,' she addressed the creature in my hair, 'no beehives! It's not the sixties anymore.'

Something tittered in my ear.

'Lol?' I asked.

'Uh-huh. She started *LOL* on the Internet. A little joke of hers—'

'If you two are done gossiping,' Oberon interrupted, 'perhaps Garet would like to focus on the task at hand.'

'But what can I do against Dee and two demons?' I asked. 'I don't even know what these demons are or what they look like.'

'They look different each time they take shape,' Oberon answered. 'In the Middle Ages they often took the shape of dragons. In ancient times they appeared as leviathans beneath the sea. No one knows what they'll look like this time, but it won't be hard to recognize their work. As they gain power, they'll sow despair and discord throughout the city, then the country, then the world. People will grow sadder and then angrier. They'll lose hope, they'll quarrel . . . before long some will even be driven to kill themselves and their families. If the box remains open for seven days, then Dee will take control. The last time the demons were abroad, Hitler came to power. If they hadn't been slain, he wouldn't have been defeated.'

'But again, what can I do? I have no powers, no

experience.' I wanted to add that I was probably lacking in courage and moral fiber as well. After all, hadn't I gotten Edgar Tolbert killed and abandoned his body in the Cloisters to be found by strangers? But I didn't even have the courage to bring up my failings.

'Yes, it's unfortunate you were never trained. Each one of your line has the ability to become a powerful guardian against evil – a protector of humanity. Encoded in your DNA are the secrets of how to defeat these demons, but you have to be trained to recognize and use those powers. But it's not too late.'

I shook my head. After everything I'd witnessed and allowed myself to believe, this part still caught me up short – that I had some special destiny to play in these events. I *was* getting used to the idea that my mother could have had a secret life; she was undeniably special. But me? I'd grown up surrounded by people of amazing talents – painters and sculptors who could make their dreams concrete – but I wasn't like that. I was an ordinary craftsman, a welder and jeweler, and even my jewelry was only a remaking of old symbols and designs. I was nothing special.

'I think you have the wrong person,' I said.

The rustling of the gathered throng – the goblins, the fire fey, and the things that still lurked outside the light in the shadows – came to a sudden halt. Oberon stared and flexed his wings, the sound echoing in the otherwise quiet hall like a great flock of birds taking off. 'Of course we understand if you are too frightened to take charge. You are right to be afraid. Even with training, there is no guarantee that you will be able to find Dee and the box and that once you find him you'll be able to get the box away from him and send the demons back to hell.'

I swallowed. *Send the demons back to hell?* He was right; I was frightened. Hell, I was terrified. I looked around the table at all these strange creatures, some beautiful, but some grotesque, and some too much a part of the shadows to make out at all. They were all waiting for my answer. All these amazing creatures were waiting for *me* to say whether I would help them or not. I felt inside me others waiting as well: Edgar Tolbert, who had been senselessly murdered, and my father lying wounded in the hospital. How many more would be hurt if I did nothing?

'Okay,' I said, my voice sounding small and hollow in the great hall. 'I'll do what I can.'

Oberon, Puck, and Fen spent the next hour arguing about who should train me in each of the skills I would need to find Dee, overpower him, and take the box from him. I wasn't clear how I was supposed to do any of that, but apparently there were guides who could teach me what I needed to do. The goblins and fire fey joined the argument from time to time, but I couldn't understand their language so I stopped paying attention, and once I stopped paying attention I started getting sleepy. After all, I hadn't slept in . . . how long had it been? I wasn't even sure what time it was. I had no sense of time down here underground. My eyelids grew heavy, the lights of the fire fey began to swell and blur, and my head began to nod . . . but then I felt a tiny hand propping my chin up. It was one of the fiery-haired fairies. I watched her as she flew over to Oberon and chattered in his ear, her orange-spotted skin undulating in the glow from her own hair and wings. As she hovered above Oberon's ear, I noticed that the markings on her wings looked like two large brown eyes with yellow irises – like the eyes of a tiger. Glimpsed among the foliage you might think you were being stalked by a giant predator. It gave me more of a sense of respect for the little creature – and the idea that she wasn't to be taken lightly. Oberon certainly seemed to be taking what she was saying seriously.

'Lol has suggested that while we decide who can teach her what she needs to know, Garet should go home and get some sleep. How does that sound, Garet?'

For an answer I yawned. I heard Lol chittering as she flew around my head. I got up to follow Oberon out of the hall. Puck bowed his farewell to me, but Fen got up to walk beside me until we reached the corridor.

'Tell Will I said hello,' she whispered in my ear.

'I don't really know if I'll see him again,' I whispered back.

A trill of laughter sounded in my ear; Lol was still clinging to my hair. Fen gave me a patient smile. 'Oh, you'll see him again,' she said. 'I don't think either of you has much choice in the matter.'

We took a different stairway up to the street. This one was more utilitarian, made of rusted steel corroded in places. The whole thing groaned with every step I took. When I paused, though, I noticed that Oberon, who was at least six feet tall and must have weighed close to two hundred pounds, made no noise at all. As if he were lighter than air.

We came out in a parking garage on Bethune Street. I was shocked to see that it was nearly dark. I'd been underground all day! I remembered my mother saying that a person could lose track of time in the Summer Country. I was beginning to suspect that might be true of any time spent with the fairies.

We were only a couple of blocks from my home, but we walked west and north to the corner of West Street and Jane Street where there was an old SRO hotel I'd passed a dozen times. I'd always admired the turret on one corner and wondered whether someone got to live there. In the lobby Oberon waved at a light-skinned, gray-haired man behind a Plexiglas-barricaded counter, then curled his hand into a fist and bumped the glass barrier. The man responded by tapping his own clenched fist against the glass.

'What up, mon?' Oberon asked, his West Indies accent back in full.

'Same ole, same ole,' the desk clerk replied, sliding several envelopes and catalogs through a narrow slit in the glass. 'Elevator's on the fritz again.'

'Tell me something new, brother.' Oberon picked up his mail. He leafed through it as we walked up the stairs. I noticed a *Sports Illustrated* and a Con Edison bill.

'So you pay your bills like everyone else?' I asked. 'Can't you just' – I snapped my fingers, but no flame appeared. I must have been too tired – 'use your magical powers for light and heat?'

'I could,' he said, glancing over his shoulder to give me a doleful look, 'but I'd probably knock out the power grid for the whole eastern seaboard.'

We came to a door on the top floor. There was a glowing silver symbol, similar to the ones Oberon had placed with Post-it notes in the doorway across from St. Vincent's, only this one was made of concentric circles. He touched it and the circles rippled and swelled into a silver disk about the size of a salad plate. A face appeared in it – that of an old woman in hair curlers and a tattered floral bathrobe. She lifted her hand and knocked on the door, waited, then scowled and left when no one answered.

'My neighbor, Mrs. Mazole,' he said.

Another face appeared in the silver mirror, this time a man in dark sunglasses and a nose ring. He also scowled at the door, but then spoke. 'Call me when you get in, O. There's something weird going on.'

'Wow, it's like video messaging.' It also reminded me of something else. 'The lines on the silver box – they moved just like that.'

'That's right.' He waved his hand over the silver circle and it shrank back to its original size. 'It's a scrying mirror. This one records images, but the box actually contains a portal between the worlds. It fell into Dee's hands in the sixteenth century and he learned how to communicate with spirits from other realms.'

Oberon unlocked two locks and a dead bolt and opened the door. We walked into a large room that ended in the rounded apse of the corner turret with four floor-to-ceiling windows. The room was dark except for the orange light of the setting sun coming through the windows. I stepped toward them and saw that they overlooked the Hudson, a view oddly similar to the one from Will Hughes's Washington Heights apartment. Did all these supernatural types like to keep an eye on the river? Or did they just use their magic to score prime real estate?

'Nice place,' I said.

'Thanks.' He tossed his keys into a ceramic bowl on a desk in front of one of the windows, then flicked on a light switch. The rest of the room leapt into light and I saw that the walls were hung from ceiling to floor with framed photographs, drawings, watercolors, pastels, and oils. A simple line drawing of a man's face morphing into a butterfly wing caught my attention. It was definitely Oberon's face – and it was definitely Picasso's signature. There were other portraits of Oberon: an oil painting of him wearing a turban and a pearl earring, his face emerging from a backdrop of rich tapestries; a silk screen of him in dreadlocks reproduced four times in different Day-Glo colors, a pencil sketch of him reclining on a cloud stretching out one finger, a black-and-white photograph of him nude curled around a long-stemmed, white lily.

'You knew all these artists?' I asked, awed, and more cowed by this evidence of Oberon's great age and acquaintanceship than by all his magic tricks.

'Like I told you before, the relationship between artist and fey is a mutually beneficial one. These were all' – he waved his hand at the dozens of priceless artworks – 'tokens of appreciation.'

I came to the painting by Santé Leone. I'd know his color palette anywhere. A woman in a shell-pink dress stood on a hill covered with purple flowers, her waist-length black hair reflecting the colors of the sun setting behind the stone tower in the background. I took a step closer. Yes, it looked like my mother – but when had Santé Leone ever seen my mother standing in a field of flowers beneath a stone tower?

'He told me it was something he dreamed,' Oberon said as if in response to my unvoiced question.

'There's one thing I don't understand.' My voice sounded angry, but that was because I didn't want to give away how close I was to tears. 'If you knew Santé – and saw this picture of my mother – then you must have known about *me*. I mean, you live only a few blocks from me! You must have known my mother died before she could tell me about this watchtower thing. So why didn't you tell me? Why didn't you try to begin my training?'

'Because your mother made me promise I wouldn't. She didn't want you to assume the role of guardian.'

For a moment I couldn't think. I recalled that drive home from RISD, my mother telling me I could be anything I wanted to be, that she didn't want me *held back*. That I had to be free to choose. It was the sort of speech that liberated mothers gave to their daughters. How could I have known that she meant me to be free of a four-hundred-year-old promise?

'So why have you changed your mind now?' I asked.

'I didn't change my mind; it was changed for me by Will Hughes . . . and *that*.' He tilted his chin toward the window and I followed his gaze out to the river, which glittered now in the last rays of the sunset. The sky above New Jersey was clear – stars were just coming out – but to the south, where I should have been able to see the Statue of Liberty, the harbor was covered by a dirty yellow fog that was creeping north up the river . . . not creeping, actually, but bulging and writhing as if the fog were a sack and whatever was in it was trying to get out.

'What *is* it?' I asked.

'Despair and Discord,' Oberon said, his smooth, melodious voice revealing for the first time since I met him the tremors of fear. 'The demons are in the fog.'

A Wandering Eye

Oberon gave me Santé's painting to bring to my father, but he told me to go home first. 'I'll look after your father tonight,' he said to me. 'You have to get some rest. Tomorrow we'll start your training in earnest.'

I didn't have the strength to argue. I just wanted to take a long shower and sleep for twelve hours. The minute I walked into the town house, though, I saw *that* wasn't going to happen.

'Where have you been?' Becky shrieked as she came tearing out of the kitchen. Her aura was a blazing orange. I wondered how I could possibly have missed seeing it all these years. 'We've been going out of our minds with worry!'

'I said you probably just needed some downtime.' Jay sauntered out of the kitchen, hands tucked into the pockets of his skinny jeans. Only the hunch in his shoulders and the skittery look in his eyes told me how worried he'd been too . . . also his aura, which was a smoky gray-blue.

'You haven't been answering your cell!'

'Damn! I turned it off when I went into—' I was about

to say 'when I went into the Cloisters library' when someone else came out of the kitchen: Detective Joe Kiernan.

'Went into where?' he asked.

'What are you doing here?' I demanded. 'Has something happened to my father?' Then I took off my coat and
slipped it over the back of a chair, but I left my scarf on.
The kitchen was chilly and drafty enough to make that
reasonable, and I didn't think it was a great idea to let the
detective – or anyone – catch sight of my bite marks.

'Not at all,' he answered quickly, 'but I'm surprised that
you'd turn off your cell phone while he's in the hospital.'

'The battery was getting low, so I turned it off when I
went into the subway.'

'I see.' He crossed his arms and leaned against the wall.
He looked like he was going to embark on a thorough
cross-examination, but Becky – God bless her – burst in.

'Can't you see the poor girl is exhausted! We shouldn't
keep her standing in the hallway.' She pulled me into the
kitchen. 'We were so worried about you that we called
Detective Kiernan. We were afraid you'd been kidnapped
by those awful men who robbed you.'

'But of course I explained to Miss Jones that those
men are in custody.' Kiernan had followed us into the
kitchen and was trying to gain control of the situation
while Jay put on the kettle and lit the burner under a
large soup pot. The detective had never had to deal with
Becky Jones before, though.

'As I explained to Detective Kiernan,' Becky said, 'those
men are obviously just hired muscle. What you've got to do
is find the kingpin, the capo, the ringleader. And don't you

try to tell me Mr. James hired them. That's just absurd.' Kiernan opened his mouth to respond to Becky's assessment of his case, but Becky interrupted him again. This time, though, it wasn't to my advantage. 'But if you weren't kidnapped, where were you? We were worried sick, weren't we, Jay?'

Jay, who'd just put down a steaming bowl of soup in front of me, grunted.

'You couldn't have been with Will Hughes the whole time.' I must have blushed because Becky clasped her hand over her mouth and then squeaked. 'Or were you?'

I caught Jay staring at me. He muttered something about needing to go out for milk and fled the kitchen. What was going on with him? I wondered.

'Were you?' Kiernan asked, using Becky's astonishment as a chance to get in a question. 'Ms. Jones here told me that you were driven uptown to Mr. Hughes's residence in Washington Heights yesterday afternoon—'

'And then Detective Kiernan told us that there was a murder at the Cloisters. And it was Edgar Tolbert, whom I know is the medieval scholar who helped you research your senior project.'

I glanced at Detective Kiernan before saying anything. He was watching me carefully. I wasn't exactly thrilled with Becky's apparent chattiness with him, but his seeming mistrust of me bothered me more. 'Edgar Tolbert is dead?' I asked. 'That's awful. What happened?'

'He had a heart attack. We think he surprised an art thief at the museum. A stone arch was badly damaged and two museum guards were killed. When was the last time you saw him?'

'I'm not sure,' I said, trying desperately to banish the image of Edgar Tolbert's stricken face from my mind. I glanced down at my hand and saw that the light blue glow around my fingers was stippled with flecks of smoky gray – the manifestation of my lies, I felt sure. I could only hope that Joe Kiernan couldn't read auras. 'Not for months. I researched some jewelry designs last summer—'

'So you didn't take advantage of your proximity to the museum last night to visit Dr. Tolbert?'

'I thought of it,' I said, hoping that the injection of a grain of honesty would fortify my lies, 'but then I stayed too long at Will Hughes's.' I felt the blood rush to my face and hoped that Kiernan would assume I'd spent the night with Hughes and that I was embarrassed to be caught in promiscuous behavior. He couldn't, I assured myself, know that the blush came from recalling the feel of Will's teeth on my neck.

'We'll have to contact Mr. Hughes and have him corroborate your story—'

'I can do that right now,' a voice announced from the hallway. I turned and saw Will Hughes filling the kitchen doorway. He looked larger in my small kitchen than he had in his own spacious apartment – or the park – last night. Perhaps it was the long, black overcoat he wore. In the kitchen light the slightly damp cashmere gleamed like an animal's pelt. When he stepped into the room I felt a spark in the air – a silver thread that leapt from him to me. It was hard to believe that Becky and Kiernan didn't see it, but when I glanced at them, I saw that Kiernan was scowling and Becky was gazing up at Will Hughes in awed silence – a state I'd never before seen her in. The first one to speak was Jay, who had trailed in behind Hughes.

'I found this dude standing on the doorstep so I told him he could come in.'

The corners of Will's mouth quirked up into a crooked smile when he met my gaze. I felt sure it was because he knew what I was thinking – that the old superstition that a vampire can't come into a private home without being invited was true. I had a feeling he knew everything I was thinking and feeling.

'You're willing to swear that Garet James was with you all of last night?' Detective Kiernan asked, shifting his weight so that the bulge of his gun holster became visible under his coat. I looked from man to man and noticed they were about the same height. Hughes was slimmer than Kiernan, more finely built, but he radiated a certain power that had the detective bristling. I could sense that Kiernan's nerves were on edge, but I couldn't see his aura at all.

'Yes,' Will said, coming to stand by my side. 'From dusk to dawn.' He smiled down at me – smirked actually – and I wasn't sure if I should be grateful for the alibi or pissed off at how thickly he was laying it on, especially since I was pretty sure it was mostly for Detective Kiernan's benefit. But then Will grinned and added, 'The poor woman fell sound asleep on my couch and I didn't have the heart to wake her after all she has been through.'

'How very gallant of you,' Kiernan remarked. 'And how

very convenient for you, Ms. James, to have such an impeccable alibi. It was lucky you went to see Mr. Hughes last night, wasn't it?'

I could see Becky open her mouth – no doubt to tell the detective off – but Will beat her to it. 'She came to me because she found my name – or rather my ancestor's name – inside a box she was hired to open. She thought I could help lead her to the man who she believed was behind the burglary and who has set up her father to assume the guilt. And she was right. I knew right away that the man she described meeting yesterday was John Dee – an internationally known art thief.'

'I've never heard of him,' Kiernan growled.

'He goes by many aliases,' Hughes replied. 'You are perhaps familiar with the Nîmes burglary several years ago?'

Detective Kiernan blanched. Everyone in the art world knew about the Nîmes burglary. A half dozen paintings – a Rubens and a Boucher among them – and some priceless antiquities had been stolen from the Nîmes Musée des Beaux-Arts and never recovered.

'Yes, of course, but I've never heard that a man named Dee was connected to it.'

Will shrugged. 'You might want to check with your superiors on that. In the meantime, perhaps you'll be interested in searching Dee's last known place of business just in case there are any clues about the burglary of the James Gallery.' Will Hughes withdrew a card from his pocket and handed it to Detective Kiernan, who held it out in front of me so I could see it. Engraved on heavy cream-colored stock were the words *John Dee, Watch Repair & Alchemist. 121½ Cordelia Street, New York, New York, 10014.* Beneath the address was a triangle with an eye in it.

Kiernan snickered. 'Alchemist? What kind of crackpot is this guy?'

'An eccentric,' Will replied. 'But don't let that make you underestimate him.'

'Is this the address of the shop you visited the day of the burglary?' Kiernan asked me.

'Yes, I think it is,' I answered.

'Okay,' he said briskly. 'That's good enough for me. Let's go see it.'

'Now?' I asked, remembering that Dee's store was covered in cobwebs and dust.

'No time like the present. If Mr. Hughes here thinks there might be evidence that will exonerate your father, then I won't waste a minute . . . unless you have a more pressing engagement.'

With my bed, I wanted to say, but didn't. For one thing I no longer felt so tired. Maybe it was the electricity coursing between Will Hughes and me. 'Okay, but I need to go change. I've been in the same clothes for twenty-four hours.'

'By all means,' Kiernan said, opening wide his arms. 'Take your time. I've got all night. How 'bout you, Mr. Hughes?'

Will Hughes smiled at the detective, but I had a feeling he was talking to me. 'Oh, yes. I definitely have *all* night.'

❖   ❖   ❖

As well as a much needed change of clothes, including a turtleneck so I didn't have to keep my scarf on, I was hoping for a few moments of privacy, but Becky followed me upstairs and into my studio. When I tried to get past her into the bathroom, she planted herself in front of the door, arms crossed, all four feet eleven and a half inches of her bristling with barely controlled energy.

'All right, Margaret Eleanor James, I'm not budging until you tell me the truth.'

'The truth?' I asked, trying to look innocent.

Becky punched me in the arm. 'Do you honestly expect me to believe that you spent the entire night with that stunning man *sleeping*?'

'Oh,' I said, relieved that Becky suspected me of first-date sex, not collusion with vampires and fairies. 'Well, not *exactly* sleeping.'

'I knew it! There's so much chemistry between you two I thought someone's head was going to go up in flames!'

'We spent the night *talking*, Rebecca Ruth Bader Ginsburg Jones.' Two could play at the middle-name game – especially when one of us had a mother who had *really* wanted her daughter to grow up to be lawyer. I ducked before Becky could hit me again – she hated her middle names even more than I hated mine – but instead of hitting me she grinned.

'I knew you didn't spend the night sleeping. What did you talk about? He's not married, is he? Does he have a rich hedge-fund-manager friend? Has he ever thought of investing in a promising indie rock band—'

'Damn, Becky, I completely forgot about that producer

who was coming to your show last night. What happened?'

Only one thing could distract Becky when she was on the scent of a potential romantic interest, and that was the band's future. 'He was definitely interested, only he thought we needed to be a little less hard-core. Tone down the shoegaze vibe a bit. Fiona and I both agree that's no problem, but Jay's going to take some convincing . . .' Becky happily chattered on about the band's prospects while I squeezed past her into the bathroom, washed up, and changed into jeans and a turtleneck sweater. I was careful not to let her see my neck, but when I surreptitiously checked out the marks in the mirror, I saw they had almost faded. When I touched them, I felt a strange thrill course through my body – as if my carotid artery had become an erogenous zone directly connected to my . . . well, to my *other* erogenous zones.

As I came out, Becky was still nattering on about the details of the record contract. 'I'm really happy for you, Jay, and Fiona,' I told her, giving her a quick hug. 'It sounds like the band's taking off.'

As we walked down the stairs – Becky bouncing in front of me – I thought to myself that here was one thing that had not been touched by the demons of Despair and Discord. Will Hughes showing up to give me an alibi for last night was another stroke of good luck. Maybe Oberon wasn't right about everything going bad – and if he wasn't right about that, maybe he wasn't right about Will Hughes.

Hughes and Kiernan were standing in the hallway when we came down, locked in a stony silence that dampened even Becky's spirits for a moment. She quickly recovered herself though. 'Where's Jay? Jay!' she shouted into the kitchen.

'Your friend said he was going upstairs to practice,' Kiernan said. 'He said to remind you that you have an appearance later tonight at the Music Hall in Williamsburg.'

'That's not until after midnight. I'm not going to miss seeing the lair of the infamous John Dee – hey! Did you know that's the name of a famous Elizabethan magician . . .' Becky happily chatted with Detective Kiernan while wrapping a scarf longer than her body several times around her neck. She winked at me as she shepherded him out the door.

'I think your friend is giving us some privacy,' Will said as he held the door open for me.

'I'm not sure Becky knows the meaning of the word.' I set the alarm code and locked the door behind me. 'But she will probably talk Detective Kiernan's ear off by the time we get there.'

I realized when I saw the detective's car parked in front of the house, though, that we weren't likely to get much privacy jammed into it. Will apparently thought the same.

'Why don't you follow us,' he said to Kiernan as he held his hand up in the air. The Silver Cloud instantly appeared. I saw Becky's eyes go wide and knew she'd be dying to ride in the Rolls, but she beamed at Detective Kiernan instead. 'Is *this* an unmarked police car? Does it have a police radio? Can I see how it works? Can we put the siren on?'

Will opened the door of the Rolls for me while Becky got into the detective's car. The minute I slid into the plush gray interior, though, I wondered if I was making a mistake. There was a smoked-glass barrier between the driver and the backseat that hadn't been up when I was driven uptown yesterday. The door closed with a heavy hermetic *clunk* that sounded as final as the lid of a sarcophagus coming down, and the car glided down Jane Street silently. Hughes was a good two feet away from me and he made no move to touch me, but I felt *engulfed* by his presence. The world outside retreated.

'So,' he broke the silence after a moment, 'how was your day?'

It was such an ordinary, mundane question that I laughed – and worse, the kind of laugh I have when I'm surprised, which comes out like a snort. 'Eventful,' I finally managed to say. 'I met Oberon, who doesn't appear to like you very much.'

Will shook his head and looked out the window. I could see from his reflection in the opaque glass that he was frowning. 'No, he blamed me for Marguerite's decision to become human.'

'But Fen doesn't dislike you. She said Marguerite asked her to watch over you.'

'Did she?' he asked, turning his head in my direction. His eyes flashed silver in the dark of the car. He leaned toward me and I felt the tug of that silver thread that connected us pulling me toward him. Without any visible motion on his part he was suddenly next to me, his hand in my hair, his body pressed against mine. I felt his lips graze my cheek and drift to my ear. His breath was warm against my neck.

'Did Oberon tell you not to see me?'

'Yes,' I admitted. 'But Fen said I *would* see you. She said I didn't have any choice about it.'

I felt Will's hand freeze on the collar of my sweater. He pulled back and looked at me, his silver eyes glowing red now. I was so startled by the transformation that I pulled back too.

'And is that how you feel?' he asked. 'That you have no choice?'

I didn't know how to answer that, but then I didn't have to. The car had come to a stop. Someone knocked on the window. Hughes powered it down and Detective Kiernan stuck his head in.

'We're here,' he said, scanning the interior of the Rolls as if looking for contraband drugs or dead bodies. 'I think you'll want to see this, Ms. James.'

I'd been so under Will Hughes's spell that I hadn't even thought to ask what he hoped to gain by bringing Detective Kiernan to Dee's shop. Once he saw that it was covered in the dust of years, he'd dismiss my claim that I'd visited a functioning antiques store just days ago.

'This place looks abandoned,' Kiernan said as I got out of the car. 'Are you sure this is where you were the day of the burglary?'

I walked up the steps to the glass door. The gilt letters glinted in the light from the streetlamp, the words *despair* and *discord* seeming to wink at me. 'Yes, this is it,' I said, sighing. 'I know it doesn't look like it was open three days ago—' I shut up when my eyes adjusted to the dark and the interior of the shop became visible. Yes, the shelves and counter were empty, but they were no longer covered with dust, nor was the counter broken. The brocade drapes, which had been torn and shredded yesterday, hung clean and whole.

Becky pushed me aside so she could see in. 'Yeah, he must have cleared out after the burglary, but hey, what's that on the floor? It looks like a scrap of torn canvas. Look, Detective Kiernan, don't you think that looks like a scrap of canvas?'

'It could be a scrap of old newspaper,' he said. 'It's not exactly a cause for a search warrant.'

'No need,' Will Hughes said. 'I've put in a call to the landlord . . . ah, here he is now.'

We all turned to find a stooped, balding man hurrying up the block from the direction of Hudson Street, a cell phone clamped to his left ear, a ring of keys jangling from his right hand.

'I would have rather contacted the landlord myself,' Kiernan muttered.

'My apologies, Detective. I was just trying to help out. I'll let you take it from here.' Will moved aside as the landlord, who introduced himself gruffly as Lochan Singh, unlocked the door and switched on the light. I looked in vain for any sign of the dust I'd seen two days ago; the shelves were polished clean. The only sign of what had been on them were pale circular shadows on the red velvet where watches and brooches had been. I startled when I found an eye looking back at me. One of the lover's eye brooches still lay on the cloth, its painted eye gazing

implacably into my own. I took a step closer to it, bent
down . . . and reared back when its long-lashed lid blinked.
I looked over my shoulder to see if anyone had noticed my
reaction, but everyone was watching Kiernan, who was
kneeling on the floor examining the scrap of canvas. I
turned back to the brooch and stepped to my right.

The eye followed my movement.

A trick left by Dee, no doubt. Okay then, I thought,
maybe it was a trick that could be turned against him. I
checked to make sure that no one was watching, then
I backed up to the shelf and palmed the brooch into my
jeans pocket. I had a second's queasy image of the eye
squelching, but banished it. Then I turned back to the
group around Kiernan. He was just lifting the scrap of
canvas off the floor with the end of a pen. He laid it on the
counter.

It was the corner of a painted canvas, not part of the
painting, but an edge where the artist had tested out his
palette. I recognized those lilacs, mauves, and honey
yellows right away. They were the colors of Pissarro's
snowy field in France.

'This came from one of our paintings,' I said. 'I'm sure
of it. If you check the canvases you have you'll see where
it's been torn off.'

Kiernan slipped the piece of canvas into a plastic bag,
then began questioning the landlord about his tenant. The
store had been leased under the name John Black just
three weeks earlier. The rent was paid up until the end of
the year. The only other address he had for John Black
was a post office box in Astoria. I listened for a

few minutes until I noticed that Will Hughes was gone.

I hurried anxiously outside, afraid he had vanished as abruptly as he had this morning, but I found him leaning on the railing at the foot of the steps, facing the river. A bank of fog was boiling at the end of the street, completely obscuring the West Side Highway and the water beyond it.

'Where do you think he is?' I asked.

He shook his head. 'Somewhere on the river, maybe. Or underground in the sewers, or out to sea. He's using the waterways to spread his contagion.' He turned around to face me. 'Why didn't you listen to Oberon when he told you not to see me?'

I could have answered that he was the one who'd come to my house tonight, that I hadn't sought him out, but I knew that wasn't what mattered. I was glad he'd come – no, more than glad. I was *relieved*. If he hadn't come, I'd have gone looking for him. 'Oberon doesn't know everything,' I answered, feeling disloyal at how peevish I sounded. 'Oh, but he did teach me this.' I looked around to make sure no one was watching, then snapped my fingers. A spark flew off my thumb and leapt up into a flame.

Will laughed at my obvious delight in my new trick, then cupped my hand in his and gently blew at the flame. Instead of going out, it flared up and I felt a surge of warmth move through my body from head to toes. The flame danced and swelled, then lifted off my hand and shot into the sky, soaring upward like a Roman candle.

'Show-off! How did you do that?'

'I'll tell you, but you have to promise that if you're ever in trouble, you'll send up a flare to let me know.'

'Sure. Now, tell me how you did it?'

'It's easy. All you have to do is put your lips together and blow.' He lifted my hand to his mouth and pressed his lips against it. I felt the graze of his fangs over my knuckles. 'I have to go. Asian markets are opening soon. But remember . . . if you need me . . .' He dropped my hand. Before I could say anything more, he'd ducked into his car. The Silver Cloud had melted into the fog at the end of the street before the heat of his lips had faded from my hand. It was just long enough for me to wonder where that warmth had come from.

Night Flight

I was relieved when we got home that Becky had a show to do. Jay and Fiona were waiting for her on the front steps, huddled in their coats, Fiona's Honda Fit packed to the rooftop with musical equipment. Fiona hugged me fiercely, her blunt, shoulder-length hair brushing against my face. It was bright red this week, but had been blue-black the last time I'd seen her. She seemed to have dyed it to match the faux-fur coat and thigh-high boots she was wearing.

'Sorry for your troubles, Garet,' she said in her lilting Irish accent. She'd been an exchange student at Pratt for a semester, then stayed on when London Dispersion Force started taking off. 'I went by the hospital today to see your dad. He was brilliant, all excited about some painter who'd been to visit.'

I didn't have the heart to tell Fiona that the painter was dead. 'That was sweet of you to visit him,' I said. 'Good luck tonight at the show. I bet that record producer offers you a huge contract.'

Jay, who was rearranging an amp in the trunk, groaned. Becky swatted him. I decided to leave before I got dragged into a band fight. I wished them all luck and climbed upstairs to my studio. When I dropped my bag on my worktable, I thought I heard something squeak, but, when after looking around I didn't detect any source for the sound, I decided it must have been my overstimulated imagination. I dug the lover's eye brooch out of my pocket, laid it on my desk, and stared at it. It didn't bat an eyelash. In fact it didn't move at all. Had I imagined that it had moved in the shop?

Keeping an eye on the brooch – I didn't like the idea of it spying on me – I reached into my bag for my jeweler's loupe . . . and felt something bite me.

I dropped the bag and it exploded. Orange and yellow flames shot up to the ceiling, scorched the plywood that was nailed over the skylight, and drifted down to my worktable in a shower of sparks. The fireball landed in front of me, rolled over and then stood up.

'Lol?'

The little creature chattered away as she shook out her wings and picked lint off her arms and legs, but I couldn't understand a word she said. She sounded angry, so I apologized for surprising her, for the state of my messenger bag – a breath mint was melted in her fiery hair, I noticed – and asked if I could do anything for her. I wasn't sure if she understood. Hands on her slim hips, she strode up and down my worktable, looking at my soldering equipment and poking into my supply boxes. She came to a dead halt when she saw the lover's eye, though. She hissed and flew into my lap.

'Pretty scary, huh?' I asked. 'I don't know why I took it from Dee's shop. I guess I thought it might come in handy.'

She started to hum . . . or, rather, *vibrate,* then she flew back to the table, hovering just above the brooch, and peered into the eye. I wasn't positive, but it seemed that the eye widened as if in surprise. Then Lol cautiously extended one pointy orange finger and poked it.

The eye blinked and teared.

Lol tittered and moved to poke it again.

'Stop it!' I cried, snatching up the brooch. 'There's no need to torture . . . *it.*' I looked down at the eye cradled in my hand and it looked back up at me. 'I think I'd better put it away until I can figure out what to do with it.'

I had some leather jewelry boxes, which I used for my more expensive pieces, that I'd had made in Italy. I took out a red box stamped in gold with the Cygnet trademark. The interior was lined with white velvet. I placed the brooch in it carefully, snapped the lid shut, then put the box in the locked metal cabinet where I kept my silver and gold. While I did all this, Lol flew around the room investigating. She explored my bookshelves, sneezing at the dust, rummaged through my junk shelves, and spilled a coffee can full of nails.

I decided it was best to ignore her. I went into the bathroom and took a long, much overdue shower. When I got out, I didn't see her anywhere, but I noticed that my bedroom door was open. I went in and found her curled up in my sweater drawer in a nest of my best cashmere sweater, snoring loudly.

I decided she had the right idea. I climbed into bed and turned the light out. For a moment I was confused by the quality of light in the room, but then I saw that it was Lol shedding her pink-orange glow like a night-light, and then I was asleep.

I slept until noon the next day. Lol was nowhere to be found when I woke up, but I did notice that all my drawers had been rearranged, and there were tiny footprints outlined in talcum powder across my bureau top. When I walked downstairs, I smelled fresh brewed coffee and something buttery. Jay and Becky were in the kitchen, lathering clotted cream on scones.

'Did you sleep with a pastry chef lately?' Becky asked me through a mouthful of scone.

'I thought it was a hedge fund manager,' Jay muttered. 'There's a baker too?'

'Well, someone is expressing his fondness in baked goods,' Becky said, holding up a grease-stained brown paper bag. 'I found this by the front door this morning . . . with this note.' She handed me a purple Post-it. *Meet me at the Empire State Building at 1:00 a.m.*, it read. 'The Empire State Building,' Becky said. 'How very *Sleepless in Seattle*. Whatever you're doing – or *whom*ever you're doing – to deserve all this, don't stop!'

'I'm not *doing* anyone, Becky,' I snapped. 'Sheesh! Tell me what happened last night with the record producer.'

'He wants to sign us up, only Jay here has *artistic reservations*.' Becky rolled her eyes.

'We already have a label,' Jay said, picking crumbs off the table. 'A label that doesn't dictate our style. I'm just not sure these guys *get* us.'

'What they'll get us is a seven-figure advance . . .'

I listened to Jay and Becky go back and forth, debating
the merits of their present label – a small indie record producer based in Brooklyn – against their new offer. It was
pretty clear who was going to win the argument. Becky had
been the captain of our high school debating team and was
prelaw at NYU before she dropped out to form the band
with Jay and Fiona. She had figures, examples, and logic
on her side. Jay had only a stubborn misgiving. His replies
became shorter and shorter as the argument went on. *He*
appeared to become shorter and shorter as he slumped
farther down in his chair.

'Maybe you can talk to the producer about your ideas
for the band,' I suggested to Jay. 'I really love the new
song, by the way. I heard it on WROX the other night.
Such a sad love song. I love how you evoke the whole
tradition of the troubadours and all their unrequited longing for the unapproachable love object.'

Jay turned a bright red at my praise and slumped down
even farther in his chair. Then he muttered something and
fled the table.

'What did I say wrong?' I asked Becky.

'Nothing. It's just . . . I think Jay might have been thinking of you when he wrote that song, and I guess he didn't
like hearing you describe his feelings as *unrequited longing for the unapproachable love object.*'

'Me? Why would he be thinking of me . . .' I stammered
to a halt under Becky's glare. 'Shit. I'm an idiot.'

'Yeah, well . . . you've had a lot on your mind.'

'Should I go talk to him?'

'Nah, I'd leave him alone for now. I think he likes

210 • Lee Carroll

to brood. Maybe we'll get some new songs out of him.'

I followed Becky's advice and left Jay alone. I couldn't help thinking as I walked to the hospital, though, that I'd taken the coward's way out. Jay was my best friend. Even more than Becky, he'd been the one who held me together after my mother died. For a whole year he'd spent every day after school with me, just hanging out while I made jewelry, ready to take me to a sci-fi film fest at the Film Forum or willing to order in Chinese food and watch old movies with me on TCM. He was the perfect company for the emotionally strung-out zombie I'd become. Restful, not too cheery, always available. I had never thought of him in a romantic light, but then I hadn't been thinking of *anyone* in that light. Although I'd had no shortage of interested men in college, none of them lasted very long. The artists I met in school and through the gallery always proved unreliable and too insecure, and the corporate types I met in the auction houses and galleries seemed to be missing something. Or maybe I was the one missing something. It occurred to me now that many of the guys I'd dated over the last ten years had been perfectly nice – some were even more than nice – but I had failed to feel anything for any one of them. And now the first man I did feel something for was a four-hundred-year-old vampire. What was wrong with me?

I was so wrapped up in my self-pity that as I rounded the corner of Twelfth Street and Seventh Avenue, I ran straight into a man coming the other way. He was middle-aged and well dressed in a Barbour raincoat and tweed cap, carrying a folded *Wall Street Journal* and a Starbucks coffee cup.

Before I could get out an apology, he snarled at me, 'You're going the wrong way, asshole!'

I was so taken aback – both by the obscenity and the notion that there was a right and wrong way to walk on the street – that I stared openmouthed and speechless as he stomped off. I looked around for a sympathetic glance from a passerby, but although the corner was busy, everyone who passed was sunk too deeply into his or her own thoughts to have noticed the incident. *Everyone.* I stood on the corner for five minutes and didn't see a single person walk by who looked happy. Even the art students on their way to Parsons looked weighed down by their portfolios. True, the day was the coldest we'd had so far this winter. Still, I couldn't remember a gloomier mood in the city since just after 9/11, and even then there'd been a feeling of shared tragedy, not this insular brooding. Was it the recession, I wondered, or was it the influence of Dee's demons making itself felt on the city?

I felt the same oppression inside the hospital. I ran for an open elevator, but no one in it held the door for me. I overheard a doctor yelling at a nurse for bringing the wrong chart and a woman snapping at her bleary-eyed toddler to 'stop whining.' The instant I walked into my father's room I could see that the malaise hanging over the city had crept into him. He looked shrunken lying in his bed, his eyes hooded and heavy, staring blankly at the ceiling. He didn't stir at the sound of my arrival, but when I said his name, his head swiveled around and he managed a weak smile.

'There's my beautiful daughter,' he said. I could have

wept for the bravery of that smile after all the gloom I'd
seen out on the streets, but I managed to smile back
instead.

'Hey, Dad, look what I brought.' I took out Santé's
painting from the portfolio I'd brought it in and propped
it up on the chair by his bed. Instantly his face brightened.

'Would you look at that? She looks exactly like she did
when I first met her.' He furrowed his brow. 'How did
Santé capture her like that?'

'Ober— Obie Smith said Santé painted this from a
dream.'

My father laughed, and the laugh turned into a cough. I
poured him a glass of water from the plastic carafe on the
tray beside his bed. When he'd sipped some water, my
father wagged his finger at me. 'That Santé, he was full of
bullshit. I know where he got this picture. There's a photograph of your mother as a young girl in France. It's in my
bedroom on my dresser. You know the one.'

'No, Dad, I'm not sure I do.'

He waved my protestation away. 'Of course you do. Santé
and your mother loved to talk about France. She was always
telling him he should go . . . that he must paint in the south
where van Gogh and Cézanne painted. She must have
shown him that picture of her in the village where she grew
up . . .' His voice drifted away. 'Santé never made it to
France, though.'

'Did you and Mom ever go back to the village she came
from?' I asked, hoping to distract him from thinking about
Santé.

'No.' He shook his head. 'We went to Paris a dozen

times and I suggested we travel south, but she said she would never forgive the people of the village where she grew up.'

'Why not?'

'I think because they didn't protect her mother from the Germans. She never would tell me the whole story, but I know her mother died in the last years of the war. She didn't want to talk about it and I respected that.'

'Of course you did,' I said, taking my father's hand. My father could barely bring himself to talk about the family he'd lost in the war.

'Sometimes I wonder if I really knew Margot at all.'

'What are you talking about, Dad? No one knew her better.'

He shook his head. 'That day she died . . .' His voice came out as a croak. He stopped and licked his lips and motioned for me to hand him the water glass.

'Don't, Dad, don't talk about that now.'

He took a sip from the straw, his cheeks collapsing. He'd lost weight since he'd been in the hospital. It made him look older.

'That day she died . . . she was planning to leave me.'

'What? Dad what are you talking about? Mom took me up to Providence to look at RISD. We were on our way home when the accident happened.'

He shook his head. 'She told me before she left that she had to leave. She was going to tell you on the way home. I wondered for a while if she had. You were so hysterical in the hospital it was hard to tell. I waited to see if you would say anything. By the time I realized she hadn't told you, I thought it was too late . . . that there was no point, it would just upset you . . . but I was being a coward. I was afraid that once you knew your mother had been leaving me that you would too.'

'Oh, Dad.' I stroked his hand. 'Even if it were true . . . even if Mom had been planning to leave, I wouldn't have left. But why . . .' I stopped, recalling the fights they'd had about money in the weeks before that trip, how angry she'd been that he'd spent my college money on that Warhol, and then the turmoil caused by the insurance-fraud accusation after the Warhol had been stolen. My mother certainly had plenty of reasons to be angry with my father, but still I couldn't imagine her ever leaving him. Then again, I'd never imagined that she was the descendant of an ancient line of supernatural guardians either.

'Maybe she wanted to get you away from me,' my father said. 'She was probably right. Look at the mess I've gotten us into now.'

'We'll be okay, Dad. The police have found a lead on the man whom they think might have been behind the burglary. They found a scrap of canvas from one of the Pissarros at his store last night. Everything will be all right.'

I wanted to say something reassuring about my mother – that of course he knew her, his wife of forty years – but I found I couldn't. I was no longer sure I knew who she was. So instead we sat in silence, gazing at the face of the woman whom we both loved, but who had kept her secrets from both of us.

❖ ❖ ❖

I spent most of the day at the hospital, sitting with my father, or talking to his doctor. Dr. Monroe told me that Roman was healing well from his bullet wound, but that he was concerned about his blood pressure. He also said he wanted my father to have a psych evaluation before he left the hospital.

'Because you think he shot himself.'

'Because I know he shot himself,' he countered.

'My father is not suicidal. He thought . . .' I floundered, aware that if I explained that my father thought that shooting himself was the only way to prevent the spirits inhabiting the burglars – the dybbuks – from getting inside him, the doctor would really think my father was crazy. And if I let on that I thought my father might have been right, then my father wasn't the only one who'd be getting a psych evaluation. 'He was confused,' I finally said.

'Then we need to consider the possibility of Alzheimer's. Do I have your permission to do a brain scan?'

I told him yes. I hoped it wouldn't alarm my father, but in a way I thought that the hospital might be the best place for him right now.

I brought dinner in from Sammy's Noodle Shop for Roman, Zach, and myself, then I went home and took a short nap so that I'd be awake for my 1:00 a.m. meeting with Oberon. I wasn't used to keeping such late hours.

When I got to the Empire State Building, I was surprised to see that there was still a line for the Observatory. I had a feeling, though, that Oberon and I wouldn't be waiting on it. At least I hoped we wouldn't. Like most New Yorkers I had an aversion to tourist sites. I'd been up to the

Observatory, but only because Becky had made me go on the day we graduated from high school 'to mark the day with something really spectacular.' I'd thought it was a silly idea, but had gone along with her because she was impossible to thwart once she was set on something. And she'd been right – it was spectacular seeing the whole island of Manhattan stretched out below us.

'It's ours for the taking, James,' she'd said, leaning into the stiff wind. 'We can do whatever we want with it from now on.'

Becky had followed her own advice. She'd started a rock band instead of following her mother's dreams for her of becoming a lawyer – and now it was paying off. The band was about to land a contract with a major record label. But what had I done in the eight years since we graduated high school? Yes, I'd started a jewelry company that was doing pretty well, but I hadn't lived on my own or had a significant relationship with a man that had lasted longer than six months. The truth was that I'd been playing it safe since the car accident.

I was startled out of my newest bout of self-pity by the appearance of Oberon striding down Fifth Avenue toward me. His long dreads were flying in the air behind him, his ankle-length coat rippling around him like a cloak. He looked every inch a king. A shimmering purple aura radiated around him. The people standing on line for the Observatory straightened up when it touched them, but they didn't stare at him.

'How do you do it?' I asked when he reached me. 'How do you blend in?'

'People see what they want to see. You'd be surprised how many pass through this world unseen. Most of us try to keep a low profile, but not the creature we're visiting tonight.'

'Creature?' I asked nervously as I followed Oberon into the lobby. I remembered that Fen and Puck had been alarmed about some of the guides I might have to seek out.

Oberon laughed. 'Don't worry, this one's fairly benign. I'm starting you out with the gentler of our kind.'

We walked past the elevator banks for the office floors of the building. Each bank had a security turnstile. When we came to the last one – for the highest floors – he took out another of his Post-its, wrote something on it, and passed it through the sensor. The light turned green. After he had passed through, he handed me the note to swipe. I took a look at it, expecting some esoteric symbol, but found instead the words *Open sesame!* I laughed, and then, because he had gone on ahead of me and wasn't looking, put the note in my pocket.

My ears popped on the way up, but I was doing fine until the elevator doors opened on the one-hundredth floor onto a glass wall that faced all of lower Manhattan and upper New York Bay glittering under a clear night sky. I had the sensation that when I stepped off the elevator I would be floating above the city, and for a moment I was frozen. Oberon had to nudge me forward. I noticed then that a sound studio was sandwiched between the first wall of glass and the outside window. Stenciled in silver on the first wall of glass were the letters WROX.

'I listen to this station all the time,' I said, stepping out of the elevator. 'Especially the night show.' I focused on the lone figure in the studio, who was seated at an equipment board so complicated that it might have been the control panel of a 747. Wearing large bulbous headphones, the DJ looked as though she were, in fact, in the cockpit of an airplane. 'Is that Ariel Earhart, the host of The Night Flight?'

Oberon nodded. 'I told her the handle was too conspicuous, but she won't listen to me. She's too in love with the sound of her own voice.' He paused with his hand on the door and glanced at the glowing red letters above the door that spelled out ON THE AIR. Ariel Earhart in her soundproof booth, her back to us, lifted up her right hand, middle finger extended. Oberon laughed.

'Do you mean that she's the same Ariel from Shakespeare's *Tempest*?' I asked, but Oberon put a finger to his lips as he opened the door. As we stepped into the studio, we were surrounded by the smooth, melodious tones of a woman's voice reading the poem she used each night to begin her show.

Night is a creature, flitting bat or owl –
mercurial in mood, from wind that howls
to starsplit balm, to sizzle in July –
and host to other sorts of wings that fly:
the feathered loft of song, of spirit-flight
invisible as thought, but pure delight.
Come soar with me, winged travelers by night;
The city far below twinkles goodbye
and we're moonward! As swift as hawks, we fly.

'Good evening, New York, this is Ariel Earhart, welcoming you aboard The Night Flight. To start us out on our flight tonight here's some new music from one of my favorite new bands, London Dispersion Force.'

She pressed a button and the studio filled with Jay's song about unrequited love. Fiona sang:

I might as well attempt to scale a tower,
a thousand miles in height, its walls slick stone,
as try to win your heart which by the hour
grows more distant, leaves me so alone.

Was Becky right? I wondered. Was Jay really talking about me?

'Yeah, 'fraid so,' the DJ said as she swiveled her chair around and took off her headphones. From her seductive voice I'd always pictured Ariel Earhart as a bombshell, but the woman in the chair barely looked like a woman. In skinny black jeans, Converse high-tops, and a long black T-shirt, she looked more like a teenaged boy. A Goth boy. Her pale blond hair stood up in spikes and she wore heavy chains around her neck, waist, and wrists. 'You're the girl in that song, Garet James,' she purred. 'I've been looking forward to meeting you.'

'Really?' I asked, unnerved that she knew so much about me. 'I've been a fan of your show for years . . . but how do you know Jay's writing about me? Do you know him?'

'No,' she said, curling her feet underneath her and gesturing at the chair by her side for me to sit down in.

'But I've been listening to London Dispersion Force for some time now.' She cocked her head to one side as if listening to something right now. 'Yes, your friends have just been offered a contract with Vista Records. I just hope that the conflict between Jay and Becky doesn't split up the band. You know how that goes.' She smiled and lifted her right hand, splaying open her fingers. The heavy chains around her wrist clanked together like bells tolling.

'Oh, I'm sure they'll work it out,' I said, 'but how—?' Before I could finish my question she had spun back to her control board and put her headphones back on.

'That was "Troubadour" by London Dispersion Force,' she whispered huskily into the mike. 'Catch them tomorrow night at the Mercury Lounge. Now I have a special request from Obie Smith to all his friends in the city. There's a storm a-brewin', children, so keep your chins up and don't give in to your darkest fears. Remember, it's always darkest before the dawn.' She hit another switch and the room filled with the sound of rain and thunder, then the opening chords of 'Riders on the Storm.'

'Okay.' Ariel launched herself out of the spinning chair, all the chains she wore crashing like the thunder on the sound track. 'I've got a twenty-minute set of storm music queued. That should give us enough time.'

'It's her first time, remember,' Oberon said, following Ariel out of the booth to the elevator.

'All the better.' Ariel grinned at me and squeezed my arm. 'The first time's the best and we have a perfect night for it. The wind's from the south and it's clear as a bell.'

'The first time doing what?' I asked, beginning to get

nervous. I didn't see why we had to leave the studio. 'A perfect night for what?'

'Here's the elevator,' Ariel said instead of answering my questions. 'The last visitors have left the Observatory.'

I opened my mouth to point out that if the last visitors had left the Observatory, then surely that meant it was closed. Besides, I was pretty sure that you had to go back down to the lobby to go to the Observatory. But Oberon was already scrawling the number 86 within a circle on a Post-it and slapping it on the elevator wall beside the other buttons. The number and circle immediately glowed green just like all the other floor buttons. He pushed it and the elevator descended to the eighty-sixth floor where the doors opened onto the deserted Observatory.

As we walked through the darkened gift shop, past models of the Empire State Building and postcards of the panoramic views, Ariel began removing the chains from her neck and wrists and draping them over the counters. When we reached the door that led to the out-side deck, Oberon turned to me. 'I believe you have the key.'

'Oh.' I guiltily extracted the *Open sesame* Post-it from my pocket and affixed it to the door, which immediately swung open. 'Here,' I said, offering him the note back. 'I'm sorry I took it before.'

'Not at all,' he replied, holding his hands up. 'I'm glad you're thinking ahead. You keep it. You're going to need all the help you can get.'

I put the note back in my pocket as I stepped out onto the open deck, just in time before the wind would have whipped it out of my hands. It had been windy when I came here with Becky, but nothing like this. Nor had the view in the daytime appeared so dizzying. The lights spread out below us were like a second night sky – a galaxy of its own whirling in inner space.

'Um . . . maybe it's not such a good idea to be out here in this high a wind,' I shouted over the shrieking gusts.

'Nonsense, the wind's perfect.' Ariel didn't have to raise her voice over the wind to be heard. In fact, the wind seemed to pick up her voice and bring it directly into my ears. 'Since it's from the south, I suggest we start on the north side.'

'Start what?' I shouted back at her.

'You'll see soon enough.'

We walked around the deck until we reached the north side. The buildings of midtown stood like a range of cliffs hewn out of light. Ariel moved to the edge of the deck and wrapped her hands around the steel barrier. The wind parted the back of her hair, exposing the nape of her neck and revealing a small tattoo in the shape of two outspread wings. Oberon came to stand beside her, his long dreadlocks whipping around his face like live snakes.

'Can you hear it?' she asked, her voice dancing into my ears on the blasting wind.

'Hear what?'

'Close your eyes,' she commanded, taking my hand. 'And listen.'

I closed my eyes and listened to the wind as it gathered, swelled, rushed . . . then slackened. Gathered, swelled, rushed . . . then slackened. Slowly I began to hear a voice in it, a voice neither male nor female, young nor old, loud nor soft. It crooned and keened, shouted and whispered. It sang a song as old as time, but always rising toward something *new*. It plucked at the hairs along my arms, bellowed my lungs, thumped the muscle of my heart, and whistled through my veins. It blew right through me as if I were its instrument. I opened my eyes and saw the city below me. It was *all* its instrument – the skyscrapers were the keys and the long avenues were the pipes of one great organ that the wind played. The wind blew through the city and each and every person in it, connecting every molecule to every other. I felt a great swell of emotion – whether fear or delight I couldn't have said – that seemed to lift me on the back of that singing multitude. It *did* lift me up, right above the curved bars of the steel railing and then out over the city. As I passed the top of the railing, I grabbed at it with my right hand, but Ariel grabbed and squeezed my other hand and clucked her tongue.

It's got you now, Ariel's voice came from inside my head. *My voice is in the wind and now the wind is inside you. Don't worry. Just let it carry you and keep listening. As long as you can hear its song, you can't fall . . . and if you fall, I'm here to catch you.*

I stole a quick glance over to Ariel, but there was nothing there but air. The panic at being alone rang in my ears so loudly I couldn't hear the wind's song anymore. Immediately, I began to drop, but a hand tugged me back up.

Never a good idea to fly visible, Ariel's voice trilled in my head. *We'd scare the living daylights out of the stargazers.*

I placed my right hand in front of my face, but I saw right through it to the lights of Fifth Avenue streaming below me. Ariel and I – we'd left Oberon behind – were moving north fast, buoyed on the wind's back. Braided into the wind's song I began to hear other voices – the murmurs of couples riding home in taxicabs, the farewells of drunkards leaving closing bars, the sighs of sleepers in high-rise apartment buildings. We passed the spires of St. Patrick's Cathedral and the green mansard roof of the Plaza Hotel, and then Central Park stretched out in front of us. Something about the park was strange, though. Although the night was dry and clear, there was a low fog coating the ground.

Hang on, Ariel's voice commanded.

I thought that's what I'd been doing, but then I felt a tug at my hand and we began to swoop down fast toward the treetops. I recognized the Wollman Skating Rink, deserted at this hour, and the Great Lawn, both slick with a coating of gray fog, like a scum of old milk on top of cold coffee. At first I thought it was deserted too, but then I began to make out faint, multicolored lights amid the trees.

'Light sylphs?'

'Yes,' Ariel answered out loud. Her voice sounded graver than before. 'They're moving much slower than they should be, though. I just want to have a look—'

We plunged so quickly my ears popped. Then we flew

through the trees, dodging the bare branches. What color would the light sylphs have to drink here? I wondered. Only a few dull brown leaves clung to the elms that lined the Promenade.

'They should have moved indoors by now,' Ariel answered my unvoiced question. 'This clutch usually moves inside to the rain-forest exhibit at the zoo or sometimes the butterfly dome at the Museum of Natural History...' Ariel's voice faded as we hovered above a bare tree branch. Something was draped over it, a scrap of trash that had been blown there by the wind...but then when we moved closer, I saw that it was actually one of the light sylphs, only all the color had been drained from its body. It lay gray and motionless against the rough bark. Its wings, stirring in the wind, made a sound like crumpled cellophane.

'What happened to it?' I asked.

'I don't know...here's another one.' We flew from tree to tree, finding one after another of the drained and crumpled creatures. Worse, some had fallen to the ground where they were wind-tossed to and fro along with the empty plastic bags, food wrappers, and cigarette butts. These sylphs were already disintegrating, turning into a chalky gray dust that sifted into the gray fog that lay over everything.

'What killed them?' I asked.

Ariel didn't answer aloud, but I heard the answer inside her head: *The fog. They drank the fog and died.* Aloud she said, 'We'd better get back and tell Oberon.'

We flew back into the wind. It was harder going this way and didn't leave any energy for speaking, out loud or not.

The exultation I'd felt on the journey out was gone now. When I listened to the song of the wind, I only heard a low keening, like someone, somewhere, weeping.

The Train to Tarascon

As soon as we touched down on the Empire State Building, Ariel told Oberon about the massacre of the sylphs.

'It was the fog,' she said.

'Yes, Despair and Discord have made their entrance into New York City now,' Oberon said in a booming voice. 'Garet and I both witnessed their fog along the Hudson from my window. And yet there's no fog on the bay or rivers tonight. So I assume they have transformed themselves into some other entity.' Oberon waved his hand at the sparkling clean vista of city that lay below us. We were on the south side of the observation deck now and could see both the East and Hudson Rivers and as far south as Upper New York Bay and the Verrazano Narrows Bridge. There was no trace of the fog that we'd seen downtown at the end of Jane Street. 'Somehow Dee must have sent a sliver of fog to the park,' Oberon concluded. 'But I don't know how he's moving it.'

'Maybe he's hiding somewhere in the park,' Ariel suggested.

Oberon shook his head. 'Not necessarily. Clearly he's

able to move it from place to place. We have to figure out how and trace it back to where he is.'

'Maybe someone in Central Park saw where it came from tonight,' Ariel suggested.

'But it killed all those sylphs,' I pointed out, shuddering at the memory of the tiny drained and desiccated corpses. 'Would anyone survive the fog to tell?'

Oberon and Ariel exchanged a look, then Oberon nodded. 'We'll go see her tomorrow. It wasn't going to be her next lesson, but there's no point putting it off.'

'My next lesson?' I asked. 'You mean flying and super-power hearing aren't enough?' It was meant as a joke, but from the worried glance that Oberon and Ariel exchanged I suspected they were wondering if anything was going to be enough.

Oberon hailed me a cab on Fifth Avenue. Before I got into the cab he handed me a Post-it note with a Midtown address written on it and told me he would meet me there at noon. 'Get some sleep,' he advised as he closed the door behind me. 'Tomorrow's going to be a long day.'

I couldn't imagine how it could be any longer than the one I'd just lived through – or how I could possibly absorb any more *abilities* than I already had. As the cab hurtled down the deserted avenue, I was bombarded by the voices around me. The cab driver was worried about saving enough money to send for his wife and three children from Mumbai. The man in the Ford Explorer at the light worried that he wouldn't get home to his house in Englewood before his wife woke up and began to suspect it wasn't his job that was keeping him late in the city . . . in fact, he'd lost his job three weeks ago, but hadn't had the nerve to tell her . . . or his mistress.

We were stopped at the light for less than a minute, but it was long enough to become entangled in this man's whole life. At least from the sky the voices had been too diffuse to get wrapped up in. They were louder at street level. Just passing the couple walking arm in arm on Fourteenth Street I learned that she was terrified that he didn't love her and he was even more afraid that he did. The late-night crowd in the Meatpacking District deluged me with fear and anxiety, lust and insecurity. Were people always this *frightened,* I wondered, or was this Dee's doing? And how could I possibly think straight to find him when I was swamped by voices on a 3:00 a.m. cab ride? What would it feel like to walk through midtown at noon?

I was so immersed in the voices in my head that I didn't notice that we'd arrived at the town house.

'Here we are, miss,' the taxi driver said aloud. *Whore,* he added in his head. I was so startled I almost dropped the bills I was passing him through the slot in the Plexiglas barrier. I saw in his head an image of Oberon – a large black man in a long black leather coat – handing me into a cab at 3:00 a.m. I wanted to spit back a retort – *That's not a pimp, you asshole, that's the King of Shadows!* – but I didn't think that would help my case. Instead I took back one of the dollars I was going to include in the tip and got out without wishing him a good-night. I tried not to listen to the epithets he mentally hurled at me as I walked up the steps to my front door.

I unlocked the door, praying for quiet, but when I stepped inside and punched in the alarm bypass code, I heard the strains of guitar music drifting down the stairs. Jay and Becky were still awake, then. As I climbed the stairs, I wondered what it would feel like to be with my friends. Would I hear their thoughts? Would I find out more than I wanted to know from the inside of their heads?

I paused outside the partly ajar door to my father's apartment and listened to Jay singing along with his guitar. He was playing the song I'd just heard on the radio, but somehow it sounded even sadder in his voice instead of Fiona's and without the band backing it up.

I might as well attempt to fly the sky,
to be a fish who dives ten thousand feet,
as try to win your love. Why lie? –
there's no recovery from love's defeat.

I felt tears stinging my eyes as I listened, but I also felt drawn toward the song. It had the same mournful pull as the wind's song. I pushed the door open as quietly as I could and padded cautiously into my father's living room. Jay was sitting alone on the couch, in T-shirt and jeans, his long, curly hair matted against his forehead and neck from the exertion of playing earlier tonight. His eyes were closed as he sang the chorus:

The troubadours wrote songs to salve heartbreak,
to let their loves know all their endless pain,

but words can't bridge our gulf, my long heartache:
I'll just keep walking in the pouring rain.

As he sang, I saw pictures . . . images inside his head. Images of me. Becky had been right. Jay was head over heels, totally in love with me. The thing that really touched me was that the images he had of me in his head were of some of the happiest moments of my life . . . stupid little moments that I'd almost forgotten about, such as ditching school and riding the subway out to Brighton Beach just to walk on the boardwalk and make up long, complicated histories for the Russian couples who sat on folding chairs warming their faces in the wan winter sunlight, afternoons combing vintage-record stores looking for rare jazz recordings and then running an extension cord out onto the roof so we could listen to them there on summer nights, watching *Monty Python* reruns late at night and me laughing so hard at the Spanish Inquisition skit that I snorted milk up my nose. *Jay cherished a memory of me snorting milk up my nose. Shit.*

I must have made a noise because Jay opened his eyes. For a moment he didn't look surprised to see me standing there, but then his eyes widened and he dropped his guitar pick. 'Oh,' he said. 'I didn't hear you come in.'

'I didn't want you to stop,' I said, sitting on the opposite end of the couch. 'Um, is Becky—'

'She went back to Williamsburg with Fiona.'

'You know you don't have to stay. They've caught the burglars.'

'I can go if you want me to.'

'No! I didn't mean it that way, Jay. You're always welcome to stay. You're my best friend—' I didn't have to have psychic abilities to see him wince at the word *friend*. 'Jay—'

He interrupted me, which was a mercy because I didn't have the slightest idea what to say to him next. 'Um, actually, Garet, I have a favor to ask you.'

'Yes?' I asked, bracing myself for a profession of undying love.

'Uh, can I crash here a little longer? I mean, even after your dad comes back? I can sleep on the couch and I can keep an eye on him. Make him soup and stuff.'

'Of course, Jay, you can stay here as long as you want . . . but why—?'

I knew the answer before he said it. I saw the whole scene in his head, the fight with Becky and Fiona and the record producer after the show tonight. Becky calling Jay a hangover from the sixties, Fiona telling him to *grow up*. The condescending smile of the record producer as he told Jay, 'Go home and mull it over, man. You'll see the light in the morning.' The peal of laughter Jay heard coming from their table as he left the club.

'I think I'm leaving the band,' Jay said, strumming a chord on the guitar. 'Who knew I'd be the Stuart Sutcliffe of the group, huh?'

I winced at the reference to the 'Fifth Beatle,' who'd died of a brain hemorrhage shortly after leaving the group. 'Oh, Jay,' I said, patting his arm, 'it's a bad time right now. People are . . . tense. Maybe you should give it some time.'

'Yeah, well. Time I've got plenty of.' He gave me a brave

smile, made all the more heartrending by the words I could hear inside his head: *That's all I've got.*

I was exhausted when I got back to my studio, but I knew right away that I wasn't going to be able to sleep. When I closed my eyes, I saw the limp, drained bodies of the light sylphs – or Jay's face, similarly drained of happiness. I sat down at my worktable and idly considered casting some molds for medallions. I had orders that were overdue. But then I recalled what had happened the last time I handled a welding torch when I was overtired. So I leaned back in my chair and stared out the window, then leaned back farther and stared out the skylight. The plywood board Becky had nailed up had come loose. Fixing it was something I could do. I couldn't hurt myself too badly with a hammer, could I?

I scrambled up on top of the table and reached for the board, but my fingers barely scraped it. Somehow Becky – a good seven inches shorter than me – had got up here. She must have done what the burglars had – and what we'd done back in high school when we wanted to go up on the roof – climbed up the metal bookshelf. As I stepped on a shelf, I wondered if I was heavier than I'd been in high school and whether the shelf would hold my weight, but then it had held the burglars' weight. Besides, I'd just flown over Manhattan. What did I have to be afraid of?

I found a hammer on the top shelf that Becky must have used and turned it around to use the claw to pull out the nails from the plywood board. They clinked, one by one, onto the metal table below me. When the board came loose, I lowered it onto the top shelf. A gust of cold air came pouring through the broken skylight. Above me I could see a clear sky studded with stars. Had they ever looked this bright over the city before – or was it my enhanced sight that made them look like a million diamonds against a velvet cloak?

All thought of fixing the skylight gone, I climbed up the rest of the shelves and pulled myself through the skylight and out onto the roof – thankfully Becky had cleared the broken glass away. I hadn't been up here since those summer nights that Jay and I had listened to jazz records while drinking bourbon purloined from Roman's liquor cabinet. I'd forgotten how good the view was and how liberating it felt to stand among the city buildings with their water towers and hidden rooftop gardens. The rooftop world of the city, like the underground world of pipes and tunnels that lay beneath the city, had always struck me as a secret world. I'd had no idea how right I'd been! Fairies and goblins held court beneath the streets, and sprites and sylphs soared above them.

I stared at the stars until they seemed to be revolving in great balls of fire. When I squinted, the sky looked like van Gogh's *Starry Night* and I remembered what Will Hughes had said about van Gogh falling in love with the colors of the night. Right now I could think of worse fates. I closed my eyes and spread my arms. I felt the wind running through my outspread fingers and through my hair. I could hear the wind's song again and on it the millions of voices in the city. I was only listening for one voice, though. I had only heard it twice – would I be able to conjure it up now?

I found I had no problem hearing it in my head. I focused on *his* voice until it was louder than all the other voices on the wind, and then I said his name aloud, letting the wind take it.

I waited, feeling foolish . . . and foolhardy. Oberon had warned me against him. He had called him a creature of the dark . . . and he was right. But I could feel his pull on me like a dark tide stirring my blood, his silver gaze the moon that moves the oceans. In his car last night he had asked me if I felt as if I had no choice in my feelings for him, and I hadn't known how to answer. I still didn't. Was I calling him now because he had contaminated my blood with his and put me under his power? Was he luring me into the world of the dark where I'd become like him – a vampire? Shouldn't I feel revulsion at that idea? Shouldn't I be fleeing from him, not calling his name to the wind?

No matter, I told myself, it probably wouldn't work anyway . . .

A current of air blowing through my hair turned warm . . . caressed my neck . . . and spoke.

'You called?'

I swirled around so quickly I lost my balance. His arm was on mine before I saw it move. 'I didn't know if that would work. You really heard me?'

'Clear as a bell. You must have met Ariel.'

'Yes. She took me flying. . . . Can *you* fly? Is that how you got here so fast?'

He smiled, his eyes flashing silver in the dark. 'Not exactly. I can move *very* fast, though. In fact, in exceptional circumstances my parts – meaning my atoms –

can move much faster than I can. But I don't routinely engage in *that* sort of motion. In any event, I wasn't far away.'

I noticed he was dressed in black jeans and a black trench coat. With his collar up he faded into the night. 'Are you stalking me?' I asked, trying to sound reproving.

'Just keeping an eye on you. You seem to forget that Dee has already tried to murder you.'

'I haven't forgotten.' I shuddered at the memory of the manticore and the stalker in the park. 'But I think he's been otherwise engaged.' I told him about the light sylphs. His eyes narrowed at my description of their drained and lifeless bodies. I couldn't tell if the look was pity or confusion.

'I don't understand why Dee would bother with such weak and helpless things,' he said. 'They may not have been his real target.'

'You mean they were just collateral damage? Then who was Dee trying to kill?'

'Not who, but *what*. Where's Oberon taking you tomorrow?'

'We're meeting in midtown on Forty-seventh Street.'

'Ah, the Diamond District . . . that makes sense. Oberon's taking things slow—'

'Slow? I jumped off the Empire State Building tonight!'

'Believe me, Ariel's a pussycat compared to some of the other elementals you'll meet. Oberon's trying to build up your powers slowly so you'll be prepared for the . . . *fiercer* guides. It's what I would do if I could.'

'And why can't you?' I said it before I knew that it was what I was thinking. 'You gave me my first power

– my enhanced sight. And that was from one tiny bite.'

'Is that how you remember it?' he asked, stroking my neck with the back of his hand. 'As one tiny bite?'

I shivered from head to foot. 'Not so tiny,' I said, leaning into his hand. 'But it didn't make me . . . like you.'

He tilted his head and narrowed his eyes, studying me . . . or preparing to bring his lips to my neck? 'Is that what you want?' he asked. 'To be like me?' He moved closer and the silver light in his eyes expanded. I could feel it filling the space between us, drawing me closer like static electricity. I felt each hair on my body standing up on end and my blood surging through my veins toward him.

'Would it be so bad?' I asked. The question seemed to come from someone else, but as soon as I asked it, I saw the logic in it. 'I'd be stronger, wouldn't I? Dee wouldn't be able to hurt me.'

He pulled his head back abruptly, a tiny spark of red glowing at the center of each iris. 'There are other ways to protect you.' His voice sounded strained. 'Less costly ways.'

'Is it so awful, then, living forever?'

He sighed. I felt his breath on my throat, but it was cold now, not warm like before. 'You'd have to watch everyone you know and love grow old and die before you.'

'I've already seen my mother die. I almost lost my father – and it's just a matter of time before I do lose him.' I thought I saw him flinch at the coldness in my voice, but it might have been that he was holding himself so rigidly. He had both hands on my arms, but I felt that he wasn't so much holding me as holding himself at bay. I could feel the tension in his body, like a bowstring drawn back.

'And what about your friends?' he asked. 'Are you so ready to give them up?'

'They're better off without me. I'm just putting them in danger as it is . . . but if you don't want me—'

'Oh no, Garet. I want you very much. I believe I've been waiting for you for four hundred years. But an eternity is a long time to feel regret. I don't want you to do anything that you don't want to do.'

'This *is* what I want,' I was startled by the certainty in my voice. *Where had it come from?* Another voice in my head whispered, *Hold on,* but it was too faint to heed. I stepped forward another inch, closing the space between us. I felt the charge of electricity sizzle against my skin. The red glow filled his eyes entirely now. He smiled . . . and drew back his lips until I could see his fangs. I did feel afraid then, but I couldn't have moved away if I'd wanted to – and I didn't want to. At that moment I wanted him to drain me of every drop of human blood, of every human feeling of fear and pain. I wanted to be cold and invincible like him. In one part of my brain I was shocked by the feeling, but in another I felt like I'd always been headed toward this.

He bent his head to my neck and breathed against my throat. The skin there turned numb under his breath, but the rest of my body seemed to be on fire. I cried out as his teeth broke my skin. He tightened his grip on my arms and pulled me hard against him. He seemed more urgent than the last time, sucking hard at the wound to draw the blood out, and I realized that was because he was being careful before not to take too much blood. He wasn't being careful now. I could feel myself growing weaker. I leaned my head against his shoulder and looked up at the sky – at the swirling waves of color unfolding from the spinning stars. Now more than ever the sky looked like van Gogh's *Starry Night* and I felt myself longing for the stars just as he had.

'Why should the spots of light in the firmament be less accessible to us than the black spots on the map of France?' van Gogh had written to his brother Theo a year before his death. 'Just as we take the train to go to Tarascon or Rouen, we take death to go to a star.'

Had that been where van Gogh thought he was going when he ended his life? Is that where I was going?

The stars blurred and swirled and changed colors . . . and, yes, they seemed to be coming closer. One – an orange fireball – seemed to be heading straight for us.

It exploded right over Will's shoulder. He reared back so quickly his teeth ripped a small gash in my throat. The pain was instant and sharp in the unanesthetized part of my skin. The cold night air stung. He batted at the flaming ball, but it darted away, then dive-bombed down into his face. Will growled and pulled back his arm to swat it. Remembering how he'd torn the stone manticore limb from limb, I grabbed his arm and he snarled at me. I took a step back, one hand on my neck to stanch the flow of blood. Lol fluttered in the air between us, chattering like an angry squirrel. An angry squirrel on fire.

Will looked from me to the angry fire fey and then, with one last regretful look, took two long strides to the edge of the roof, and vanished. I watched him disappear, wondering what that look had meant. Was he sorry he had snarled at me? Or was he sorry he hadn't finished me off?

The Diamond Dairy

I woke up the next morning to the sound of someone screaming. I was so startled that I was out my door and down the stairs – in the sweatpants and T-shirt I'd slept in – before I realized that the screaming wasn't *out loud*. Someone was screaming very loudly inside her own head. The 'sound' was coming from the gallery.

I grabbed a jacket off the coatrack and, remembering last night, a long scarf, which I wrapped around my neck. Then I pushed my feet into a pair of boots left in the hall-way and unlocked the door into the gallery, hoping I didn't look too deranged. It was the first time that I'd gone into the gallery since the burglary, and it wouldn't do our reputation any good for the proprietor's daughter to look like an insane bag lady.

Maia was seated behind the reception desk looking lovely and poised as always. She was wearing a short, chocolaty-brown sweater dress, ornate Mexican silver ear-rings, and thigh-high suede boots in the same fawn shade as her tights. She was smiling politely at the woman hover-ing over her desk, but inside her head she was yelling, *Shut up! Shut up! Shut up!*

I turned to the woman causing this uproar in Maia's head. Was she threatening Maia? But the woman hardly looked threatening. She looked, rather, like one of the Long Island matrons to whom I sometimes sold my pendants: expensively coiffed hair brushed the corduroy collar of her quilted Burberry jacket, a Louis Vuitton tote bag – large enough to hold a ten-pound bag of rice – dangled from her arm.

'Is there something I can do to help?' I asked. 'I'm the acting manager of the gallery.'

The woman eyed my sweatpants suspiciously and crinkled her brow in confusion. She glanced back at Maia, but when Maia didn't denounce me as an impostor, she sighed. 'I was just explaining to your *gallerina* that there's a recession going on.'

The screaming in Maia's head went up a notch. She hated the term *gallerina*.

'Oh really?' I said as if I hadn't read a newspaper in a year.

'*And,* in light of the recession, most businesses are accommodating their clients by . . . well . . . by reducing their prices.'

'Mrs. Birnbach likes the Dufy watercolor,' Maia said helpfully when I continued to stare at the woman. 'But she thinks it's overpriced for the current market.'

'I've had my eye on it for some time,' Mrs. Birnbach added. 'It would look lovely in our condo in Boca. I just wondered if you could do a little better on the price.'

It wasn't the first time a client had tried to bargain down a price. Roman usually handled those negotiations –

and usually came away ahead. But the idea that this woman with her $800 bag and condo in Boca would use the economic woes of the country to get a deal on a Dufy – a piece of décor to her – made my blood boil.

I opened my mouth to let loose a withering tirade when I heard something. A little-girlish voice saying, *Please don't yell at me!* was coming from inside Mrs. Birnbach's head. I was so surprised that my mouth hung open for a minute, then I snapped it shut. A jumble of images flooded through my brain: a harried-looking man holding up a bill and yelling, a beautiful teenaged girl pointing to an expensive pocketbook, a younger boy with braces . . . *Aaron will go to med school, or maybe law school* . . . a whole life teetering on the edge of collapse. Then why was she here trying to buy a Dufy?

I looked toward the painting in question – a watercolor of a beach scene full of brightly colored umbrellas. Mrs. Birnbach's gaze followed mine toward the painting. When I turned back to her, I saw in her mind's eye a beach scene not unlike the one in the painting. It was probably New Jersey or Long Island, but it was as radiant as any beach in the south of France. Children were playing at the edge of the surf, seagulls careened in the bright blue sky, an old man . . . *Papa Rosenfeld* . . . handed a young girl a gleaming pink seashell. I blinked and the vision evaporated like spray from the surf. Focusing back on Mrs. Birnbach, I noticed that her nail polish was the same shade as the seashell her grandfather had given her.

I named a price 30 percent below the asking price for the Dufy.

Maia stared at me. Even Mrs. Birnbach seemed surprised, but she reached for her wallet quickly enough. As I passed her American Express card to Maia, I wondered if I was doing any of us a favor. Her husband was going to be furious with her, Roman was certainly going to wonder why I let the Dufy go for so little, and Maia could justifiably resent my generosity since it obliterated her commission, but for this moment Mrs. Birnbach and I were smiling at each other as if neither of us had a care in the world.

Despite my euphoria, I realized I did have to do something equitable for Maia regarding her lost commission. After Mrs. Birnbach left with her Dufy, I told Maia that she would still get a commission based on the original sale price. Her grateful smile put me at ease, and then I went back upstairs to shower and dress for my noon appointment with Oberon. At the door to my father's apartment I stopped and listened for any sound – audible or mental – from Jay, but there was nothing. He must still have been asleep. I supposed I should have been thankful that I hadn't started hearing and seeing people's dreams.

My apartment was quiet too – no sign of Lol. After she'd chased off Will Hughes last night she'd chattered at me for a few minutes and then flew off, probably to report back to Oberon about my near conversion to vampirism. If she hadn't interfered, would I already be on my way to becoming a vampire? In the cold light of the morning – a light I'd almost given up – it was hard to believe how close I'd come. I leaned over the bathroom sink and swept my hair off my neck to examine the marks. There were two angry red puncture wounds just above my jugular vein, with a small gash where Will's teeth had torn my skin when he'd pulled away from me. These marks hadn't faded as the first ones had – probably because he hadn't had the time to heal them. The sight of the torn flesh – which I had offered up to him of my own free will – shocked me. Was this really what I wanted? For this man . . . or *creature* . . . to rip my flesh and drain the life out of me?

The body is the sanctuary of the soul. Roman's words came back now reprovingly. I blanched to think what my father would think if he could see these marks – these nearly *self*-inflicted marks! I might as well have torn my own flesh. If I had let Will Hughes drain me of blood, would I have lost my soul?

Did Will Hughes have a soul?

I thought of how I felt when I looked into his eyes, the pull of that silver thread that connected us. What did it connect if not our souls?

After I'd washed the wounds and applied Neosporin to them, I lifted my eyes from my throat to meet my own gaze in the mirror . . . and gasped at what I saw there. A red flame flickered in the center of each iris, swelled and swayed as I held my breath, and then, as I breathed out, expired. My own eyes stared back at me wide with shock, but for a moment I'd had the strangest feeling that someone else had been looking out through them.

The address Oberon had given me turned out to be the National Jewelers Exchange in the Diamond District.

Were the fey in the jewelry business? I wondered, wandering the floor of the crowded showroom. I'd always thought it was the Hasidim. Whoever was in the business, they were doing well. The place was busy; no sign of a recession here.

As I walked from booth to booth, though, I noticed something. Although some of the customers were buying – young couples on their lunch breaks picking out engagement rings, office workers selecting Christmas and Hanukkah presents – many more were actually selling. It wasn't always easy to tell who was who because the sellers often started out by browsing the merchandise, asking to see a watch or ring, and then, as if as an afterthought, pulling out a pouch from their bag or pocket and asking, casually, if the vendor also *bought* jewelry. As if the signs WE BUY GOLD AND DIAMONDS weren't perfectly visible to the naked eye.

I watched one transaction in which a tired-looking woman in her fifties sold an engagement ring. 'From my ex-husband,' she told the vendor, 'the schlemiel.'

'Who needs bad memories?' the dealer replied. He was short and bald but for a fringe of white hair, and had a long white beard. His potbelly strained against a shiny black vest. When he smiled at the woman, a gold tooth glinted in the showroom's fluorescent lights. 'Take yourself on a cruise, *bubeleh*,' he said, adjusting his loupe over the two-carat diamond. 'You'll meet a new man who'll buy you a ring twice as big.'

The woman laughed and years fell away from her face. I hadn't been focusing on auras today, but I saw hers brighten to a crystal blue under the gentle teasing of the diamond dealer. His aura was pure white. 'Maybe I'll do that,' she said, leaning her elbows on the counter as the jeweler used a caliper to measure the diamond. 'What do you think of the Bahamas this time of year?'

'Too cold,' he said, taking the loupe out of his eye. 'Aruba's better.' He wrote something down on a scrap of paper – a number with a lot of zeros – and slid it across the counter. The woman looked back and forth between the number and the ring for a few minutes, measuring the distance between them as if they were two points on a map. Where she came from and where she'd arrived, maybe. I couldn't hear any words in her head, just numbers.

'That seems like a fair price,' she said at last.

'Of course it's a fair price, darling! And I'll tell you what – I'll throw in a twenty percent discount for when you meet Mr. Right on that cruise and come back here next year for a new ring.'

The woman smiled and the dealer wrote out a check for her. When she reached for it, he took her hand in his and brought it up to his lips, bowing his head to plant a kiss on her knuckles. His bald scalp gleamed under the fluorescents as brightly as one of his diamonds. Then he pressed the check into her palm, clasping both his hands over hers. 'To better times, dearheart.'

As she passed me on her way out, I could hear that her thoughts were still full of numbers: tallies of rent and electricity, food and phone bills. She was trying to figure out how long she could stretch out the money she'd gotten from the ring. There were no plans for a cruise in those calculations.

Oberon came into the showroom as she left. For the first time since I'd met him – had it only been four days? – he looked tired. As he crossed the floor, I noticed that his skin was ashy, as if something had drained out of him when the light sylphs had been drained of their lives.

He nodded to me when he reached me, but he spoke to the white-bearded jeweler behind me. 'Hello, Noam. How's business?'

The dealer shrugged, holding his hands palms up to the sky. 'Can't complain. And if I did, what good would it do, eh? I'm buying more than I'm selling – never a good sign – but at least I've got the capital to weather the storm. Others aren't so lucky.'

'No, others haven't been lucky at all.' Oberon looked around the showroom, then gestured for me to come closer to the counter. 'Noam Erdmann, meet Garet James.'

'Ah, the Watchtower. I thought it might be you.' He took the hand I'd extended to shake in both of his – they were cold and dry – bowed his head, and touched his lips – also cold and dry – to my knuckles. 'It's an honor to meet you.'

'It's an honor to meet you, Mr. Erdmann.'

'Please, call me Noam.' He lifted his head and smiled at me. The gold tooth winked in the light, but his brown eyes retained a look of melancholy despite the smile. They were surrounded by deeply etched lines that looked like furrows in a dry field. Looking into them, I felt as if I were looking down into a deep well that went into the very bowels of the earth. Although he held my hand lightly, I could feel a current running from his fingers up into my arm, down into my body into the ground, right through the showroom floor and into the bedrock below the building. '*Erdmann?* Doesn't that mean . . .'

'"A man of the earth,"' he said, letting my fingers drop and thumping his barrel-shaped chest with his right hand. 'My people have mined the wealth of the earth for millennia.' Then he shrugged. 'It's a living. And speaking of living . . . we've all got to eat. Why don't we get a bite while we talk?' He cocked his thumb toward the mezzanine where a kosher dairy restaurant overlooked the floor. 'C'mon. There's a waitress there who's sweet on me. She'll give us extra pickles and coleslaw.'

He winked at me, slid off his stool, and came out from behind his counter. I was surprised to see that the top of his bald head barely came up to my shoulder. He wasn't any taller than Becky, but he led us across the floor like a prince surveying his kingdom, waving and exchanging pleasantries as he went. Oberon might be king of the fairies, but this was clearly Noam Erdmann's domain.

'I get the Erdmann part,' I whispered to Oberon as we started up the stairs to the mezzanine, 'but his first name . . . Noam sounds a lot like . . .'

'*G-n-o-m-e?* Yes, that's exactly what he is – an elemental who guards over the treasures and resources of the earth.'

'And what power am I supposed to learn from him?' I asked, looking at the squat little man. Now that I thought of it, all he needed was a pointed cap to look like the statues people put in their gardens.

Oberon turned to me at the top of the stairs. Noam was a few feet ahead of us enthusiastically greeting a buxom waitress with hair dyed the color of a ripe eggplant. 'We're going to ask him to ground you,' he said. 'But at this point I'd be happy if you'd learn to choose your company better.' Oberon looked meaningfully at my neck – covered by a turtleneck sweater. Before I could ask him if Lol had told him about last night, he turned away to join Noam at a vinyl-upholstered booth with a view over the showroom. I sat next to Oberon, across from Noam, preferring to look into the jeweler's sad brown eyes than to endure Oberon's glowering gaze.

'The blintzes are delicious,' Noam told me as the aubergine-haired waitress, whose name tag read SADIE, brought us plastic cups full of lukewarm water. 'And so is the borscht.'

'Then that's what I'll have,' I told Sadie. 'And a cup of hot tea.'

'The lady has good taste,' Noam said, winking at me. 'Make mine the same, but with a cream soda.'

Oberon ordered chow mein – I had a feeling just to be contrary – and an iced tea.

When Sadie had taken our orders, Noam turned back to face Oberon, his features becoming grave. 'We heard about what happened last night up at the park. Is it true the sylphs were killed by Dee?'

Oberon slid his eyes over to the Hasidic man eating soup at the counter, then toward an elderly couple in the booth behind us, and lifted his eyebrows. Noam nodded and took out a gray velvet pouch from his pocket. He untied the drawstrings and spilled the contents of the pouch into his broad, lined palm. A half dozen diamonds glittered against his weathered skin, along with an assortment of multicolored stones, some smooth, some cut. He selected a clear crystal lozenge and placed it in the middle of the table. I looked closer and saw that it was veined with feathery black lines branching out like miniature fern fronds.

'Dendritic quartz,' I said. 'One of my favorite stones.' I knew from my college gemology class that the fern design was made from iron trapped inside the rock when it was formed, but it always looked to me like a fossilized plant.

'Yes, and very useful for privacy.' Noam lifted his water cup and poured a drop onto the stone while muttering a few guttural syllables. The stone sizzled, vibrated, spun twice counterclockwise, then came to a standstill. Nothing happened for a minute. Then, looking closer, I noticed that the worn linoleum table was covered with fine feathery lines branching out to the edges of the table. They didn't stop there, but continued sprouting upward, covering our booth with a crystal dome supported by a tracery of black branches. I gasped at the beauty of it and heard the echo of my gasp rebound off the walls. I looked around the diner to see if anyone noticed the new addition to the décor, but the Hasidic man continued placidly eating his soup, the elderly couple picked at their omelets, and the waitresses gossiped by the kitchen window.

'So you were going to say?' Noam asked, spilling the other stones back in the gray pouch.

'Yes, what you heard was true. At least one hundred

sylphs were killed. They appear to have died by drinking a fog that we think was sent by John Dee.'

Noam Erdmann shook his head. His eyes looked heavier and sadder than before. 'A tragedy. What kind of beast does a thing like that? Do you know how he moved the fog?'

'I was hoping maybe you knew something. Your people spend a lot of time underground.'

'Not so much anymore, at least not in the city. It's gotten so crowded lately with all the work being done down there, from the building at Ground Zero to the new water tunnel and the Trans-Hudson Express train tunnel. You can barely hear yourself think belowground anymore. I go up to the Catskills on the weekends to get a little peace and quiet – most of my people have relocated up there year-round. There's a bit of natural-gas drilling going on up there, unfortunately, but nothing too deafening so far.'

'As to New York City, that leaves the tunnels free for Dee,' Oberon pointed out.

'You're right about that, but if I call my people back to the city to man the tunnels, how do we know they won't be poisoned like the sylphs?'

'We don't, but someone has to keep an eye on the water tunnels. If Dee gets into them—' Oberon was interrupted by Sadie coming back with our orders. I wondered how she'd get the food through the dome, but the plates moved right through the crystal as if it weren't there. When her lips moved, though, I couldn't hear a word she said.

Noam grinned at her and gave her a thumbs-up, then he

turned back to Oberon. 'Okay. I can get some workers to guard the Croton Reservoir, and the Independent subway lines down to midtown. But no one's going to go below Fourteenth Street with you-know-who down at City Hall.'

'Understandable. What about the IRT?'

While the two men went back and forth over the best way to guard the city's underground water tunnels and subways, I ate my borscht and blintzes. The borscht was bright red and vinegary, pink where the dollop of sour cream melted into it. The blintzes were crisp at the edges and filled with soft, sweet cheese. I ate every bit, then sat back to drink my tea from its plastic cup. The men had divided up most of underground Manhattan; there didn't seem to be much for me to do, and no one had mentioned *grounding* me, whatever that entailed. I had a feeling it didn't mean making me stay in my room for the duration of the battle with John Dee, although given the grim expressions on Oberon's and Noam's faces that didn't sound like a bad idea.

Finally Noam glanced up at me and then looked over at Oberon. 'It's pretty confusing down there. If she does have to battle Dee below the ground, she'll need help finding her way.'

Battle Dee below the ground? I didn't like the sound of that. As scary as it had been to fly over the city, I'd prefer that to facing an adversary below street level where, aside from Dee's minions, there might be giant rats and mutant cockroaches.

'Um . . . I suppose you could give me a map,' I suggested.

Noam smiled wryly and took out his gray pouch again. 'I can do better than that, *bubeleh.*' He spilled out the stones into his hand. Maybe I was going to get a magic diamond, I thought, leaning forward to peer into Noam's palm. The stone he picked out, though, wasn't a diamond; it was gray and shiny and shaped like a teardrop.

'Hematite,' I said. 'The blood stone.'

'Yes!' Noam crooned approvingly. He took my right hand in his left and dropped the stone into my palm. It felt heavier than it looked. 'We call it the compass stone. It possesses both ferromagnetic and antiferromagnetic properties. Excellent for telling directions.'

I felt something twitch in my hand and looked down to see the stone spinning. It came to a halt pointed toward the showroom floor. 'It's pointing north, isn't it?' I asked. I nudged the stone with my finger until it pointed in the opposite direction. When I removed my finger, it swung around to face north again. 'Cool! So I just carry this with me?'

Noam shifted his melancholy gaze from my palm to Oberon. I glanced over at Oberon to see him nod once. Noam covered my hand, which he still held in his left hand, with his right hand and squeezed both of his hands around mine. It was like being caught in a vise. His short, squat fingers were as cold and rigid as steel. I thought he was going to break my hand. I could feel the hematite pressing into my palm like an arrow carved out of ice.

'Hey!' I cried, trying to pull my hand away, but Oberon blocked my way out of the booth and I couldn't have gotten my hand out of Noam's grip even if he hadn't. I looked desperately around the diner for someone to help me, but of course no one had heard my cry of pain. So I looked back at Noam, into those soulful brown eyes, to beg him to stop. His eyes were glassy with tears, but he only squeezed harder.

'Sorry, *bubeleh*,' he said, and gave one final iron-gripped squeeze that sent an excruciating stab of pain into the palm of my hand that traveled up my whole arm and lodged in my chest. Then he released his grip and still cradling my throbbing hand in his, he bowed his head.

If he kisses my hand, I'm going to slap him, I thought.

But he only unclenched my fingers and blew into my palm. Looking down, I expected to find a mutilated stub, but my hand was whole and unharmed, the skin soft and white as if I'd just had a manicure; the only change was that something tear-shaped glowed under the skin of my palm. I lifted my hand to have a better look, and the tear shape moved under the skin, realigning itself to point north. As it moved, I felt my whole body – the blood in my veins, the hairs on my skin, the very atoms in my cells – shift with it, yearning toward north. Noam hadn't only inserted the compass stone into my hand; he'd turned *me* into a compass as well.

Angel of the Waters

'Was that really necessary?' I asked Oberon out on the street. 'Couldn't we have gone over to Circuit City and bought a fracking GPS?'

Oberon grabbed my hand and spun me around to face him. 'Is that all you think this does? Give directions?'

'No,' I said, pulling my hand back, 'it also hurts like hell. My whole arm is numb. I can feel it *here*.' I thumped my hand over my heart.

'Of course you feel it there.' Oberon leaned so close I could feel his breath in my face like an angry wind. 'Your heart beats in sync with the gravitational pull of the tides and the rotation of the earth now. That's what it means to be *grounded*. You could find your way through the Amazon jungle without a compass—'

'Great. Only I live in New York City. North is that way.' I pointed straight up Fifth Avenue, but my arm twitched and shifted a few degrees to the left. 'Okay, so the grid's not perfect, but I've never needed a compass to get around. Well, maybe in Brooklyn . . .'

'Where you're going is a little more confusing – and dangerous – than Brooklyn,' he said, turning to walk north (well, northeast) up Fifth Avenue. Although I walked as fast as I could, I didn't catch up with him until he hit a red light at Fifty-seventh Street.

'You could have at least warned me,' I said while we waited for the light to turn.

Oberon glared at the traffic light on Fifth and it abruptly changed from green to red, causing a line of taxis to screech to a halt. 'Would that really have helped?' He glanced at me out of the corner of his eye as we crossed the street. 'I find with patients that the anticipation of pain is often worse than the pain.'

'So do you sneak up and surprise them with hypodermic needles?'

'No,' he admitted, stopping and turning to face me. 'They'd never trust me again.' He looked down at me, studying my face. 'I'm sorry. You're right. You deserve to know what's coming. . . . It's just that much of what I see is jumbled and confused. I'm not sure how much to tell you.'

'You can see the future?' I was shocked as much by the fact that anything could still surprise me as by his answer. We were standing in front of the Bergdorf Goodman holiday windows. Oberon was framed against an arctic backdrop between a woman in a white evening dress playing an accordion and a white wolf in black tie playing a trombone. A white swan was flying toward the couple, bearing a page of sheet music in its beak. Oberon belonged to that world, not out here on the sidewalk apologizing to a mere mortal like me. For the first time since I'd met him, I saw the sadness in his eyes – the same melancholy that afflicted Noam Erdmann and that I had heard in the wind's song last night. I recalled what he'd said to me in the underground passage below Puck's. *We may have once been a great people – there were those among us who were revered as gods.* What did it feel like to have been a god once and now to stand on a busy street in Manhattan unnoticed by the crowds?

'I see glimpses of the future, but it's always changing. Whenever someone changes the path they're on, their future changes.'

'Can you see if I'll be able to find Dee?' I asked.

'No. I see you wandering in the dark. That's why I wanted you to have the compass stone – to keep you from getting lost. But you're right – I should have told you what was coming and given you a choice.'

I raised my hand. The compass stone adjusted by shifting back to north. A stone was moving underneath my skin, but suddenly it didn't hurt. It felt, rather, as though I had a small bird cradled in my palm, a homing pigeon that I could launch into the sky to lead me home.

'Okay,' I said, looking back at Oberon. 'You're forgiven. But next time give me a heads-up, okay?'

He grinned as broadly as the leering white wolf in the Christmas window. 'Absolutely. I'll start right now. You'd better answer your phone. Your friend Becky's calling and she's pretty upset.' As he turned to continue walking up Fifth, my cell phone rang. I retrieved it out of my bag and followed Oberon as I answered it.

'Garet?!' Becky's voice screeched. 'Thank God! I've been calling you all morning, but I kept going to voice mail. Did you turn your phone off again?'

258 • Lee Carroll

'Um, no, I was in' – I looked to Oberon to see if he had any acceptable substitute for *dendritic quartz dome of silence*. He mouthed *subway* and took my elbow to keep me from tripping over the curb as we crossed Fifty-ninth Street – 'the subway. Sorry. Is anything wrong? Is it my father?'

'No, your dad's fine. I stopped by earlier and he and Zach were happy as clams planning a *show*. No, it's Jay. Did you talk to him last night?'

'A little,' I admitted warily. I tried as much as possible to stay out of Jay and Becky's fights. 'He told me you had some creative differences about the direction the band's going in.'

'Going in?' Becky snorted. 'The direction he wants to go in is backwards. If he had his way, we'd be playing balalaikas and recording on eight-track cassettes.'

'Yeah, well, Jay's a little old-fashioned. You know that.' I glanced over at Oberon and rolled my eyes to express exasperation with Jay and Becky. We had entered the park and were walking toward the zoo. We passed a street artist drawing on the sidewalk in multicolored chalk, a calypso band playing on steel drums, and a woman on stilts dressed up as the Empire State Building. It was a little hard focusing on Becky with so much going on around me.

'It's not just old-fashioned this time. He's stuck in the past. It's not healthy. I think he's suffering from depression.'

I moved the phone away from my mouth so Becky wouldn't hear me sigh. Ever since she took AP psychology in our junior year of high school, she'd been an armchair analyst, dissecting the psyches of everyone around us. For some reason, the tendency worsened when she was under stress, as if she needed to control and catalog the neuroses of the rest of the world in order to keep herself under control. I listened to her list Jay's symptoms – not sleeping (I didn't know how any of them got any sleep with the performance schedule they kept up), avoiding friends (as far as I knew, Becky was the only friend he was avoiding), failure to maintain a romantic relationship (she could have said the same about me or herself) – with a growing sense of concern, but for her, not Jay. Just to be sure, though, I decided to cash in on my recent promise from Oberon.

'Hold on a sec, Becky.' Covering the phone, I turned to Oberon. 'Do you see anything bad happening to Jay?'

Oberon stopped and closed his eyes, tilting his face to the sky. We were at the beginning of the tree-lined Mall, the shadows of the bare elm branches playing over his face. I wondered if that's what the future looked like to him: shadow branches spreading out into the void.

He flicked open his eyes. 'No, I don't see anything bad happening to Jay.'

'Thanks.' I uncovered the phone. 'Becky, I think Jay's going to be just fine. And to tell you the truth, I've got too much on my plate right now to mediate a band fight. Maybe you should worry about the direction *you're* going in.'

The phone was silent so long I thought we must have gotten disconnected, but then Becky said, 'Oh. Maybe you're right. I'll talk to you later.' Then she hung up. I'd rarely heard Becky give such a terse response to anything.

'Do you think I was too hard on her?' I asked, putting the phone away and turning to Oberon, but Oberon was too engrossed with the scene in front of us to answer. It took me a few minutes to make sense of what he was looking at. Where the sun shone through the branches, the pavement glistened with smears of multicolored glitter. It looked like a third-grade crafts project gone horribly wrong.

'Is this what's left of the sylphs?' I asked.

Oberon nodded. Then he knelt down on one knee and gathered a handful of glitter. He raised his hand to his nose and sniffed. 'Iron. Dee sent a fog laden with iron molecules. That's what killed them. The smaller fey can't stand the touch of iron.' He said something else in a language I didn't understand and then, rising, flung the glitter into the air. A gust of wind caught it and carried it up to the treetops. I heard a song in the wind – a keening that raised the hair on the back of my neck – and the air above us began to swirl. The leaves and bits of trash on the ground stirred and spun about our feet in quickening eddies that climbed toward the gathering vortex in the sky. Where Oberon and I stood, the air was dead still. We were in the eye of the funnel. I stared up, spellbound, unable to move. *This is what it must feel like to be at the center of a tornado,* I thought. If I moved even a millimeter, the wind would pick me up and tear me apart. All I could do was watch the currents of air racing above us. One minute they were transparent and then the next they thickened – the way pudding thickens on the stove as you stir it. The air turned into glossy ribbons, within which the sylphs, their bodies distended, their faces stretched in pain, were borne up into the sky . . . and then they were gone. They broke apart into a million bits of glitter and in one horrendous, ripping wrench, the vortex broke free of the earth and flew up into the sky.

I turned to Oberon and saw his lips moving, but I couldn't hear what he was saying. Then my ears popped and sound came rushing back in.

'They're gone,' he repeated. 'I've sent them back into the ether.'

He turned and walked north up the Mall, and I followed him. As he walked, a cloud of glitter shook free from his hair and lit the air around him like a psychedelic halo.

Oberon walked to the end of the Mall to the upper section of Bethesda Terrace, then down the stairs to where the Angel fountain presided regally over the lower terrace and the lake. The Angel of the Waters was one of my favorite statues in the park. My mother had told me the biblical story of the angel who moved the waters of a sacred spring in Jerusalem to heal the sick. The statue showed up in the play *Angels in America* and most recently on the television show *Gossip Girl,* but I never got tired of looking at the angel's calm face, her hand extended over the fountain as if blessing the water. No water flowed from it today, but plenty of people were sitting on its rim, eating lunch, chatting, or just soaking up the winter sunshine. Oberon sat down on the rim of the fountain and turned his face up to the sun. Glitter spangled his skin.

'What you did just now for the sylphs . . . was it some kind of funeral?'

'I freed their spirits from this world. Their atoms will be reabsorbed in the earth and appear again in flowers and plants and trees, perhaps one day to be drunk by another sylph.' He opened his eyes and smiled. I'd almost forgotten what it felt like to be smiled at by him, like having a warm tropical breeze waft against your face. 'That's a sylph's idea of reincarnation – to be reborn as a flower and drunk by another sylph, only . . .' His smile faded and his brows drew together. He looked away.

'Only what?'

'Every year there are fewer and fewer sylphs. Each winter their population diminishes by hundreds. When the last sylph dies, there will be none to drink its reborn spirit and then their race will be truly dead. Like the sleigh beggy and the Irish merrows.'

'You mean fairies can become extinct?'

'Of course. I told you we diminish. This world is too hard for most to survive in . . . but then there are some who hang on despite all obstacles.' His smile had returned and he was looking over my shoulder toward the upper terrace. I followed his gaze to the stairs where a heavily bundled figure (it was impossible to tell if it was a man or a woman) was dragging an overladen shopping cart down to the lower terrace. At the bottom of the stairs the figure looked up and I recognized the bag lady I had seen three mornings ago on Greenwich Avenue – the woman with the nut-brown face who conversed with steam and had greeted me by spitting in her hand and waving. As if to remind me of that greeting she cleared her throat and hawked up a great gob of spit that landed six inches from the polished loafers of a lunching businessman. He mimed gagging to his lunch partner and crumpled his sandwich wrappers into a ball, which he launched over the bag lady's head toward a garbage can. Halfway there, a gust of wind caught the ball and flung it back at the man. The missile exploded against his chest, splattering his suit with mayo, ketchup, and lettuce shreds. He wiped himself off and fled in disgust.

I laughed before I could stop myself, and the woman looked up, grinned at me toothlessly, and headed in our direction. The lunchtime picnickers around the fountain began clearing out as she approached – in fear of being spit on, I guessed, or maybe it was the distinctly *fishy* odor that became detectable a few feet away. By the time she reached us the whole terrace was deserted except for Oberon and me.

'Mel,' Oberon said, spitting into his palm and lifting his hand in greeting. 'Good to see you still have your aim.'

She grunted. 'I was aiming for his face.' She hawked spit into her crabbed, arthritic hand and touched it against Oberon's palm. Then she looked at me.

'This is her?' Mel pointed a crooked finger in my direction. 'She don't look like much.' She shambled closer to me until her face was inches from mine. Her face smelled like the East River at low tide. I stayed very still and prayed she didn't spit on me.

'This is Garet James, descendant of Marguerite D'Arques, Watchtower. Garet this is Mel.'

Mel sniffed at my credentials – or maybe she was sniffing at the borscht on my breath. I was glad I hadn't ordered the gefilte fish. '*She's* going to go up against John Dee?'

'First we have to find him. He moved a fog here last night. Do you have any idea where it came from?'

'Could be the steam tunnels,' she replied, turning from me to Oberon. 'I've noticed that the steam coming up onto the streets is tainted.' She sniffed again, rattling the phlegm in her throat.

'That's what you were doing on Greenwich Avenue?' I asked, taking a discreet step backward in anticipation of another spitting incident. 'I thought you were talking to the steam.'

I laughed at my misapprehension, but Oberon and Mel didn't join me.

'Mel has the ability to communicate with water,' Oberon explained to me. Then, turning back to Mel, he said, 'I was hoping you could have a look around and see if you can tell how Dee is moving fog around the city and where he's doing it from. I thought you might also initiate Garet into the mysteries of water.'

'Is there anything else his lordship would like me to do while I'm at it?' Mel asked in a mincing falsetto. 'Maybe pick up his dry cleaning and spit-shine his shoes?' I heard the phlegm gurgling up in her throat and I moved away. The glob headed straight toward Oberon's face, but he calmly pursed his lips, blew, and redirected the missile into the dry basin of the fountain. I thought he'd be furious, but he only smiled and spread his arms out toward the miscreant.

'Mel,' he crooned, 'who else could I ask? Who else

would I entrust but the daughter of Elinas and Pressina, Queen of Columbiers and Poitou, and Banshee of Lusignan?'

She made a noise in her throat and looked away, but I thought I saw a smile appear under the influence of Oberon's blandishments.

'Melusine!' he sang the name like a hymn, and years seemed to fall away from her face. I'd heard the name before. It was in one of the stories my mother used to tell. A prince wandering in the forest came upon a beautiful maiden sitting by a fountain. He asked her to marry him and she agreed, but on one condition: that he never look upon her on a Saturday. He agreed and they married. She brought him prosperity and ten children and built for him the castle of Lusignan. They were happy until one Saturday his curiosity got the better of him and he spied on her in the bath and saw that from the waist down she was really a serpent. Still he kept her secret until their son – a tusked monster – massacred a hundred monks. Then he turned on his wife, blaming her for their child's tainted blood. Realizing her secret had been betrayed, Melusine turned into a serpent and flew away. She would appear at the castle, though, whenever one of the descendants was about to die, gaining her the title Banshee of Lusignan.

Could this be the same creature, crusted with grime and hobbled with age? As if in answer to my unvoiced question, she straightened up and stepped daintily into the fountain basin. She lifted her crabbed hands up toward the statue of the angel, and water spouted from the pipes and rained down onto her upturned face. She clawed at her clothes, shucking off layers of shirts and sweaters, pants and long underwear, until she was completely naked . . . and beautiful. Under the streaming water her skin gleamed in the opalescent purples and grays of an abalone shell, her hair fell long and sea-green to her shapely waist where blue and green scales flashed in the sunlight. Her long, muscular tail smacked the water and propelled her out of the fountain, through the air, and to the edge of the lake, where she perched, admiring her reflection.

'It's not her reflection she's looking for,' Oberon said, hearing my thoughts. 'It's Dee. She has the power to see in the water. Go and she'll teach you.' Oberon nudged me forward, taking my bag off my shoulder as I cautiously approached her. Of all the creatures I'd seen so far, she was the most amazing. No image of a mermaid that I'd ever seen began to do justice to the strangeness of that tail joined to pearly flesh . . . although as I moved closer I saw that even her skin wasn't precisely flesh. It was coated with chitinous shell like a . . .

I took a step closer and bent down to see her arms, which were folded under her breasts. She turned toward me, her seaweed-green eyes blinking, and I saw the slits of gills on her throat and the long pincerlike claws where her hands should have been. I started to back away, but then I saw an image forming in the water – a face, but not Melusine's face. It was familiar. I knelt beside her and bent over the edge of the lake to see better. For a moment I thought I was looking at my own reflection, but then

I realized it was my mother's face. She was moving her lips, speaking to me. I bent closer to hear what she was saying . . . or to read the words on her lips . . . but then her face vanished and was replaced by the face of John Dee, looking straight at me, laughing. I reared back, gasping. Beside me, Melusine made a sound – a kind of caw that sounded like the cry of a raptor before it seized its prey. Then, before I knew what was happening, she seized my wrist tightly in her lobster's claw and dragged me with her into the water.

The Source

My gasp of surprise was the last breath I took before the water closed over my head. I tried to hold on to that breath as Melusine pulled me down through the cold, murky water. I tried to get free, but her grip was pincer tight and only hurt more when I struggled. I looked to see where she could be heading so fast. The artificial lake couldn't be all that deep, after all. The sun filtered down to the bottom, turning the water a muddy green sparked with gold motes racing past us as we plummeted downward. A shape was beginning to emerge out of the gloom – a round, gaping hole covered with a perforated grill festooned with plumes of algae. A drain? A pipe that brought water into the lake? Whatever it was, we were going to end up grated like cheese when we hit it.

I closed my eyes and brought up my free arm over my face to protect it against the impact. It was worse than I expected, worse than when that Ford Expedition rammed into my mother's car. It felt as if every part of my body had hit a steel wall at the same time, as though I were being torn apart, not just limb from limb, but atom from atom. And then, just when I thought I'd lose consciousness from the wrenching pain, it was gone. I felt nothing but the flow of water and weightless buoyancy.

I opened my eyes – or at least I thought I did. I was surrounded by blackness. Was I dead?

No, a silky sibilant voice whispered. *You're waterborne.*

I tried to find the source of the voice, but it was all around me . . . and by *all around me* I realized that the voice permeated my entire body . . . no, that wasn't quite it, because I didn't have a body.

You're borne on the flow of water. Can you feel it? We're in the reservoir. From here we can go into the main water tunnel and travel through the city. Dee is sssomewhere in the water system. We must find him.

How? I asked, thinking the words. *I can't feel – or see – anything.*

You will. It takes a little time to get used to the incorporeal stage. I ssspent centuries in the springs beneath the forest of Brocéliande, percolating in the rock layers far below the earth. Here, before we go into the tunnel, let'ssss evaporate.

Evaporate? That sounded dangerous. But I could already feel myself growing lighter, rising to the surface. I became aware of light, then I was floating above the shimmering skin of water, merging with the air, dodging dragonflies and watergliders, and then, rising quickly, I was above Central Park. I could see the joggers running around the reservoir and the towers of the Dakota against the skyline. Then we were above the towers, heading for the clouds . . . but then I felt myself grow heavier.

We fell in a light drizzle back to the reservoir and sank

down again into a pipe, caught up in a strong current. Although it was dark, I could sense where we were. The compass Noam Erdmann had implanted in my hand pulsed in every cell so that I could tell we were traveling southwest through the island of Manhattan in a wide tunnel . . . through Water Tunnel #1, I suddenly knew. Not only had the compass stone given me a sense of direction, it gave me a sense of specific location, as if a map of the city were imprinted within my cells. I really was my own GPS! Even though we were deep beneath the bedrock of the city, I knew what streets we were under. When we soared up through the vertical shafts, pushed by the insistent flow of water that had been running downhill from the mountains, and into the water mains, I knew exactly where we were. I knew the apartment numbers we passed as we soared high up into buildings. When we reached the rooftop water tanks, I could identify every landmark within a ten-mile radius. And when we plunged down again through a maze of pipes and back into the main water tunnel, I could have stated our exact longitude and latitude.

We traversed every inch of the city in the time it usually took me to take the subway from the Village to midtown, but nowhere did we catch a glimpse or scent of Dee. Then at the end of the island we veered southeast and plunged into deeper darkness. I heard rushing water and boats moving above us. We were below the bay, heading for Brooklyn. Melusine was quieter while we were under the bay, and I sensed a tension in her that I hadn't as we coursed through the city. If she had lungs instead of gills,

I would have said she was holding her breath. When we made landfall in Brooklyn, she seemed easier even though we had to swim against the current upstream, northeast through Brooklyn and Queens, then northwest toward the Bronx.

At the Hillview Reservoir, Melusine took us on a lap around the lake. I felt her exulting in the wider expanse of water, freed from the pressure of the tunnels.

Are we going back to the city now? I asked.

Instead of answering my question she had us plunge into the Delaware Aqueduct and race upstream toward the Kensico Reservoir in Valhalla. Although we were fighting the current, we went faster and faster. Melusine remained stubbornly silent, but I could sense her desire now. I could feel her because as we had traveled together our molecules had crossed and crisscrossed, braiding and unbraiding like long strands of DNA. She yearned to go farther north, up to the mountain springs from which the streams and rivers had sprung. She was a creature of the springs – not the sea – and that was why she had felt uneasy beneath the salt-water bay. She was the goddess of the spring, the sprite of the source. I saw her worshipped at Roman springs and Celtic wells, heard the names she had been worshipped by on the water . . . Sulis, Sequana, Coventina, Egeria, Sinann, Laga. I felt the love she'd had for Raimond de Lusignan and the anguish of betrayal when he turned away from her in disgust. I saw the long years she haunted the Château de Lusignan, her banshee cry serenading the last of her descendants. And, finally, I felt the sadness of exile, a craving to return to her source.

I was so wrapped up (literally) in Melusine's history that I forgot our mission, forgot that we had to head back to the city. I wanted to travel north into the Catskills and join the fresh springs below the snowcapped peaks. But while my molecules had merged with Melusine's so that I learned her history, she had been listening to mine as well. She saw everything: my mother's face, the car crash, the shriek of tearing metal, my father falling apart . . . She raced through my whole life until she got to the moment that I walked into Dee's shop, then she paused and lingered. She watched him bending over the silver box, his shadowmen invading my house, the yellow fog that crept into my studio and animated the demon Jaws, and the fog that gave life to the manticore in the Cloisters. I heard her weep at the sight of the dead sylphs and felt her anger rising against Dee. He had infiltrated her waterways like a virus, used her currents to carry death. The anger pulled her up short and sent her back, tugging me along with her. We joined the southward flow down the Delaware Aqueduct, racing the current into the Hillview Reservoir and back into Tunnel #1.

Although we moved fast, Melusine paused at every shaft, sniffing for Dee's presence. I had the feeling she was homing in on his location, scenting him in the water. I could smell him too, that trace of sulfur I'd detected in the fog four nights ago. We caught a whiff of it near the park and then again below the West Village, but it was faint and fading. Melusine pushed us back into the main tunnel, forcing us on, even though I could sense her repugnance as we headed underneath the East River again. She picked up the pace, eager to cross the salt water quickly. In her haste she dismissed the possibility that Dee was here. There were no shafts leading to the surface here, only a straight run under the river to Brooklyn, no connecting pipes . . . or, at least, there shouldn't be. About halfway across the river I caught the sulfur scent again, lingering on a metal joint. Melusine scented it too, and wrenched herself to a stop. I could feel how hard it was for her. It was like being in a subway car when it stopped between stations . . . and the lights went out . . . and you smelled smoke . . .

There are no shafts here, I thought, *how could he be here?*

There aren't ssssupposed to be any shafts, but if Dee got into the minds of the men who made the tunnels, he could have compelled them to build a shaft. What better place to go unnoticed than deep below the river . . . ssssee here?

Since neither of us had bodies, Melusine couldn't very well point to where she meant, but I felt the force of her attention directing me toward a spot on the tunnel wall. Glowing faintly in the rushing water was a familiar symbol – an eye surrounded by a spiral. It was the same symbol that Oberon had pasted on the columns on either side of the doorway outside St. Vincent's so that no one would see us.

A spell of misdirection, Melusine explained. *There's sssssomething here we're not ssssupposed to see, but if I sweep it away . . .* A current of water pulsed against the wall. The spiral eye flickered and faded. In its place appeared a metal valve.

I don't get it, I said, *why bother to disguise it? No one comes in this tunnel.*

The undines swim through here ssssometimes . . . and I should patrol all the tunnels regularly, only I've avoided this one because it's under salt water. Sssstupid, she hissed, angry at herself. I could feel her ticking off the mistakes she'd made in her long, long existence, marrying a mortal chief among them, although I also sensed that she still longed for the mortal man she'd married and borne children to.

You shouldn't blame yourself. We all make mistakes.

I felt a pulse in the water, a warm current, and then a glimmer of light, as if a school of phosphorescent plankton swarmed around us.

Yesss, but this is one I can fix.

The current revolved around the valve, spinning into a fast-moving eddy that churned the surrounding water into a white froth. The wheel began to move, creaking and groaning as if it hadn't been opened in many years. Even the steel of the tunnel walls creaked and groaned. I felt a sudden horror at the idea that the tunnel might cave in. What would become of us then? Would we seep into the bedrock or float out to sea? I probed Melusine's consciousness for an answer, but hit a wall around the question. Clearly she was unwilling to contemplate that outcome, which made me all the more frightened.

At last the wheel stopped spinning. With one final wrenching shriek the valve opened. We were sucked into the vertical shaft, propelled by the water pressure upward, too quickly to consider what we were being sucked into. It looked like the maw of a giant squid as envisioned by Jules Verne – that horrible horny beak edged with razor-sharp teeth. This beak was made of perforated steel sieves that churned the water as it rose. We were spun through a spiral of interlocking doors. First I felt myself lose touch with Melusine's consciousness . . . then I began to lose touch with my *own*. Bits of my past and present were spewed up like chum – my mother telling me a bedtime story about fairies who guarded me while I slept, Santé's painting of my mother, Jay laughing on the boardwalk in Brighton Beach, Becky spreading her arms in the wind on top of the Empire State Building . . . they were more than memories. For a fleeting second I was in each moment and then spit out of it. It felt as if a ravenous creature were chewing up my memories and sucking them dry. What would be left when it was done but a hollowed-out shell? I could feel the moments detaching from one another, the way thought becomes more random and disconnected as you're falling asleep. One by one they floated away . . .

Hold on to them.

The voice cried across the churning water, startling me awake. *How?* I tried to ask, but Melusine's voice was gone. I plucked at the moments that were spinning away – my father holding my hand on a rainy day as we walked up the long marble steps to the Metropolitan Museum, Jay sliding an Ella Fitzgerald record out of its worn cardboard sleeve, Becky's hair flying in the wind . . . I plucked each memory out of the maelstrom and held on to it, focusing all my attention on each face that spun by – my mother, Jay, Becky, my father, Zach Reese, Santé Leone, and even, flickering

276 • Lee Carroll

through the others but coming more often, Will Hughes. These were the pieces that made up who I was. As long as I held on to them, I wouldn't be lost.

At last the steel maw spit us out into a shallow pool under a steel dome. Citrinous light filtered through an open oculus.

Are you all here? Melusine asked.

Yes, I answered, but was I? How could I know? Were bits of me still floating out in the water tunnel now heading for Brooklyn? An image of my molecules watering geraniums in Carroll Gardens and then seeping into the Gowanus Canal was interrupted by a hiss from Melusine.

And what of it? Do you think I haven't ssssloughed off bits of myself over the centuries? You'll have held on to the important parts. Ssssome you'll wish you'd been able to get rid of. Now come, we have to go up.

We floated to the surface – where a dirty yellow scum clung to the top skin of water – then evaporated. The air was so humid we rose easily up through the oculus and into a marble space shaped like the inside of a nautilus shell. The inside of a nautilus shell as decorated by Gianni Versace circa 1990s Miami Beach. The floors were covered in heavy Persian rugs, the furniture was carved mahogany, heaped with antiques – Greek amphorae and Roman bronzes – the walls themselves were lined with gold. Hanging on the gold walls were paintings that I recognized as lost masterpieces: Leonardo da Vinci's *Leda and the Swan,* Caravaggio's *Adoration of the Shepherds,* Vermeer's *Concert,* van Gogh's *Portrait of Dr. Gachet.* Among all this opulence I noticed a rather unprepossessing late eighteenth-century portrait of a woman in an empire waist dress hanging above a fireplace. Something about her looked familiar. I hovered closer to her, looking into her soft almond-shaped eyes, but I still couldn't place her.

'She's a beauty, isn't she?'

The voice startled me so badly I nearly dissolved into a puddle of condensation on the floor. I'd heard it only once before, and he'd been hiding his power then. Now as I turned my attention to the man seated below me, I could feel every ounce of his power radiating in the air around him, an aura unlike any other I'd seen so far. Its contours were sharp and jagged, like a sunburst. He was wearing the same maroon cardigan, but it didn't disguise the strength of his build. Sitting in a high wing-backed red chair, he looked coiled to strike. The yellow-nailed finger-tips of one hand perched on the arm of the chair like a long-legged spider. In the other hand he held a cigar, which he brought to his lips and drew on. He exhaled a long stream of smoke directly at me. I felt the edges of my molecules crisp and singe. Melusine pulsed in the air beside me.

Sssstay out of my waterwayssss! she hissed. *You don't belong here.*

'Don't I?' Dee asked, fanning his long fingers out. 'I've had this little pied-à-terre – or should I say pied-à-mer – for over fifty years and you've never noticed me here. Maybe it's you who don't belong here, Melusine. Isn't it a little too . . . salty for your taste?'

The fog that was Melusine condensed into a long-winged serpent coiled in the air above Dee's head, its long tongue flicking out from between sharp fangs, its jaws snapping inches from Dee's face. He regarded her with his cool amber eyes and flicked the ash of his cigar into an ashtray on a table beside his chair. Drawn by the motion, I looked down and caught a gleam of silver. Lying beside the ashtray was the silver box. Dee smiled and rested his hand on top of the box.

'Is this what you've come for Garet James? Did you want another look inside?' His fingers caressed the lid of the box, coaxing the engraved lines into motion. They writhed like a nest of snakes awakened. I felt myself drifting closer, following the path of each line . . . if I could just follow one of them to its conclusion, I would know . . .

I snapped back. Know what?

'You would gain dominion over the elements and know the secret of everlasting life,' he said. 'And, what might be more important, you'd know how to escape that everlasting life. That's what your boyfriend wants to know. Do you think he's helping you for your pretty face alone? He wants the box too. It's the only way he can be mortal again . . . although I can't imagine why he'd want that. He's counting on you to lead him to the box. Why don't you call him now and see how fast he comes . . . oh, I forgot. You can't very well do your little fire trick in your current state. Why don't you materialize?'

Don't lisssten to him! Melusine sputtered around me.

I hadn't realized that I *could* materialize on my own. As soon as he put the idea in my head, I felt my cells growing heavier and I longed for the solidity of flesh.

'I always find the watery element so very cold and

damp.' Dee shammed a convulsive shudder. 'Wouldn't you like to sit by the fire and have a glass of brandy?'

Now that he mentioned it, I *was* cold. And empty. So empty.

'You and I have much to talk over, Garet James. You have nothing to fear from me. After all, I could have told my shadows to shoot you when I sent them to your house.'

You shot my father!

'No, dear.' Dee clucked his tongue and shook his head like a kindly uncle correcting a favorite niece. 'Your father shot himself. A regrettable accident. How was I to know he was afraid of dybbuks?'

'You sent the manticore to kill me – it killed Edgar Tolbert!'

'Did I? Whose word do you have for that? The vampire's? Convenient that the manticore's bite allowed him to drink your blood, wasn't it?'

I shook my head – or at least I shook the molecules that had once made up my head. 'Will saved me . . .' I stopped, recalling Will's mouth on my throat, how he'd almost made me one of his last night . . . but then I'd asked for that, begged him to make me like him—

'Of course you asked him to make you a vampire. Once he's contaminated your blood, you long for more. He's gotten you hooked.'

He's trying to trick you into materializing so he can destroy you, Melusine sang in my ear. *Don't forget what he did to the ssssylphs.*

'Oh yes, the sylphs. That I freely confess to, but it was self-defense. Have you ever met a sylph, dear? Nasty creatures, like those nasty creatures you saw lurking in the shadows with Oberon and Puck. Why do you think they call Oberon the Prince of Shadows? He's using you just like the vampire is using you – to get the box for himself and gain control over the human race. Do you think Oberon's creatures *like* being relegated to the shadows? Do you think our watery friend here enjoys living in the sewers? They ruled the world once and they'd like to once more. How much room for humans will there be once they do?'

Is that true? I asked Melusine.

She didn't answer. Instead I saw an image of a man in royal robes, a crown upon his head, his features contorted in disgust. He stood in a hall soaked in blood and gore. *This is all your fault,* he cried. *It is your foul blood that runs in his veins.*

It is you humans who have no room for ussss, she said at last.

'And what wouldn't you do to revenge the wrongs perpetrated on you and your people, Melusine?'

She flicked her long tail and hissed. She had grown more corporeal in the last few minutes, anger and bitterness weighing down her cells like an oil slick on a seagull's wings. Melusine was right – Dee was trying to make both of us materialize by invoking our anger. I was tempted to do so on the off chance I could take the opportunity to destroy Dee. But I didn't feel I'd been properly trained to launch such an attack yet, especially with him having some access to my immaterial thoughts, which could remove the advantage of surprise.

We should go. I tried to make it a whisper, a mere trill

of water, but Melusine was too far gone to hear anything below a torrent. Not Dee, though.

'Yes, perhaps you *should* go, my dear. Your friends need you. I believe there are eleven more voice mails on your phone from your friend Becky. I'm afraid that the argument between her and Jay has gotten rather *nasty*.' He opened the lid of the silver box. A condensation of mist appeared on the inside of the lid. Dee rubbed his hand over it and a picture emerged of Jay and Becky sitting at my kitchen table – or at least Jay was sitting, his bony shoulders hunched up to his ears, his hair falling over his face. Becky was half in, half out of her chair, crouching on her knees as if ready to spring at Jay, her arms spinning like windmills. No sound accompanied the picture, but I could guess by the way that Jay became smaller and smaller as she shouted what kind of things Becky was saying to him.

Stop it! I cried. *You're doing this to them! They've never argued like this before. Make her stop!*

'Shall I?' Dee asked with a low chuckle. 'Perhaps you're right. You know how fragile your friend is, suicidal even. Shall I make her stop?' He extended his index finger and stroked the image of Becky on the silver screen, with the same motion you'd use to control the touch screen on an iPhone. Immediately Becky sank down in her chair, her arms fell, and her face drained of color. I'd never seen her look so still.

Dee touched the screen again, just above Becky's heart, and she opened her mouth, gasping like a fish.

No! I rushed through the air toward Dee, my cells gaining weight as I moved. I sensed Melusine coming with me, a splatter of water against my solidifying flesh, and then I felt her emerging claws digging into my arms. We were both corporeal again by the time we reached Dee, but he wasn't. His body dissolved as we landed in his chair . . . and then so did the chair. Where it had been was a gaping hole in the floor that sucked us in. Melusine and I were both squeezed into a pipe with barely enough room to breathe. Melusine struggled to dematerialize, but before she could, we were ejected out of the pipe into ice-cold salt water, flushed out into the East River like a bit of sewage.

Deliquesce

I'd been underwater for so long without having to breathe that I hoped I still didn't have to, but the pressure on my chest soon told me otherwise. I didn't have long to get to the surface – and I couldn't even see the surface. I tried to stroke upward, but the only direction I moved in was southwest. The tide was going out, sweeping me out to sea.

I struggled against the current fruitlessly for a few moments, but I couldn't break free. Then I stopped. I remembered my father telling me when I was little and we took trips out to the beaches on Long Island that if I ever got caught in a riptide, not to fight it. Eventually it would bring me back to shore. But was that true in a tidal strait like the East River? And what good would it do me if I drowned before being spewed out somewhere in New Jersey? But there *was* landfall before New Jersey – Governors Island – and it wasn't far away. If I could relax and let the current take me there, I might survive.

I concentrated on making my muscles relax, limb by limb, just as my yoga teacher instructed at the end of class for *shavasana* . . . corpse pose. The thought that I might literally be a corpse soon made it hard to relax, but I banished the image from my mind and tried to concentrate on releasing each muscle. *Imagine you are melting into the ground,* my yoga teacher would say, *let your feet go, your calves, your thighs* . . .

Something grazed my leg.

I flinched and flipped over, frantically beating the water with my hands, dreading but needing to see what was behind me.

A pale silvery shape loomed out of the murk.

Shark. The word slammed through my nervous system, every primeval fear of the deep awakened. But then as the shape drifted closer, I made out arms and legs and a dead-white face.

A corpse, I thought, before noticing the gills and claws. It was Melusine. I had thought she had evaporated again, but the salt water must have stunned her and rendered her unconscious. Or dead. There was probably nothing I could do for her . . .

But I had to try. In the time our molecules had intertwined I'd gained a fondness for the strange creature. Despite her outward show of bitterness – her brittle, chitinous shell – she still mourned for the man who had betrayed her and the children she had been forced to abandon. For centuries she'd haunted the Château of Lusignan just for a glimpse of her children's children, even if they shrieked in fear when they saw her, until she fled to a new country. I couldn't just let her die here in the polluted murk of the East River when she'd been born of the purest springs.

And she was dying. I could feel it. More than that, she

was dissolving. Her pearl-bright skin was sloughing off in the current leaving a trail of phosphorescent dust behind her like the tail of a comet. As she floated by me, her eyes wide-open and staring sightlessly, I grabbed her arm. Her skin dented and slipped greasily under my fingers. I was afraid her arm would come off in my hand, but it didn't. I pulled her closer to me, so I could throw my right arm over her head to secure her in a lifesaving hold. Her body felt light, like a shell that's been abandoned by its molluscan inhabitant. I tried not to think of that as the current bore us on, but images of snails crawling out of bony eye sockets and eels nibbling on drowned flesh plagued me. At least the phosphorescence that surrounded Melusine acted like a giant flashlight. I could make out rocks ahead of us, and above them, lit up by Melusine's phosphorescence, discarded water bottles and driftwood bobbing on the surface. If I could catch hold of one of the rocks, perhaps I could climb out of the water.

I hadn't figured on how much holding Melusine would hamper me. I had only one hand to reach out with – a clumsy left hand. I grasped at the rocks . . . and came away with handfuls of green mush.

Let her go, a voice inside my head told me. *She's gone anyhow.*

But I held on, maybe only because I was afraid of being alone here in the dark. At last the current drove me up against a jutting rock. It scraped my left hip, but I was able to loop my left arm over its jagged edge, and from there to start the climb up. I still couldn't see any light above me. I began to think that the blackness all around me was a

286 • Lee Carroll

much deeper abyss than the bottom of the East River. Perhaps I was dead already.

Still I climbed, dragging the limp, empty hull of Melusine with me like a snail dragging its shell on its back. I lost track of how long or how far. I think I must have blacked out for a little while. When I came to, I was still surrounded by blackness, but it was the blackness of night and the cold was the chill of December wind on naked skin. I was lying on a rock slab next to a smear of pale silver gelatinous flesh – like a shucked oyster. Bile rose in my throat and I turned to vomit salt water over the other side of the rock. Everything came up. I retched until my throat burned and my stomach felt as if it had been turned inside out . . . I pictured it looking a little like the pile of goo by my side . . . which made me retch some more. I couldn't look at it again. I started crawling onto the next rock . . .

Marguerite . . . don't leave me . . .

The voice came from behind me, but also from inside my head. It came from the puddle of ooze that had once been Melusine. She was still alive, but she wouldn't be for long. I couldn't bear to look again at that mess and know there was still a consciousness inside it. I crawled another few inches . . .

Marguerite . . . my sister . . .

Sister?

It was just a figure of speech, I told myself. But even as I crept farther away I knew different. An image bloomed in my head. A girl in a forest glade crouched beside a pool, looking at her reflection in the clear water . . . only it wasn't a reflection, it was another girl looking up from the water, her face identical to the one above her save for the color of her hair.

I turned around. The pale flesh quivered on the rock. Something glittered in its folds. I leaned closer and saw to my horror that it was her eyes. Green eyes that fastened on to mine.

'You and Marguerite – the Marguerite who was my ancestor – were sisters?'

A ripple moved through the glutinous gel and I felt a corresponding chill crawl over my flesh.

Yesss . . . sisssters . . . Only she was called to the Watchtower and I became . . . I became thisssss.

This was a part of the story Oberon hadn't told me.

When Marguerite became mortal . . . A rattling gasp shook what was left of Melusine's body. Air bubbles percolated through her disappearing flesh.

'What? What happened when she became mortal?'

Helped her . . . showed her . . . the way . . . The green eyes swiveled in the goo, then slid sideways, but they remained focused on me. *Help me . . . now!*

'How? How can I help you?'

Catch me! She hissed, her flesh sizzling on the rock. *Bring me . . . back!*

'Catch you? But how?' Her flesh was dissolving fast now, pooling into a depression in the rock and oozing toward a crack on the sea side. If she spilled into the salt water of the bay, I feared she would be lost forever. I looked around frantically and spotted a plastic bottle wedged between the rocks. I dived for it and brought up a plastic Poland Spring bottle, half-full and still capped. The bane of environmentalists everywhere – but I was glad to see it. I spilled out the old water, shaking out the last drops. *At least it's spring water,* I thought as I made my way around the rock to the seaward side. I placed the bottle beneath the crack.

'It's okay,' I said. 'I'm going to catch you. You can . . .' I struggled for the right word. *Deliquesce* leapt to mind out of some old SAT study guide, but I didn't use it. 'You can let go. I've got you.'

After I capped the bottle that held what remained of Melusine – daughter of Elinas and Pressina, Queen of Columbiers and Poitou, Banshee of Lusignan – I stood up and looked around me. I was on a rock outcropping not far from a paved walkway. Beyond the walkway loomed brick buildings, dark against the skyline of Manhattan. I'd been to Governors Island on a school trip and knew that it had once been a military base, but was now a national monument. The buildings were abandoned, which was a good thing because I was stark naked.

There must be security guards, though, patrolling the island. One would come by eventually and see me. Then I'd have to come up with a reason for being naked on Governors Island, which I now remembered was closed for the season. They would assume I was a failed suicide, or crazy, or both. I'd probably end up in the psych ward at Bellevue.

And then I would be powerless to stop John Dee.

No doubt that's what he intended by flushing Melusine and me out of his lair once he saw I didn't buy his claims of innocence. Which I didn't, did I?

I shook the thought aside. I had no time for doubt. I had to get off this island somehow without getting myself arrested or committed.

I walked inland, clutching the water bottle that held what remained of Melusine. On the other side of the paved pathways was a lawn leading up to a brick house. The grass felt good on my bare feet after the wet rocks, but I was still freezing. If I didn't find some way to warm up soon, I'd get hypothermia. Could I break into one of the houses? Find some old curtains to wrap myself in? An image of an old Carol Burnett skit, which Jay had shown me on YouTube, of the comedian as Scarlett O'Hara dressed in full curtain plus curtain-rod regalia popped into my head. Laughter bubbled up from my aching stomach, as improbable as everything else that had happened to me, and somehow irresistible. I doubled over from it and sank down on the lawn in the shelter of a towering pine tree. Jay would love that I was laughing at this. Remembering Jay, I recalled what Dee had said about Jay being fragile, *suicidal even*. Was he lying? Was Jay in danger of killing himself?

I shook my head, spraying cold water over my shoulders. It was no use thinking about that now. I drew my knees up to my chest and wrapped my arms around them to stop my teeth from chattering. If only I could get warm, I could think straight. . . . But I could. Oberon had taught me that trick. I brought my fingers together, but my hand was shaking too much to snap them. I tried again and again, focusing on the little bit of heat left in my flesh, until a spark appeared. The flame wavered . . . and went out. I had nothing to light with it.

I ran back down to the shore for driftwood. I gathered up armfuls and carried them back to the lawn, near the pine, but not so close that a fire would catch in its boughs. My hands shaking from the cold, I piled them up and then ran back down to the rocks to collect whatever stray paper I could find. Then I crouched in front of my pyre, snapped my fingers, and using a sheet from the *Wall Street Journal* stock pages, lit my bonfire. The flame snapped and crackled and then spread to the wood. Only when the flames leapt higher than my head did I realize the fire was bound to bring park security.

But Oberon had taught me one other trick, although not intentionally. I snapped my fingers again and seared a pattern into the grass: an eye surrounded by a spiral. The design glowed red-gold against the grass and then turned silver. I got up and drew three more in a square around my bonfire. When I was done, a silver pyramid formed over the fire. I noticed that a trail of smoke snaked out a hole in the top of the pyramid, but I just had to hope no one would notice it. I sat down again and rubbed my hands in front of the fire.

At least now I wouldn't die of hypothermia, but I was no closer to finding my way home. I sat for a while, watching the smoke from my fire trace a spiral path into the night sky above me. If only I could follow it, but I didn't think I could fly without Ariel, just as I didn't think I could turn myself into water again without Melusine. Even if I could have, the idea of entering that state again after watching Melusine melt made me shudder. No, I wanted warmth, and not just the warmth from a fire, but the comfort of warm flesh.

The answer was there, but I kept circling around it. Will Hughes. He had shown me how to call him. But should I? I heard Dee's accusations – *Once he's contaminated your blood, you long for more. He's gotten you hooked* – as clearly as if Dee sat beside me. It was true that I'd acted like a possessed woman last night. Had that been Will's plan? Was he using me to get to the box? Did I want to call him now because he had enslaved me with that first bite?

I ran my thumb over my fingers again and again, debating whether to call him. A voice kept repeating in my head, *What other choice do you have?* It was Will's voice and I knew it might be lying to me . . . no, I didn't really have any choice, but that wasn't the reason I'd call him. It was desire, pure and simple, that finally made me snap my fingers together.

The flame leapt higher than before, startling me. I must have stoked it by running my thumb across my fingertips for so long – or maybe it was my desire that fed it. I blew on it and it shot into the sky through the smoke hole, beyond the barrier of my pyramid, where it exploded in a burst of fireworks. My desire writ large across the night sky for all the world to see. I might as well have posted it on Twitter.

There was nothing to do now but wait, which I did with agonizing impatience as minutes passed by. Maybe he wouldn't see it. Maybe he'd see it and not come. . . .

I felt something stir the night air. A shadow moved under the boughs of the pine tree. A dark shape separated from the shadow the tree cast on the lawn. Will, in a long black overcoat that billowed behind him like a cape, walked toward me, a dark figure that remained dark as he approached the fire without catching any reflection of the light. Was he made up of such dark stuff that not even the light could touch him? But then I realized the firelight didn't touch him because of the screen I'd erected. He scanned the lawn, his pale face tense and alert, without seeing me. Well, at least I didn't have to be embarrassed that I was naked.

'Garet?' he called at last.

'I'm here.'

His head swung around and he looked directly at me – he had the senses of a tracking animal. He looked directly into my eyes – I felt sure he saw me – but then he looked an inch to the right and his mouth twisted into a smile. 'Ah, you've mastered the spell of misdirection,' he said. 'You're learning fast.'

I thought I detected a trace of bitterness in his voice. Was he afraid I'd learned enough not to trust him? All of Dee's warnings came back to me.

'Not fast enough to get me out of here. . . . Um . . . would you mind lending me your coat?'

'My coat? Ah, you must have met Melusine and learned the trick of turning into water.' He took off his long black overcoat and ran his hand across the fabric. 'Hm . . . I'm afraid this will feel rough against your delicate skin. Here.' He unbuttoned his white dress shirt and took it off. His skin was as white as the fabric and gleamed like cold marble in the starlight. 'You'll have to say something again so I'll know where you are,' he said.

'Marco.'

'Polo,' he replied, grinning as he dropped the shirt an inch from the barrier of the dome.

I reached out of the dome and took the shirt. I saw his eyes widen as it must have disappeared in front of him. The fine polished cotton slid over my arms like cool water. My hands were shaking as I did the buttons, but I wasn't as cold anymore.

'Are you going to invite me into your parlor?'

'I'm not sure I know how to do that,' I said, equivocating. What I really wasn't sure about was whether I *should* do it.

'You simply have to give me your hand.'

I stood up. He was standing only a few inches from me, but he couldn't see me. I looked into the wide silver eyes and followed the chiseled line of his cheekbone down to his jaw, his collarbones, the sweep of his broad chest, the sculpted ridges of his abdominal muscles . . . he didn't look like a creature who had been dead for four hundred years. He looked alive . . . and dangerous. Was it really a good idea to invite him into my . . . *parlor*, as he called it. But then I had called him here and I still needed his help.

I extended my hand outside the silver wall of the dome. His eyes lit on it as soon as it appeared, but instead of taking it right away he bowed. 'Thank you, my lady,' he said. Then he laid his hand in mine and stepped across the silver screen.

As soon as he was inside the dome his skin, which had been white a moment ago, turned gold in the glow of the fire. I could feel warmth radiating off him.

'You're warm,' I said, stepping back and sitting down by the fire. 'Does that mean . . . ?'

'Yes, it means I've fed recently.' He sat down beside me, leaving a few inches between us. 'You have nothing to fear from me.'

'I see. So I have nothing you want.'

'I wouldn't say that.' He lifted his hand to my face, but I turned my head away from him before he touched me.

'You want the box, don't you?' I asked.

His hand froze in the air. 'Did Dee tell you that?'

'He said that you want the box to free you from immortality. Is that true? Does the box have the power to make you' – I turned my head toward him so I could see his face – 'human?'

He flinched. A flash of red moved across his silver eyes, like a streak of sunset across the horizon, then subsided. 'Yes, that part's true. Dee used the box to summon the demon who turned me into . . . *this*. But Marguerite also used the box to summon the creature that turned her into a mortal. I believe that the box might lead me back to that creature . . . or at least to the place where it dwells. Can you blame me for wanting to be human again when you look at me like that . . . as if I were a monster?'

'I don't see you as a monster. But perhaps you see me as a means for finding the box.'

'I confess when you first showed up at my apartment and told me that you had found the box, I wondered if you were the incarnation of Marguerite come back to save me. But then when I saw your horror at what I was, I wondered if you hadn't been sent to torture me. It feels like torture, to be offered a chance to be with you, but to know I can't take it. If you did find the box, if you did take it from Dee . . . would you blame me for wanting to use it to become human again?' He sighed and his hand, still balanced in the air like a hummingbird, lit on my face. A vision sparked under his touch – like the vision I'd seen earlier of Marguerite and her sister Melusine. I recognized Marguerite from the earlier vision, only she was older. She stood on the shore of a lake – the same lake beside the tower I'd seen in my dream of the two swans. She held the silver box in her hands. She was calling something from the lake, the creature that could turn her into a mortal. She was frightened, but she was doing it so that she would be with Will. I could feel the love she had for him in every cell of my body, as if it had been encoded there with my DNA. I leaned into his touch. He slipped his hand under my chin, tilted my face up, and touched his lips to the edge of my jaw. 'Would you blame me for wanting to be with you like this?' he murmured into my skin. I waited for his mouth to slide down my neck, but instead he found my mouth.

His lips pressed against mine, opening them. I melted into the warmth of his mouth and felt the heat of his skin as it touched mine. *A heat that came from feeding on someone else's blood.* I pulled back and traced the vein on his throat with my finger. 'Can we . . . ?' I began, feeling the blood rush to my face. 'Can we be together without . . . ?'

'Without you becoming like me? It's . . . difficult. If we make love, I'll want to drink from you. But you're not under my power here.' He waved his hand at the silver dome above us. 'This dome is of your making. I have no power here. It's your choice. You don't have to become like me.'

'Even if you drink from me?'

He inhaled sharply, a gasp that made his skin tremble. 'Not if I'm careful . . . only . . .'

'Only what?'

He buried his head in my neck, grazed my throat with his teeth. I strained against him.

'Only it will be hard to stop once I start,' he said, his voice hoarse.

I shivered and closed my eyes. I saw Marguerite again, standing at the shore of the dark lake calling a super-natural creature to make her mortal so she could be with the man she loved. I didn't have half as much to fear as she'd had.

'I trust you,' I said, opening my eyes. 'I trust you not to hurt me.'

He raised his head. His eyes were wide and burning red at the center, his skin glowed gold in the firelight, his lips were parted, the tips of his fangs showing. With one swift motion he slid me down onto the ground and pressed him-self against me. I ran my hand down his back, feeling his skin beginning to cool despite the heat of the fire. I stroked my hand along his hip bones to the waistband of his pants. He guided my hand to buttons and zippers and then below his waistband. I understood then why the rest of his skin was cooling and where all his blood had gone. I felt the length of him rub against me and I arched up to meet him. And then, just as he entered me, I felt his teeth pierce the skin at the base of my throat. A flood of heat coursed through my body . . . then I felt the same heat moving through him. He was inside every inch of me . . . just as I was inside him. We moved like one person rocked by one tide, like water moving again and again against the shore.

When he pulled his mouth away from my throat, we both cried out with the same voice. It was the cry of the swan that rose from the lake when its mate was shot, the banshee cry that rocked the castle walls of Lusignan. A cry that turned every bone in my body into water.

The Red Shoes

We lay together by the fire until it burned down to ashes, Will's coat draped over both of us now like a blanket. I lay on my side, his body curled protectively against my back, his skin warmer than the fire in front of me. I told him about finding Dee's lair and how he'd ejected Melusine and me into the water after he vanished.

'He may not have been physically there at all,' Will said. 'Over the years I've found that he's able to project himself into different surroundings. He uses each place as an observation post.'

'But then we're no closer to finding him?'

'There might be clues in what you saw there to find where he really is. It's remarkable that you found one of his observation posts at all.'

'It seems a small gain for the price.' I told him how I'd dragged Melusine to the island and watched her melt, and of the vision I'd had of Marguerite kneeling beside a pool looking down at Melusine. I showed him the Poland Spring bottle that held Melusine's essence.

'I suppose they could have been sisters,' he said. 'Marguerite told me very little about her origins, but it would explain . . .' His voice trailed off. He was quiet for so long that I turned to look at him. He was staring up at the sky, but he looked as though he were contemplating scenes farther away than the stars.

'Explain what?'

'Remember when I told you that I followed Marguerite to France?' I nodded although he still wasn't looking at me. He didn't need my response, though, the story was already calling him. 'When she left London, I went to her abandoned lodgings. There I found a painting of an old church in Paris. It was the only clue I had, so I went there. I spent weeks visiting that church, hoping that she would come, but there was no sign of her. Just as I was going to give up, I received a sign there that led me to another site. I thought she would be there, but instead I found another sign . . . that led me to *another* place. I believed that she had left these signs for me and devised the chase as a test of my love and that once I found her she would relent and grant me immortality. I followed her all over France. One of the places the signs led me to – not the last, but near to it – was the Château of Lusignan, the legendary home of Melusine.'

'You think she left that sign because she was related to Melusine?' I asked.

'It's possible. Several of the places the signs led me to were springs . . . or sacred wells above which churches had been built. The place where I finally found Marguerite was a tower beside a sacred pool in which lived a creature who could grant eternal life . . . or take it away. I think that creature had been one of her sisters too.'

I thought of my vision of Marguerite standing beside a pool, summoning a creature who lived beneath the water to make her mortal. 'I think I dreamed of that place,' I told Will.

'I dream about it every day when I close my eyes at dawn. It was the last place on earth where I was ever happy. I spent three days there with Marguerite, convinced that I had found the fountain of youth.' He laughed bitterly, a sound that made me feel suddenly cold. 'On the third night she made me stay in the tower while she spent the night beside the pool. She came back exhausted and fell into a deep sleep. While she slept, I stole the silver box and the ring and took them to John Dee. I thought it was what I had to do to become immortal and live with her forever.'

'But she had already become mortal,' I said. 'That night must have been when she summoned the creature from the lake to make herself mortal. That's the vision I saw. I could feel how frightened she was, but she did it because she loved you.'

He looked at me for the first time since he had begun his story. 'You must think I'm a fool.'

'We all do foolish things. It seems to me you've suffered for your mistakes more – and for longer – than most.'

He laughed. 'Yes, that's one way of looking at it. The night she found me in Paris she told me that she'd given up her immortality for my sake and she was pledged to destroy my kind was the worst moment of my then short life. I spent years – decades – searching for her. I waited for months in the church where I had found the first sign, but no sign appeared to me. Marguerite had told me that the path to the Summer Country always changed and that unless you started in the church and followed the signs, you could never find it, but still I tried to find the pool by which we had spent those three nights, but in vain. It was as if it had never existed. It was maddening. I truly thought at times that I *had* gone mad. I wondered if I had dreamt up Marguerite.' He cradled my face in his hand and looked into my eyes. 'When you walked into my apartment, it was the first time in four hundred years that I felt anything resembling hope – hope that I could be mortal again.'

His eyes burned into mine, but the hand that lay against my face was cold. My blood was already cooling in his veins. Soon he'd feel the cold of the grave again. It was unbearable to think of him suffering that.

'Is there any reason why you can't just continue to' – I struggled for the right phrase – 'feed from me?'

He stroked my hair away from my neck and touched his lips against the new wound there. 'It will get harder and harder for me not to drink more each time. Already I'm addicted to your taste.' He ran his tongue over the bite marks and I felt a tingling sensation on my skin that crept into my veins. 'And the more I drink from you, the more you will grow dependent on the venom I release into your system. Now it heals your skin and takes the pain away, but like an opiate you'll want more and more of it. I'm afraid that vampire/human intimacy doesn't usually end well for the human.'

I thought of what it would be like to never walk outside during the day, to hunt for blood, and to live forever. Last

night I had thought it didn't sound so bad, but since then
I'd experienced Melusine's consciousness and felt how
weary she was of eternal life. In the brief glimpse I'd had
of Marguerite standing on the shore of the Swan Pool
(as I'd begun to think of it), I'd felt her willingness to
give up her immortality for one lifetime with the man she
loved.

'If I can get the box away from Dee, can you use it to
make yourself mortal?' I asked.

'I think so . . . only your friend Oberon won't like the
idea. He's always blamed me for Marguerite's decision to
become a mortal. He won't want me to have the box – even
for a second.'

I thought of what Dee had said about Oberon – that he
wanted the box for himself to control the human race and
to make the fey powerful once more. 'Well, it won't be up to
him,' I said, clasping the hand Will held to my face with my
own hand. 'If he needs me to get the box, then he has to
listen to what I want done with it. And what I want' – I
pressed my lips against Will's – 'is to be able to do this over
and over again.'

'Again?' he asked, stroking his hand down the curve of
my hip. 'At this rate you'll be a vampire in a week.' He
wrapped his arms around me and drew me hard against
him. 'We'd better find that box soon.'

Although I couldn't see any change in the sky, Will knew
when dawn was approaching. 'We have to go,' he told me.
'I have just enough time to get you back.'

The fire had burnt down to ashes, but the four spiral

eyes still glowed in the grass. I wasn't sure at first how to put them out, but when I waved my hand over them, the silver faded to gray, then white, and then turned to mist, leaving no sign on the grass. Then I picked up the water bottle that held what was left of Melusine and turned to Will, wondering for the first time how exactly he was going to get me home.

'The boat's just around the bend,' he said.

'Boat? I didn't know you came on a boat.'

'As I may have mentioned, I don't fly. But I do keep a boat at the West Seventy-ninth Street Boat Basin and it's very fast.'

When we reached the dock, I saw what he meant. Every line of the sleek craft had been designed for speed. Even moored, it rode the waves impatiently. The name on the bow was *Marguerite*.

Will helped me on board, then went down below. He came back with a pair of jeans and a striped fisherman's sweater, which I put on over his shirt. He made a call on his cell phone before untying the boat and steering out into the bay. 'I've told my driver to meet us at the Chelsea Piers. He'll take you home from there. I regret that I won't be able to escort you there myself.'

'You're very old-fashioned, you know,' I said, laughing and shaking my hair free in the sharp salt breeze. 'I hardly need an escort.'

'You tracked Dee down to one of his observation posts. He knows you're getting closer. Once he realizes you're still alive, he'll try to kill you before you can find him again. I don't like the thought of leaving you alone.'

'I won't be alone. My friend Jay's at the house.' I
laughed. 'I guess he's not the best protection.'

Will shook his head. 'Your friend Jay is very fond of you.
I believe he would defend you to the death – only I'm
afraid he wouldn't last long against John Dee.'

Will's words came back to me when I got home. I called
Jay's name as I walked up the stairs, my voice echoing
hollowly in the stairwell. No one was in the living room or
the bedroom, or the little room that my father used as a
study. The door to the bathroom was closed.

'Jay?' I called, knocking on the door. 'Are you in there?'
Visions of Jay falling asleep in the bathtub, slipping under
the water, made my hand clammy as I turned the knob. My
eyes went straight to the old-fashioned claw-foot tub. The
shower curtain was pushed back far enough that I could
see it was empty. Someone must have used it recently,
though, because there was a pile of wet towels on the
floor. . . . Had Jay brought his own towels with him? I was
pretty sure my father used only white towels, and these
were a floral red and pink. And soaking. I noticed then
that the shower curtain was moving slightly, stirred by a
breeze from the open window above the tub, which was
half-hidden by the shower curtain. Maybe water had
gotten in . . . although it hadn't rained on Governors Island
last night . . . and Jay had put the towels on the floor to
clean up.

I closed the window, then knelt down to pick up
the towels. The floral pattern on one turned into
splotches of blood. I looked down at the floor. The tile was

smeared with blood, even the grout was red with it.

My heart pounding, I got to my feet and left the bathroom, still holding a bloody towel, then crossed my father's living room to the phone. My idea was to call an ambulance, but when I got the phone in my hand, I realized I couldn't call an ambulance for a bloody towel. Then I looked down at the phone and saw that the message light was on. I jabbed at the PLAY MESSAGES button with a shaking finger. The machine's digitized voice told me I had twenty-two new messages.

I let out a relieved breath when I heard Jay's voice. *He's okay,* I thought, as I listened to his characteristic hemming and hawing, maybe he'd cut himself shaving or . . . *something* . . . and was calling to tell me not to freak out when I saw all that blood in the bathroom. 'Um . . . Garet . . . I've been trying your cell phone . . . yeah, this is Jay.' Jay, God bless him, was the master of the long rambling message. He'd once left me a fifteen-minute voice mail telling me the plot to a silent movie he'd just seen in his film class. 'But I guess you're not getting those messages, because I think we would have heard from you by now. So when you get this message . . .' A sound in the background interrupted him, something that sounded like a loudspeaker making an announcement in an echoing hallway. 'Uh . . . yeah . . . well . . . you should get over here as soon as possible.' The message ended.

'Where's *here,* Jay?' I shouted at the phone while waiting for the next message on the queue. It was Jay again.

'Hey, Garet, I realized after I hung up that if you hadn't gotten my previous messages you might not know where I am . . . or what's happened. Anyway, I'm at St. Vincent's. It's Beck—' His voice cracked on Becky's name. 'She tried to kill herself. Please get here as soon as you can.'

I ran to the hospital without bothering to change my clothes. Only when I was riding the elevator up (to the psych ward – that's where the information desk told me Becky was) did I realize I smelled like the East River, a swampy miasma that seemed to capture my situation perfectly. I was slowly being drowned. Dee had got to my father, and then he'd got to my best friend. Who would be next? Would I lose everyone and everything if I continued to try to stop him?

I found Becky's room, but when I first stepped in, I was sure I had gotten the number wrong. The person in the bed couldn't be Becky. Sure, Becky was short, but this person barely swelled the tightly drawn sheets. And when had Becky ever lain that still? I'd shared a bed with her on lots of overnights and spent the night fending off her thrashing limbs. This person lay flat on her back, her white, muffled arms lying on top of the sheets on either side of her like large cotton Q-tips. Even her hair, which usually bristled with electricity, lay limp and dead against the white hospital sheets.

But then I noticed the slumped form in the chair beside the bed and recognized Jay. The minute he saw me he sprang to his feet – Jay, who ambled through life, *sprang* to his feet and threw his arms around me.

'Garet, thank God. I thought something had happened to you too.'

'I'm okay. I lost my phone . . . and I couldn't get home last night. . . . Damn, Jay! What happened? Is she going to be all right? Has she been unconscious since . . .' I looked down at Becky's heavily swaddled wrists. The bandages went up to the crooks of her elbows.

'She was out when I found her,' he said. 'The EMTs said she'd lost a lot of blood, but she came to for a little while after they gave her a transfusion.'

'You found her?' I looked hard at Jay. He'd fainted in biology class when we had to prick our fingers to test our blood types. I noticed dark stains on the knees of his jeans and a red smear on the cuff of his plaid flannel shirt. 'Oh, Jay, I'm so sorry. What happened?'

He shook his head, his hair swaying lankly against his pale cheeks. He had dark rings under his eyes. 'She came over last night to talk about the record contract. I thought she'd come to argue with me some more, but she was . . . contrite.'

'Contrite? Becky?'

'Yeah, I know. It was really weird. She brought a bottle of wine and told me she was sorry she'd been trying to pressure me into signing the contract. She said it didn't matter, that getting a big contract wasn't worth it if it was going to screw up our friendship. That it was okay if we spent the rest of our lives warming up for bigger bands and playing small-town gigs. We drank the whole bottle and watched a movie on TV . . . *The Red Shoes* . . . which was funny, because it wasn't in the newspaper listings or the cable guide. Becky was really excited because she said it was her favorite movie. She even insisted that we TiVo it for you. Becky opened up another bottle of wine that we found in your dad's cupboard and we microwaved popcorn. It was nice . . . like those nights in high school when we used to stay up late watching old movies. It was foggy outside and Becky said that made it cozy—'

'Foggy? It wasn't foggy where I was,' I said, remembering the clear sky above Governors Island.

Jay gave me a funny look. 'I don't know where *you* were last night, but it was foggy here in the Village. We couldn't even see out the windows. Becky said it was a good thing we weren't watching a horror movie . . . only, well I'd forgotten how creepy that movie is . . . you know that scene where the girl in the story puts on the red shoes and she dances herself to death? Well, Becky said sometimes she feels like she's wearing those red shoes and she just wishes she could stop . . . stop touring, stop promoting the band, stop worrying over whether we were going to make it big or not. Just stop. And then when we got to the scene where Moira Shearer throws herself in front of the train, I noticed that Becky was crying. I should have realized something was wrong, but somehow it all just made me tired. I kind of felt like I'd been dancing my feet off like Moira Shearer. I fell asleep on the couch, and when I woke up, Becky wasn't there. I almost went back to sleep, but I heard a sound coming from the bathroom. A tapping noise. It got all confused in my head with the movie and I thought it was the ballerina from the story . . . dancing. It was so annoying I finally got up and went to see . . .'

He covered his face with his hands as if he could block out the memory of what he'd seen in the bathroom.

'The tapping came from the shower curtain blowing in the wind. Becky must have opened the window, because I'm pretty sure it was closed earlier. Maybe she thought about jumping, but not even Becky could fit out that tiny window. She'd found a razor blade in the medicine cabinet. She'd lined the floor with towels, so the blood wouldn't get on the tile. You know how neat she can be.' Jay gulped air. I put my arm around him and patted his back until he was able to talk again. 'I wrapped the towels around her wrists as tight as I could and called 911 right away. The EMT said that if they hadn't gotten to her, she'd have been dead in another half hour. When I think that I almost turned over on the couch and went back to sleep—'

'But you didn't, Jay! You got up and saved her.' I didn't know how to explain to Jay what forces he'd been battling to stay awake. I was sure that the fog Becky had let in the apartment had both coaxed her into trying to take her own life and lulled Jay asleep. 'And it's not your fault she did this—'

'My fault . . .' The voice came from the bed. Jay and I looked down and saw that Becky's eyes were open. They looked huge in her white face. 'I'm so sorry . . .'

'It's okay, Becky.' I sat down on the bed next to her and reached for her hand. Her fingers felt limp and cold. Looking down at those huge eyes in that pale face reminded me of Melusine as she had melted into the rock. I squeezed Becky's hand as if I could keep her from slipping away by holding on to her tightly. 'You didn't know what you were doing.'

Becky licked her dry, chapped lips. 'But I did. I just thought it would be easier. . . . I felt tired of trying so hard. I mean, who am I kidding, trying to be a rock star? I should have gone to law school like my mother said . . . Oh, *shit*! Is my mother here? Does she know?'

'She's on her way up from Fort Lauderdale,' Jay said. 'I'm sorry, Beck. I had to call her.'

Tears slid down Becky's face. I plucked a tissue from the box on the bedside table and dabbed at them. 'This is going to kill her. What was I thinking?'

'You weren't thinking, sweetie. You were' – the words *under a spell* occurred to me, but I bit them back – 'under too much pressure. You'll get some rest . . . and some help . . . and you'll get better. I promise.'

Becky nodded, but her eyes were already drooping closed again. I sat by her, holding her hand, trying to think how I was going to make good on that promise.

I stayed with Becky through most of the morning, taking turns with Jay watching her. When Jay relieved me, I went to see my father. I had a bad moment when I walked into his room and found it empty, but then a nurse came in and told me that my father and his friend had gone to the sun-room. I hurried down the hall and found Roman sitting up in his wheelchair playing bridge with Zach and two Chinese ladies whom he introduced as Minnie and Sue. His color looked good and he was smiling. After they finished their hand, I took Zach aside and told him about Becky.

'Poor thing,' Zach said, shaking his head. 'I know she's been under a lot of pressure.'

'Has she?' I asked, but then without waiting for an answer, went on, 'I don't know if we should tell Roman. I'm afraid it will remind him of when Santé killed himself.' As I said it, I realized that maybe I shouldn't have told Zach. I'd always worried that he might be suicidal.

But although he looked saddened by the news, Zach seemed remarkably calm. 'I see what you mean,' he said. 'It *is* similar. Santé killed himself just before his biggest show, and Becky's band is right on the edge of making it really big.' He smiled ruefully. 'Sometimes I think it's easier to be a failure.'

The remark startled me. All these years that Zach hadn't painted, I'd thought he was lacking in inspiration. I'd never considered that he was protecting himself from heartache by not trying too hard.

'You're not a failure, Zach,' I said, putting my hand on his arm. 'You're . . . family. I don't know what I would have done these last few days without you.'

Zach's eyes widened and gleamed. I was instantly afraid he might start weeping, but he squared his shoulders and pulled himself out of his characteristic slouch. 'Don't worry about Roman and Becky,' he said. 'I'll keep an eye on both of them. You do whatever you have to do. I'll hold down the fort here.'

Despite Zach's assurances I hated to leave Becky, but at eleven a nurse delivered a message to me from Oberon.

Meet me at 2:00 on the steps in front of City Hall. Wear your welding clothes.

My welding clothes? Then I remembered that the only elemental I'd yet to meet was fire. Will had said that Oberon was saving the *fiercer guides* for last. I couldn't begin to imagine what would be more dangerous than jumping off the Empire State Building or traveling through the city's water system in purely molecular form, but I did know that I'd be better prepared for whatever was in store for me if I got some sleep.

What finally prompted me to get out was spotting Joe Kiernan. I was coming back from the cafeteria when I saw him heading into Becky's room. I stopped in the hallway and waved Jay down when he came out immediately afterward.

'What's *he* doing here?' I asked. 'Does he think what happened to Becky had something to do with the robbery?'

Jay stared at me. 'How could he?' Then he shrugged. 'He came by earlier too. He said he just wanted to see, as a friend, how Becky was doing.'

I didn't trust Detective Kiernan to do anything casually, but I couldn't imagine how he'd know that Becky's suicide attempt was connected to John Dee – and I wasn't about to try to explain it to him. 'I think you'd better keep an eye on him,' I told Jay. 'I have to go home for a while.'

Jay nodded. 'I think you'd better get some rest. You're beginning to sound paranoid.'

I went home and took a long hot shower (in the third-floor bathroom; I didn't think I'd be using my dad's bathroom for a while). I put on sweatpants and an old T-shirt and then, for no good reason, Will's shirt over that. When I lay down, though, I heard Jay's voice describing what had happened last night.

Becky and I had watched *The Red Shoes* at a Film Forum festival when we were sixteen. She'd loved it so much that she'd dragged me back to see it a second time – and gone back by herself a third. I'd liked the movie too, but I'd thought at the time it was strange how obsessed with it she became. It *was* peculiar that it had come on last night when it wasn't even on the TV schedule. *Becky was really excited. . . . She even insisted that we TiVo it for you.*

I got out of bed and padded barefoot downstairs to the second floor. When I opened the door to my dad's apartment, I was assailed by the coppery tang of blood. I almost shut the door and fled up the stairs, but I went to the couch instead and sat down facing the TV. There were two open bottles, two empty glasses, and a large bowl on the coffee table. I picked up one bottle of wine and read the label: Woop Woop, an Australian Shiraz that the liquor store on Hudson sold and Becky loved to buy because it was cheap and she loved saying the name. That would have been the bottle she brought. I picked up the other bottle, the one Jay said they'd found in my dad's cupboard. The bottle was so covered in dust that I had to wipe off the label to read it. *Le Vin du Temps Perdu*. The wine of lost time. I was pretty sure that it wasn't a bottle my father had bought, but how had Dee managed to sneak it into the house? Had the shadow-men left it the night of the burglary? I lifted the bottle and noticed a little was still left. I poured a few inches of deep

314 • Lee Carroll

red liquid into one of the empty glasses and held it up to my nose. A heady aroma of chocolate and cinnamon wafted up from the glass. Before I could remind myself why it was not a good idea, I took a sip.

The wine was so dry that it seemed to evaporate as soon as it hit my tongue and turn into a mist that filled my mouth . . . a mist that tasted of chocolate and lavender and some unnamable spice. I took another sip and tried to roll the flavor on my tongue before it evaporated. I closed my eyes and I was standing in a vineyard in southern France. I could feel the sun on my skin and smell lavender in the air . . .

I snapped my eyes open and pushed the wineglass away. *Le Vin du Temps Perdu,* indeed! Talk about the dangers of drink! And Becky had drunk a whole bottle of this . . . while watching a movie that shouldn't have been on.

I looked around for the remote and then dug in the couch cushions until I found it. I switched on the TV and pressed the button for the DVR menu. The most recent recording was *Bringing Up Baby* with Katharine Hepburn and Cary Grant, but it was the only recording made last night so I selected it and hit PLAY. I fast-forwarded through a commercial for a Turner Classic Movies DVD collection until I saw Robert Osborne, TCM's movie critic, standing in front of his brick fireplace in his clubby den full of oil paintings and overstuffed red chairs. Becky and Jay would have watched the intro – Jay loved Robert Osborne and could do a pitch-perfect imitation of his glib movie intros. I hit PLAY.

'Hi, I'm Robert Osborne and our movie tonight is' – the

screen flickered for half a second and Robert Osborne's broad, friendly face froze. His hooded eyes (*You can tell he's spent his life in dark movie theaters,* Jay always said) seemed to darken – 'our movie for tonight is Michael Powell and Emeric Pressburger's *The Red Shoes* with the incomparable Moira Shearer as the doomed ballerina, Victoria Page, and the devastatingly charming Anton Walbrook as the diabolical impresario Boris Lermontov.'

I leaned closer to the set. Something was wrong with the sound quality. Robert Osborne's words didn't quite match the movements of his mouth. Or maybe I was just tired. I pulled an old afghan throw over my knees and slid down in the couch, lulled by Robert Osborne's mellifluous voice as he explained that the movie's producers had wanted to create a manifesto for the power of art. He described with relish how the *diabolical* (he used the word several times) Lermontov drove Vicky Page to suicide.

Funny, I thought, Robert Osborne didn't usually give out spoilers like that. But it was okay since I had seen the film before. I hadn't remembered, though, how hallucinatory and vivid were the dream sequences in which Vicky Page reenacted the story of the girl who puts on a pair of red shoes crafted by a mysterious shoemaker and then dances herself to death. It was downright psychedelic . . . and Freudian. The face of the shoemaker became the face of her lover and then the face of Lermontov. I hadn't noticed before how much Lermontov looked like John Dee . . . but of course I hadn't met John Dee when I first saw the movie.

I could see how the movie must have affected Becky. In

her own way, Becky was as driven to succeed as the ballerina Vicky Page. She even looked like Moira Shearer with her abundant red curls. And it suddenly struck me that the actor who played the composer who falls in love with Vicky looked a lot like Jay.

I must have fallen asleep for a bit because the next thing I knew I was sitting up, wineglass in hand, watching the penultimate scene in which Lermontov tells Vicky she must choose between the life of a great dancer and the mundane life of a housewife. I dimly remembered arguing with Becky about this scene when we first saw the film.

'Why does Vicky have to choose?' I'd asked.

'Because she does!' Becky had answered. 'No one gets to have it both ways.'

Now I saw Lermontov's – and Becky's – point. Most of the great artists were no good at love – unless they had relationships with people who subjugated their own desires and goals to theirs. People who tried to lead ordinary lives – like Zach and Jay and me – failed in their art. In truth, we failed at everything. I'd been so busy running around trying to save the world that I'd ignored the signs that my best friend was in trouble. Now she was in the hospital along with my father. How many of the people I loved would have to suffer because of my carelessness? I really wasn't any good at art *or* life, I thought as I watched Vicky Page run from the theater and throw herself in front of the Paris-bound train. I could see why she did it; it was just too hard to choose. At least now she could take off those red shoes and rest.

I picked up the remote to turn off the set, but Robert Osborne came back on. He was sitting in his red chair in front of a crackling fire with a glass of red wine in his hand.

'*The Red Shoes* was a failure when it was released in 1948,' he said. 'Many moviegoers couldn't stomach the film's final message – that it's better to die for art than to live for nothing. But we know what the right choice is, don't we?' Robert Osborne smiled – even the woman in the portrait above the fireplace seemed to smile – and I nodded in agreement. I was sitting on the edge of the couch now, so close to the TV set that I could see the amber glint in Robert Osborne's eyes. He was looking right at me, waiting for me to do the right thing. It *was* the right thing. After all, Robert Osborne knew *everything*. It occurred to me that Robert Osborne had been sent to me as a spirit guide. This was an unfamiliar, and vaguely uncomfortable, sensation, but totally compelling. I needed to follow Robert Osborne.

I got up and walked into the bathroom. The razor that Becky had used was still on the rim of the sink. As I picked it up, I met my eyes in the mirror. My pupils had swollen to cover all of my irises, making my eyes look black and empty, a cold emptiness that rose up inside me like water filling up a dark well. I would drown in that emptiness if I didn't do something soon.

I looked down and saw that my left hand was holding the razor blade over my right wrist. *Funny*, I thought, as I dragged the blade tentatively across my skin, *I'm right-handed*. A faint crimson line opened up in my skin. *Letting out the dark*. I could hear the surge of my blood, hammering against my skin as if eager to get out. But the sound came from the bathtub. It was the shower curtain rings rattling against the rod. Jay had said something about the shower curtain . . . the sound of the curtain moving in the breeze had woken him up . . . only the window wasn't open now. I had closed it when I first came into the bathroom this morning. I stared at the curtain, the hand that held the razor blade arrested above my wrist, puzzled. Later I would wonder why it was this discrepancy that got to me – not the appearance of a bottle of wine called Lost Time or the new décor on the TCM set or the oddity of Robert Osborne suggesting suicide – but a shower curtain moving in a windless room. I'm still not sure why, but something in its *wrongness* penetrated the black fog that had swamped my brain.

I put the razor blade down on the edge of the sink, stepped over to the tub, and looked down. There, sprawled on the bottom of the tub was a perfect miniature version of Vicky Page in the last scene of *The Red Shoes* – from wild red hair to tattered, stained tutu and red shoes. I bent down to look closer and recognized Lol. She lay limply on the bottom of the porcelain tub, one tiny hand jerking the edge of the shower curtain. When she saw me she opened her mouth, but no sound came out. Then she let go of the shower curtain and pointed at her feet.

What I had thought were red shoes were actually Lol's bare feet stained red with blood.

The smaller fey can't stand the touch of iron. I recalled what Oberon had said in the park when he scattered the remains of the sylphs. And blood was full of iron.

I quickly scooped her up and carried her to the sink. I rinsed her feet in cold water, then filled the sink with water so she could soak her feet in it. While she sat on the edge of the sink, I found a Band-Aid in the medicine cabinet and put it on over my scratched wrist. When I looked back down into the basin, I saw images forming in the water, just as I had in the park with Melusine. So she *had* left me with one skill, only instead of seeing the present, I saw the past in the water: Lol finding Becky in the bathroom and trying to stanch the blood, but when the blood had got on her feet, she had fallen in the tub. She'd rattled the shower curtain to alert Jay.

'Thank you,' I said. 'You saved Becky – and me.' She squawked and splashed water in my face. 'I don't know what I was thinking.'

Lol folded her arms over her chest and huffed. Then she flexed her wings and flew into the living room and hovered above the TV set. The image of Robert Osborne was still frozen on the screen, only it wasn't Robert Osborne. It was John Dee.

'He tried to make Becky kill herself and then he did the same thing to me.'

Lol fluttered in the air and pointed at something on the screen.

'Yes,' I said. 'I see. It's John Dee's lair. The paintings and the rugs are the same as the ones I saw in the cavern under the river. I'll tell Oberon – damn!' I looked at the time on the cable box. It was 1:33. I had less than half an hour to make it down to City Hall. 'I have to go meet the fire elemental,' I told Lol, and then, remembering that she was a fire fey, added, 'Do you want to come with me?'

Lol's tawny skin turned powder white. She shook her head, for once rendered mute. She had dive-bombed a vampire and risked the contagion of poisonous blood. I wondered what could possibly scare her so badly.

The Exchequer

Riding the subway to City Hall, I couldn't quite shake the dirty feel of Dee's presence in my brain. If the shadowmen's breaking into my home felt like a violation, this felt like mind rape. The worst part was wondering if he was still inside me, subtly influencing my thoughts in ways I couldn't imagine. When I looked at my fellow passengers on the subway, I sensed fatigue and despair, but was I projecting my own bad mood on them? Were the murky auras I saw hallucinations? Were the voices I'd heard since my flight with Ariel my own demons speaking to me? Was I imagining everything?

Perhaps you're simply losing your mind, a voice that sounded somewhere between John Dee's and Robert Osborne's said inside my head. I'd taken each spectacular manifestation I'd experienced as proof that what was happening was real, but what if it was all a hallucination? How could I possibly know?

I got off at Park Place. As I was leaving the subway station, I passed several mosaic eyes embedded in the walls. I'd seen them before, but today I glanced at them nervously, as if they were following my progress. I couldn't quite shake that feeling of being watched as I walked east on Park Place. Even seeing Oberon waiting for me – in a beige sweatshirt and baseball cap – at the security checkpoint on Broadway did nothing to reassure me of my sanity. He could simply be part of the whole elaborate hallucination. I greeted him politely, though, just in case.

'I'm sorry about your friend Becky,' he said. 'I knew Dee might try to get to you through one of your loved ones, but I thought it would be your father, whom I'm watching much of the time at the hospital, or Jay, whom I told Lol to watch.'

'Becky would have died if not for Lol.' I told him how I'd found Lol in the bathtub with her feet soaked in blood. I didn't tell him, though, about my own close call with the razor blade; my long sleeves covered the Band-Aid. I saw him studying me closely so I quickly went on to give a full report of everything that had happened yesterday with Melusine. A shadow of pain crossed his face when I told him about Melusine melting into the rock, and he had no idea what could be done to bring her back from her current state inside the bottle. The only question he asked me was about John Dee's lair.

'Were there any windows?'

'Windows? Why would there be windows? We were under the East River.'

Oberon shook his head. 'That was a projection of his real location into a space where he could lure you and Melusine and then flush you out into the river. He knew the salt water would destroy Melusine.'

'If you knew all that, why didn't you stop her?' I asked,

my voice rising with anger now. A group of women – also wearing beige sweatshirts and caps – glanced in our direction as they walked through the metal detectors, but no one paid much attention to us.

Oberon only laughed at my outrage. 'Stop an elemental? I'd as soon try to stop the tides of the ocean or the earth from turning. Melusine knew what she was doing. If there was anything useful you learned from that glimpse you had of Dee's lair, she'd want you to use it. If there were windows you might have seen something from them that indicated where he really was.'

I shook my head. 'The walls were covered with paintings,' I said. 'If there were any windows, they were covered.'

'Did you notice what the walls were made of?'

'Some kind of gold paneling. It was a complete waste of time – and a waste of Melusine.'

Oberon tilted his head and regarded me through his slanty green eyes. 'I doubt that. Something will come to you. But for now, we have something else to do.' He handed me a sweatshirt and baseball cap. 'Here, put these on.'

I noticed now that both the sweatshirt and the cap bore the logo of the Queens Public Libraries. 'Are these our cover?'

'I don't need cover,' he replied, 'but I thought it would be nice to show our support. A lot of the fey work in the public libraries – or use their resources. It would be terrible to see them closed.'

We told the guard that we were joining the protest on

the steps and passed through a metal detector into the courtyard. I hadn't been at City Hall since a third-grade trip and had forgotten what a pretty building it was. The limestone façade glowed in the midafternoon light. But as we approached the building, I looked up and saw that though the statue of Justice on top of the clock tower still gleamed, the sky was darkening to the east. The statue on top of the Municipal Building to the east was already obscured by fog.

As we walked past the protesters on the stairs – carrying banners that read SLOW ECONOMY = BUSY LIBRARIES and DON'T LET LIBRARIES GO DARK – Oberon started chanting, 'Save our libraries! Save our libraries.' The rest of the protesters took up the chant immediately, but we kept going, through the arched doorway, past the bronze statue of George Washington and the marble rotunda, but then instead of taking the sweeping, cantilevered stairway up, Oberon led me to a service elevator that went down to a subbasement. The elevator door opened up onto a dimly lit hallway. We turned right and walked down to the end of the corridor, where there was a door with a frosted-glass window stenciled with gold letters that read THE OFFICE OF THE EXCHEQUER OF THE ASSESSOR. A small wooden sign, hanging from a hook above the window, read ONE AT A TIME PLEASE, and another wooden sign held up by an elaborate cast-iron stand read LINE FORMS HERE. A dozen or so people stood waiting in an orderly line, each one clutching a yellowish sheet of paper in his or her hands. Oberon went to the head of the line and reached for the doorknob.

'Hey, buddy,' the beefy-looking man at the front of the line said. 'There's a line, y'know!'

'Yes, I see, Mr. . . .' Oberon plucked the sheet of paper the man held from his meaty hands. The paper, which was nearly transparent and the color of old nail clippings, crackled as though it had been ripped, but was intact. 'Mr. Arnold A. Herkimer of Kissena Boulevard, Flushing, New York,' Oberon said without looking at the sheet. I looked at the letter and saw that the name and address were correct. 'Let's see what kind of trouble you're in.'

Dear Mr. Herkimer:

You have been found to be in violation of city code #73197-PYT-C2. Please present yourself to the Office of the Exchequer of the Assessor, Room B7, City Hall, where your fine will be assessed.
    Note: All fines must be paid in coin.

Sincerely,
Ignatius T. Ashburn III
Exchequer of the Assessor

When he finished reading, Oberon held the letter up to the light, revealing a watermark of spiral lines, which began to spin. I looked away when I started getting dizzy and saw that Mr. Herkimer's eyes were moving rapidly back and forth.

'Well then,' Oberon said, handing Arnold Herkimer his letter, 'that all appears to be in order. I'll just have a word with the exchequer on behalf of your case.'

'Thank you, sir,' Arnold Herkimer said, his eyes still flicking back and forth as if he were watching a game of table tennis, 'I'd appreciate it. I can't think what I've done wrong—'

'Oh, can't you, Arnie?' Oberon clucked his tongue. 'Why don't you try while I go ahead.'

Arnold Herkimer blushed bright pink as Oberon bent down and whispered in my ear, 'He uses his ninety-seven-year-old mother's Social Security money to gamble at Atlantic City and tells her the money pays for his son's college tuition.'

Oberon opened the door, leaving Arnold Herkimer contemplating his sins. Inside was a short hallway and another door, divided horizontally in half. The top section was open onto a counter at which sat a thirtyish man in a red-striped oxford shirt, with receding ginger-colored hair and heavily freckled skin. A brass nameplate identified him as IGNATIUS T. ASHBURN III, EXCHEQUER OF THE ASSESSOR. Another sign, photocopied on pink paper, said IF YOU ARE GROUCHY, IRRITABLE, OR JUST PLAIN MEAN, THERE WILL BE A $10 CHARGE FOR PUTTING UP WITH YOU. Oberon closed the first door behind us and pulled me to one side of the narrow corridor. A young girl in skinny jeans, a leather bomber jacket, and UGG boots was standing in front of the counter rummaging in an enormous pocketbook.

'I had it just a second ago,' she said. 'Can't you just look up my case by my name?'

'No, I cannot,' the clerk said, tilting his head back so that he was literally looking down his nose at the girl. The angle revealed unusually large nostrils that widened farther as the girl started unpacking the contents of her bag on the counter. An iPhone, makeup case, and a handful of gum wrappers appeared before the ivory-colored letter was found.

'Here it is,' she said, shoving the paper across the counter. 'But I don't have any idea what it's about. I mean, I live at home when I'm not at school and my car is in my parents' names, so anything to do with it or them should go to my home address in Scarsdale.'

'This has nothing to do with your parents, Jenna Abigail Lawrence,' the clerk said, holding the paper up to the light. 'Ah, I see, a code 4801929-XNT-8R violation. That's a violation-of-privacy code.' He lowered the paper and looked across the counter at Jenna Lawrence, a thin trail of smoke curling out of his nostrils. His eyes, which were the color of cinnamon gum, had begun to revolve in the same pattern as the watermark lines on the paper. Looking at them I was overcome with a sick sense of guilt. I recalled cheating on a seventh-grade French test, a thank-you note I had never sent, and a library book I had never returned to the library. 'Your fine will be lowered if you volunteer the information yourself.'

Jenna Lawrence shifted her purse from one shoulder to another and flipped her perfectly straight, highlighted blond hair over her right shoulder. 'I really don't know what you're talking about, but if this has to do with my freshman roommate, then you just have to know that you can't believe a thing she says. I certainly never read her stupid paper on Dante—'

'No, you didn't. If you had, you might understand a thing or two about *punishment,* Miss Lawrence. No, this has to do with reading your boyfriend Scott's cell phone messages while he went into the 7-Eleven to get you an iced coffee.'

Jenna Lawrence opened her mouth. 'How—? But . . .' she spluttered. And then, finally getting some control of herself: 'Did Scott tell you that?'

'Scott has no idea that you read his cell phone messages. He does wonder, though, why you've been so angry with him.'

'He called me a spoiled brat!' Jenna wailed. 'And he told his so-called best friend from high school, Angie, that I didn't care about anything but clothes.' Jenna started digging in her bag, and Ignatius plucked a tissue from a box on the counter and handed it to her. He waited patiently while she blew her nose.

'I don't really understand how you know about this, but what are you going to do about it? You're not going to tell Scott, are you?'

'No, Jenna, but you are. And you're going to spend the summer volunteering at the battered women's shelter instead of lying on the beach in the Hamptons.'

'Okay,' Jenna said, sniffling. 'I suppose it will look good on my résumé.'

Ignatius sighed, sending a stream of smoke out of his flared nostrils. '*And* you'll spend more time with your grandmother Ruth.' He stamped the letter with a large wooden mallet. 'And of course there is a fine—' He craned his neck over the counter to look in Jenna's oversize pocketbook. When he leaned forward, I caught a glimpse of a scaly tail behind the counter. 'Is that the new iPhone?'

'Yessss . . . ,' Jenna moaned, 'but you can't—'

The tail snapped over his head, reached into Jenna's bag, and retrieved the iPhone. 'Ah, Peggle. He will be pleased.' The tail vanished behind the counter. Ignatius handed the letter back to Jenna, who held it up to look at the stamp. It was in the shape of a red dragon breathing fire into a spiral pattern that grew, glowed red, then burst into flame, incinerating the letter and singeing the ends of Jenna's hair. As she turned to leave, the look on her face was as blank as a newborn baby's.

'Will she remember any of this?' I asked Oberon, but it was Ignatius who answered.

'Only what she's supposed to do. She'll think she spent the morning browsing through Bloomingdale's and that she lost her phone in a cab. Did you need something, Oberon? As you can see, I've got a long line this morning.'

Oberon reopened the outside door and waved his hand over the gold letters on the glass. They faded and disappeared, replaced by the words JANITOR'S CLOSET. The line of people waiting outside filed down the corridor, scratching their heads. I heard Arnold Herkimer ask someone the way to the Tropicana Casino.

'Sorry, Nate, this can't wait,' Oberon said. 'Is His Honor in?'

'"His Honor"?' I echoed. 'I thought you said we weren't going to see the mayor.'

Both Ignatius and Oberon smiled. 'Oh, he's much more important than the mayor,' Ignatius answered, opening the bottom half of the door to let us in. As I stepped through the door, I saw that the lower part of the clerk's body was covered in coppery scales. When he turned around, his massive tail writhed across the linoleum floor of the tiny office. The space, small to begin with, was further cramped by numerous bulging sacks, cartons of ivory-colored paper, and what looked to be a year's supply of ramen noodles. Ignatius used his tail to sweep away a carton of paper from a low arched door fitted with several brass locks, which he unlocked using three different keys from a ring he wore around his neck. The door opened onto a dimly lit stairwell. Ignatius picked up one of the sacks and waved for us to follow him.

'He doesn't seem so bad,' I whispered to Oberon as we went through the door. 'Why is everyone so afraid of him?'

'It's not him everyone's afraid of. He's just the exchequer. It's the assessor you have to worry about. That's whom we're going to see.'

The Assessor

Although we were already in the subbasement of the building, the steps from Ignatius's office went down another two flights, through a long dimly lit corridor, then down another short flight of stairs. I was expecting another basement at the end, but when Ignatius opened the door to a barrel vault of herringboned bricks and green and white tiles, which was surmounted by a frosted glass oculus, I knew exactly where we were.

'Wow! The City Hall subway station. I've always wanted to see this!' I'd read about the station in histories of the city. Opened in 1904 and designed by Rafael Guastavino, it was called the 'crown jewel of the system.' 'I heard they closed it because the tracks were too curved to be extended.'

Ignatius and Oberon exchanged a look. 'That was the official reason,' Ignatius said, waddling across the vaulted space to a sealed doorway.

'There were also the incidents,' Oberon said.

'Incidents?' I asked.

Ignatius unlocked the door but didn't open it and turned to me. In the dim subterranean light his eyes glowed red. 'Purse snatchings, child abductions, workmen injuries, burns . . .'

'Burns?'

'From steam vents,' Oberon said. 'A confidential task force decided that the station was built over a "geologically unstable area" and was best closed to the public.'

'Since then there have been minimal incidents,' Ignatius added. 'As long as I bring him a sufficient amount of loot, he hardly ever goes afield.'

'Hardly?' Oberon asked. 'I thought you had the area secured, Ignatius.'

'There are tunnels that even I don't know about. I'm only one dragon. If you want better service, hire more help.'

'Wish I could, Nate, but we've had budget cuts too. He's here now, though, right?'

Ignatius sniffed the air, his broad nostrils dilating. 'I'd say so.' Then he opened the door and ushered us into another flight of stairs. These were cut into the granite bedrock; veins of silver and gray glimmered in the light from Ignatius's red eyes. As we descended, I noticed a strong odor rising from below us – a mixture of burnt toast, copper, and something faintly sweet. The other thing I noticed was that Ignatius was changing as we went deeper into the earth. His back hunched over more, dragging the upper part of his body farther down to the ground with each step until he was walking on all fours. A spiky ridge of scales broke through his oxford shirt along his backbone. Underneath the torn shirt his skin gleamed copper. When he reached a barred door at the bottom of the stairs and turned around, I saw that his face had turned into the long snout of a dragon. I still recognized the red eyes, the distended nostrils, and the voice, which admonished us to hurry.

'Something has him agitated,' he said, unlocking the three bolts on the door. 'We'd better see what it is.'

As the door opened, a roar filled the stairwell. It sounded like a subway train headed straight for us. I wondered how many times I'd heard the rumble of a train underfoot and it had really been this creature stirring in the bowels of the earth.

'Are you sure this is a good idea?' I whispered to Oberon. 'I mean, if he's agitated—'

'If Ddraik is agitated, then we'd better find out why,' he answered. 'He's very . . . sensitive.'

Sensitive? It wasn't the word I would have used to describe the creature I saw as I went through the door. The room was huge; like the station above, it was vaulted and tiled in Guastavino's characteristic herringbone pattern, only these tiles were encrusted with a mosaic of various metals and jewels and the top of the vault was nearly two stories high. But the creature who crouched at its center took up almost all the space. Just one of its copper-red scales was the size of a Hummer door, and the red-glowing eye that fastened on me was as large as a manhole cover. What frightened me the most, though, was that I recognized him. He was the spitting image of Jaws, the dragon I had welded out of my worst nightmares.

'Aaahhh,' he breathed, his hot breath lapping against my face. 'Garet James. I've been wanting to' – he paused to extend a long forked tongue over his crooked jaw – '*meet* you.' He huffed three times rapidly – a sound I supposed was his version of laughter.

'How does he know who I am?' I turned to ask Oberon – but I found that Oberon and Ignatius were several feet behind me in front of the doorway.

'Ddraik the Assessor knows everything,' Oberon said. 'He's a hoarder of information.'

'Knowledge is power,' the dragon roared. 'Have you brought me some?'

Ignatius tossed the sack he'd brought toward Ddraik. Coins and jewelry – I saw a Rolex smash against the floor and caught the glitter of several wedding bands – sprayed across the floor as the dragon rooted in the bag, but it was the iPhone that Ignatius had confiscated from Jenna Lawrence that he plucked out of the heap. Holding it in one six-inch claw he used the tip of his tail to touch the screen.

He chuckled. 'Snoop Dogg's twitters really crack me up.' He typed something using two claws and chuckled again. Then he whisked his tail across the screen and growled. 'The euro's bubbling up again. Sell the dollar short. The greed of these currency traders amazes me. It puts a dragon to shame.' He cracked open the iPhone like a clamshell and using two claws like a pair of tweezers delicately extracted its circuit board. He scanned the ceiling above him, blew a stream of fire at a spot until the metal glowed red-hot, and then pressed the circuit board into the molten metal. Looking up, I realized that the whole room was paved with circuit boards among the jewels and coins and melted precious metals, the copper tracings on all those circuit boards creating an intricate filigreed pattern.

'What's he making?' I hissed at Ignatius.

'A supercomputer,' Ignatius said with a sigh.

'Did you get me any more RAID cards?' Ddraik growled.

'Not yet, sir, but I've summonsed a couple of Mac employees for hacking violations and suggested they could pay their fines in terabytes.'

'Heh heh, tell them they've been pwned!' Ddraik chuckled. Then he touched the tip of his claw to one of the copper lines in the circuit board and the whole network lit up. It spanned the breadth of the vaulted ceiling, ran down the columns, and spread across the floor – a pulsing red web. Images and numbers flashed through the air, too fast for me to identify.

'Traditionally dragons hoard gold,' Oberon said. 'But since the dawn of the information age Ddraik has been hoarding data.'

'Knowledge is power,' the dragon repeated, 'at least most of the time. Every once in a while, like this past autumn, you humans screw up so badly that knowledge, and the patterns it reveals, doesn't work anymore.' He touched his claw tip to the groove again. The network pulsed and flashed even faster, until its information was an intense blue blur. Then it was nothing but blinding white light for a millisecond as if chaos had coalesced into a vision, then it went back to spewing images and numbers, but more weakly now. Almost wanly. Ddraik grinned. 'The trend is your friend,' he rumbled. 'Until it ends with no warning. But go on,' he said, fixing me with a glowing red eye. 'Ask me something.'

'Where's Dee?' I asked without a moment's hesitation.

Ddraik reached a claw up into the air and intercepted a stream of bright light. A picture shimmered in the air of John Dee seated in a red chair before a fireplace. It was the same setting I had seen him in beneath the river – and, I realized, the same as the TCM set – down to the silver box on the table beside his chair and the portrait of the sad-looking eighteenth-century lady above the fireplace.

'But this doesn't tell me where to find him,' I complained.

'Doesn't it?' Ddraik asked, cocking his huge head at the image. 'I only provide the data. What you do with it is up to you.'

I stared at the picture of Dee. Although the fire crackled behind him, he was motionless – static. 'It's not a live shot, is it? It's as if he's posing.'

'I think we can look at it as a sort of "away message" he's left for us,' Oberon said. 'But Ddraik's right. Knowing Dee, he's left some clue to his real whereabouts in the image.'

I stared harder at the picture, examining every brick in the fireplace, then moving up to the portrait. The subject regarded me dolefully out of almond-shaped eyes. I felt sure I had met that gaze before, but I couldn't for the life of me remember where. I noticed, though, that a name was engraved on a brass plate affixed to the frame. MADAME DUFAY it read. Might her identity provide some clue to Dee's location? I looked in her eyes again and felt a stirring of recognition just as the image faded from the air.

'Enough!' Ddraik roared. 'I don't give information for free. What have you to offer me?'

'Me?' I looked back to Oberon and Ignatius, but they had backed away farther into the doorway. 'I don't think I know anything that you'd be interested in.'

The dragon stretched his neck until the tip of his nose was level with my face. I nearly gagged at the sharp odor of burnt hair on his breath as he sniffed at me, but I didn't move. 'Mmmm . . . I think you might have one or two very tasty memories. If you would allow me to warm them up a little—'

'Remember, Ddraik, this is a descendant of the Watchtower,' Oberon said. 'We need her.'

'If she's a true descendant of the Watchtower, she'll be in no danger. What say you, Garet James? Shall we explore the past together?'

'Oberon? Is this . . . safe?'

Ignatius made a sound that might have been a stifled giggle. After a pause too long for my peace of mind Oberon sighed. 'The important thing to remember is that the fire reveals the truth – but not *all* truths.'

'The fire?' I asked, but the only answer I got was the click of the door latch. I turned, but Oberon and Ignatius were gone. I heard the bolts on the other side of the door sliding home, then heard a gasp and felt something tugging me backward. I whirled around to find Ddraik reared up on his hind legs, his head bent under the high, domed ceiling, his cheeks and belly swollen. The force I'd

felt pulling me back was the intake of his breath, which he
now released on me.

The fire hit me so hard it knocked me back against the
door. I opened my mouth to scream, but that only sucked
the fire inside me. I felt it burn the cilia on my windpipe
and scorch the lining of my lungs, and then it was in my
blood, racing through my heart like brush fire through dry
grass, then striking out through my veins to the tips of my
fingers and toes. The pain was horrendous, but it was only
when it reached my brain that I started to scream again. It
reached into every synapse and exploded them like firecrackers. Each explosion sparked a memory: I was three,
on a swing in the park, my mother's hand firm on my back
as she pushed me up to the treetops; I was six, eating an ice
pop on our front stoop; twelve and waking up scared from
a nightmare and wanting to call for my mother, but knowing I was too old. Random memories flashed by so quickly I
had no time to process them. I was sixteen smoking a
cigarette at a bar in the East Village; I was seventeen
standing on top of the Empire State Building with Becky;
twenty-six and begging Will Hughes to drink my blood.
The fire circled briefly there and raced on. I was four,
waking up in a warm puddle in my bed; I was eight and I'd
broken an expensive Lalique vase that my father had given
my mother for their anniversary and I hid the pieces so she
wouldn't know about it; I was still eight and lying to my
mother about what had happened, watching her face go
slack with disappointment; it was last night and I was lying
in Will Hughes's arms on Governors Island. *I'm not
ashamed of that*, a voice – my own? – called out.

In an unnerving moment of recognition I realized that faint, faraway voice was my *present* self. The fire had cut me off so thoroughly in the past that I needed to strain desperately to hear my present self, like the faintest of crackling radio signals on a stormy winter night. I was desperate not to let go of that voice, but it only came through on occasion. I clung to it the way Melusine had to her dissolving form, with a fear of the oblivion that lay beyond it.

The fire only laughed and plunged onward. I could feel it seeking, scouring my brain for something it wanted. I was fourteen and making out with a boy I didn't really like; twenty and losing my temper with a checker at the ShopRite; sixteen and sitting in the back of a rented car wishing my mother dead—

The fire circled and pounced.

No! that faint voice inside my head screamed. *I never wanted my mother dead.* To my relief the fire left the car and flipped back through my memories of my mother – her hand on my back as I swung at the playground, her face when I won an award at school, her expression when I lied about the vase, her face in the rearview mirror watching me sulk in the backseat.

Aaaahhh, the fire crooned with a satisfied sigh (I heard its thoughts with the same staticky distance as my own thoughts, but I could tell the difference), *back here again. We're always here, aren't we?*

It was right. I was in the back of the rented car coming back from Providence, watching the snow fog up the windows, hating my mother . . . and, yes, wishing her dead.

I knew I'd do what she wanted in the end or hate myself for not. I loved her too much. I'd never be free as long as she lived.

That's not the same as wanting her dead! my present voice called out, barely audible over the slap of the windshield wipers and the hum of the defrost fan.

'This fog is really thick,' my mother said. 'I think I'll pull off at the next exit.'

I didn't answer. I knew my mother would do the safe thing, the right thing – she always did. She always knew what ought to be done. As long as she lived, I'd do what she wanted rather than see her disappointed.

A red Ford Expedition passed us.

Tell her to pull over now, my present self screamed, but my sixteen-year-old self only turned up the volume on her Walkman.

When the Expedition slammed into us, I tried desperately to wrench myself out of the memory – to tell myself it *was* a memory – but I was pinned in the hurtling carapace of metal as surely as I was trapped in my sixteen-year-old body; the little bit of extra consciousness that flickered in Ddraik's cave only made it worse. I knew that the fire would circle this moment until it had burnt a hole in my brain. Already I could feel the conflagration of this memory spreading out, overtaking all other memories, reducing them to ash. What did it matter how much I loved my mother? I had wished her dead and she had died. This was the truth at the core of my being. This is where I'd spend eternity.

'Garet, can you hear me? Are you okay?'

It was my mother calling me from the front seat. My sixteen-year-old self was answering that she was okay. My twenty-six-year-old self was shouting that *she* wasn't okay. *Your mother is going to die and you will spend the rest of your life trapped in this moment!* But that voice was drowned out by the screech of the Jaws of Life tearing through the metal. The fireman was pulling me out . . .

And then I was in the backseat of the car watching the snow fog up the windows, wishing my mother dead, turning up my Walkman, watching the red Ford Expedition pass us . . . I watched it all happen again and again, helpless to change a thing no matter how loud I screamed. The fire cackled happily. It had found the perfect fuel to keep it burning for eternity: my guilt.

On the tenth . . . or was it the hundredth? . . . time I stopped screaming and merely listened instead, lulled by the cadences of my mother's voice as she lied and told me that everything would be okay. 'Always trust your instincts,' she told me.

Right, see how well that's turned out!

'You're a rare bird . . . unique . . . think for yourself . . .' But I always missed what she said next in the wail of the sirens. It became, amidst all the horror, a small annoyance. *What was she saying?* Would I be doomed to relive this experience for the rest of eternity without catching my mother's last words?

I started trying to listen *harder,* but that didn't work. The sirens were too loud. Perhaps she hadn't really said anything at all.

But then I recalled that my older self had gained a skill

or two in the last few days. I knew how to find true north and see pictures in a pool of water . . . and I knew how to listen to thoughts. Could I listen to my mother's thoughts in a memory?

And if I could, would I like what I heard there?

Then I recalled what Oberon had said: the fire reveals the truth, but not all truths. Unless I learned something new here, my only truth would be that I was a girl who had killed her mother by wishing her dead. Almost anything had to be better than that.

The next time around I focused on trying to read my mother's thoughts . . . and got nothing. I tried the next time, and still got nothing, but on the third time, right after she said, 'The fog is really thick. I think I'll pull off at the next exit,' I heard, clear as a bell, two words in my mother's head. John Dee.

John Dee? My mind stuttered on the words. *What about John Dee?*

My mother's eyes flicked up to the rearview mirror and met mine. *That* hadn't happened the last time – or the hundred times before.

Garet? Is that you?

I could hear the fire roaring in my brain, trying now to drown out her voice in my head. I had to scream over it. *Yes! Mom, it's me – ten years later me – there's going to be an accident –*

Out of the corner of my eye I saw the red Expedition pass us. I couldn't look at it, though. I couldn't look away from my mother's eyes in the mirror, which were now filling with tears.

But you survive? she asked. *You're okay?*

Yes, but you won't. Mom, you have to stop—

But the Expedition was already ramming into us and we were flipping over, spinning into space. Still, I had changed something this time. If I tried harder next time . . .

'Garet, can you hear me?' It was my mother's voice inside my head, not in my memory. 'Are you okay?'

'I'm here, Mom,' my sixteen-year-old self answered. 'I'm okay, but I can't move. Are you okay?'

She's not! She's not! I screamed at myself, but it was my mother who answered; in that pause before she spoke now I clearly heard her say inside my mind, *It's okay, sweetheart, you can't change the past.*

'Marguerite,' she said aloud, 'always trust your instincts.' *I love you so much, sweetheart, I am so proud of you,* she thought. 'You're a rare bird . . . unique . . . think for yourself . . .'

I heard the sirens blaring, drowning out her next words, but my eyes were on her face in the rearview mirror, and I could see her lips moving and hear the words she spoke aloud echoed in her thoughts.

I know you love me. Don't be afraid, my mother told me.

'There's something else I need to tell you,' my mother shouted aloud.

I wanted to tell you about the Watchtower, she told me now. *I shouldn't have kept it from you, but I saw it kill my mother. I thought that if I pretended it didn't exist, I would be free of it and then you would be free of it. But it came looking for me again . . .*

The Jaws of Life was tearing apart the car now.

That's why I wanted you to go away to college.

The fireman was pulling me out of the car.

That's why I was going to go away. Tell your father I was only leaving to protect him and you . . . tell him . . .

My sixteen-year-old self was fighting the fireman, but inside I was calm. I only had to wait for the next loop and I would break into my mother's head sooner. I would make her pull over. I would stop the accident. I would keep her alive. *You'll tell him yourself,* I thought as I was pulled out of the car. *I love you, Mom. I'm going to save you next time.*

But instead of going back to the car, I was actually getting farther away from it. I turned and saw the car blow up, the *whoosh* of the explosion eerily echoed by the crackle of the dragon's flames in my own head. But I could already hear the fire inside me dying down, retreating from my brain, smoldering in my veins. The scene in front of me was fading like an overexposed photograph. I screamed along with my sixteen-year-old self, desperate to stay in the moment. I could go back! I could change this! I fixed my eyes on the flames, willing the dragon's fire back into my brain, but it was already gone. I could already feel the cold floor of Ddraik's cave against my skin.

Just before the scene faded completely, though, I noticed a figure standing behind the fire, on the far side of the median among the EMTs who had arrived to help the owner of the Expedition. His shape wavered in the heat waves from the fire giving him the appearance of a mirage. But he wasn't a mirage. He was there. He had always been there. John Dee stood beside the fire that had killed my mother and stared through the flames directly at me.

The Lover's Eye

I awoke on the floor of Ddraik's cave screaming, 'Send me back! Send me back!' I flung myself at the dragon, pounding my fists against his scaly hide. For answer he wrapped his tail around my back and held me firmly in his grip.

'It took great strength to break free of your worst memory, but it shows even greater strength to be willing to go back. You are truly a descendant of the Watchtower, Margaret James. I am proud to have shared your memories.'

'Then send me back!' I sobbed.

'That I cannot do. Nor would it make any difference. Your mother was right – you cannot change the past. But you did a rare thing – you sent a message back.'

'Did she?' I heard Oberon's voice from behind me. At some point he and Ignatius had come back into the room.

'Yes, she did. This one's stronger than you thought,' Ddraik answered, then he said to me, 'Your mother died knowing that you survived and grew into a strong woman. No mother could ask for more.' He stroked my face with the surprisingly soft tip of his tail, brushing away my tears. His stroke kindled a flame in the pit of my belly and I realized that Ddraik's fire had not left my body. It had retreated deep inside where it smoldered – a hearth fire banked against a long winter's night – for me to draw on if need be.

I drew on it now, pulling it into the palms of my hands. I pictured Dee as I'd just seen him, standing behind the car fire that had consumed my mother. Of course, I realized, that's why my mother had thought of Dee when she saw the fog. Dee had sent the fog that pushed the Ford Expedition into our car, killing my mother, and then he had watched me while my mother burned to decide if I was anything to be afraid of. Clearly he'd decided I hadn't been. I pictured him now *inside* the fire I summoned into my hands. A huge ball of fire sprung from my palms and grew to fill the room. I heard Oberon and Ignatius scurrying backward, but Ddraik only chuckled.

'Yes! Much stronger than you thought!'

I smiled at Ddraik, letting the fireball shrink back to a spark that slipped into my veins. 'Thank you,' I said, bowing. Then, turning to Oberon, who was cowering near the door with Ignatius, I said, 'Let's go home. I think I know how to find Dee.'

On the subway ride back Oberon wanted to know what I'd learned that would help us find Dee, but I told him that I had to show him. That was only half-true. Really, I wanted to talk about something else.

'Did you know that Dee killed my mother?'

'What makes you think that?' he asked, glaring at a man whose legs were spread out so wide he was taking up three seats. The man got up and walked to the end of the car.

'I saw him at the site of the accident.'

Oberon shook his head, then patted me reassuringly on the shoulder.

'I was afraid that was where Ddraik would take you. That must have been very painful.' He laid his hand on mine. It felt cool against my overheated skin, soothing. A green glow flowed from his skin to mine. I felt it quenching the fire that still smoldered in my veins.

I took my hand away. I wasn't ready to have my anger quenched. 'You haven't answered my question.'

'I suspected,' he said. 'In the days before your mother's death she came to me and told me that she thought John Dee was in New York. She told me she was going to send you away to school and then leave the country – that there was something she had to do back in France.'

'Did she say what?'

'No, she didn't. I'm afraid she didn't trust me entirely. She resented how the Watchtower had ruled her mother's life and believed that she had died because of it. She made me promise not to initiate you if anything happened to her. And then she died. I suspected Dee might have been behind the accident, but I found no sign of him in New York afterward. Then I heard through contacts abroad that he'd been spotted in France. Perhaps Dee learned that was where your mother had been headed and he went to find out why.'

We'd reached our stop. I followed Oberon out of the station. When we got up to the street, I was surprised to see that it was nearly dark already. I checked my watch and saw that it was four thirty – sunset at this time of year, but there should have been a lot more light. When I looked up at the sky, I saw why there wasn't. A heavy fog obscured the western sky, smothering any last rays of the setting sun.

'We'd better hurry,' Oberon said. 'If you saw Dee in your memories, he probably knows you've been to see Ddraik. He's not going to bother going after your friends anymore – he's going to go straight for you.'

We walked briskly, but at the last street corner on the way to my house we had to slow up because a large crowd had congregated, blocking the pavement. The crowd and thick strands of fog obscured our view at first, but soon we could see that, near the curb, a half dozen police officers had surrounded two well-dressed men who, from their bloodied faces, had been in a fistfight. Police were hand-cuffing them but the taller man was still screaming expletives at the shorter man. The shorter man's attaché case lay open on the sidewalk near his feet, the pile of papers in it beginning to be strewn about by the wind. I observed that his face seemed to be streaked with tears as well as blood. I thought of helping the man with his wafting-away paper pile, but as I took a step toward him, the police deepened their ring around them with some new arrivals.

Then Oberon and I started to slip through the crowd, and I overheard a pale, slender woman in a quilted red riding jacket say to her companion, 'It's been the darndest day, Angelique. I also saw a fight like this on the way to my subway station in Queens this morning. Also normal-looking businessmen. And Chris called me at work this afternoon – he's off today – to tell me there were two separate house fires raging at opposite ends of our block. What a bleak coincidence; there hasn't been a fire on the block in ten years! Both have been put out, but still, I'm starting to get the creeps. Is something in the air?'

'Back in the islands we call it voodoo wind,' Angelique answered in a soft but somehow emphatic voice. 'It is creepy, but I haven't run into anything today until now.'

'Discord,' Oberon muttered under his breath. 'A some-times erratic but always most poisonous demon.' He glanced around at the fog, which was starting to break up in the wind, but was still coiling around lampposts and trees with the sinuousness of multiplying snakes. In the east, the sky was graying. 'Angelique may not have much longer to wait,' he rumbled, taking my hand briefly as we walked on.

At the town house I told Oberon to stay on the second floor and wait for me while I got something from my studio on the third floor. I found him sitting on the couch, sniffing the empty wineglasses.

'Mandrake root and hellebore,' he said. 'The combin-ation increases melancholy and makes the user susceptible to suggestion.'

I sat down next to him and used the remote to turn on the TV and select the movie Jay and Becky had watched. I fast-forwarded to the end where Robert Osborne came on and paused. 'There,' I said, pointing at the portrait of Madame Dufay. 'I knew I'd seen this woman's eyes before, but really I'd just seen one of her eyes.' I opened my hand and showed Oberon the lover's eye brooch.

He jumped up, knocking over the wineglasses on the table. 'Where did you get that thing? Cover it up!'

I closed my hand. 'I got it at Dee's shop. Why are you so afraid of it?'

'Dee can see through it.' Oberon moved closer to the TV screen and bent down to look at the portrait. 'Yes, you're probably right about the eye matching the portrait. They're a pair. An enchantment was placed on both the portrait and the miniature, so that if you look through the eye of the portrait you can see what the lover's eye looks upon – sort of like a remote camera. In fact, I remember when this particular portrait was painted.'

'You do? Did you know her? She looks so sad.'

'Madame Dufay? Yes, she had good reason to be sad. I knew her in Paris in the days just before the Reign of Terror. Now *there* was a time when the demons of Discord and Despair ran rampant! Madame Dufay was a young woman at the court of Louis the Sixteenth. She fell in love there with a young man of mysterious birth and questionable repute. He commissioned a painter to do her portrait, but she knew that because the king frowned on the romance, he would not be able to display it. So she asked the painter to do a miniature of just her eye, so that her lover could wear it and no one but she would know to whom he was professing his devotion. While the artist was painting the eye, she said to him, "If only I could see through this eye, I would always be with my lover."

'And the painter, who had fallen in love with her, thought to himself, "If she could see how her lover conducts himself while away from her, she would see he was unworthy of her." So he went to a man in Paris who was rumored to know how to make spells. The magician agreed to give him a magical pigment to use in his paintings to effect the spell, on the agreement that he would be named the painter's beneficiary in the event of his death. The painter agreed, completed the portrait and the lover's eye, and gave the portrait to Madame Dufay and the lover's eye to her lover. The first night he wore it, though, an attempt was made on his life. Seeing this through the eye, Madame Dufay, who was nearby, ran to his aid and was killed herself. When the painter learned what had happened because of him, he hung himself, and his paintings – including the one which Madame Dufay had yet to pay for – became the property of the magician—'

'Wait, don't tell me . . . the magician was John Dee.'

Oberon inclined his head. 'He must have left the eye in his shop hoping you would pick it up and that he'd be able to spy on you. You must destroy it.' Oberon reached for the brooch in my hand.

'No!' I said, pulling my hand away. He looked at me in surprise. I was surprised myself. Since the ordeal in Ddraik's cave I'd felt a shift in my relationship with Oberon, but I hadn't realized until now that I knew something he didn't . . . or at least I thought I did. 'I think the eye wanted to be left behind. I think it – she – wanted me to find her. There's a link between us. I can feel it.'

Oberon sucked in his breath and narrowed his eyes at me. 'Ddraik was right. You *are* stronger than I thought. But still, you don't have my experience. I agree that there might be a link between you and Madame Dufay, but how is that going to help us find Dee?'

'Like this.' I opened my hand. The eye blinked in the sudden light. Oberon backed away. *Why is he so freaked out by it?* I wondered. Something in the way he had told the story seemed . . . *off* to me. As if he were reciting from a script. But I didn't have time to ponder the question right now. Oberon was correct about one thing: Dee could be using the portrait to watch us. I was hoping, though, that the portrait was still hanging over his fireplace.

I held the lover's eye between my thumb and forefinger and looked at it. The almond-shaped brown eye narrowed, as if studying me, and then, to my amazement, winked. I laughed out loud and then, turning the eye away from me, lifted the brooch and held it up to my own right eye, fitting it into my eye socket like a jeweler's loupe.

For a moment my vision blurred and doubled. A kaleidoscope of images revolved across my field of vision. When I covered my left eye, the disparate images resolved into one. It was not Dee's lair, though. I stood in a garden at night, lit by gaily colored paper lanterns and peopled by men and women dressed in eighteenth-century costume. The men and women both wore wigs, the women's hair piled high on top of their heads and crowned with flowers and birds' feathers.

'What do you see?' I heard Oberon ask.

'I think I'm watching one of her memories,' I said. 'I'm in a garden . . .' I was walking down a dark path bordered by white roses. At the end of it was a marble fountain, its water jets aglow in the light of a hundred torches. 'I think

I'm in Versailles! At some kind of party.' A girl in a yellow silk dress rushed by me, laughing, pursued by a young man in blue silk. They both wore masks. 'A masquerade party! You said Madame Dufay was at the court of Louis the Sixteenth. Does that mean I might see Marie Antoinette?'

'This isn't a sightseeing trip,' Oberon said primly. 'Can you ask Madame Dufay to show you Dee?'

'Could you show me John Dee, please?' I asked, and then, resurrecting my high school French, *'Je voudrais voir John Dee, s'il vous plaît.'*

I felt the body I was in stumble. *Well, no wonder,* I thought, looking down at the dainty, petal-pink, high-heeled slippers on Madame Dufay's feet, *who could walk in these? They are gorgeous, though.*

Madame Dufay pointed her toe and turned her heel, showing off the spray of feathers on the heel of the shoe. She knew I was there! She could hear me.

'John Dee, s'il vous plaît,' I repeated.

She picked up her head and started walking toward the fountain at the end of the path. A circle of revelers surrounded a man in a fawn-colored frock coat and black cloak. He wore a mask shaped like an owl's face and seemed to be performing some sort of magic trick. He waved his hand above a crystal goblet and a bouquet of roses appeared. The crowd applauded and he swept down in a low bow, revealing that the top of his head was bald. When he looked up, I saw amber eyes glinting through the slits of the owl mask.

'John Dee!' I gasped. 'He's at the party.'

'Tell her you want to see John Dee *now*! In 2008.'

'Will she understand that?' I asked, but she was already turning away from Dee and walking toward an open pavilion where couples danced a minuet. She was headed toward a man in a dark peacock-blue coat with white lace at his throat and a black-feathered mask over the top part of his face. He bowed low and I felt myself – or Madame Dufay – curtsying in return. Then I was placing my hand in his and I was swept into the dance. The brightly colored lanterns blurred into a rainbow circle around us, the gray eyes behind the mask the still focal point in the swirling world. I felt I knew those eyes.

'This must be the man she fell in love with,' I said. 'The one she gave her portrait to.'

Oberon sighed. 'Can't you hurry her along?'

'I don't think so. I think she wants to show me these things. She's been trapped in this painting for over two hundred years. Who am I to rush her?'

The truth was I didn't want to rush her. I could feel my body swaying in time to the music, those gray eyes holding me as tightly as an embrace. I wanted to dance forever, but suddenly I was jolted out of the moment. Someone had bumped into Madame Dufay on the dance floor. As she turned to see who it was, I caught a glimpse of a black man in a long green silk caftan, a white turban on his head, and a thin white mask over his eyes. 'Hey—' I began, but the feeling of being jostled transposed itself to present-day New York. The brooch came dislodged from my eye, shattering the vision into a million fragments of flowers and fountains and masked faces.

I quickly put the brooch back to my eye, but the scene

had changed. I – or Madame Dufay, rather – was sitting in a cold, bare room facing a wall of windows that framed a view of tiled rooftops. A little to my right a pale young man with tousled blond hair and a paint-spattered blue smock stood behind an easel, dabbing paint to a canvas with a paintbrush.

'She's having her portrait done,' I informed Oberon.

'Wonderful,' he remarked drily. 'Perhaps we'll be treated to a visit to her hairdresser next.'

'No, this is important. She's telling the painter that she wishes she could see through the eyes he is painting so that she might watch *his lordship* while she's not with him.'

The painter looked up from his painting and met her – my – eyes. 'Perhaps, madame, you would not like what you saw,' he said.

'I would always rather know the truth,' Madame Dufay replied.

A shadow fell over the young man's face. The sun had moved below the roof of the building opposite the painter's garret. 'We'll have to stop,' he said. 'The light's gone for today.'

The scene went dark and then I was standing on a street – or rather in a doorway – sheltering from the rain. A carriage passed by and splashed cold water on my feet. I looked down and saw that the hem of my dress had been muddied, and then, when I looked up, my attention was drawn by a flash of blue across the street. It was the young painter going into a shop. There was a sign of a dis-embodied eye hanging over the doorway.

'It must be Dee's shop,' I said aloud. 'The painter must

be going to find out how to give the lover's eye the power of sight. If I could see inside—'

As if in response to my wish, Madame Dufay stepped out onto the street. I felt the rain falling on my head and shoulders, smelled the dank odor of sewage and refuse. The glass window of the shop was fogged over but I could make out the outline of the painter as he approached a counter where a man was bent over something.

'A mortar and pestle,' I said aloud. 'The shopkeeper is grinding something. It must be an apothecary's.'

'Yes!' Oberon said impatiently. 'Dee often posed as an apothecary. Now ask her to show us Dee *now*!' He said the last word so loudly I jumped. On the street in Paris Madame Dufay tripped. A view of rain-slicked cobble-stones swam up toward me, then the scene abruptly shifted. I was sitting up high, as if in a balcony, looking down on a small amber-colored room, the floors covered with Persian rugs, walls lined with paintings. Somewhere below me a fire crackled; it reflected on the face of the man sitting before it in a red chair.

'This is it!' I cried, recognizing the room I'd glimpsed below the East River and seen on the TV set. Only the angle was different. I was looking down at the room because I was in the painting above the fireplace. From this angle I could see now that the room was shaped like an octagon.

'It's a tower room, I think,' I said aloud.

'Are there any windows?' Oberon asked.

I scanned the wall opposite me. It was covered with amber panels and paintings . . . but then I noticed a narrow gap between two of the panels. 'It looks like a tall, skinny window, like the kind you'd have in a medieval tower . . . only . . . damn!'

'What?' Oberon demanded. 'Can't you see anything?'

'No.' The window was dark. 'Of course not. It's already dark outside.' As I spoke, though, I realized I *did* see something. 'There's a red light in the distance . . . some kind of beacon.'

Oberon made a sound of disgust. 'That could be anything! She showed you her memories before, can't she show you the room in daylight?'

'I don't think so,' I answered. 'Those memories all had meaning for her. I don't think much if anything that happens in this room matters to her.' I was startled to hear my voice crack. The sadness had stolen over me stealthily, the agony of spending eternity trapped in paint and canvas seeping into my own bones. I could feel tears gathering in my eyes. One welled in the space between the brooch and my eye. The scene of John Dee's lair wavered and swam in front of me, the red light outside the window swelling like a dying star. But suddenly, with a small gasp, I recognized the light. I couldn't tell if my perception came through sight or memory or stirred somewhere deeper – in the flickering embers of knowledge that Ddraik had bequeathed me, perhaps.

'I know what that light is!' I said, letting the brooch slip out of my eye. 'It's the beacon on top of the Cloisters. I saw it from Will Hughes's apartment.'

'Perhaps John Dee's tower is in Will Hughes's apartment building,' Oberon suggested.

'No, I don't think there's an octagonal tower on that

building. There's only one tower I recall in that neighborhood.' I got up and went to my father's bookshelves. My father loved New York City history, and I'd given him many books over the years on various topics about New York. I picked out one and quickly looked up what I wanted and brought the open book back to the couch for Oberon to see.

'The High Bridge Water Tower,' I said, pointing to a picture of the tall skinny tower that stood beside the Harlem River. I had asked my father about it once, and he had explained that it had been built along with the Croton Aqueduct to provide water to higher elevations in Manhattan. 'See, it's octagonal *and* it's connected to the water system – or at least it once was. It hasn't been used in years, but the tunnels that connected it to the old Croton Aqueduct are probably still there.'

'And those tunnels meet the new water system at Jerome Park Reservoir in the Bronx,' Oberon finished for me. 'He might not be able to send water through the old tunnels, but he could send fog. Yes, it makes sense.' As he was speaking, Oberon had taken out a pack of Post-it notes from his pocket and now he sketched an octagon on it.

'It's at 174th Street and Amsterdam Avenue,' I said, pointing to a map next to the picture of the tower, thinking that Oberon would want to write that down. But instead Oberon drew a sideways *S* through the octagon – like half an infinity symbol – and added a dot to the center of the picture.

'Wha—?' I began, but then Oberon slapped the note on my forehead and my mouth – my vocal cords, my throat, my whole body – turned to stone.

The Wrong Way

'I'm so sorry, Garet,' Oberon said. 'But Ddraik is right: you are becoming much stronger, much more quickly, than I'd anticipated.'

He leaned forward until his face was only inches from mine. Instinctively I wanted to put more space between us, but I couldn't even blink.

'Nor had I anticipated that you would be able to communicate with former Watchtowers who might explain to you why you shouldn't let me have the box. Your mother was bad enough, but once you were able to contact Marguerite Dufay, it was only a matter of time before you found out that I'm not supposed to have the box again.'

If I could have gasped and widened my eyes in surprise, I would have, but I couldn't even breathe . . . *I wasn't breathing! How long could I stay alive in this state?*

'For about an hour,' Oberon said, apparently reading my thoughts. 'Now what was I saying? Oh, yes, Marguerite Dufay – now there was a most uncooperative Watchtower and, like you, foolishly attracted to that vampire.'

An image from Madame Dufay's memories replayed before my frozen eyes: a man in a peacock-blue coat and feathered mask bowing low and then sweeping us into the dance, familiar silver eyes behind the mask . . . it was Will! He'd been the man whom Madame Dufay had loved.

'I had no choice but to keep them apart,' Oberon said.

Now I recalled the rain-soaked Paris street, but when I looked at the fogged-over apothecary's window, I recognized the figure at the counter – it was Oberon. It was he, not John Dee, who had sold the painter the magic paints to paint the lover's eye.

Oberon smiled. 'Sometimes I think I will spend eternity keeping you two apart. A hundred years will go by and I'll think I've finally broken the bond between you two and then—' Oberon reached his hand up to my neck. I couldn't feel a thing, but from the tilt of his head I guessed he was looking at the bite marks on my neck. When he moved his head, I saw something else out of the corner of my eye – a flutter of wings. 'Voilà! Here you two are again!'

He sat back. The flutter of wings moved closer. It was Lol, hovering on top of a bookcase a few feet behind Oberon.

'You keep finding each other, life after life.' I was paying more attention to Lol than to what Oberon was saying, but that comment distracted me. What did he mean that we kept finding each other? Will had said he'd had almost no contact with Marguerite's descendants since they'd parted in the early seventeenth century. But I couldn't very well ask Oberon what he meant. And then my attention was taken up by Lol, who looked as if she were doing some kind of yoga pose on the top bookshelf. She was bent over at the waist, both her arms stretched out behind her like a swimmer warming up for a race. Then she lifted herself onto the tips of her toes and sprang off the bookshelf into the air, soaring so fast that she became a blur of yellow and orange – a meteor hurtling toward my forehead. She was going for the Post-it note, to remove the spell, only before she reached me, Oberon raised his right hand and without even so much as breaking eye contact with me swatted Lol aside.

I heard a sickening thud as she slammed into something, but I couldn't even turn my head to see if she was still alive.

'Poor Lol,' Oberon said, clucking his tongue, 'she's always been attached to you. But she knows the price of taking the side of a human over one of her own.'

He got to his feet and I lost sight of his face, but then he bent down to look at me and I was surprised to see the pain and regret on his face. 'As should you by now.' Then his face disappeared and I heard his footsteps going down the stairs and the front door opening and closing.

Oberon had left me in front of the TV set, as if I were parked there to watch my favorite show. The image on the set was as frozen as I was, though, and not on a channel I would have chosen: John Dee in his guise as Robert Osborne sitting by the fire, with Marguerite Dufay looking down at me with her sad eyes as if waiting for me to expire. Oberon had said I could live like this about an hour – and already five minutes had gone by. The clock on the cable box read 5:34 . . . then 5:35. I had until sometime around 6:30. Had he purposely left me here in front of the clock so I could watch the last minutes of my life slip away? It seemed cruel. How had I so misjudged him? In the hospital he had seemed so kind. I'd watched him use his green aura to heal Zach Reese and my father – *damn! My poor father!* Who would take care of him if I died?

I felt a prickling in my eyes, but even my tear ducts were frozen. I couldn't cry. I could still think, though. And what did I have to think about but to wonder why Oberon had done this to me? He had looked genuinely grieved, as if he were doing something he was forced to do. What had he said? *It was only a matter of time before you remembered that I wasn't supposed to have the box again.* Dee had said that Oberon wanted the box to gain control over the human race and gain power for the kingdom of the fey. Apparently he had been using me all along to find the box, and now that I'd told him where it was, he didn't need me anymore. And once I'd made contact with Madame Dufay he was afraid I would learn why I had to keep him from getting the box. All that made a sort of sense, but I still found it hard to understand how he could kill Lol and leave me to die.

Nevertheless the clock now read 6:03. I had only half an hour left. Maybe Jay would come back from the hospital – he'd been there since the middle of last night, surely he'd come back to shower and change. But then I remembered Jay's grief-stricken face as he sat beside Becky's bed and realized that he probably wasn't going anywhere. And no one else had the key to get in the town house.

There was one person, though, who wouldn't need a key. Will had said he'd see me tonight, but when tonight?

The sun had already set, but he'd have to feed. How long would that take? Where did he find his victims . . . or did he have willing donors? The thought of him taking blood from some other woman while I sat here dying would have brought tears to my eyes if my tear ducts hadn't been frozen.

If I could have moved my fingers I could have sent up a flare, but all I could do was *think* about him and hope that some vampire radar picked up my mental distress signal. After all, Oberon had said that Will and I kept finding each other *life after life.* Didn't that mean we shared some spiritual bond?

That bond hadn't helped Madame Dufay any, I reflected. She'd run to Will's rescue and been killed.

The numbers on the cable box melted from 6:15 to 6:16.

I tried to picture Will's face as he'd looked last night in the glow of the firelight, his eyes hungry for me . . . I saw Will, but it wasn't as he'd looked last night. This man had longer hair, tied back in a ponytail, and there was lace at his throat. The glow on his face came not from the firelight, but the orange of the setting sun. His eyes were filled with grief, not hunger. Somehow I knew that this was Madame Dufay's last memory of him – a remnant of her sight that she'd left for me – her lover arriving seconds too late to save her.

Is that what would be my last memory as well?

I banished the picture and focused on the man – well, *vampire* – I'd been with last night.

The clock read 6:23.

Will, I love you, I said to myself, surprised that the words were true. *Come quick.*

Upstairs in my studio came a metallic clang, like wind chimes. The wind knocking something over?

The clock moved soundlessly from 6:25 to 6:26, the red numerals glowing like the last light of the setting sun.

I heard the wind now. It was inside the house, whistling down the staircase. Perhaps this was what death sounded like when it came for you. A great wind. But didn't I still have a few minutes? I could no longer read the clock. A shadow had fallen between me and the TV set, like an enormous black wing spreading itself over me. Death come to take me away. And why not go with it? Death had a beautiful face . . . like an angel . . . white as marble, eyes the silver of new coins.

Death touched my forehead and I could feel my soul pouring out of my body through a spot between my eyes. My yoga teacher was right – the third eye *was* the seat of enlightenment and vision! I could see everything now. A million memories – from my own life and a dozen others – flashed by me with astounding speed, but I recognized all of them. I was all of the Marguerites that had come before me. At last the slide show stilled on one image: the round pool beneath the stone tower, the black swan gliding on the water. *Yes,* I heard myself – *all my selves* – thinking, it always came back to this. An arrow split the still air, an anguished cry broke the silence . . .

'Garet!'

The sound mingled with the swan's cry, both anguished. I could feel myself slipping under the dark water, but then I felt strong hands pulling me out, shaking me, calling my name again.

'Garet!'

I opened my eyes and saw Will's face above me. 'You came,' I said, my voice as hoarse as if I hadn't spoken in a hundred years. 'You heard me.'

'I *did* hear you,' he said, shaking his head in wonderment that I'd been able to summon him. 'Where did you learn to do *that*?'

'From Marguerite Dufay, I think,' I said as he helped me sit up.

'Dufay?' Will whispered the name. 'But how?'

I opened my right hand and found the eye brooch looking up at me. Will looked down at it. His skin, already white, turned a shade of pale blue. He picked up the brooch and held it up to his eye. I noticed that unlike Oberon he wasn't afraid to touch it. 'Where did you get this?' he asked, his voice as hoarse as mine had been a moment ago.

'From Dee's shop. I realized it matched the portrait in Dee's lair and I used it to find out where he was.'

'I thought he might have taken it. I suspected that he was the one who gave poor Auguste Regnault the ability to paint it.'

'Dee must have stolen the brooch at some point, but it was Oberon who gave the painter the magic to make it.'

'Oberon?' Will frowned.

'Because he wanted to keep you two apart.'

Will shook his head. 'But Oberon wouldn't have wanted Marguerite dead.'

'Well, he certainly wanted me dead . . . and I think he might have killed Lol!' I jumped to my feet, dismayed that I hadn't thought to look for Lol immediately. I scanned the floor and finally found her behind a potted fern, her body limp and her wings crumpled like discarded cellophane wrappers. I touched the tip of my index finger to her sternum and felt a faint flutter.

'I think she's still alive,' I said to Will, who knelt beside me. 'Is there anything we can do for her?'

'I saw Marguerite tend to a wounded fairy once. She said they could heal themselves with the energies from certain plants.' He reached over my shoulder and yanked out a handful of fern fronds. 'Here, you'd better do it. I don't think a vampire's touch will do her much good.'

I wrapped the fronds around Lol's limp body as gently as I could, not wanting to jar any broken bones. Then I lay her in the pot beneath the fern. She looked a little like the Vietnamese spring rolls they served at Saigon Grill. After a moment I heard a faint humming noise and saw a pale green glow surround her.

'I think it's working,' Will said. 'The best thing we can do is let her rest. You say Oberon did this? I've seen him be ruthless before, but to harm one of his own . . .'

'He said it was what she deserved for siding with a human, and then he said something else.' I frowned, trying to remember Oberon's parting words to me. 'He said I should know well the price of taking a human's side. Did he mean the first Marguerite's decision to become mortal in order to be with you?'

Will looked away, a pained expression on his face. 'I suppose. Sometimes I think that the reason Oberon hates me so much is that he was in love with Marguerite and he blames me for her decision to become human. But still,

I'm surprised he would hurt you.' His eye fell on the crumpled Post-it note that he'd peeled from my forehead. He picked it up and unfolded it. 'See,' he said, pointing at the symbol, 'he only drew half an infinity sign through the octagon. If he wanted you dead, he would have drawn a full one. He knew I'd get here in time.'

'Really? He could have told *me* that.'

'Maybe he wanted you to have to call me, or maybe he was just messing with you.' Will shrugged his shoulders. 'Oberon is fond of tricks, but not evil. He wanted a head start. You say you were able to find out where Dee is?'

'He's in the High Bridge Tower – or at least he was an hour ago – here, give me the brooch.'

He seemed reluctant to part with it – or maybe, I thought, reluctant to have me looking through Marguerite Dufay's eyes again. He needn't have been. Madame Dufay didn't treat me to any of her memories this time; she took me straight to Dee's lair. Dee was sitting in the chair beside the fire. He seemed curiously still.

'He's there,' I told Will.

'Is the box still there?' Will asked.

I looked down at the table beside the chair. 'Yes.'

'And Oberon?'

'No, I don't see him.'

'Then I'm afraid Dee has already disposed of him. Come on, we have to hurry.'

I took the brooch from my eye and slipped it into my pocket. 'But how are we going to get up into the tower. Can you scale it?'

Will had been watching where I put the brooch. He

looked up, distracted, then smiled. 'I'm afraid not, my dear. I know another way.' He looked down at my feet. 'Ah, good, you'll need those,' he said, pointing to my Doc Martens, which I'd put on earlier today because Oberon had told me to wear my welding clothes. 'The way we're going is a bit damp.'

Will's driver was waiting outside in the Rolls. The fog was so thick that I wasn't sure how he was going to drive through it, but he seemed unperturbed when Will told him to drive to Van Cortlandt Park in the Bronx.

'Why are we going there?' I asked Will, who was sitting in the backseat to my right as the car glided down Jane Street. 'The High Bridge Tower is in the 170s in Manhattan.'

'If we try to approach the tower from the ground, Dee will see us.'

'How can he see anything in this pea soup?' I asked. We'd come to the corner of Jane Street and the West Side Highway. To our right was the SRO hotel where Oberon lived, the corner tower lost in the heavy fog. A man came out of the lobby and shivered when he breathed in the fog. He pulled up the corduroy collar of his Barbour raincoat and coughed into his hand, his face turning a sickly gray. With a start, I recognized him as the man whom I'd bumped into on Twelfth Street a few days ago, the one who'd called me an asshole for going 'the wrong way.' He started walking to the corner, but then abruptly lurched into the street and fell against the hood of the still stationary Rolls.

'Is he all right?' I asked, starting to open the door. 'He looks like he needs help.'

Will reached his arm over me and pulled the door shut. 'I don't think that's a good idea,' he hissed.

The man's face was suddenly at my window, his features contorted with rage. *'You're going the wrong way, asshole!'* he screamed, pounding his fists against the glass. 'D'ya think 'cause you have a fancy car you can just run people over?'

'Go on,' Will instructed the driver. 'And don't stop for any reason.'

As we turned onto the West Side Highway, I looked in the rearview mirror. The man in the Barbour coat had run out into the middle of the highway and was waving his fist in the air and shouting obscenities at us and at the other cars that careened around him.

'You asked how Dee could see us in this fog, well, there's the answer.' Will pointed to a plume of fog pouring out of a manhole cover beside the raving man. The fog billowed above the man and assumed the rudimentary shape of a creature with great bearlike arms and legs. The only clearly delineated part of the fog-monster was its glowing yellow eyes. 'The fog has eyes,' Will said. 'John Dee's eyes.'

I shuddered as the fog-monster wrapped its paws around the man and began pulling him down through the holes in the manhole cover. Even as the man disintegrated, I could still hear his voice shouting, *'You're all going the wrong way, assholes!'*

The Transmigration
of Atoms

We rode uptown a few minutes in relative calm, though I was startled in the West Forties by a large foggy smear in the middle of the Hudson River, to our left from the highway. Gazing at it, I saw that it had enough substance to it to be floating up and down with the river's tidal swell – the Hudson was moved by ocean tides for a hundred miles of its length – and that in a vague way it resembled an airplane. It was a cylinder at least a football field in length with two winglike protuberances midlength and a tail-like upward swing at its end. How bizarre, I initially thought, but then it occurred to me that many planes flew not very high over the Hudson after taking off from La Guardia. And this fog could rise into the air without warning.

'Will.' I nudged him with my elbow. 'What is that thing in the river?'

He glanced out the window so swiftly I could barely follow the motion of his eyes. His pupils widened in alarm, nearly effacing the silver glow of his irises. 'Dee's nearing mass murder now as part of his mayhem. Despair and Discord made that fog. But I don't think 911 will believe us if we call in to get all flights grounded. All the more reason . . .' He urged his driver to speed up. The driver stepped on the gas so hard that even the Rolls, smoothest of all cars, lurched ahead. But the acceleration didn't last long.

Already I could see a dim, large shape looming up about a half mile ahead in the moon-silvered road. Brake lights were glimmering in front of it, blooming like little luminescent flowers. At first faintly, then more distinctly, I could hear a series of thudding crashes from beyond the shape. I nestled closer to Will as the Rolls slowed sharply. 'What the . . .' he muttered. His eyes brightened and his gaze penetrated the darkness ahead as if transformed to a searchlight, but it shed no light for me, and he hushed me when I asked him what was going on.

In another ten yards or so I could see for myself. The shape was a growing pyramid of mangled cars – their front and rear ends all badly crashed in – centered in the opposite, southbound side of the road but spilling over onto our side now. From a greater distance to the north, I began to hear the high-pitched sirens of emergency vehicles. The pyramidal shape of the wreck surprised me, as if it displayed some tendency to order in even the most twisted and jumbled metal, and I also couldn't understand why the crashes seemed to be occurring only on the south-bound side of the road.

'What the hell is that?' I queried Will again.

'Hell is right,' he said, but now squeezing my hand re-assuringly. 'Discord at its worst. The demon's put down a force field, an invisible barrier, at Ninety-sixth Street, and then Dee's draped a fog over it so oncoming southbound drivers can't see it or the wreckage in front of them. So the crashes keep on coming. The demon's either not potent enough yet to block both sides of the road, or it's got a worse catastrophe in mind for when there's a big enough backup northbound. We can't afford to wait to find out, though. Can you call 911 while we detour?'

'Detour?' I replied, my eyes widening. The deserted southbound side of the highway looked appealing for a U-turn detour to the southbound exit, but access was blocked by a four-foot-high wall between the lanes. To the right were the bare trees, shadowy grass, and graffitied lamps of Riverside Park; none of the paved walkways were wide enough to allow a car access.

I tried 911 as the driver pondered the detour dilemma as well. The number was busy, something that was never supposed to happen again given the circuit expansion after 9/11 . . . I didn't want to speculate on how many disasters could be happening now around the city, given that we had encountered one on just our one small route – tens of thousands of calls were certainly required to fill up the circuits. Then Will's patience with his driver lapsed. He jerked open the partition between the front and rear seats, ordered the driver one seat over, and clambered legs first through the partition opening, nimbly as the sleekest of jaguars. He floored the gas pedal while steering sharply to the right, maneuvering the Rolls between several cars in the middle and right northbound lanes in a way that seemed impossible, and jumped the curb into the park with only the slightest of bumps. Then he maneuvered on grass with surprising smoothness, between the gaunt, winter-stripped trees, as effortlessly as if he had been out there in the park jogging.

At one point, though, for all his dexterity, I thought we were about to smash into a majestic oak that appeared in our path as if out of nowhere. For a fleeting instant I had the impression that the oak had in fact slid into our path, its roots sliding like coiling legs beneath the frozen ground, the twigged ends to its branches featuring tiny eyes that allowed it to position itself properly. I cringed and closed my eyes, bracing for an awful impact. And in that moment of closing my eyes, I felt an enormous wind sweeping through the car, sending us all hurtling into a void deeper than darkness; when I opened my eyes again, I couldn't see a thing. The temperature seemed to have plunged massively, but the only motion in the total darkness was my own shivering; the wind had vanished. I briefly heard the faintest of high-pitched whining sounds. The thought came to me that I was now reduced to subatomic size and was standing on the chilly nucleus of a single atom, listening to electrons whir. I even located the atom, near the edge of the universe. Without warning the reality of the car then returned – for a moment it seemed to be still spinning itself, though it hadn't crashed – and then Will was calmly driving it back over another curb onto Riverside Drive heading north. He made a right onto West Seventy-sixth Street as blithely as if he were driving to the Fairway supermarket on Broadway, then a left onto northbound West End Avenue. I remained speechless with relief and astonishment. When we stopped for a light behind a long line of cars – no doubt there was significant overflow already from the trauma on the highway – Will nodded to the driver, got out of the car, and then they both took the seats they'd started up the West Side Highway in.

'What on earth was that?' I asked.

'Transmigration of atoms,' Will said casually. He smiled, and there was a sense of triumph in his smile.

'And what is that?'

'As I mentioned on Governors Island, I can't exactly fly but . . .' He draped his left arm over me and gave my left shoulder an affectionate squeeze. 'Atom-transit can be the next best, or an even better, thing. You have already experienced a waterpower similar to it with Melusine, but atom-transit belongs to the air. I was initiated into it long ago by one of the fey, but not quite correctly, and thus I always invoke it with mixed results. In any event the intensity of will – no pun intended – required for it is enormous, and so it can only be resorted to in the direst of emergencies. The malevolent tree attacking us, manipulated by Discord – a tree which was one of the French botanist Jean Robin's experiments that got away from him, its seed blown here on a transoceanic wind current centuries ago – certainly qualified. Especially with Dee trying to destroy New York City in the background. But even under the most dramatic of conditions, it doesn't always succeed. I've had both sorts of outcomes with it over the years. Anyway, it's benign when it works – we all slept right through it. Just as well. Those trillion-mile journeys can get a little dull.' He laughed as if he'd been on one too many.

I pondered whether to tell him that I hadn't quite been asleep – or else my moment on the surface of the nucleus had been a dream, but it had seemed real – when a titanic boom from a nearby explosion shook the car and brought both traffic and thinking to a halt. Slowly, as my eardrums reestablished equilibrium, I shook all my limbs to make sure they were still attached to my body. They were. There was no sign of blood on my coat, either, always a good omen for surviving a disaster. My companions looked unhurt and the car seemed undamaged, though the boom had exploded through the car just as overwhelmingly as the wind of transubstantiation had blown through it minutes before. As best I could tell, the sound had come from farther north on West End Avenue, a bit to our left, either on the west side of the street or nearby on an intersecting side street. But far enough away that we hadn't been hurt. Except traffic was once again at a standstill. Another victory for Dee.

Fire engines were already racing up the southbound side of West End Avenue, against traffic, causing a number of southbound cars to pivot wildly or seek refuge on the northbound side. It looked like it could be a while before the confusion got sorted out. And it looked as if Despair's and Discord's mayhem would only escalate as we were further delayed. Perhaps New York City was going to be taken apart tonight, road by road, block by block. I dreaded what incidents like this boom or the car pyramid meant for their immediate victims. But I dreaded even more the momentary despair in Will's eyes as he directed an agonized glance at me. Had he run out of ideas?

'The tower entrance is ten miles from here,' he said. 'We'll never get there.'

It was the first moment since I'd met him that I'd known him to seem without hope. Mournful, yes. Regretful, yes. But never hopeless. 'Trans – what is it – migration?' was all I could think of in response. Maybe he needed me to encourage him to get to the necessary level of will. If it could work once, why couldn't it work twice? The trip around the tree had taken no more than an instant, really, but if I'd been right about the location of the atom I stood on midtrip, we could have gone anywhere in that instant. It'd been pretty cold wherever we went, but it held nothing like the pain of entering water with Melusine. I didn't know the physics of the other world well enough to guess what the problem could be.

Then my thoughts were interrupted again when, several blocks to the east – perhaps above Central Park West – I could see a huge arc of white and gold flame suddenly sear the sky, dropping sparks and what looked like tiny flaming cylinders everywhere. A low boom resonated seconds later, like thunder following lightning. The very sight of the fire was so intense that it stirred a blood memory of my time with Ddraik, as if we had formed an ashes-to-ashes bond beneath City Hall. A wave of heat coursed through my veins as if my flesh could actually catch fire. I shuddered; certainly we didn't have a moment to lose in getting away to the north. But the next words out of Will's mouth were not encouraging.

'I've just never known it to work twice within a short period of time. And I have tried it.'

The fiery reflection of the conflagration to the east highlighted Will's features as he turned to me while speaking. His flesh took on an eerie cast, as if the silver tint of his skin were merging with bronze in an alchemy of Discord. He observed the tremor in my expression and tried to sound more hopeful. 'We could try calling in my helicopter, but I didn't like that fog on the river.'

A particularly loud, flaring thump echoed then from the roof of the car, which I thought might have been falling debris from whatever had happened near Central Park West. But then I was astonished, and elated, to see Lol's tiny face appear upside down near the top of Will's passenger-side window. She started to crawl down from the roof while jabbing a finger at him along the glass, gesticulating wildly, and jabbering at him continuously. Slowly, as if reluctantly, he lowered the window. She flew into the backseat and hovered in the air, wings whirring faster than a hummingbird's, and went on lecturing Will in adamant fashion.

I pulled on his sleeve to get his attention. 'What's she saying?'

He turned briefly to me, though she squawked loudly at his inattention. 'She's saying that if she helps, we can transmigrate a second time. She can't go with us, as her knowledge and skills are required here to give what help she can in fighting the fires. But she can help the atom-travel. She claims she knows a part of the incantation I've never been able to obtain.'

First of all I was relieved that Lol had recovered, and quickly, from Oberon's brutality. And as to Lol's offer, I didn't have to give it any thought. 'We can do it!' I shouted. And I was thrilled to say 'we.' If this was a power we both could participate in, Will *couldn't* be all bad, no matter what Oberon or Dee or the reputation of vampires or anything else claimed.

Things moved quickly then. Will ordered the driver out of the car, and he disappeared into a throng of people streaming up West End Avenue toward the site of the explosion. No doubt the idea of expelling him was to lighten the molecular load. Will occupied the driver's seat and had me sit up front with him. He lowered the driver's-side window and Lol hovered exactly where the glass had been, ready to both transmit instructions into Will's left ear and, I assumed, peel away at the last possible instant before transmigration. Will glanced at Lol, then took his right hand off the steering wheel to clasp my left hand tightly.

'Don't you need that to steer?' I asked, glancing from hand to wheel. But I didn't take my hand away.

He grinned. 'If all it took were two hands on the wheel, we already would have toured galaxies, you and me!'

He floored the gas pedal and veered into the now empty southbound side of West End Avenue. I was then jarred back into my seat by more acceleration than I'd ever felt in my life. My eyelids slammed shut. At the very last instant of sight I thought I saw Lol's green and gold flash as she soared skyward in a different direction from our motion. I fastened on the idea of her scurrying through the air to fight the Central Park West fire by whatever ingenious means she had, then flowed once again into extreme cold

and a sense of standing on a nucleus while electrons
whirled faintly around it like distant planets, even though
the entire atom including their orbits was an infinitesimal
scrap of matter itself. But then the cold went away and for
a searing moment I was standing on near-infinite, pulsing
heat, vaster than the sun's in a sunstorm, more akin to the
original white-hot surge that created matter. Had we
burned up this time? I couldn't help wondering, while
vertigo began to afflict me from watching the circling
electrons. But if I was asking the question I was alive, and
I could also separate and distinguish the warmth and life
in Will's grasping hand from the sudden sizzle of the atom.

The next thing I knew the atomic landscape had
vanished, and we had come to a bumpy stop. Rougher than
the last landing, but I was all right even if the car, from a
variety of groaning metallic sounds I had last heard in the
accident with my mother, wasn't. As my eyelids struggled
open, I observed that another massive tree had split open
the car's engine block this time, the violent cleavage
ending only a few inches from the windshield. I had the
most fleeting sense of tiny eyes on the twig tips of
branches sprawled all over the windshield like a spider
web of wood. Much more important, Will was okay,
a quick glance told me. He was already trying to open the
driver's-side door. The door only budged a few inches, but
he then shattered the window glass with a sharp jab of his
elbow, exiting through the shard-edged, empty window
frame as lithely as he'd climbed through the car's open
partition earlier. He planted himself firmly on the ground,
extended his arms to me, and gathered me up and lifted

me out the window in one supple motion, with a delicacy that left me unscratched by the slivers of glass. Will had the strength in his forearms to split steel.

'My aim was a little bit off,' he said sheepishly in reference to the car, as he settled me on the ground.

We were in front of an entrance to Van Cortlandt Park near the Old Croton Aqueduct Trail, a sign told us. I didn't know the neighborhood at all, but I was struck by how deserted the street seemed. I didn't want to dwell on the possibilities for why, but certainly the bigger the disaster, the bigger the audience watching on TV at home.

'Or else that tree splitting the car is a very recent arrival,' Will went on. 'It certainly didn't appear on the geoscreen I used in plotting the landing. If that's the case, that's a shame about Jean Robin's capacity for error. I knew him and liked him way back when. But sometimes his botany could get a little out of control.'

I was too drained to ask for examples of Jean Robin's 'past errors.'

But I wasn't too drained for a kiss.

The high Tower

We entered Van Cortlandt Park and started along the Croton trail. As I followed Will's increasingly fast pace on the wooded trail, I began to wonder what we were going to do when we found Dee. If Dee was so powerful that he could cause massive traffic accidents with invisible force fields, blow up buildings, and start huge fires, what chance did we have against him?

'I don't understand how we're going to get to the High Bridge Tower from here,' I yelled to Will on a more immediate point. He'd stopped up ahead at a small, square, stone building and was standing in front of a boarded-up and padlocked door. 'What's this place?'

'The Weir,' he said, leaning his shoulder against the door. The wood groaned, splintered, and suddenly just wasn't there anymore. Through the dust of the shattered door I saw stone steps leading down into the ground. 'We're going underground,' Will said, taking my hand. 'Come on. There's not much time.'

As I followed Will down the stone steps, I snapped my fingers to produce a small flame to see by. At the bottom of the stairs the flame danced off a sheet of black water, sending ripples of light up into an arched brick tunnel hung with stalactites. Tree roots snaked out of chinks in the brick, twisting across the arched roof in an intricate weave. It looked like the entrance to the underworld, but I had figured out what it was by now.

'The old Croton Aqueduct,' I said aloud.

'Yes. It leads straight to the High Bridge Tower.' Will stepped off the last step into the water, which I was glad to see was only a few inches deep. Still, I felt an innate dread of stepping into that dark water.

'Come on,' he said, holding his hand out for me. 'You traveled through the whole water system yesterday.'

'As disembodied molecules,' I answered, stepping gingerly into the water, 'and that was clean drinking water. *This*—' The water eddied around my feet, rippling in long ropes of black and white in the firelight. 'This looks like it could have—'

'Don't say it!' Will ordered, grabbing my arm and pulling me into a fast walk. 'As we get closer to Dee, we'll be susceptible to his influence. He'll pick up on any fears you voice – or even think – and make them real.'

Great! I thought; I hadn't said the word *snakes*, but now it was the only word in my head – except maybe for *rats* and *giant mutant crocodiles.* 'I thought you said that Dee wouldn't see us if we approached the tower underground.'

'I'm *hoping* he won't see us, but even if he doesn't, he'll have set some traps in the tunnels. Don't think about it – just stay close.'

Will set such a fast pace that soon I didn't have the breath to talk anymore. That left a lot of room for my

384 • Lee Carroll

imagination to roam over all the potential horrors that
might be lurking in the underground, disused aqueduct. I
tried to focus on the blinding white-hot anger I'd felt for
Dee when I learned he'd killed my mother. I pictured him
standing by the car fire, his face impassive and cold as my
mother burned to death. But then, instead of feeling
anger, I felt horror as I imagined my mother burning in
that fire. I tried to push the thought away. It was the one
image I had forbidden myself from ever picturing. She
was already dead when the car exploded, I'd told myself.
Or the explosion happened so quickly she wouldn't have
felt anything. But now when I pictured John Dee standing
beside that fire, I heard my mother's screams as well and
knew that her last minutes on earth had been a living hell.

'We're almost at the bridge,' Will's voice broke into the
painful image. I was glad for the distraction, but when I
focused on the scene ahead of us, my heart sank. The
aqueduct sloped steeply downward and disappeared in a
sea of fog. 'This is the gate chamber that pumped the
water upward to the bridge. Dee's filled it with fog to
make it more difficult to cross. We'll have to be especially
careful. There are dead ends and siphons that plunge
down into the hillside. Can you use your flame to shine
through the fog?'

I held up my thumb and willed the small flame into a
larger torch. The flame swelled up a foot high, but instead
of lighting a path through the fog it revealed shapes in the
murk – bulging blobs like giant amoebas, writhing,
swelling, dividing . . . then swelling again.

'What are they?' I asked, horrified to see that some of

the blobs were acquiring the rough shapes of human beings.

'It's the cellular matter of the fog. The fog shapes itself into images using negative energy. It's still at a protozoic stage, but as it grows stronger, the fog will be charged and then it will form into whatever mental images it encounters.'

'So basically people all over the city will get to meet their worst nightmares mentally even if they manage to avoid them physically.'

'Exactly. Even now if it encounters a strong enough mental image, it will shape itself to that. Since you've been exposed to training from the four elementals, your mind can send images powerful enough to spark life into it. So try to keep your mind blank.' He turned to me and smiled, but in the ghastly yellow light of the fog it looked more like a snarl. 'And please stay close. We'll have to feel our way across.'

Will tucked my arm under his and we started down the slope. The ground underfoot was slick and, once we were in the fog, invisible. I slipped several times, but each time he caught me. I tried to hold on tighter, but my hands were dripping from the fog and shaking from the cold. His hands felt as chilly and brittle as bare bones, flesh that had been dead a hundred years – and of course he had been dead for much longer than that.

'It's not much farther.' His disembodied whisper came from beside me. The fog was so thick I couldn't even see him ... did I really even know it was Will I clung to? I peered through the thick clotted air for Will's face. Even the face of a vampire – a creature of the undead – would be a welcome sight right now. I leaned closer . . . and a white skull loomed out of the fog, leering at me with empty eye sockets. I screamed and backed away, wrenching my hands out of the skeletal fingers I now saw clutching at me.

'Garet!' the voice came from the loose-flapping jaw.

I took another step back . . . and fell. Will – or whatever that *thing* by my side was – was too far away to catch me. I slid down the steep slope, through muck and ooze, and landed in a pool of foul-smelling water at the bottom. I heard Will's voice calling from above me, but all I kept seeing was that horrible leering skull.

It's the fog, I told myself, but another voice said, *But that's really what he is – a four-hundred-year-old corpse.*

So I stayed quiet. I didn't answer Will's call. I got to my hands and knees and began to crawl up the opposite slope. I would go on to the tower myself, get the box from Dee, and then this pernicious fog would soon evaporate and Will – the real Will – would catch up to me. Everything would go back to normal, then. That's what I had to focus on – my old life returned to stability and normalcy. My father would come home from the hospital and we'd find a way to pay off that loan. Becky and Jay would make up and find a way to compromise on the band's direction. And I'd prove to Detective Kiernan that my father had had nothing to do with the robbery. I continued to climb, keeping my mind on these mundane problems, which had seemed so huge a few days ago but were now somehow comforting. In fact, my everyday worries seemed to be an antidote to the fog. When I reached the top of the slope, the fog cleared and I could see the tunnel entrance to the High Bridge. I snapped my fingers and produced a small, flickering flame that I held up to the mouth of the tunnel . . . lighting up the figure of a man standing just inside.

I screamed. The man turned around and aimed a flashlight into my face, blinding me.

'Garet James, is that you?'

The voice was familiar, and when the man lowered the flashlight, I saw that he was Detective Joe Kiernan. 'What are you doing here?' I gasped.

'We saw that you looked up the High Bridge Tower and figured you'd come here,' the detective said. Then turning, he shouted into the tunnel, 'She's here. I found her.'

Two figures emerged from the gloom: Jay and Zach Reese. I'd never been so happy to see anyone in my entire life.

'We figured out what was going on,' Jay said. 'And we came to help.'

'You shouldn't have tried to do it all by yourself,' Zach said.

'I wasn't—' I began, looking behind me. What had happened to Will? 'I didn't think anyone would believe me,' I said instead.

'It *is* pretty unbelievable,' Kiernan said, 'but some pretty unbelievable things are happening up above. Fires and explosions everywhere. Come on. Let's find this guy Dee and stop whatever he's doing to this city.' Joe Kiernan smiled encouragingly. It was such a clean, honest smile that I wondered why I had taken such a dislike to the officer before. He was only trying to help. He took my arm now and led me into the tunnel. Jay took my other arm and Zach walked behind us. I could hear his steps reverberating on the iron supports of the bridge, a pounding that made my head hurt.

'This is really cool,' Jay said, pointing his flashlight onto the floor. 'Look, the pylons of the bridge are hollow. You can see all the way down to the river.'

A dizzying abyss opened beneath us and I gasped.

'Don't worry,' Jay said. 'I wouldn't let anything happen to you.' Then he whispered into my ear, 'You know how I feel about you, don't you?' His breath, so close to my face, smelled coppery. I turned to look at him, but he'd turned away so all I could see was his profile.

'She doesn't feel that way about you,' Joe Kiernan said. 'She doesn't really care that much about you or Becky. Look at what she let happen to Becky.'

'And to her father,' Zach added from behind us. I tried to turn around to face Zach, but Kiernan tightened his grip on my arm.

'That's right,' Kiernan said. 'You led those men to your house so they could shoot your father, didn't you? If he had died, it would have been a convenient way out of your troubles. And you wouldn't have to waste the rest of your life catering to a senile old man who gambled away your inheritance.'

'You wished him dead just like you wished your mother dead,' Zach's voice came from behind me. But it wasn't Zach. The two things marching me across the bridge weren't Joe Kiernan and Jay, either. They were demons I'd conjured up out of the fog. I closed my eyes and said aloud, 'You're not real.'

The three men laughed. 'Aren't we?' the one in Jay's shape said. 'We know all about you. Remember the time we cut school and took the ferry to Staten Island? I wanted to kiss you that day, but all you talked about was some boy you had a crush on.'

'And remember what your father said at your mother's funeral?' Zach asked. 'I was the only one close enough to hear. He said he wished it had been you who died instead.'

'That's not true!' I yelled, struggling to break free and turn around to face Zach. 'He said if I'd been in the passenger seat I would have died.'

'But that's what he was thinking.' Kiernan clucked his tongue. 'What a terrible thing for a father to think, but then your father always has been a selfish man. If he really cared about your well-being, he wouldn't have gambled away all your money.'

I pulled my arm away from Kiernan and he suddenly let go. Jay let go of my other arm. I took a step forward, but then I looked down and saw that we were at the edge of one of the bridge's pylons. Far below me I could see the churning water of the Harlem River.

'Go ahead, Garet,' the three men whispered together. 'Jump!'

I braced myself, waiting for them to push me over the edge, but nothing happened. They didn't have that power, at least not yet. They were made of air and water and, I suddenly remembered, I had power over both. I turned around and faced the three of them. 'You're just water,' I said aloud. The shapes turned gray and began to waver in the air. I lifted both arms up – the way I'd seen Ariel summon the wind – and listened for the wind's song. I felt it rushing over the High Bridge and skimming the water below, insinuating itself into the cracks between the bricks. Then it came through the tunnel like a freight train, lifting me off my feet for a moment. The shapes of the three fog-men began to disintegrate until there was only a trail of smoke that the wind blew out the other side of the tunnel.

'Thank you,' I said aloud.

A sigh stirred the air and then was gone. In its place I heard my name.

'Garet? Are you there?' It was Will.

'I'm here.' I saw him coming out of the gloom, his face pale and drawn but whole. The fog was gone now. This was the real him.

'Thank God!' he said, pulling me into his arms. 'I thought I'd lost you.'

'It was the fog. It made me see terrible things, but it's gone now.'

'Not for long,' Will said, holding me at arm's length and turning me toward the Bronx side of the tunnel where a curl of mist lay at the entrance like a coiled snake. 'We'd better hurry.'

At the end of the bridge was another gate chamber leading to the base of the tower. Without the fog it was easier to navigate, but still it was a difficult climb. My legs were shaking by the time we reached the base of the tower. I leaned against the brick wall for a moment to catch my breath, and then I looked up and saw a stairwell made of perforated iron spiraling up as far as my eye could see.

Just past one of the spirals was a narrow vertical opening in the wall; it looked like one of those slits in medieval fortresses built for archers to fire arrows through. There was a muted orange and yellow glow in it which baffled me, so I took a few steps to scrutinize it more closely, and then I gasped. The glassless window looked out on a block of apartment buildings, and two buildings at the end of the block were in flames. I shuddered with the thought of how many spark-sprouting tentacles could be growing throughout the city now, and how much of the city could be ashes by the time we subjugated Dee, if we did, but there was nothing to be done but try. Turning back to Will, who had enough on his mind, I pretended to be distracted only by profuse amber light, thick as honey, that was flowing down from the top of the tower.

'At least there isn't any fog,' I said to Will.

He nodded, but I noticed that he looked drained.

'Have you fed tonight?' I asked. 'I thought that's where you were before you came to me.'

'Your call interrupted me,' he said.

'Do you need—'

He waved me away. 'You need your strength. There's something in this tower that drains energy. Can't you feel it?'

Now that he mentioned it, I did. It felt as if gravity were stronger here, exerting a downward pressure on us. I had to grip the iron railing of the stairs to pull myself up onto the first step. As soon as my feet touched the iron staircase I felt the charge – an electrical current running down through the metal slammed into my body with the force of a Mack truck.

'Whoa,' I said, sinking down to my knees. 'What *is* it?'

'Dee has set up an energy coil. The spiral stairs are the perfect vehicle for it. This is what's pushing the fog out into the city – it's like a giant fan.'

'How are we going to get past it?'

Will didn't answer. I looked behind me and saw him slumped to the ground, his face ashen gray. 'Will!' I called, and reached down to take his hand. A current of energy leapt from my hand to his.

Instantly his skin lost the gray tint and he opened his eyes. He sat up and looked at me, his silver eyes flashing like mirrors. 'How did you do that?' he asked.

'I don't know.' Without losing contact with his hand I turned my palm up and saw that the compass stone embedded there was glowing. 'Oberon said that the stone *grounded* me. I can still feel the energy, but now it's flowing through me.' I stood up, pulling Will to his feet effortlessly. I felt the energy coursing through my body, but it no longer weighed on me. It felt, rather, as if I were standing beneath a cool waterfall. It felt . . . well, *energizing*. 'Come on,' I said, 'keep ahold of my hand.'

Climbing the spiral stairs was easy now. It was as if I were being carried upward on a spiral escalator. The whole stairway thrummed with energy, producing a low hum that reminded me of the song I'd heard in the wind. 'There's one thing I don't understand,' I said to Will over my shoulder. 'I thought Dee was summoning demons, but this energy wave doesn't feel evil – it feels great!'

Will laughed. 'And what makes you think that evil can't feel good? You made love to a demon last night. Are you telling me that didn't feel good?'

I looked back at him and saw that he was shining like an alabaster vase filled with light. He looked more like an angel than a demon. 'You're not a demon,' I said.

'There are those who would disagree.' He smiled sadly and touched my face. The energy connection set off sparks. 'At any rate, this energy isn't good or evil – it's just a conveyer, the engine behind whatever you send with it. Compared to the two demons that Dee has conjured, I *am* an angel. We'd better hurry.'

He looked so beautiful that I hated to turn away from him, but he was right. I continued up the stairs, but after the next flight Will put his hand on my arm to hold me back. 'Wait.' He pointed to something above my head. 'There's someone – or something – on the stairs up ahead.'

I looked up and saw what he meant. Because the stairs were perforated you could see through them all the way to the top, but on the next level just below the top something blocked the flow of light – something large and dark. I watched it for a few moments without seeing any movement. 'We'd better see what it is,' I whispered.

We took the remaining loops toward the top slowly and quietly. When we came around the last turn, I saw that the inert, dark mass was Oberon. He was pinned to the iron steps by a mesh of metal chains, as if a spider had spun a web of fine iron and trapped him in it. His eyes were open, staring vacantly toward the top of the tower.

'Is he dead?' I asked.

'It takes a lot to kill a fairy. I think he's just *iron-klampt*.'

'But he said it was just the little fey who were susceptible to iron.'

'Usually it is, but this is a lot of iron and Dee must have rigged a net to catch him.'

I knelt down and looked into Oberon's face. His eyes were the opaque white of milk glass – lifeless marbles. And his face was contorted in a rictus of pain. He had tricked me, left me to die, but I didn't like seeing the King of the Fairies pinned and trapped like a housefly. I laid my hand on his chest to feel for a heartbeat, and the blind milky white eyes revolved in their sockets toward me.

'Marguerite?' It was a hoarse croak, barely audible through dry, cracked lips.

'It's Garet. Here, let me take these chains off you.' I plucked at one of the chains with my fingers, but it was weirdly heavy. I pulled harder, but I couldn't budge it. I turned to Will to ask his help, but he shook his head.

'He left you paralyzed. Why should we help him?'

Oberon shook his head weakly back and forth. 'He's right. You have no reason to trust me again. Besides, as long as the box is open, the force of its energy keeps these chains pinned to the iron beneath me. But once you close the box, the chains will fall away.'

'And then he'll try to take the box from you,' Will said. 'We should finish him off.'

'No!' I said with more force than I'd intended. 'I won't

kill the King of the Fairies. He only did what he thought he had to, and besides, I think he'll be too weak from the iron to do anything to stop me once I have the box.'

'You're right,' Oberon said. 'Go! Just one thing. . . . When you get to the box . . . close it right away . . . don't look into it.'

It felt like a fairy-tale admonition, but then, it came from a fairy. I was tempted to ask why not, but there wasn't time for that. It seemed an easy enough thing to promise. 'Okay,' I said. 'We'll come back for you.'

Oberon stretched his cracked lips over his teeth and I realized he was trying to smile. 'Sure,' he said. 'I'll be waiting right here.'

The Amber Room

The room I stepped into was the same room I had seen
under the river and on the TCM set, and through Madame
Dufay's eyes, but none of those perspectives had prepared
me for what the room looked like now. I had noticed
before that the walls behind the paintings were gold-
colored, but now I saw that they were actually lined with
panels of translucent, glowing amber. And I recognized
the panels – they were from the famed Amber Room, built
for the Catherine Palace of St. Petersburg in the
eighteenth century, looted by the Nazis, then mysteriously
lost in the aftermath of World War II. I had seen pictures
of the ornate panels, but I had never heard that they
glowed. It was as if some energy source had filled them
with light. The whole room was pulsating with a honey-
gold energy that set my teeth on edge and made my blood
fizz.

The energy came from the shallow silver box sitting on
the table in front of the fireplace. I looked up from the box
and saw all that energy reflected in the amber eyes of the
man seated before me.

'Welcome, Garet James. I had hoped you would make it.

When I saw Oberon, I was afraid he'd already disposed of you.'

'Will saved me,' I replied. 'You were wrong about my not being able to trust him . . . but then spreading dissension and doubt is what you're best at, isn't it? When you're not preoccupied with physical destruction, that is.'

Dee smiled. 'Oh, my dear, you really haven't known me long enough to judge what I'm *best* at . . . nor should you be so certain that I was wrong about Will Hughes. I notice that he's let you take the lead here.'

I glanced back to see that Will stood on the threshold of the room, his hands braced on either side of the doorframe.

'I can't come any further,' Will said. 'This energy field he's created is too like sunlight.' To demonstrate, Will extended one hand a few inches into the room. Instantly his skin blistered and crisped.

'Stay back!' I cried, trying to go to him, but I couldn't. I was stuck. The amber light filling the room wasn't just light, it was made up of some kind of viscous substance – like the prehistoric sap that amber came from – and I was trapped like an insect in its sticky grasp. Or at least I thought I was. Although I couldn't go back to Will, I found I could turn back around to face Dee. And when I tried, I found that I could take a step toward Dee. Or, rather, toward the box. The energy flowing out of the box created a pathway I could walk on. In fact, it seemed to be pulling me forward. I had to dig my heels into the carpet to keep from going any farther.

'Go on,' Dee said, slowly lifting his right hand and

splaying his fingers toward the box. 'It's what you've come for, isn't it? I'll not get in your way.'

'Why not? You've certainly thrown enough obstacles in my way so far.'

Dee smiled . . . or, rather, he was *still* smiling, his lips frozen in a lifeless grin. I noticed too, that his hand remained in the air, fingers fanned open. 'I was curious to see how hard you would try to retrieve the box and whether you'd be able to make it here. I'm a very old man who's lived a very long time. There's not much that entertains me anymore, but your activities these past few days have been quite diverting.'

'Is that why you've unleashed the demons of Discord and Despair on the city? For entertainment?'

Dee shrugged. The gesture was supposed to look casual, but I noticed that his right shoulder remained hunched up to his ear. His hand was still in the air and his face was frozen in the same smile. 'Let's just say that every once in a while I like to shake things up and see what falls out. This time it's you who's landed on my doorstep.'

'So you don't mind if I take the box?'

'If you can take it, my dear,' he said, lifting one eyebrow, 'you're welcome to it.'

The eyebrow remained cocked. I realized now what was wrong with the way Dee was moving. Each motion was labored and, once made, he was fixed in that position. He'd been sitting in the amber electric field so long that he was stuck in it, while I could still move – as long as I moved toward the box. He wouldn't be able to stop me from taking the box.

I took a step forward. It was like walking on those moving walkways in the airport – one step seemed to take me three steps forward. I was inches from the open box . . .

Which Oberon had told me not to look in.

But if I closed the box, then the energy field might disappear and Dee would be able to move. Even though he'd told me I was welcome to take the box, I had no reason to believe he wouldn't spring on me the minute he could. I'd have to wait to the last minute to close it. Of course that didn't mean I had to look in it.

I stepped forward and raised my hands to the box, keeping my eyes above the open lid. As soon as I touched the lid, though, I had that feeling I'd had when I first touched the box in Dee's shop – as though it belonged to me. What harm could it possibly do me? I looked down.

At first the light was so bright it blinded me, but then, slowly, my eyes adjusted to the glare and I could see perfectly. I could, in fact, see for miles. For inside the box was another world – a world of green meadows starred with wildflowers and stitched with clear streams. I could hear the purl of the running water and smell the wildflowers.

I leaned closer to the box and the meadows rolled toward a stone tower that looked familiar. I came closer – I felt as though I were flying over the hills, skimming the high summer grass like a lark – and saw that the tower was reflected in a still, clear pool. It was, I realized with a thrill of recognition, the tower and pool from my dreams, only instead of one black swan, a dozen white swans glided across the crystal surface.

'Do you recognize it?' Dee's voice came as if from far away although he was only a few feet behind me.

'I've dreamed about this place' – another memory prickled at the edge of my consciousness – 'and heard about it. This is the place my mother used to tell me about. The Summer Country, she called it, or the Fair Land. I thought it was just a story she made up.'

'No, it's a real place, a beautiful place, yes? It is always summer there and no one ever ages.'

I saw now that there were men and women in the woods surrounding the pool. I couldn't see them very clearly – they seemed to slip in and out of the green shadows – but I had an impression of great beauty.

'Once our world and the Summer Country existed side by side and the fey and humans could pass from one to another,' Dee went on, 'but then our world grew more populous and humans stopped believing in the Summer Country and the doors between the two worlds began to close.'

How had my mother put it? *The door to the Summer Country opened in a glimpse, never in a second look.* Yet here I was staring into the heart of it – and I knew, somehow, that the tower and the pool *were* the heart of it.

'There are very few places where one can still cross over into the Summer Country, but this marvelous box can open a door anywhere if you know how to use it. Do you see those silver necklaces around the swans' necks?'

I leaned in closer. Dee was right. Each of the swans wore a silver chain with a large oval pendant around its neck. I remembered that the black swan in my dream had worn such a pendant. I touched the medallion at my own throat, the one I'd made from the ring my mother had given me, and felt it grow heavier.

'Those are the swan maidens. Perhaps you've heard the stories. When the silver chains are removed from their necks, they become women and they can step into the human world, only they need the chain to go back. One of those swan maidens strayed into the human world a very long time ago and fell in love with a mortal man. But he betrayed her and stole her silver chain and medallion. He had them melted down and made into this box, and that is why the box can open a door between the worlds.'

I pictured the black swan gliding on the pool at sunset and remembered the cry it made as it was shot by an arrow. Something was wrong with the way Dee had told the story, but I couldn't remember what. I was listening to what he was saying. 'If you like, you can step into that world right now.'

I could? I became aware that the light pouring out of the box had surrounded me in a glowing halo. I looked down and saw that I was no longer standing on a Persian rug, but green grass. I looked up and saw not the amber panels of the tower room, but blue sky. I was standing on the threshold of the Summer Country, the magical place my mother had told me about when I was little . . . and if my mother told me about it . . . ? If she *knew* about it . . . ? I looked ahead of me and saw standing, on the far side of the swan pool, a woman with long dark hair. It was my mother as she looked when I was a child: young, beauti- ful . . . not burnt and mangled in the car wreck, but whole and alive, waiting for me in the Summer Country. She reached out her hand and called my name. *Garet,* she called. *Garet . . .*

'Garet!' The third call came from behind me. It wasn't my mother's voice. It was Will's. 'Garet, don't go. You'll never be able to come back.'

So? I wanted to say, only it seemed like too much effort to speak out loud. Why would I want to come back to this world of strife and pain? Why wouldn't I want to join my mother in a land of ease and perpetual summer?

Again I heard Will's voice behind me calling my name, but instead of calling *Garet* he was calling *Marguerite.* The anguish in his voice made me turn around. Will was behind me, but he stood at the edge of a wood and he was dressed in a green tunic and slim, fawn-colored pants. His hair was longer and blonder, his skin was golden from the reflection of the setting sun and, I realized, ruddy with the glow of mortality. This Will wasn't a vampire, but neither was he the Elizabethan young man who had fallen in love with Marguerite D'Arques. This man, I felt sure, was an ancestor of that man and this time was a much earlier time. Nor were we in the Summer Country. We stood on the edge between the worlds. I also knew that this man was not supposed to be here. The sun was setting behind me, and once it set, something would happen that he was not supposed to see. He had promised me in that long-ago time that he would never follow me to the pool at sunset, but he had broken that promise. And now I would lose him forever. I already felt myself changing – my neck lengthening, my arms stretching wide, the skin between my toes growing webs, the prickle of feathers sprouting from my skin. I saw the look of horror on the youth's face. And then, as I glided out onto the lake, I saw him lift a great curved bow to his shoulder and pull an arrow back.

Why? Did he think it was the only way to keep me from leaving him? Had he heard all the stories of the enchanted animal wives – the selkies, the undines, the swan maidens – who left forever once their mortal lovers had broken the one admonition – never to look upon their wives in the moment of changing?

The arrow pierced my wing and I felt myself changing back, my human limbs sinking into the water, the heavy silver chain around my neck weighing me down . . . and then I was being dragged out of the water, the chain torn from my neck, the arrow pulled from my arm.

The man was weeping. 'Don't go!' he cried in a voice like Will's. 'Don't go!' But I was already going. I was turning into something else.

'I have to go,' I told him, 'but I will always watch over you and your sons and all the sons and daughters of your race. I will become like a watchtower guarding the border between the two worlds.'

And then all was black . . . but I still heard Will's voice calling me, 'Don't go, Garet! Don't go!' and I knew that I was back in the high tower and I knew who I was. I was the Watchtower pledged to stand on the border between the worlds and protect humanity, because of the love I had for one man even after he broke his promise to me.

I opened my eyes and saw the silver box in my hands. The

world of the Summer Country beckoned green and gold, my mother standing on the far shore, one hand raised – but whether in greeting or farewell I didn't know.

I closed the box. Instantly the amber light in the room swirled around me like a funnel cloud. I turned in it, feeling its power move with me like a great cloak. John Dee flexed his fingers, gathered a ball of the glowing stuff into his hands, and hurled it at me like Mariano Rivera closing out a tight game with a fastball.

It hit me square in my sternum and I collapsed. Dee leapt from his chair and was on me, wrenching the box from my hands, but I held on to it. His face was close to mine, his sulfurous breath hot on my skin.

'You fool! You'll be sorry you didn't take your chance to leave this world when I'm done with it. What you've seen so far is nothing!'

I felt my grip on the box loosening, but then Dee's hands lost their grip instead. He flew off me, as if he'd been plucked up by a giant forklift, and hit the wall. The amber panel shattered and all the electricity it had soaked up exploded. Dee's body jerked as if he'd been electrocuted and he slumped to the floor, unconscious. Will stood over him, his lips spread back over his fangs in an angry snarl. He lunged at Dee, straight toward his neck, but then recoiled, sparks flying between them. I smelled something burning and realized it was Will's flesh. The panel behind Dee was aflame and so was the next panel. An electrical fire was racing from panel to panel, and the light of the fire was burning Will's skin.

'Leave him!' I cried, struggling to my feet with the

box still cradled in my arms. 'We have to get out of here.'

Will turned to me and for an instant I don't think he knew me. His eyes glowed red in his fire-scarred face and his teeth were bared. But then the red in his eyes subsided, replaced by the flickering glow of the amber fire. He nodded once and reached out his hand for me, but I couldn't take it while I held the box, so I let him put one arm around my back and the other under my knees to pick me up. He had just stepped out of the room with me when I shouted for him to stop and put me down.

Something in the command in my voice made him listen to me. I handed him the box and ran back into the tower room, which had become an inferno. I looked over to where Dee had been lying a moment ago but he was gone. Had he vaporized from all the energy he'd absorbed? Or had he somehow escaped? I didn't have time to find out. I hadn't come for him.

I crossed the room and reached over the mantel for the portrait of Madame Dufay. The frame was singed and the canvas had browned in one corner, but her image was intact. When I grabbed the frame, it was so hot that it seared my hand, but I tucked it under my arm and ran onto the metal landing just as the tower room was engulfed in flames. An explosion shook the iron stairs and filled the tower with a noxious yellow smoke. I could barely see through it to the other side of the landing where Will stood leaning against the railing. I rushed to him, afraid that he'd been hurt in the explosion, but when I reached him, I found that the man wasn't Will. It was Oberon, freed from his metal chains, but still weakened.

'What have you done to Will?' I demanded.

Oberon laughed pathetically. 'Do I look like I'm in any shape to do anything to a vampire? No. He released me from the chains – only for your sake, he said – and asked me to get you out of here safely.' He gave me a sad smile. He looked sorrier for me than when he'd left me paralyzed in my father's apartment. 'And he told me to tell you he was sorry. Then he left, taking the silver box with him.'

The Summer Country

For weeks after, when I thought about that night, the part that was hardest to remember wasn't the glimpse I'd had of the Summer Country – that remained painfully and tantalizingly clear – but the walk back through the aqueduct with Oberon. I did remember going down the spiral stairs with him and that he was talking about Will.

'I knew he'd take it if he got a chance. He believes he can use it to make himself human again. He'll take it to the border of the Summer Country and summon the creature of the lake to make himself human again – and if that creature makes it into this world, it will be worse than if Dee had succeeded completely in unleashing the demons of Despair and Discord. I have to follow him and stop him.'

A quick glance through the slitted window we were again passing strongly suggested that Dee had, at least, been thwarted in completely unleashing the demons of Despair and Discord. Nothing was burning now. One of the buildings that had been aflame before had clearly sustained damage, but the other appeared to have been untouched.

I blinked, wondering if I was seeing accurately, but, no, only one building seemed to have had a fire. I could only speculate that at the moment I had acquired possession of the box – when the demons had presumably been annihilated – there'd been some small reversal in the progression of time, some reverberating recoil so powerful that the minutes in which the second building had caught fire had been erased. I felt a sense of triumph wash over me. New York City likely wasn't burning anymore, and maybe in some places lives had been saved by the time retraction.

Who was I, Garet James, to battle the darkest demons of the universe? I had asked myself what seemed like only hours before. Now the question had an answer at least for me. I was in fact up to it. I was the Watchtower, and a worthy one. Even if I was still – and at the same time – that frailest of humans, Garet James.

'I'll go with you,' I called after Oberon, who was marching ahead oblivious of my pause. I hurried to catch up with him.

He hadn't answered at first. We were entering the gate chamber and we had to be careful not to slip down the steep slope . . . then we were on the bridge and we had to be careful not to fall into the hollow pylons. Only when we'd navigated the gate chamber on the Bronx side of the bridge did he turn to me and say, 'Perhaps it's better if I take it from here.'

The next thing I knew I was lying in the woods beside the Weir house in Van Cortlandt Park, watching the sun coming up through the bare trees. My clothes were soaked and torn and smeared with mud. My right hand was throbbing with pain, and when I looked at it, I saw the skin was swollen and blistered. I remembered burning it when I grabbed the portrait of Madame Dufay, and I sat up to look for the picture . . . but my head started spinning and I had to lie down again before I could find it. I patted my jeans pocket for the lover's eye and felt a lump there, but my fingers were too tender to dig into the pocket. It could wait. I would rest awhile before trying to go home. There was no rush. Dee had been defeated and Will was gone. No one was waiting for me at home.

I drifted off again and awoke sometime later to the sound of a woman's voice. 'Ma'am, are you all right? Have you been injured?'

'She looks like her hand's been burned,' a male voice said. 'There's that psychopath who's been setting homeless people on fire.'

Homeless? Me? I wanted to tell him that I had a home, but when I opened my mouth to speak, all I could do was croak like an agitated frog. My throat felt as if it had been seared. I opened my eyes and saw a young man and woman dressed in the khaki uniforms of the urban park rangers. 'I think she inhaled a lot of smoke,' the man said. Then he spoke into a walkie-talkie to request an ambulance.

I tried to tell him that wouldn't be necessary, but I must have fallen asleep again because the next thing I knew I was being lifted and carried out of the woods. Things got jumbled after that. I was in an ambulance, but I was with my father and he'd been shot. I was lying in bed in a hospital room looking out the window at steam rising from the streets – great white plumes that assumed the shapes of dragons and serpent-tailed women. My father was there, hovering over my bed, his face creased with anxiety and grief.

'Don't worry,' I told him in a hoarse voice that didn't sound at all like my own, 'I took care of John Dee. Everything will be all right now.' But that only made my father look more worried so I tried not to talk any more.

Detective Kiernan came and told me that he was sorry he had ever suspected my father. 'The men who were hired to rob your gallery no longer claim that your father hired them. They seem to have no memory of who did, but we matched the canvas we found at Dee's shop to the canvas of your Pissarros. A man matching Dee's description has been tied to an art theft in Paris which Interpol is investigating.' That worried me, but I didn't say anything. I certainly couldn't explain to Joe Kiernan that Dee had vanished from a burning tower.

I knew the burning tower itself had been real, though. A front-page headline in the first *New York Times* I read in my hospital bed told me that the High Bridge Tower was going to be completely restored after a severe fire on what had come to be called Arson Night left it 'looking like a charred and smoldering ziggurat.' The cost would be upward of $300 million, the article went on, but that was just a small portion of the more than $5 billion Congress, the NYS Legislature, and the NYC Council had appropriated to repair and restore damage from the worst urban fires since the Great Chicago Fire of 1871.

Miraculously, only fourteen people (including five fire-fighters) had been killed in the more than one hundred separate fires set, but property damage was in the billions and more than two thousand people had been left home-less. An additional nine fatalities, with twenty-four people seriously injured, had occurred in the massive traffic accident on the West Side Highway that same night, the largest single car accident in New York City history.

Wow, I couldn't help thinking; I had to stop reading for a moment, with a shudder. *If we hadn't gotten to Dee . . . would anyone have survived?*

Becky came, long sleeves covering the bandages on her wrists. 'I'd slap you if you were up to it, James,' she said, plopping herself down on the side of my bed. 'What were you thinking of wandering around a New York City park at night? On Arson Night of all nights! You could have gotten yourself killed. And your poor hand!' She cradled my bandaged right hand in hers. 'You won't be able to weld for months!'

I had second-degree burns on my right hand and double pneumonia from lying out in the cold all night.

'Joe – Detective Kiernan says he thinks you were follow-ing some lead on the gallery robbery. Was that it?'

I nodded and pretended to be too weak to say more, but the next time Detective Kiernan came to visit (he came almost every day even though my father was no longer a suspect in the robbery), I told him I had spotted Dee on the subway and followed him uptown and into the park and then been ambushed by his hired thugs. The story sounded pretty silly even to me, but it was more plausible

412 • Lee Carroll

than the truth, and Kiernan only shook his head sadly and told me to stop playing detective. I promised him I would.

Although I had no lack of visitors – Jay and Zach came frequently, too – the one person I wanted to see the most never came. I knew it was foolish to hope that Will would regret taking the box and come back, but every evening, as soon as the light faded from the sky through my west-facing window, I waited. I insisted that the night nurse leave my window open a crack, even though she said the cold air wasn't good for my recovering lungs. Sometimes too, I would take out the lover's eye (which had been in my jeans pocket) and try to look through it, hoping for at least a glimpse of Will from Madame Dufay's memory, but when I placed it to my eye, all I saw was the silver backing of the brooch. Perhaps Oberon had destroyed the portrait – or perhaps smoke had destroyed the eye's ability to see.

And maybe Will was wary of visiting me in the hospital – as were Lol and Fen and the other fey and elementals I had met (I had asked for RN O. Smith, but drew only blank stares from the staff). I wanted to get home and look for them to see if any of them knew where Oberon and Will might have gone, but it was mid-January before I was released from the hospital. When I got back to the town house, I checked the DVR and found that the only movie recorded on it was *Bringing Up Baby*. I watched Robert Osborne do the introduction from his usual clubby-looking set, in his usual congenial manner. I couldn't detect any sign of recent demonic possession.

The next day I managed to slip out of the house while my father was in the gallery, and walked over to the hotel on the corner of Jane Street and the West Side Highway where Oberon lived. I found the façade covered with scaffolding, a large sign proclaiming that it was the future site of The Jane, a tony boutique hotel from the looks of the picture on the sign. I went inside and asked the clerk behind the refurbished desk (no longer protected by bulletproof Plexiglas) if any of the former SRO residents still lived in the hotel, and he told me that yes, some did, but when I asked about the tower room he told me that it was being turned into a bar.

'What about the man who lived there?' I asked.

The clerk shrugged and told me he'd only been working there since the first of the year.

I went to Puck's afterward and found that it had become a Starbucks.

I took the subway to City Hall and snuck into the basement, but Ignatius T. Ashburn III's office had gone back to being a janitor's closet.

I went to the National Jewelers Exchange and found that Noam Erdmann's stall was manned by a Hasid named Saul Levy, who told me that the previous tenant had retired to Miami.

As to Lol, I had no idea where she lived – if she lived anywhere – so there seemed no point in trying to search for her. I was still immensely grateful for her assistance with the second transmigration (and would never forget the sight of her upside-down face at the top of the window in Will's Rolls just in the nick of time), so out of that gratitude and some sense of obligation, I did stare on more than one occasion into a wind in which I'd heard some rustling, but the source of that was inevitably dried brown leaves, or the morning's newspapers, or discarded candy wrappers, or my imagination. If I ever crossed paths with Lol again, it would be her decision, not mine.

By the time I got back to the town house I was exhausted. I expected to find my father fretting over where I had been, but instead I found him glued to the TV set. 'I just heard that a plane's gone down in the Hudson,' he told me.

I had a sinking feeling as I sat down beside him. I might have got the box away from Dee, but the world was still a perilous place where planes crashed and people died. But when the CNN broadcaster came on, we learned that the airplane had, amazingly, landed safely on the Hudson near West Forty-second Street, navigated by a resolute and calm former fighter pilot named Chesley 'Sully' Sullenberger. My father and I watched the coverage for hours, listening to the testimony of witnesses who'd watched the plane's miraculous water landing, and those on the ferries and tugboats that immediately came to the rescue of the stranded crew and passengers. As we watched, I kept imagining what the story could have been – how many people could have died if the plane had, instead of landing safely, crashed into a Manhattan high-rise.

'It makes you feel hopeful,' my father said, wiping away a tear.

'Yeah,' I answered, my own voice husky, 'it does.' What I couldn't tell my father was that it gave me hope that what I had experienced meant something. It had gradually dawned on me while watching the coverage that the stretch of river where the plane had landed was exactly where I had observed a cylinder of fog suggesting a plane during our ride uptown on Arson Night. It chilled me to think of it. As far as I knew, there hadn't been any aerial catastrophes on Arson Night, so that roll of malevolent fog had likely never reached its critical mass. And it went to oblivion with the annihilation of Despair and Discord, but now it sounded like something even better than annihilation could have happened. As if the positive forces out there, the same ones that allowed us to transport our atoms to so much more quickly confront Dee, had protected that part of the river after its possession and made it a refuge. Which the plane had found.

And if the world was in this way and many others a better place now, wasn't it because I had gotten the box away from Dee? It was difficult to tell much from the news, though. The economy still looked bad, with home prices falling, car companies faltering, and unemployment claims reaching new weekly peaks, but there also did seem to be a mood of cautious optimism. Five days after Captain Sullenberger's landing on the Hudson, I sat on the couch between Jay and Becky watching Barack Obama being sworn in as the forty-fourth president and felt myself tearing up when he said, 'On this day, we gather because we have chosen hope over fear, unity of purpose over conflict and discord.'

There were more private, personal signs of hope as well. Becky was happier than I'd seen her in months – mostly due to the influence of Joe Kiernan. He'd visited her every day in the hospital and then, when she was let out, gone to every show London Dispersion Force played. At first Becky had scoffed at the idea of dating a cop, but Joe endeared himself to her by constantly expressing his delight that she was *not* a lawyer. He endeared himself to Jay by agreeing that the big commercial record contract was a mistake and what they should really do was start their own indy recording label. He had a cousin in Brooklyn who had the equipment and space. I couldn't begrudge Becky her happiness with Joe, even as the weeks passed without any sign from Will.

And, perhaps inspired by Becky's hopeful example, I woke up one ice-blue morning with the warm inspiration that perhaps Will was skittish about contacting me exclusively because of how angry I might be about his theft, and that it was time for me to reach out. He could simply be too embarrassed to get in touch. With that in mind I contemplated paying a surprise visit to him one evening, but his silence had produced enough hurt – and caution – that I hit instead on the compromise of sending him a brief note. I selected a blank card with care at Barnes & Noble – the cover showed a young couple holding hands on the observation deck of the Empire State Building in the 1940s – and wrote that I had enjoyed our adventures together and I missed him. One sentence, no mention of the box. After further debate, I chose *Warm thoughts, Garet* over *Love, Garet* as my sign-off, mailed it to his apartment, and got it back a week later stamped ADDRESSEE MOVED – NO FORWARDING ADDRESS.

That was a pretty bad jolt – I cried all the next day – but

then I realized Black Swan Partners might have been harder to shut down than his apartment was to vacate. I wasn't quite up to calling the office, but I did call Chuck Chennery and get a list of hedge fund websites where I might be able to get additional contact information for Will's fund by pretending to be an investor. The first site I went to, Hedge World, reported Black Swan as having closed on the last day of the year, with a PO box in the Cayman Islands as an address for any partner needing further information. I mailed the old note in a new envelope, with low expectations this time that were fulfilled, although it did come back faster with its ADDRESSEE UNKNOWN stamp even though it had traveled thousands of miles as opposed to eight miles along Manhattan Island.

In a final act of semidesperation, I called Hedge World's offices, hoping that by some wild chance I would speak to someone who knew Will or Black Swan and might just be in a mood to talk. The HW phone receptionist, a very young-sounding woman, was pleasant enough but told me, 'Will Hughes was a famously reclusive manager when he was running a fund. Someone here once tried to set up an investor with him and he'd only meet with him between two and three in the morning. Not much chance of finding him now that he's closed his fund, I'm afraid.'

So I finally had to give up on finding Will. Like Lol, I'd hear from him at a time of his own choosing – if ever.

In the last week of February my father brought me to Zach Reese's studio. 'He's been painting nonstop since mid-December,' Roman told me in an uncharacteristically vague and halting manner, as if he wasn't quite sure how to describe what he had seen. 'What he's doing is . . . different . . . more controlled than his early work, but also more lucid . . . and luminous . . . Well, you'll see. I want you to tell me what you think . . . whether I'm biased.'

Zach Reese had lived and worked in a loft on Mercer Street since the late seventies – one of the first lofts in the area converted from warehouse space into studio and living space. I remembered visiting with my father when I was little and being scared by the giant hook that hung on the first floor and the rattling metal steps that led up to the studio, but once in the studio it was like being at the circus or in a tropical garden. There were huge canvases splashed with color, cans of paint lined up like vats of ice cream, and everywhere – on the walls, the floors, the canvas drop cloths – multicolored paint splatters like confetti after a parade. Over the years the paintings had vanished, the cans of paint were closed and stacked against the walls, the drop cloths tossed away. Only the splatters on the floors and walls remained, mute testimony to the creative spirit that had once dwelled in this space, but as they faded with age, they began to look like blood splatter from some horrible slaughter. The smell of turpentine had also faded, replaced by the medicinal reek of vodka.

But when I walked up those stairs with my father on a cold, sunny day in February, I smelled turpentine and paint again. Zach greeted us at the door, a paintbrush held steady in his hand, his clothes speckled with fresh paint, his eyes shining. As soon as I stepped into the studio, a large canvas drew my attention . . . and immediately took my breath away. Incandescent colors glowed against a dark background that wasn't quite blue or black or purple but somehow all of those. At first I thought the splatters were abstract, but when I looked closer, I saw shapes in the canvas – figures, flowers, wings. It took me a few minutes to realize what it reminded me of – the heather garden at Fort Tryon Park the night I first walked through it with Will, my sight heightened by his blood in my veins.

My eyes brimming with tears, I turned to Zach. 'How did you—?' I began, wanting to ask him how he'd seen through vampire eyes, but when I turned to him, I saw my father standing beside him looking at the painting with his eyes also full of tears.

'When I look at this,' Roman said, 'I see the Luxembourg Gardens on the first evening I walked through them with Margot.'

Zach nodded and I realized that the sight Zach had used to paint this wasn't supernatural, it was the sight of first love. But whom had Zach loved like this? I watched him as he showed us painting after painting – he'd done more than a dozen since December – each one a breathtaking explosion of color and form. After the first one, my father stopped looking at the paintings and watched me looking at them instead. When Zach raced to the other side of the loft to retrieve something he said he wanted to give me, my father turned to me.

'So,' he said in a low voice, 'am I crazy or are these' – he waved his hand at the light-filled canvases – '*something*?'

'Oh, these are *something*, all right. These are *everything*. There are whole worlds in these paintings. Only' – I

420 • Lee Carroll

too, lowered my voice – 'was Zach in love with somebody he lost?'

I thought my father would ask what gave me that idea – how could I see the history of a lost love affair in abstract splatters of paint? – but he didn't. He only smiled sadly and said, 'Didn't you know? Zach was in love with your mother.'

I opened my mouth to ask questions. How long? Did you know? Were they lovers? But Zach had come back with a rolled-up piece of paper. 'I came across this when I was going through some old sketchbooks,' Zach said, handing me the paper. 'I thought you'd want to have it.'

I knew Zach had had a classical art education before he'd become an abstract painter, but I'd never seen anything he'd done that wasn't abstract. This was a portrait of my mother, sketched in pencil. She was sitting by a pond looking into the water at her own reflection.

'Thank you, Zach,' I said. 'It's beautiful.' When I looked up, my father was smiling at Zach. I saw now why the two men were so close – why my father had stood by Zach all these years when he couldn't paint a thing, and why Zach had sat beside my father every day he was in the hospital. They were united in having loved the same woman and having lost her. I might not have understood once, but I understood now. If I had known someone who had loved Will the way I did – Marguerite D'Arques or Madame Dufay, say – I would gladly have stayed by her side.

As the long winter lost its grip and spring finally began, I found that there was plenty to keep me busy. To our surprise, Sotheby's in Paris had expressed an interest in offering the Pissarros in their spring Impressionist auction, so I had to oversee the paperwork, catalog copy, and their shipping.

I also had a lot of signet medallions to make. Rather than hurt my business, the recession had made moderately priced jewelry with mottoes such as HOPE, FAITH, and HARD TIMES MAKE ME STRONGER more popular than ever. It was difficult, at first, to work with my scarred right hand, but I eventually got enough mobility back to handle the soldering iron. What I couldn't do, though, was snap my fingers on that hand, so I didn't know if I could still produce fire, but I did feel a tug in the palm of my hand that pointed toward true north. That and my ability to see auras and hear thoughts were the only proofs I had that what I had been through was real. I sometimes wondered if those talents might be figments of my imagination, but I squelched such worries (along with any temptation to test those powers by playing mental guessing games or jumping off the Empire State Building) with more hard work.

What kept me busiest was getting the gallery ready for Zach's show, which was scheduled for the last week in May, on the same day as the Sotheby's auction in Paris. I was worried at first that my father had given us too little time to publicize the show adequately, but I needn't have been; the show seemed to publicize itself. The entire art community was fascinated with the idea of a fading star making a comeback. 'I think they want good news,' Captain Sullenberger modestly said of the public's response to his heroic landing, 'I think they want to feel hopeful again.' Perhaps watching a washed-up, alcoholic painter pick himself up and create beautiful work again was just such another sign of hope. There was so much preshow buzz, in fact, that I worried Zach might crack under the pressure, but he took it all in good humor, radiating a calm and steadiness I'd never seen in him before. When the paintings were hung, I saw at last that there was nothing to worry about. In the empty gallery moments before the show was scheduled to begin, the paintings themselves radiated an aura of peace and beauty.

'Surprising,' I heard an NYU professor lecturing a group of art students, 'given the artist's turbulent past. But the riot of color and movement seems to lead the viewer through great cataclysms of experience into a hard-won serenity.'

I wondered what experience the professor saw in the paintings. The show was called 'Elements,' and the four largest canvases were entitled *Air, Earth, Water,* and *Fire.* I saw in them my flight over the city, the pain in Noam Erdmann's eyes when he pressed the compass stone into my flesh, the longing of Melusine for the pure springs, and a bonfire burning on the shore of Governors Island, its flames reaching toward the stars. I saw too, the last flight of the sylphs when Oberon had released their souls into the ether, and a torch-lit garden party in eighteenth-century Versailles. As I circulated around the gallery, I heard a jaded art critic enthuse that one piece brought him back to his grandmother's garden and a young hedge fund manager say that another made her think of an idyllic summer she'd spent lifeguarding on the Jersey shore when she was a teenager. Whatever they all saw in Zach's paintings, they wanted them. Every painting was sold before the end of the show.

When I finished helping a jubilant Maia (she'd earned enough on her share of the commission on Zach's paintings to put the down payment on a studio in Williamsburg) clean up and had locked up the gallery, I found my father and Zach drinking champagne in the kitchen.

'Join us in a toast, sweetheart,' my father crooned as I sat tiredly down at the table.

'Of course,' I said, taking a Baccarat crystal flute (one of a set my parents had brought back from their honeymoon in Paris) from Zach's steady hand. I gazed at my father and remembered how tense and worried he had looked five months ago, on the night I'd come home from John Dee's shop with the silver box. Now, despite his gunshot wound and his week in the hospital, he looked happy and rested and glowing from the success of Zach's show.

'Here's to a successful show,' I said, lifting my glass. 'The paintings are amazing, Zach. I'm almost sorry to see them all go.' I meant it even though I knew that what we'd earned on our commission from the sales would go a long way toward paying off our debt and putting us on the road to financial stability. Zach had been that generous with his commissions and the prices had gone wildly high.

'We've got more good news,' my father said, exchanging a look with Zach. 'I just heard from Pierre Benoit at Sotheby's. The Pissarros sold for twice their reserve.'

'Really?' I said. 'That's great! Who bought them?'

'An anonymous buyer,' Roman said. 'So much for snow scenes not selling in a recession!'

I thought of the mauve-and-blue-tinted snow in the Pissarros, remembering how on the night of the robbery

I'd longed to slip into those snow-covered French fields, and I wished I could see the paintings one more time, but I raised my glass and said, 'To Anonymous, then, whoever he or she may be!'

We clinked our glasses, the old crystal chiming like church bells. Then my father said, 'There's something else strange. Anonymous insisted on sending us a gift along with his money. A package was delivered earlier today. I was so busy getting ready for the show I didn't have time to open it.' He pointed to a wooden packing crate on the floor beside the safe door.

'That *is* strange,' I said. 'It must have been sent before the auction. Anonymous must have been pretty sure he was going to get the paintings. And why send the seller a present? I've never heard of that.'

Roman shrugged. 'Me neither. Why don't we open it?'

Zach got out a screwdriver from the tool drawer and went to work dismantling the wooden packing case. I searched the outside of the box for an address or shipping label, but there was nothing. It was clear, though, that the gift was a small painting, professionally packed.

'Maybe it's another Pissarro that he wants us to sell for him?' I wondered aloud as Zach removed the last layer of packing foam from the painting. I could see that the gilt frame was mid-nineteenth-century, but the front of the canvas was facing away from me and toward Zach.

'Not a Pissarro,' Zach said. 'A Vuillard maybe? There's no signature. The subject's Parisian, though. I'm sure I've seen the place before.'

He turned the painting around and propped it up on a

kitchen chair, just as he and my father had propped up the Pissarros that night in December. As on that night I felt as if the painting opened a window onto another place, but this time it was a rain-soaked park in Paris in shades of blue and lilac, lamplight gleaming on bits of marble statuary and the leaves of trees. A small stone church loomed dimly in the mist at the back of the park.

'It's pretty,' I said, moving closer to the painting. 'An old church in Paris.' As I said the words, something pricked at my memory.

'The *oldest* church in Paris,' my father said with a far-away look in his eyes as he gazed at the picture. 'That's Saint-Julien-le-Pauvre. Your mother and I stayed at an apartment nearby in Saint-Germain lent to her by one of her old friends – Marie Du something or other – after the war. When I came back from the galleries, I'd find your mother sitting in that church and then we'd have dinner at the café across the street. After the war the neighborhood of Saint-Germain-des-Prés was where one would go to listen to jazz or to Sartre and de Beauvoir arguing about existentialism . . .'

My father went on for some time, reminiscing about the days he and my mother had spent in Paris in the fifties, and trips they later took there to buy paintings. I listened contentedly, gazing at the painting and sipping more champagne than I should have. By the time Zach went home and my father went up to bed, it was almost dawn. I continued to sit at the kitchen table and gazed at the painting as the gray light of dawn slowly stole across the canvas.

A painting of an old church in Paris. That's what

Marguerite D'Arques had left for Will in her London lodgings when she left him. He took it as an invitation to find her – and eventually he had, by following a clue he found in the church that had led him to another clue . . . and then to another, until he traced her back to the pool beside the tower – to the place where she summoned the creature that made her mortal. Isn't that where Will would have taken the silver box now? He said that he'd tried to retrace his steps over the years and failed, but maybe he'd found a way this time, and perhaps he'd wondered if I could follow the trail if I had the starting point.

I reached into my pocket for my loupe, but brought out the lover's eye instead. I'd taken to keeping it in my pocket and holding it up to my eye every once in a while, always hoping it would show me something other than the blank silver back of the brooch. I held it up now over the painting. For a moment I wondered if I'd gotten the loupe after all because I saw, as though through glass, the scene in the painting in front of me . . . the rain-slicked park, the stone church . . . but then I saw that the rain was actually falling and, as I watched, a dark-cloaked figure walked by, his boots stirring the lamplit puddle.

I blinked and the vision abruptly faded. The brooch was opaque and the painting was still. Perhaps I had imagined it, or perhaps Madame Dufay's eye, although damaged by smoke, had revived for a moment at the sight of a familiar place.

I brought the painting upstairs and leaned it against the window behind my worktable so I could look at it while I searched the Internet. By the time the morning light had fully filled my studio, I'd reserved a seat on a flight to Paris. I looked up from my computer screen and noticed that the Poland Spring bottle that I'd brought back from Governors Island – the one I'd filled with the last of Melusine – was glowing in the light, as if it knew that it was on its way home. Then I looked at the painting. In full sunlight it glowed like an opal, each raindrop glistening as if the sun in my studio were actually shining on that rain-soaked park. Like the vision I'd had before, the illusion only lasted for a moment, but long enough for me to know that once I set foot in that park, I'd be on the path to finding Will Hughes and the Summer Country.

Garet's extraordinary adventures continue in

THE WATCHTOWER

coming in August 2011 from Bantam Press

Here's a sneak preview of the first chapter . . .

Chapter One

The Pigeon

The park outside the church smelled like pigeon droppings and cat pee. At least I hoped it was cat pee. After my first week in Paris, I realized that I hadn't seen any cats. Pigeons, yes. Each morning I sat with the pigeons and the still sleeping homeless people, waiting for my chance to sit inside the smallest, and surely the dimmest, little church in Paris in order to wait some more . . . for what I wasn't sure. A sign. But I didn't even know what form that sign would take.

It had all started with a silver box I found in an antiques shop in Manhattan, which I had unwittingly opened for the evil Dr. John Dee – yes, John Dee, Queen Elizabeth's alchemist who should have been dead almost four hundred years, but wasn't – unleashing the demons of discord and despair onto New York City. With the help of some fairies – Oberon, Puck, Ariel . . . the whole Shakespearean crew plus a diminutive fire sprite named Lol – I had gotten the box back and closed it, only to have it stolen by Will Hughes, a rather charming four-hundred-year-old vampire whom I'd fallen in love with. Will had taken it to open a door to the Summer Country and release a creature who could make him mortal again so we could be together, so I supposed I could forgive him for that. But why hadn't he taken me with him? I would have followed Will on the path that led to the Summer Country. Will had told me on the first night we met wandering through the gardens outside the Cloisters that he had taken the path once before, following signs left behind by his beloved Margeurite, who turned out to be my ancestor. The first sign had appeared outside an old church in Paris. The path always changed, Will had told me, but it always started in that church. You just had to wait there for a sign that would tell you where to go next.

So when, months after Will disappeared, just when I thought I'd gotten over him, an anonymous art buyer sent to my father's gallery a painting of an old church in Paris, which my father identified as Saint-Julien-le-Pauvre in the Latin Quarter, I knew the painting must have come from Will and that he was asking me to join him on the path to the Summer Country.

I made my plane reservation right away and booked my room at the Hôtel des Grandes Écoles, the little Latin Quarter pension where my parents had spent their honeymoon. I told my father and friends Jay and Becky, that I was going to Paris to research new jewelry designs at the Louvre and in the Museum of Decorative Arts. I read in their eyes how thin the pretext was, but they hadn't questioned me too deeply. After the events of last fall – a burglary, my father getting shot, me ending up burned and battered in Van Cortlandt Park in the Bronx – they didn't need to know more to think I could use a couple of weeks away. And what more diverting place to go than Paris?

If they had known I planned to spend my mornings sitting in a dim, musty church waiting for a sign from my vampire lover, perhaps they would have suggested a month in the Hamptons instead.

On my seventh morning in the church I had to admit that the old women with their string bags and the old men with their copies of *Le Monde* were all more likely to receive a sign from the doe-eyed saints on the walls than I was. I slipped out of the quiet church, avoiding the eyes of the black-robed priest who, after seeing me here for seven mornings in a row must have wondered, too, what I was looking for, and escaped into the only slightly more salubrious air of the Square Viviani.

Like the church, the Square Viviani needed something to boast of besides its homeless inhabitants and free Wi-Fi access. For Viviani, it was the oldest tree in Paris, a *Robinia pseudoacacia fabacées* planted in 1602 by the botanist Jean Robin, now leaning so perilously towards the walls of Saint-Julien that I found myself worrying that one of these mornings, on which I would no doubt still be sitting here waiting for my sign, the oldest tree in Paris would fall onto the oldest church in Paris and collapse with it, like the two old drunks curled up like nesting spoons.

To keep such an event from happening, the city of Paris has propped the twenty-or-so foot-tall tree up with a cement girder ingeniously sculpted to look like a tree itself, and the actual tree has been fortified against some blight with an unsightly patch of grey cement, one large enough that I probably could have squeezed into the hole it filled.

It made me feel sorry for the tree ... or perhaps it's just that I was feeling sorry for myself.

To make my self-pity complete, a pigeon landed on my head. I was so startled I let out a yelp and the pigeon flapped indignantly down to my feet and squawked at me. It was an unusual one, brown and long-necked, perhaps some indigenous European variety. I looked closer ... and the bird winked at me.

I laughed so loud that I woke up one of the sleeping drunks. She clutched her ancient mackintosh around her scrawny frame, pointed her bent fingers at me and gummed a slurry of words that I interpreted to mean *He fooled you, didn't he?* Then she put her fingers to her mouth and I realized she was asking for a cigarette.

I didn't have a cigarette so I offered her a euro, and she slipped it into an interior pocket of her mac, which I noticed was a Burberry *and* her only garment. She pointed again to the brown pigeon who had taken up a command-ing pose atop the *Robinia pseudoacacia*, from which it regarded me dolefully.

'Amélie,' the woman said.

I pointed to the pigeon and repeated the name, but she laughed and pointed to herself.

'Oh, you're Amelie,' I said, wondering if it was her real name or one she'd taken because of the popular movie with Audrey Tatou.

'Garet,' I told her, then gave her another euro and got up to go. If I needed a sign to show me that I was spend-ing too much time in the Square Viviani, it was being on a first name basis with the homeless there.

I decided to go to the other place I'd frequented this week – a little watch shop in the Marais. The owner, ninety-year old Horatio Durant, was an old friend of my parents. On the first day I had visited him he took me on what he called a horological tour of Paris.

'They should call Paris the City of Time,' he declared, striding down the rue de Rivoli, his cloud of white hair bobbing like a wind-borne cloud, 'instead of the city of light.' He showed me the enormous train station clock in the Musée d'Orsay and the modernist clock in the Quartier de l'Horloge composed of a brass-plated knight battling the elements in the shape of savage beasts. He took me to a watch exhibition at the Louvre, then to the Musée des Arts et Métiers to see the astrolabes and sundials, where I fell in love with a timepiece that had belonged to a sixteenth- century astrologer named Cosimo Ruggieri. It had the workings of a watch revealed through a transparent crystal, but its face was divided into years instead of hours. Stars and moons revolved around the perimeter and, inset into a small window, a tree lost its leaves, gained a snowy mantle, sprouted new leaves, and turned to blazing red. I sketched it again and again, making small changes, until I found I had an unbearable itch to cast it into metal. Monsieur Durant told me I was welcome to use his workshop. He leant me not only his tools, but also his expertise with watchmaking. A week later I had almost finished it.

After I left the park and took the metro to the Marais, I spent a few hours happily etching the last details on the timepiece. I had modified the design by adding a tower topped by an eye with rays coming out of it.

'That's an interesting motif,' Monsieur Durant remarked when I showed him the finished piece. 'Did you copy it from someplace?'

'It was on a signet ring I saw once,' I replied, without mentioning that it had been on Will Hughes' ring. Will had explained that the ring had belonged to my ancestor, Margeurite D'Arques. The symbol represented the Watchtower, an ancient order of women pledged to protect the world from evil. Four hundred years ago Will had stolen the ring from Margeurite and left in its place his own swan signet ring, which had subsequently been handed down from mother to daughter until my mother had given it to me when I was sixteen, just months before she died.

'A watchtower for a watch,' Monsieur Durant remarked, squinting at it through his jeweler's loupe. When he looked up at me his eye was freakishly magnified and I felt exposed. Did Monsieur Durant know about the Watchtower? But he only smiled and said, 'How apropos!'

After I left Monsieur Durant's I stopped on the Pont de la Tournelle. As I watched the sun set behind the turrets of Notre Dame, I realized I hadn't made my evening vigil at Saint-Julien-le-Pauvre. Checking my new watch, which now hung around my neck, I saw that it was almost ten o'clock. The long days of the Paris summer had fooled me. I felt a twinge of guilt then, followed by a pang of grief. I wasn't going to get a message. If Will really had sent the painting of the church – and even that certitude was fading fast in the limpid evening light – perhaps he had only sent it as a farewell. An apology for betraying my trust and stealing the box. A reminder that he'd needed it to embark on his own quest for mortality. Perhaps it served no more purpose than a postcard sent from a foreign land with the message *Wish you were here*. It hadn't been an invitation at all.

With another pang I recalled another moment by a river. That very first night I had spent with Will we had sat on a parapet above the Hudson and he had told me his history. 'When I was a young man,' he had begun, 'I was, I am sorry to say, exceedingly vain of my good looks, and exceedingly shallow. So vain and shallow that although many beautiful young women fell in love with me and my father begged me to marry and produce an heir, I would not tie myself to one lest I lose the adulation of the many.'

I remembered looking at his profile against the night sky and thinking that he might be forgiven a little vanity, but that surely he had gained depth over the centuries.

But had he? Might I not be just another one of those young women who had adored him and whom he had spurned?

The sun-struck water blurred into a haze of gold light in front of my eyes. I thought it might be one of my ocular migraines, but then I realized it was only my tears blurring my vision.

He isn't coming, he isn't coming. I heard the words chiming inside my head as the bells of Notre Dame began to toll the hour.

How many disappointed lovers had stood on this bridge and thought those words? How many had leaned a little further over the stone parapet and given themselves to the river rather than face another day without their beloved?

Well not me, I thought, straightening myself up. As I did I felt the timepiece ticking against my chest like a second heart. I looked at it again, pleased with the work I'd done. The week hadn't been a total waste. The timepiece would be the basis of a new line of jewelry when I got back to New York. I'd found exactly the inspiration I'd told my friends I'd come here looking for. Could I hate Will for calling me to Paris if this was the result?

No. The answer was that I couldn't hate him. But that didn't mean I had to spend the rest of my vacation sitting in a dark, musty church waiting for him.

I walked slowly back toward the Square Viviani. I had never tried to go to the church after dark, mostly because of the concerts that were held there at night. Tonight was no exception, but I thought if I waited until after the concertgoers left I might be able to sneak in. I felt I had to go tonight while my mind was made up. I had to go one last time to say goodbye.

The concert was still going on when I got there so I waited in the square for it to finish. At first the square was crowded enough with tourists that I didn't worry about being safe here at night. This area by the Seine, across the river from Notre Dame, was especially popular with the students who filled the schools on the Left Bank during the summer. I listened to a group of American girls laughing about a man who had approached them outside Notre Dame that day.

'Was it crazy pigeon man again?' a girl with wavy, brown hair and a dimple in her left cheek asked.

'No,' a redheaded girl answered. 'It was crazy pigeon man's friend, Charlemagne man!'

'Oh yeah!' a third girl with black bangs low over her forehead replied. 'The one who went on about how Charlemagne was a great man and he founded the schools so we could come here to study art. Don't you think he's got Charlemagne mixed up with Napoléon?'

'I think he's got more than that mixed up!' the dimpled girl responded.

I listened to them dissect the crazy ranting of the two street characters – I'd seen them myself in the square in front of Notre Dame – and then go on to talk of the paintings they'd seen at the d'Orsay that day, the eccentricities of their art teacher ('What do you think he means when he says my lines need more *voce*?'), the accordion players on the metro ('I like the one at the Cluny stop whose accordion sounds like an organ.') and I thought, how wonderful to be a student in Paris! Why shouldn't I enjoy myself the way they were, reveling in the whole scene instead of waiting for a sign that wasn't going to come?

The girls talked until the one with the brown wavy hair looked down at her watch and gasped. 'We're going to miss the midnight curfew if we don't run!' she said. I was as startled, looking at my watch, as she was by how much time had passed. As they hurriedly left the park I noticed that all the tourists were evaporating into the night. The last of the concertgoers were hurrying away – all except one tall man in a long overcoat and wide-brimmed hat who paused at the gate staring in my direction. Perhaps he was just waiting for someone – or maybe he was a thief waiting for the park to clear out so he could rob me – or worse. Certainly the homeless people wouldn't be of any help. The ones who were left in the park – Amélie curled up in her raincoat with her companion – were already asleep or passed out.

I got up to go, my movement startling a pigeon roosting on a Gothic turret. It was the long-necked brown pigeon. He landed a few feet from me and fixed me with his strangely intelligent eye. Then he fluttered up to the leaning tree, landing on the scarred bark just above the cement gash. His claws skittered for purchase there for a moment. His glossy brown wings gleamed in the streetlight, revealing a layer of iridescent colours – indigo, mauve and violet – beneath the brown. Across the Seine the bells of Notre Dame began to chime midnight. The pigeon steadied himself and began to peck at the cement. Startled, I noticed he pecked once for each toll of the bells.

Okay, I thought, someone has trained this bird and is having a laugh at my expense. Could it be that man in the long coat and hat waiting at the gate? But when I glanced over I couldn't see the man at the gate anymore. I couldn't even see the gate. A ring of darkness circled the square that was made up of the shadows of trees, but also something else . . . some murky substance that wasn't black but an opalescent blend of indigo, mauve and violet – the same colours in the pigeon's wings – a colour that seemed to be the essence of the Parisian night.

As Notre Dame chimed its last note, I looked back at

the tree. The grey cement was gone, peeled away like a discarded shell. In its place was a gaping hole, pointed at the top like a high Gothic arch. The brown pigeon stood at the centre of the arch staring at me. With a flick of its wing – for all the world like a hand waving me in – he turned and waddled into the vaulted space inside the tree as if going through his own front door. Clearly that's what the gap in the tree was – a door. But to what?

Perhaps I had misread my invitation to come to Paris, but surely this was an invitation. Maybe even a sign. I might not get another. I got up and followed the pigeon into the oldest tree in Paris.

The Watchtower

Lee Carroll

What secrets are hidden in her past . . . ?

Jewellery designer Garet James is still coming to terms with the astounding revelation that she is a Watchtower, the last in a long line of women sworn to protect the world from evil. Now she has received a sign from Will Hughes, the four-hundred-year-old vampire who vanished having helped her defeat the evil threatening to destroy New York City. The clue he has left points to his having fled to France where, Garet knows, he believes he will at last find the means to rid himself of the curse of vampirism and to become mortal once more.

While looking for Will in Paris, Garet encounters a number of mysterious, mythic figures – an ancient botanist metamorphosed into the oldest tree in the city, a gnome who lives under the Labyrinth at the Jardin des Plantes, a librarian at the Institut Oceanographique, and a dryad in the Luxembourg Gardens . . .

Each encounter leads Garet closer to finding Will but she realizes that she's not the only one who's trying to find the way to the elusive, magical world of the Fey, called the Summer Country. As Garet struggles to understand her family legacy, each answer she finds only leads to more questions – and to more danger . . .

9780593065976

COMING SOON FROM BANTAM PRESS

A Kiss of Shadows

Laurell K. Hamilton

Meet Meredith Gentry: exotic, decadent, deadly.
Private investigator, princess-in-hiding.
Half human, half faerie.

Sometimes you have to stop running to start fighting back.

Three years in hiding and it looks like Merry Gentry's secret is out.

Can she keep her real identity hidden to live the life she wants to lead? To live full stop?

A Kiss of Shadows – rich, sensual and brimming with dangerous magic.

'Gloriously erotic, funny and horrific . . . probably not
one for your granny'
SHIVERS

LAURELL K. HAMILTON
Unleash your fantasy

9780553813838

A Caress of Twilight

Laurell K. Hamilton

Meet Meredith Gentry: exotic, decadent, deadly.
Private investigator, princess-in-hiding.
Half human, half faerie.

*I know I must confront an ancient evil that could destroy the
very fabric of reality . . .*

Merry Gentry is in a race with her cousin for the Faerie crown –
whoever bears the first child can claim the throne.

But while she tests lovers to be future king, others start to die in
mysterious and frightening ways . . .

A Caress of Twilight – a time when earthly delights and dangerous
magic meet.

'Oozing with sensuality . . . steamy sex scenes that
are wonderfully touchy-feely'
STARBURST

Laurell K. Hamilton
Unleash your fantasy

9780553813845

Succubus Blues

Richelle Mead

Succubus (n.) An alluring, shape-shifting demon who seduces and pleasures mortal men.
Pathetic (adj.) A succubus with great shoes and no social life. *See*: Georgina Kincaid.

When it comes to jobs in hell, being a succubus seems pretty glamorous. A girl can be anything she wants, the wardrobe is killer, and mortal men will do anything just for a touch. Granted, they can often pay with their souls, but why get technical?

But Seattle succubus Georgina Kincaid's life is far less exotic. Her boss is a middle-management demon with a thing for John Cusack movies, and she can't get a decent date without sucking away part of the guy's life. At least there's her day job at a local bookstore – free books; all the white chocolate mochas she can drink; and easy access to bestselling, sexy writer, Seth Mortensen, aka He Whom She Would Give Anything to Touch but Can't.

But dreaming about Seth will have to wait. Something wicked is at work in Seattle's demon underground. And for once, all her hot charms and drop-dead one-liners won't help because Georgina's about to discover there are some creatures out there that both heaven and hell want to deny . . .

'Sexy, scintillating, and sassy!'
MICHELLE ROWEN, AUTHOR OF *BITTEN & SMITTEN*

'Deliciously wicked!'
LILITH SAINTCROW, AUTHOR OF *WORKING FOR THE DEVIL*

9780553818925

Storm Born

Richelle Mead

Just typical. No love life to speak of for months, then all at once, every horny creature in the Otherworld wants to get in your pants . . .

Eugenie Markham is a powerful shaman who does a brisk trade banishing spirits and fey who cross into the mortal world. Mercenary, yes, but a girl's got to eat. Her most recent case, however, is enough to ruin her appetite. Hired to find a teenager who has been taken to the Otherworld, Eugenie comes face to face with a startling prophecy – one that uncovers dark secrets about her past and claims that Eugenie's first-born will threaten the future of the world as she knows it.

Now Eugenie is a hot target for every ambitious demon and Otherworldy ne'er-do-well, and the ones who don't want to knock her up want her dead. Eugenie handles a Glock as smoothly as she wields a wand, but she needs some formidable allies for a job like this. She finds them in Dorian, a seductive fairy king with a taste for bondage, and Kiyo, a gorgeous shape-shifter who redefines animal attraction. But with enemies growing bolder and time running out, Eugenie realizes that the greatest danger is yet to come, and it lies in the dark powers that are stirring to life within her . . .

A Dark Swan novel.

9780553819861

Twelve

Jasper Kent

Autumn, 1812. Napoleon's triumphant Grande Armée continues its relentless march into Russia. City after city has fallen and now only a miracle can keep the French from taking Moscow itself.

In a last, desperate act of defiance, a group of Russian officers enlist the help of twelve mercenaries who claim they can turn the tide of the war. It seems an impossible boast but it soon becomes clear that these strangers from the outer reaches of Christian Europe are indeed quite capable of fulfilling their promise . . . and more.

But the fact that so few seem able to accomplish so much unsettles one of the Russians, Captain Aleksei Danilov. As winter closes in, he begins to understand the true, horrific nature of the twelve and the nightmare he unwittingly helped to unleash . . .

'Rich, detailed and enjoyable . . . a great read and a
breath of fresh air'
FANTASYBOOKREVIEW

'An accomplished, entertaining blend of historical
fiction and dark fantasy'
LISA TUTTLE, *THE TIMES*

'A fantastical blend of historical novel and
supernatural chiller'
DEATHRAY

9780553819588